PLAY OF PASSION

'Compelling characters and wonderfully dense plotting are two reasons
why Singh's books continue to enthral'

Romantic Times

KISS OF SNOW

'An unforgettable tale that is rich with complex, vivid emotions and
edge-of-your-seat danger'

Romantic Times

TANGLE OF NEED

'One of her strongest episodes to date'

Publishers Weekly

HEART OF OBSIDIAN

'*Heart of Obsidian* stands as one of the best books Singh has
penned in her career'

Fresh Fiction

Also by Nalini Singh from Gollancz:
Guild Hunter Series
Angels' Blood
Archangel's Kiss
Archangel's Consort
Archangel's Blade
Archangel's Storm
Archangel's Legion
Archangel's Shadows
Angels' Flight (short story collection)

Psy-Changeling Series

Slave to Sensation	Bonds of Justice
Visions of Heat	Play of Passion
Caressed by Ice	Kiss of Snow
Mine to Possess	Tangle of Need
Hostage to Pleasure	Heart of Obsidian
Branded by Fire	Wild Invitation
Blaze of Memory	(short story collection)

SHIELD OF WINTER

A PSY-CHANGELING NOVEL

NALINI SINGH

First published in Great Britain in 2014 by
Gollancz
An imprint of the Orion Publishing Group
Orion House, 5 Upper St Martin's Lane, London WC2H 9EA
An Hachette UK Company

This edition published in Great Britain in 2014 by Gollancz

1 3 5 7 9 10 8 6 4 2

A CIP catalogue record for this book is available
from the British Library

ISBN 978 0 575 11150 9

Printed in Great Britain by Clays Ltd, plc

The Orion Publishing Group's policy is to use papers that are
natural, renewable and recyclable products and made from wood
grown in sustainable forests. The logging and manufacturing
processes are expected to conform to the environmental regulations
of the country of origin.

www.nalinisingh.com
www.orionbooks.co.uk
www.gollancz.co.uk

CAST OF CHARACTERS

In Alphabetical Order by First Name
Key: SD = SnowDancer Wolves; DR = DarkRiver Leopards

Abbot Arrow, teleport-capable telekinetic (Tk)

Aden Arrow, telepath (Tp)

Alice Eldridge Human scientist, placed in forced cryonic suspension for over a century, now living with SD

Amara Aleine Psy member of DR, former Council scientist, twin of Ashaya, mentally unstable

Anthony Kyriakus Member of the Ruling Coalition, former Psy Councilor, father of Faith

Ashaya Aleine Psy member of DR, former Council scientist, mated to Dorian, mother of Keenan, twin of Amara

Ben SD pup

Brigitte Empath (E), home base: Amsterdam

Carter Hirsch Father of Ivy

Chang Cardinal empath (E), home base: research station in Kenya

Concetta Empath (E), home base: Paraguay

Council (or Psy Council) The former ruling Council of the Psy race, no longer extant

Cristabel Rodriguez Arrow, sharpshooter

CAST OF CHARACTERS

DarkMind Neosentient psychic entity and dark twin of NetMind

Dechen Empath, home base: Tibet

Devraj Santos Leader of the Forgotten (Psy who defected from the PsyNet at the dawn of Silence and intermingled with the human and changeling populations), married to Katya Haas

Dorian Christensen DR Sentinel, mated to Ashaya

Faith NightStar Psy member of DR, gift of Foresight (F), mated to Vaughn, daughter of Anthony, cousin to Sahara

Gwen Jane Mother of Ivy

Hawke Snow SD Alpha, mated to Sienna

Indigo Riviere SD Lieutenant

Isaiah Empath (E), home base: Niue

Ivy Jane Empath (E), daughter of Gwen Jane and Carter Hirsch

Jaya Empath (E), home base: Maldives

Judd Lauren Psy member of SD, Lieutenant, mated to Brenna, uncle of Sienna, Toby, and Marlee

Julian/Jules DR cub, son of Tamsyn, twin of Roman

Kaleb Krychek Cardinal Tk, leader of the Ruling Coalition, former Psy Councilor, psychically bonded to Sahara Kyriakus

Keenan Aleine Psy member of DR, child, son of Ashaya

Kit DR Soldier

Lianne Empath (E), home base: Kuala Lumpur

Lucas Hunter DR Alpha, mated to Sascha, father of Naya

Marlee Lauren Psy member of SD, child, daughter of Walker Lauren, niece of Judd Lauren

Mercy Smith DR Sentinel, mated to Riley

Ming LeBon Former Psy Councilor, military mastermind, cardinal telepath (Tp)

CAST OF CHARACTERS

Naya Hunter DR cub, daughter of Sascha and Lucas

NetMind Neosentient psychic entity said to be the guardian and librarian of the PsyNet, twin of the DarkMind

Nikita Duncan Former Psy Councilor, part of Ruling Coalition, mother of Sascha

Patton (deceased), Arrow, teleporter (Tk-V), trained Vasic

Penn Empath (E), home base: Scotland

Pure Psy Fanatical and violent pro-Silence group

Riley Kincaid SD Lieutenant, mated to Mercy

Roman/Rome DR cub, son of Tamsyn, twin of Julian

Ruling Coalition Formed after the fall of Silence and of the Psy Council. Composed of Kaleb Krychek, Nikita Duncan, Anthony Kyriakus, and the Arrow Squad

Sahara Kyriakus Unclassified designation, psychically bonded to Kaleb Krychek, niece of Anthony Kyriakus, cousin to Faith

Sascha Duncan Psy member of DR, cardinal empath (E), mated to Lucas, mother of Naya, daughter of Nikita

Sienna Lauren Psy member of SD, possesses lethal psychic abilities (X), mated to Hawke, niece of Judd

Tamsyn SD Healer

Tatiana Rika-Smythe Former Psy Councilor

Teri Empath (E), home base: Houston

Vasic Arrow, teleporter (Tk-V)

Walker Lauren Psy member of SD, telepath (Tp), father of Marlee, brother of Judd

Zaira Arrow, in charge of the covert Arrow compound in Venice

Zie Zen Psy elder, telepath (Tp)

Splintered

THE SILENCE PROTOCOL has been the defining aspect of the Psy race for over a hundred years. Conditioned not to feel emotion from childhood, they are known for their icy practicality, acute mental abilities, and adherence to strict codes of behavior. It is all they know and all they've been since the inception of the Protocol . . . until now.

The twilight of 2081 will be forever remembered as the time when Silence fell in a crash of violence brutally leashed by the furious abilities of the most powerful Psy in the Net. With the fall comes a hush across the world, as the Psy race seeks to understand who they are in this new reality where emotion isn't a crime punishable by a vicious psychic brain-wipe, and the heart is no longer an organ simply used to pump blood. For though Silence was a deeply flawed construct, it existed for a reason.

Insanity, blood-soaked death, murderous aggression, this is who the Psy were before Silence. No other race, it is said, bred more vicious, more intelligent, or more sadistic serial killers. But worse was the clawing madness that destroyed so many of them, saints and sinners alike, until it became known as the flip side to their incredible psychic gifts.

Is the past their future?

Will the Psy race once more devolve into endless nightmare?

No one can answer that question. Not yet.

Chapter 1

To be an Arrow is to be an island, devoid of attachments that create vulnerability.

First Code of Arrows

THERE WAS NOTHING left of the man he'd been.

Vasic stared through the glass wall in front of him as the computronic gauntlet biologically fused to his left forearm hummed near silently in the diagnostic mode he'd initiated. Sleek black, the new invention remained relatively unstable, despite the constant and ongoing refinement by the medics and techs, but Vasic wasn't concerned about his life.

He hadn't been concerned about anything for a long time. At first it had been his conditioning under Silence that kept him cold, his emotions on ice. Now, as the world navigated the first days of a new year, he was beyond Silence and into a numbness so vast, it was an endless grayness.

The only reason he kept waking up in the morning was for the others, the ones in the squad who still had some hope of a normal life. It was far too late for him, his hands permanently stained with blood from the countless lives he'd taken in pursuit of a mandate that had proven false in a very ugly way.

"What is it?" he said to the man clad in a black combat uniform who'd just entered the common area of Arrow Central Command. None of them were sociable, yet they maintained this space, having learned through bitter experience that even an Arrow couldn't always walk alone.

Today the room was empty except for the two of them.

"Krychek has a theory." Aden came to stand beside Vasic, his dark eyes on the vista beyond the glass. It wasn't of the outside world—the Arrows were creatures of shadow, and so they lived in the shadows, their headquarters buried deep underground in a location inaccessible to anyone who didn't know the correct routes and codes.

Even a teleporter needed a visual lock, and there were no images of Arrow Central Command anywhere in the world, not in any database, not on the PsyNet, nowhere. Which made it all the more notable that Kaleb Krychek had demonstrated the ability to 'port into the HQ when the squad first contacted him. However, despite the subterranean nature of the squad's base of operations, on the other side of the glass lay a sprawling green space full of trees, ferns, even a natural-seeming pool, the area bathed in simulated sunlight that would change to moonlight as the day turned.

It had been difficult to acquire that technology without tipping their hand—the SnowDancer wolves were very proprietary of their tech, usually installed it themselves. But the squad had managed, because that light was as necessary to their sanity and their physical health as the captured piece of the outside world on which it shone.

"Krychek's theory—it's about the disease in the Net," Vasic guessed, aware that the broken remnants of fanatical Pure Psy and the sporadic new outbreaks of violence notwithstanding, that was the most dangerous threat facing their race.

"You've seen the reports."

"Yes." The disease, the *infection*, was spreading at a phenomenal pace no one could've predicted. Rooted in the psychic fabric that connected every Psy on the planet but for the renegades, it had the potential to devastate their race . . . because to be Psy was to need the biofeedback provided by a psychic network. Now that same link could well be pumping poison directly into their brains.

There were some who whispered that the fall of Silence a month prior was behind the acceleration, but Vasic didn't believe that to be the truth—the decay was too deeply integrated in the PsyNet. It had had over a century to grow, feeding on the suppressed psychic energy of all the dark, twisted emotions their race sought to stifle. "Krychek's theory?"

Aden, his hands clasped loosely behind his back, said, "He believes the empaths are the key."

The empaths.

An unexpected idea from Kaleb Krychek, whom many considered the epitome of Silence . . . but that was a false truth, as the entire Net had learned when he had lowered the shield around the adamantine bond that linked him to Sahara Kyriakus. Of course, it was a false truth only when it came to Sahara Kyriakus. That was a fact Vasic didn't think everyone understood, and it was a critical one.

Kaleb Krychek remained a lethal threat.

"Krychek," Aden continued, "theorizes that the fact the empaths are so prevalent in the population speaks to their necessity in subtle ways we've never grasped. Stifling their abilities has thus had a dangerous flow-on effect."

Vasic saw the logic—empaths might've been publicly erased from the Net, but every Arrow knew the E designation had never been rare. Except once. Their emotion-linked abilities contrary to the very foundations of the Protocol, the Es had been systematically eliminated from the gene pool in the years after Silence was first implemented, only for the ruling Council to realize almost too late that it was attempting to excise a vital organ.

No one truly understood why the Net needed the Es, but it was incontrovertible that it did. The Council that had first come face-to-face with that truth had named it the Correlation Concept—the lower the number of E-Psy in the population, the higher the incidents of psychopathy and insanity. However, while the current generation of Es might've been allowed to be born, they'd never been allowed to *be*, conditioned to suppress their abilities since birth. "Has Krychek considered the fact that it might not be a case of merely awakening the Es?"

"Yes. You see the critical problem."

It was inescapable—if the empaths had to do something active to negate the infection, then the Psy race might well disintegrate to ash, because there was no one left to teach the Es what to do. By the time the ruling Council of the time had accepted their mistake in attempting to cull the Es from the gene pool, all the old ones were dead and information about their abilities had been erased from every known archive.

"How many?" Vasic asked, knowing they couldn't simply begin to nudge the empaths awake on a wholesale level. Their deaths had almost collapsed the PsyNet. No one knew what would happen if they woke all at once, disoriented and unable to control their abilities.

"A test group of ten." Aden telepathed him the list.

Scanning it, Vasic saw the short-listed Es were all high Gradient, from cardinal to 8.7. "No," he said, before Aden could make the request. "I won't retrieve them."

"You don't have to retrieve them all. Just one."

"No," Vasic said again. "If Krychek wishes to abduct empaths, he's capable of doing so himself." Vasic was no longer on anyone's leash but his own.

Aden's response was quiet. "Do you think I'd bring you such a request?"

Turning at last, Vasic met the eyes of the telepath who was the one individual in the world he considered a friend, their lives intertwined since childhood—when they'd been paired up to do exercises designed to turn Vasic into a stone-cold killer. To their trainers, Aden had simply been a useful telepathic sparring partner, a well-behaved complement to Vasic's erratic temperament at the time, an Arrow trainee only because his parents were both Arrows who'd worked to hone his skills since the cradle.

As such, Aden had been put into classes that eventually qualified him as a field medic. He'd been given the same harsh training all inductees were given, but was never deemed worthy of any extra interest—except when it came to punishments designed to "harden" a boy who'd been small for his age. Always, the ones who would use the Arrows had under-estimated Aden, and in so doing, they'd given the squad a leader who'd saved countless lives and who they would follow into any hell.

"No," Vasic conceded. "You wouldn't." Aden knew exactly how close Vasic was to the edge, that the destruction of, or damage to one more innocent life could snap the razor-fine thread that bound him to the world.

"Krychek," Aden continued into the quiet between them, "doesn't think his proposed experiment as to the impact of the empaths on the infection will work if the Es are forced to participate." A pause. "I'm not certain if that's his personal view, or if it's Sahara's, but whatever the case, each of the Es must volunteer."

Vasic agreed with Aden that the compassion was likely to emanate from the woman who had appeared out of nowhere to forge an unbreakable bond with the otherwise cold-blooded dual cardinal, and who, their investigations told them, was in no way Silent. "Where does Krychek intend to run his experiment?"

"SnowDancer-DarkRiver territory."

Very few things had the capacity to surprise Vasic, on any level. This, however, was unexpected. "The SnowDancer wolves have a tendency to shoot intruders on sight"—"shoot first and ask questions of the corpses" was their rumored motto—"and the leopards aren't much friendlier."

"I've told Krychek the same, yet I can see his point as to the area's suitability."

"An isolated location, no other PsyNet connected minds for miles in any direction." As a result, that part of the Net, too, would be quiet, giving Krychek a clean canvas on which to run his experiment.

However, that was a factor that could be replicated elsewhere.

Which left a single critical element that could *only* be found in the changeling-held territory. "Sascha Duncan." Access to the only active E in the world no doubt played a crucial part in Krychek's plans.

"There's no infection in that section of the Net," Aden said, instead of nodding to confirm what they both knew must be true. "However Krychek has the ability to shift the infection in that direction, or seed the area with it. He says he can't control it beyond that, but I haven't yet decided if he's lying." The other Arrow turned to acknowledge another member of the squad who'd just entered, walking over to her when she indicated she needed to speak to him.

Alone, Vasic considered the misleading simplicity of Krychek's proposed experiment. An isolated group of empaths surrounded on the Net by the infection. If the experiment failed and the infection threatened to overwhelm them in a wave of murderous madness or more subtle mental degradation, it would be relatively easy to relocate all ten men and women at short notice. As well, the deterioration of an empty part of the Net would cause few ripples.

In that sense, it was a clean plan, with no threat of major losses.

Of course, no one could predict how the infection would move, what it would do to the empaths. "I can't, Aden," he said when the other man returned to his side, their fellow Arrow having left the room.

Aden waited.

"You know what happened when I had cause to pass near Sascha Duncan prior to her defection. It was a deeply . . . uncomfortable experience." Councilor Nikita Duncan's daughter had been pretending to be Silent at the time, but even then, there'd been something about her that had made his instincts bristle.

It was one of the few times he'd felt true pain as an adult—at first, he'd thought he was under attack, only to realize it was Sascha's simple presence in a room separated from the one where he stood by a *solid wall*, that was sandpaper along the insides of his skin. As if some part of him knew she was the antithesis to everything he had ever been taught to be, the rejection primal.

It wasn't until her defection and the resulting revelation of her empathy that he'd realized the reason behind the strange effect; the knowledge had made him recall the numerous other times he'd felt a faint irritation against his skin as he moved through the shadows in populated areas. Sleeping empaths, their conditioning not as badly degraded as Sascha's must have been.

He also knew he was an anomaly in sensing them in such a way—according to Aden, no one else in the squad had ever reported the same. Vasic had a theory that the awareness was an undocumented adjunct of being a Tk-V, a born teleporter. Patton, the only other Tk-V Vasic had ever met, had often complained about an "itch" under his skin when he was in the outside world.

Regardless of whether that was true or not, the effect continued unchecked for Vasic, causing deeper and more frequent serrated scrapes over his skin as the conditioning of the Es in the Net fractured further with each passing day.

Aden took several minutes to reply. "Uncomfortable, not debilitating." The words of a leader evaluating one of his men. "The empaths will need a protection squad—their designation has never been aggressive according to the historical records I've been able to unearth so far, and none of this group are, either."

The telepath's tone remained even as he added, "I want you to run it. You're the only man I trust to get them all out of danger if there's a sudden spike in the infection, or if the pro-Silence elements in the Net seek to do them harm."

Vasic knew that wasn't quite the truth—the squad had other teleport-capable operatives in its ranks. No one as fast as Vasic, but fast enough. None of them, however, stood so close to an irrevocable and final descent into the abyss. "Are you trying to put me on soft duty?"

"Yes." Eyes on the greenery outside, but his attention on Vasic, Aden continued to speak. "You don't see it, but you're one of the core members of the squad, the one we all rely on when things go to hell. Outside emergency situations, the younger Arrows turn to you for guidance; the older ones use you as a sounding board. Your loss would be a staggering blow to the group . . . to me."

"I won't snap." Even though he knew the oblivion of death was the only peace he'd ever find. "I have things to do yet." And it didn't only have to do with helping to save those Arrows who might still have the chance to live some kind of a real life.

You don't have the right to be tired. When you can write her name on a memorial, when you can honor her blood, then you'll have earned the right.

A leopard changeling had said that to him over the broken body of a woman whose death Vasic had been sent to erase. The leopard couldn't know how many names Vasic needed to write, how many deaths he'd covered up when he'd believed that what he was doing was for the good of his people . . . and later, when he'd known it was too early for any revolution to succeed. Each and every name had a claim on his soul.

"Nevertheless, I want you away from the violence, at least for a short period." Again, Aden's voice was that of the leader he was, and yet it was no order, their relationship far too old to need any such trappings. "There's another reason I want you on this detail—and why I'm going to ask you to consider certain others for your team. Being near empaths may be uncomfortable for you, but it will likely be soothing for the Es."

Because, Vasic realized, he and the others like him, were ice-cold, permanently cut off from their emotions. Unlike the fractured, they would leak neither fear nor pain, eliminating one source of stress on the newly awakened Es. "How does that tie in with being so close to the changelings?" The shapeshifting race was as rawly emotional as the Psy were not, their world painted in vivid shades of passion.

"If Krychek manages to negotiate access to part of their land, he intends to agree to full satellite and remote surveillance, while asking them to keep a physical distance the majority of the time." Aden paused as a butterfly flew from the lush green of the trees to flutter its scarlet wings against the glass before returning to more hospitable climes. "It'll take time for negotiations to be concluded, a location to be settled on, whether it's in changeling territory or elsewhere. Take the invitation to your nominated E, gauge whether you could remain in her proximity for the duration."

"You've already decided who I'm to approach."

"According to Krychek, all the empaths on the list but one have already begun to wake to their abilities, even if they aren't cognizant of it."

Vasic didn't ask how Krychek could've known that, aware the cardinal telekinetic had an intimate link with the NetMind, the vast neosentience that was the librarian and guardian of the Net. The NetMind had no doubt informed Krychek of the Es who were coming to an awareness of their true designation.

"Your retrieval, however, first broke conditioning at sixteen and was given aggressive reconditioning to wrench her abilities back under. Two months later, she and her parents quietly disappeared."

It was the second surprise of the conversation. "The NetMind can't locate the family unit?"

"Not that type of disappearance," Aden clarified. "We know where they are geographically, but they've done an impeccable job of making themselves of no interest to anyone. Her mother was a systems analyst for a cutting-edge computronic firm in Washington; her father held a senior position in a bank. Now they run a large but only moderately successful farm in North Dakota, in cooperation with a number of other Psy."

Psy preferred to live in cities, near others of their kind, but that wasn't to say none of their race ever chose outdoor occupations. Like humans and changelings, Psy needed to eat, to put a roof over their heads, and work was work. Such a massive career change, however, was an indication of a conscious decision. "Protecting their child?" It wasn't impossible, the parental instinct a driving force even in many of the Silent, though Vasic had no personal experience of such.

"Possible but unconfirmed."

Vasic knew there was more to come.

"What's also unconfirmed is if she still has access to her abilities—or if they were terminally damaged by the reconditioning process." Aden stared unblinking through the glass. "I watched the recording, and it was one of the most brutal sessions I've ever seen, a hairsbreadth from a rehabilitation."

"Then why is she on the list?" The ugliness of rehabilitation erased the personality, left the individual a drooling vegetable, and if this E had come so close to it, she had to bear major mental scars.

"To be valid, the experiment needs not only Psy who have never been reconditioned, but those who've been through the process. She's one of six in the group who have, but the others underwent only a minor reset."

It made absolute sense . . . because the majority of empaths in the Net would've undergone reconditioning at some stage, the process designed to force their minds back into the accepted norm, in denial of the fact those minds had never been meant to be emotionless constructs. Which meant the PsyNet had to deal not only with Es who didn't have any idea of how to utilize their abilities, but also ones damaged on a fundamental level.

"The flip side to their problematic conditioning," Aden added, faultlessly following Vasic's line of thought, "is that they'll suffer no pain breaking it."

"Of course." The process known as dissonance was designed to reinforce Silence by punishing any unacceptable emotional deviation with pain, but clearly that approach wouldn't work on an individual whose mental pathways were structured with emotion as the core. It would simply kill. "The details of the retrieval."

Aden handed Vasic an envelope. "A letter to her directly from Krychek, setting out the parameters of her engagement, as well as the payment schedule."

"He's offering them jobs?" The Council had always just taken.

"We both know how intelligent he is. Why coerce when you can contract?" With that cool statement that perfectly described the way Krychek's mind worked, Aden sent Vasic a telepathic image.

It was of a small female with black hair to her shoulders, the strands shaping themselves into soft natural curls, and eyes so unusual, he took a second look. The pupils were jet-black against irises of translucent copper ringed by a fine rim of gold. They stood out against the golden cream of her skin, somehow too old, too perceptive.

As if she saw beneath the skin.

Storing the photograph in a mental vault after imprinting a geographic location on his mind using her appearance as a lock, he looked down at the envelope. Her name was hand-written across it in black ink: *Ivy Jane*.

He wondered what Ivy Jane would think of the Arrow about to enter her life, a man who could never again feel anything. Even were it physiologically possible, Vasic had no intention of allowing his Silence to fragment . . . because behind it lay only a howling madness created of blood and death and endless horror.

Chapter 2

Ruling Coalition or not, Kaleb Krychek is now the effective leader of the Psy race. It remains to be seen where he will take us.

Editorial, *PsyNet Beacon*

KALEB CAME TO a halt, his upper body gleaming from the martial arts drill he'd been doing in the cleared living room of his and Sahara's home on the outskirts of Moscow. The terrace, his usual practice ground, was currently under several inches of snow and being pounded by screaming hail.

That had never before stopped him, but Sahara would follow if he went out there now, and she had a tendency to shiver even under a telekinetic shield. So he'd temporarily teleported the living room furniture into another part of the house instead.

Seated not far from him, her legs stretched out over the carpet as she bent over in a toning exercise she'd learned as a dancer, she said, "What is it?"

Kaleb watched her rise back into a sitting position, then get lithely to her feet, her body clad in black tights paired with a white T-shirt, and felt a deep sense of possession in his blood. She was here. *Safe*. No one would ever again cause her harm. He considered whether the news he'd just received from the NetMind would disturb her, thought about how much to share.

Her lips quirked as she redid the tie that held back the silky dark of her hair, the hidden strands of red-gold not apparent in this light. "You do realize I know you?"

Yes, she knew him, saw him, and still she loved him.

And he'd made her a promise that he'd never hide anything. "Subject 8-91 is dead." Sahara didn't agree with the way he'd left the man to slowly sicken, oblivious of the infection in his brain, but Kaleb didn't see the point in informing the male of his certain demise—because there was no cure.

Subject 8-91 had functioned as a barometer of the infection that was crawling into countless minds in the Net. It would torture and kill millions if left unchecked. Not only was the biofeedback toxic in affected parts of the Net, the infection had begun to corrode the actual fabric of the psychic landscape itself in the worst-hit sections. If—*when*—any of the heavily populated sections collapsed, the death toll would be in the thousands each time.

"Calling it an infection," he said to Sahara now, "is useful shorthand, but inaccurate."

A slow nod. "It's a corruption, isn't it?" The dark blue of her eyes filled with sadness. "It's risen from within, no bacteria or virus or other outside source involved."

Kaleb cupped her jaw, rubbed his thumb over her lower lip. "Subject 8-91 was the most deeply infected. If he's dead, we're now on a countdown."

Kissing his thumb, Sahara broke contact to walk to the corner where he'd discarded his T-shirt, and picked it up. "You need to go check the scene," she guessed, returning with the camouflage green cotton in her grasp, frown lines marring her brow. "You'll be careful." It was an order.

He nodded after pulling on the T-shirt, still unused to the fact that he once again had her in his life—the one person who cared about him. Every time she showed that care, whether through her words or her actions, it curled around the dark part of him that lived in the void, a petting caress.

"I'll be home soon," he said. "Don't link telepathically." She was always with him, but he didn't want her seeing what he was sure awaited in 8-91's home. Since he'd never reject her psychic touch, he had to have her promise.

Rising on tiptoe, she kissed him sweet and soft, the way she had of doing sometimes—as if he was the vulnerable one. It was true. But only when it came to Sahara, his obsidian shields mist against her touch; her slender fingers could cage him more effectively than any chain or prison.

"I won't," she promised. "We'll talk about it afterward." Her gaze held his own in a trust he'd never break, the charm bracelet on her wrist catching the light. "Take care, Kaleb," she repeated. "You belong to me."

He teleported out with the warmth of her a lingering kiss against his skin, and into a bloody hell. Subject 8-91 hadn't simply died. He'd gone critical. And he'd taken someone with him. Crouching by the body that lay just inside the closed doorway, Kaleb attempted to count the stab marks that had sliced through the man's pin-striped shirt, got to nineteen before it became impossible to separate the wounds.

The flicker came to the right of him a second later. "We have a situation," he said to the two Arrows he'd telepathed on arrival. "Subject 8-91"—he pointed to the slender male who sat slumped against the opposing wall, his face bruised and cut, a streak of red behind his head, as if he'd slid down the wall after being thrown onto it—"was infected. The most advanced case in the Net."

Vasic stayed in place as Aden stepped over the nearest body, skirting the blood that splattered the room to scan 8-91 using a small medical device. "He suffered blunt force injuries to the face as well as a cracked skull, but my initial judgment is that he died of an implosion in his brain."

Rising to a standing position, Kaleb considered the facts. "Sunshine Station," he said, dead certain both Arrows knew of the remote Alaskan science station where the disease had first claimed Psy lives. "The infected didn't die that way."

"No." Aden came across to scan the stabbing victim. "The staff of the science station went mad, bludgeoned, stabbed, and otherwise assaulted one another. The survivors were weak but still psychotic by the time we arrived. A number were so aggressive they died during the containment process; the remainder were put into involuntary comas."

Aden's first-person account jibed with the details Kaleb had been able to dig up, though former Councilor Ming LeBon had done his best to conceal the scale and nature of the deaths. As a result, Kaleb knew that none of the comatose victims had ever woken up. Brain death had followed within a week of the incident. "Does 8-91's mode of death mean the infection's become more virulent?"

The Arrow medic got to his feet. "Possible—but it's also possible he had a genetic vulnerability that coincided with the final stages of the infection. A full autopsy will be necessary to know for certain." Aden held Kaleb's eyes. "You have his history?"

Kaleb telepathed across the detailed files he'd kept on 8-91's disintegration, even as he stared at the room, analyzed the damage, then returned his gaze to the stabbed male. "It's possible 8-91's victim was also infected. I recognize him as 8-91's closest neighbor." Meaning there was a high chance they'd been next to each other on the psychic plane as well.

"Do we need to evacuate this region of the PsyNet?"

"I'll quarantine the area for the time being, but it's a stopgap measure." The oily black of the infection was crawling across vast swathes of the Net.

Vasic spoke for the first time. "I'll teleport the bodies to the secure morgue where they can be autopsied, clean up this room."

He's so close to the edge; I don't know if anything can save him.

Words Sahara had spoken about Vasic, hurt in her voice for a man she saw as kin to Kaleb. He didn't disagree. He might've been trained by a sociopath, but the same was true of many Arrows; the only difference was that Kaleb's trainer had slipped the leash into unsanctioned murder. In the end, they'd all grown up under a regime that attempted to turn them into tools for the use of others—tools meant to be discarded once they passed their use-by date.

Kaleb had no illusions about himself, knew he'd use anyone and everyone if it would keep the world safe for Sahara, but he also had no intention of becoming the Council he'd destroyed. "No," he said in response to Vasic's offer. "Let Enforcement handle this scene as a murder.

"If we don't find a way to halt the infection, such incidents will become all too common soon enough." Even if Enforcement discovered the truth of what had happened here tonight, they'd only be ahead of the curve by weeks at most. News of the infection hadn't yet made front-page news, but it was already being whispered of in hidden corners of the Net. "I'll make sure the autopsy is done by one of my people."

Aden's eyes connected with Kaleb's at that instant, and he knew the leader of the Arrows understood why Kaleb had made this choice. Part of Kaleb, the part that was always coolly calculating with anyone but Sahara, saw in Aden's understanding leverage to gain a stronger hold on the squad. However, the calculation was offset by the part of him that saw in the Arrows who he would've been but for Sahara, his life an endless darkness.

He would still execute them without hesitation should they threaten him or Sahara, but until then, he'd do as Sahara had asked.

Don't they deserve lives, too? Her voice had been husky as she said that, her back against his chest and his arm curved around her shoulders where they lay on the lounger on the terrace, looking up at the starlit night sky.

They've given up everything for their people. And maybe they believed in the wrong mandate once, did things for which there might be no forgiveness, but they've also protected the world from monsters for over a century. Her hands clenching on his forearm, voice passionate with emotion. *Shouldn't they have a chance to try and find redemption?*

"Focus on the E-Psy," he said to the two men now. "That's your highest priority."

Waiting until the Arrows left, Kaleb made the report to Enforcement before returning to Moscow.

Sahara was waiting for him beside the internal koi pond that was her favorite spot in the house. "How bad was it?" she asked, walking into his arms.

It was where she should've always been. Seven years she'd spent in hell. Seven years he'd been alone. Seven years he wanted to torture payment from those responsible. One was dead, torn apart by changeling claws and teeth, but one remained. He'd locked Tatiana Rika-Smythe in an underground hole she could never escape, but he could hurt the ex-Councilor in so many other ways, make her scream and scream.

"Kaleb." Sahara's breath against his lips, her kiss in his mind. *Don't go there. Be here. With me.*

He'd never wanted to be anywhere else.

Slamming the door shut on the evil that had sought to tear them apart, he told her about 8-91's final minutes. "If I'm right," he said afterward, "the empaths hold the answer to the Net's survival."

Sahara tilted back her head to look at him with eyes that spoke of her piercing intelligence. "But?"

He gloried in the sensation that was the possessive warmth of her hands at his waist, in the feel of her vibrant and alive and with him. "If I'm wrong or if the empaths are too damaged to function as they should"—a vicious possibility—"there'll come a time when I'll have to excise the rotten and unstable sections of the Net."

Bleak understanding dulled the light in Sahara's expression. "Like slicing away gangrenous flesh so the healthy segment can survive."

"It's a worst-case scenario." Millions would die during the excision, but to allow the infection to advance unchecked would mean the collapse of the PsyNet and the death of every single person linked to it.

Including Sahara.

That, Kaleb would never accept, never permit. The world had taken seven years from them. It would get nothing else.

Now she lay her cheek against his chest, her arms sliding around his torso. "How did this happen to our people, Kaleb?" A kiss pressed to the beat of his heart, as if she needed the reminder that they were alive, unbroken. "We created heartbreaking art once, discovered star systems and new species of butterflies with equal joy. We were explorers and musicians and writers of great works. Now . . . how did the Psy become such a ruin?"

Kaleb knew the answer wasn't as simple as Silence, and yet Silence was the core. "We attempted to become a race without flaws."

Chapter 3

E-Psy have never been rare, but not much is known about them, perhaps because we study that which we are afraid of. And no one is afraid of the empaths.

Excerpted from *The Mysterious E Designation: Empathic Gifts & Shadows* by Alice Eldridge

IVY WENT CAREFULLY over the bark of the slumbering apple tree. She was on alert for any signs of the fungus that had appeared two weeks earlier, but found nothing. "The treatment worked," she said to Rabbit. "The other trees are safe."

Involved in sniffing the snow at the roots of the tree, tail wagging like a metronome, Rabbit gave a small "woof."

"Glad to see you agree this is a good thing." Noting down the result on her datapad, she continued on through the trees, Rabbit scampering after her a second later, his paws soft and soundless on the carpet of white.

For such a small dog, she thought as his furry white form streaked past, he could certainly go fast when he put his mind to it. Shaking her head, she left him to his adventures and went to check another apple tree she'd been worried about . . . when Rabbit began to bark. Hairs rising on the back of her neck, she fought her instinctive revulsion and reached into a pants pocket to retrieve the tiny laser weapon that fit neatly into the palm of her hand. Rabbit *never* barked, not like that. As if he'd scented a predator.

Ten seconds later, she broke out of the trees and knew her dog was right.

There was a man standing on the path between the snow-kissed trees. No, not a man. A soldier. Over six feet tall with broad shoulders, his posture was unyielding, his stillness absolute, his eyes a chill gray, and his hair black.

His uniform, too, was black, stark against the backdrop: rugged pants, a long-sleeved T-shirt of some high-tech and likely bulletproof material that hugged the muscle of his arms, a lightweight armored vest that covered his chest and back as well as the lower part of his neck, heavy combat boots, what appeared to be an electronic gauntlet strapped to his left arm.

They'd come for her again.

A trickle of icy sweat ran down her spine. She'd always known this day was inevitable. Her emotions were too volatile, had no doubt leaked past the tightly woven network of interlinked shields that protected those who called this remote location home. All she could hope for was that she'd betrayed herself alone.

Mother, Father, she telepathed, *we have a situation. Tell the others to keep their heads down and ensure their shields are airtight. I'll handle this.*

Fear squeezed frozen fingers around her lungs as she sent an image of the soldier to her parents, but she was no longer a scared sixteen-year-old girl who thought she was going insane; she was a twenty-three-year-old adult who understood that while she was defective and unstable, she didn't deserve to be violated and tortured. No one would ever again strap her down and attempt to break her. Not even this deadly stranger.

Datapad held to the side of her body with one ice-cold hand, her heavy jacket and thin thermal gloves suddenly useless, she slid away the weapon in the guise of putting her datapen into her pocket. It seemed a counter-intuitive act, but her every instinct screamed she'd be dead before she ever got off a shot. She couldn't win this battle by force, and it was probable she couldn't win it at all, but she'd fight to give the others as much time as possible to prepare.

Breath tight, she closed the distance between her and the soldier whose uniform bore a silver star on one shoulder. Councilor Kaleb Krychek's emblem, though he no longer laid claim to the title, the Council in pieces.

Simple semantics, however, couldn't change the fact that as of just over a month ago, Kaleb Krychek effectively ruled the Net.

"Rabbit." She tapped her thigh, curling her fingers inward to hide the slight trembling she couldn't seem to control.

Still quivering with outrage, but no longer barking now that she was here, Rabbit ran back to her side and once again pinned his eyes on the intruder.

The man glanced at her dog. "He clearly isn't of the Leporidae family."

It was the last thing she'd expected to hear. "It's because he's so energetic," she found herself saying. "It seemed appropriate at the time." When she'd been half-destroyed, a zombie sleepwalking through life.

"He's protective but not dangerous. You should get a bigger dog." Eyes of winter frost met her own, the gray so cold, her skin pebbled with a bone-deep chill.

"He's perfect," she said, reaching down to stroke her pet's stiff form once before rising back to her full height. "You didn't come here to talk to me about my dog."

"No."

"You're an Arrow." Part of the squad of assassins long thought of as myth but who were now aligned with Kaleb Krychek—though they remained shadows, nameless and faceless for the majority of the population. *No one* wanted to meet one in the flesh.

A slight nod that confirmed the unnerving truth. "I am Vasic."

"Silence has fallen," she said, holding her ground because this was *her* place, her home. "You have no right to take me in." No right to strap her down in a reconditioning chair and stab psychic fingers into her mind, ripping and tearing.

"No," he said again, so emotionless that she couldn't see a single element of the person behind the soldier. "I've been charged to deliver an employment proposal."

Ivy just stared at him for several long seconds. "An employment proposal?" she said at last, wondering if she had gone insane after all and was now having a very realistic delusion.

"Yes."

She shivered. He was too hard, too lethal to be a delusion. Testing him by taking a step back toward the trees, Rabbit growling beside her, she said, "Can we walk and talk? I need to finish checking the trees."

The Arrow—Vasic—watched in silence as she completed her examination of the apple tree she'd been heading toward before Rabbit's warning bark. When he did speak, his voice was as deep as the ocean. He didn't raise his volume or change his pitch in spite of Rabbit's continued growling, and yet she heard every word with crystal clarity.

"You've been identified as having an ability that could be useful in stabilizing the Net."

"Me? I'm a Gradient 3.2 telepath." No matter if she sometimes felt a huge stretching inside her mind, as if there was *power* there, if she could only find a way to touch it, hold it. The mirage had led to her near destruction as a teen.

"Are you aware of rumors of a hidden designation? Designation E?"

Her fingers halted in the act of tapping information into the datapad, her blood cells coated in ice, fine and crystalline. "E?"

"Empath."

The word resonated in a keening note inside her, as if it spoke to a deep-rooted knowledge of which she was unaware. "What does an empath do?" she said through a throat lined with grit and gravel.

"I'm not certain," he answered, "but it has to do with emotion."

Staggering inside, she thought of the chaos of wrenching emotions— pain, loathing, anger, sadness, loss, such tearing loss—that had threatened to crush her mind in the minutes before the cruel agony of the reconditioning. Her nose had bled, the fine blood vessels in her eyes bursting to leave the whites swimming in red, her head pounding and pounding and pounding as her stomach revolted.

It had been the worst episode she'd ever suffered.

"Emotions almost killed me once." Terrified, she'd been *happy* to submit to the medical tech at the local center, never realizing the hell that awaited.

In the aftermath of her "treatment," it had felt like she was just . . . gone, the Ivy who'd lived for sixteen years erased. There had been a quiet horror at the back of her mind at the loss of herself, but that horror couldn't penetrate the nothingness, not for a long, long time.

"That incident"—Vasic's voice slicing through the nightmare of memory—"resulted from a catastrophic and sudden breach of your conditioning. The built-up pressure smashed it to pieces."

That's exactly what it had felt like, a violent explosion in her head.

"Most Es tend to awaken more slowly," he continued. "Small fractures that leach off tension rather than a catastrophic collapse."

Most . . .

"How many?" she asked, her voice hoarse.

"Unknown, but E is a significant grouping." His gaze scanned her face with clinical precision. "You're in shock. Sit." When she did nothing, he went as if to touch her . . . and Rabbit lunged at him.

"No!" she screamed.

Rabbit never reached his target, was left swimming frantically in the air. Reaching down, she gathered her pet into her arms and sat down at the foot of the nearest tree, uncaring of the cold, the datapad forgotten on the ground. "I thought you were going to hurt him," she said to the Arrow, the *telekinetic* Arrow.

Vasic didn't defend himself. As an eight-year-old, he'd resisted using his abilities on living creatures, but an eight-year-old boy can't withstand torture of the kind used to burn all humanity out of Arrow trainees. He knew he held within himself the capacity to snap the neck or crush the spine of the small creature who was so attached to his mistress. That he'd never done such an act of his own free will meant nothing. Death was death. "Do you wish me to continue?"

Ivy looked at him, her jet-black pupils hugely dilated against the clear copper of her eyes. "Yes."

"In all probability, your already damaged pathways were further damaged during the reconditioning process." Needing to be aware of what he faced, Vasic had watched the recording Aden had referenced, witnessed the brutality with which her mind had been yanked back into line.

It was a miracle she'd survived without severe brain damage. The psychic trauma had been vicious regardless. That she was functional and whole and strong enough to stand firm against an Arrow was a testament to what must be an iron will.

"However," he added, "it's clear that your Silence has fractured again." No one who was Silent would have the capacity to care for a pet, or to look at Vasic with fear a staccato pulse in her throat. "The buildup is happening again inside you."

Ivy set her pet down on the snow, murmuring at the dog to hush when it began to growl at Vasic once more. "You're saying I could be in the same situation I was at sixteen?"

"Yes." He crouched down beside her, having realized she couldn't comfortably look at him if he remained standing. "The technician in charge of your reconditioning was incompetent." A point Vasic had already made to him in person—and a point the male would never, ever forget. "He simply smashed everything back down inside your mind and slammed a lock over it. That lock is apt to rupture soon, given the amateurish nature of it."

He saw he'd come too close to the truth when she avoided his eyes, her jawline delicate in his vision . . . easily breakable. "You risk nothing by telling me," he pointed out, "I'm already aware of both your problematic Silence and the nature of your ability."

Expression pensive, she rubbed a gloved hand over her face before nodding. "The nosebleeds have begun again, and yesterday, while I was getting supplies from the township, it was as if I was drowning under a wave of happiness and anger and excitement and curiosity and other emotions I couldn't separate out." Her fingers shook as she stroked her pet. "It only lasted a second or two, but it was enough."

Vasic held her gaze, noting that the rim of gold around her irises was more vivid than in the image he had of her. "You may learn how to manage your E abilities during the course of this contract. However, should you decide to turn down the proposal and continue to remain shielded against your abilities, I know a medic who can remove the broken shards of the malfunctioning lock and replace it with a far more subtle, complex construction."

She stared at him, this woman whose presence caused him physical pain the same way Sascha Duncan's had. But he wasn't going to ask for another assignment if Ivy agreed to Krychek's proposal. Seeing her, speaking to her, had made him understand that aside from children, the empaths were the closest thing the Net had to innocents.

He'd spotted Ivy's weapon, noted her distaste in holding it, seen her get rid of it. Her features were so expressive it was as if she'd spoken aloud—he'd known she'd made the decision to use herself as a distraction in an effort to protect the others who lived here. Perhaps he was wrong, perhaps her face wasn't as devoid of deceit as it appeared, but he couldn't take the risk that he *was* right, that she was that vulnerable. Because he didn't trust Krychek to keep his word when it came to the safety of the empaths; the other man's priority was the Net as a whole, not the individuals within it.

Ivy and the others needed the protection he could provide. Unlike her, he'd have no compunction in using lethal force if someone meant her—or any other E—harm. Keeping them safe wouldn't earn him absolution, but perhaps it would give him peace for a splinter of time. "Whatever your choice," he told her, "it will be respected. I give you my word." His honor was close to worthless, but he'd never broken any of the rare promises he'd made.

IVY stroked Rabbit's coat when he nudged at her hand with a worried nose. She felt as if her life had skewed sideways in the minutes since she'd first heard him bark. So many years she'd lived believing there was something fundamentally wrong with her. Now, this Arrow with his cold eyes and icy calm was telling her she had never been flawed.

Except she was terrified it was far too late. "I lost something in that reconditioning room"—perhaps the very thing for which he'd come to her—"and I don't think I can get it back. I broke."

"Do you wish to give up, then? Admit defeat?"

Anger uncurled inside her at that flat statement, though she knew his words hadn't been a judgment but a simple question. That anger was a raw, wild thing that had been growing and growing inside her since the day she'd become herself again. Vasic had inadvertently made himself a target.

Pushing up onto her knees, the snow a chilling dampness through her jeans, she fought to keep her shields from fracturing under the weight of her emotions. Kaleb Krychek might have declared the fall of Silence, but neither Ivy nor the others in the settlement were planning to expose themselves until they were dead certain the new regime would hold, that it wasn't just a trick to bring the fractured out of hiding.

"What do you know of emptiness?" she asked him, her body vibrating with the fury inside her. "What do you know of having your mind violated as if a steel brush is being scraped over your every nerve ending, every sense?"

He took so long to answer that the world was beyond silent when he said, "I am an Arrow. I was placed in training at four years of age. I know everything about having my mind torn open."

Four years old.

Anger shattering as if it had been hit with an anvil, the wreckage tearing holes through her, she rubbed a fisted hand over her heart. "I'm sorry."

"Why? You caused me no harm."

She saw from his expression that he meant that, as if the hurt of that small, vulnerable child was nothing. "Do you truly feel nothing?" she whispered. "Are you without fractures?"

"It's better this way." His eyes kissed her with frost. "The day I feel is the day I die."

Chapter 4

I'd like to propose a cooperative venture.

Kaleb Krychek, in a conference call to DarkRiver alpha Lucas Hunter and SnowDancer alpha Hawke Snow

ACROSS FROM SASCHA, Hawke shook his head, the silver-gold of his hair bright in the noon sunlight slanting through the skylight. "I'll say this for Krychek," the SnowDancer alpha muttered, "he has the balls of an elephant."

Splurting coffee, Mercy coughed, eyes watering. "An elephant?" She stared at the SnowDancer alpha as her mate, Riley, rubbed her back. "Are you serious?"

Hawke shrugged. "What has bigger ones?"

"Man has a point," Lucas drawled from beside Sascha, the six of them seated around Mercy and Riley's dining table, the land beyond the windows a sprawl of tall green firs draped with snow that turned it into a winter postcard.

The snowfall was nothing like the heavy coating up in the higher elevations of the Sierra Nevada range, while farther down, there was no precipitation at all, the air cold but dry.

"Whatever the size of Krychek's balls," Mercy said after catching her breath, "this is one hell of a request."

Lucas ran his fingers absently over Sascha's nape as he looked toward the male who sat on Riley's other side. When Sascha had first met Judd Lauren, she couldn't have imagined that the distant and self-contained former Arrow would end up a SnowDancer lieutenant mated to another member of the wolf pack. And never in a million years would she have predicted that he'd become a favorite with the pups and cubs both.

"The information Krychek sent us," Lucas said to Judd now, "about the infection in the Net, were you able to corroborate it independently?"

Judd nodded, the fine dark gray wool of his pullover sitting easily on his shoulders. "Kaleb's been up-front."

"Too up-front." Sascha *wanted* to believe love had altered Kaleb Krychek for the better, that he'd found the same joy with Sahara that Sascha had with Lucas, but the fact of the matter was, he continued to be a deadly threat. There was a reason he'd become the youngest ever individual to hold a seat on the Council, a reason why his name caused men and women across the world to tremble in naked terror.

Biting down on her lower lip as her mate continued to stroke her nape with the tactile affection that was so natural to the cats, she said, "He has my unqualified gratitude for putting his own life at risk to save countless people in San Francisco a month ago"—when the cardinal telekinetic had helped disarm a toxic weapon—"but I think it would be foolish to think we can predict anything when it comes to him." The other man remained as opaque as ever, an enigmatic figure who held near-total control of the PsyNet.

No one, Sascha thought, should have that much power, hold that many lives in the palm of his hand. Yet, if not Kaleb Krychek, then who? His staggering psychic and military strength was the only reason the Psy race hadn't collapsed into anarchy and death in the aftermath of the fall of Silence. It was as unavoidable a truth as the fact he'd risen to power with ruthless, blood-soaked determination.

Hawke narrowed his eyes. "The news about the infection." He glanced at Judd. "Is it a secret?"

"No. It's not headline news in the Net yet, but the knowledge is gathering steam."

Lucas shook his head. "So, Krychek isn't exactly giving up anything by offering us the data."

"And," Riley said in his quiet, direct way, "it's not as if we didn't already know about the existence of empaths."

Everyone looked at Sascha.

Hands cupped around the mug of hot chocolate Mercy had offered her in lieu of the aromatic coffee the others were drinking, Sascha leaned a little into Lucas. "I have no hesitation in helping other Es," she said, able to sense Lucas's panther rising to the surface to rub against the insides of his skin . . . against her.

It made her feel safe and protected even before her mate wrapped an arm around her shoulders and tucked her close. "There's nothing I want more than to stretch my psychic muscles with others of my designation," she said, making no attempt to hide the depth of her hunger.

She adored working with Judd's nephew, Toby, but while the young boy was a cardinal telepath who could blow her out of the water when it came to telepathy, the reverse was true when it came to their E abilities. "I want to learn from the others," she said, "even as I teach them what I know." Things she'd figured out through often frustrating trial and error. "But most of all," she whispered, "I want to help those of my designation accept that they're not broken"—her fingers tightened on the mug, her eyes wet—"that they aren't flawed."

Lucas pressed a kiss to her temple. Her strong, loving, protective mate had been with her when she'd understood the truth about herself, understood that she wasn't a defective cardinal as she'd been told all her life, but a woman with a gift meant to help the hurt and the lost.

It was Mercy who said, "Yet something's making you hesitate," the red of her hair vivid against her fitted blue shirt.

"I'm a mother as well as an E." Sascha's heart bloomed with love at the thought of her and Lucas's sweet baby. "And Naya is only one of the children in DarkRiver and SnowDancer." Pups and cubs who were painfully vulnerable. "We can't justify putting them at risk." Even to help men and women who were as bruised and as wounded as Sascha had once been.

The thought made her chest clench in agony, but she couldn't see a way around the threat posed by those coming in with the empaths.

"Kaleb won't harm anyone in either pack."

Lucas stirred at Judd's confident statement. "Exactly how much of an *ex*-Arrow are you?" he asked, panther-green eyes intent.

"It's been pointed out to me that an Arrow who has never broken faith with the squad continues to be considered an Arrow regardless of his location or belief otherwise." The lieutenant's lips curved up unexpectedly at the corners, the light reaching the deep brown of his eyes, the gold flecks in them bright.

It struck Sascha then that Judd existed on the same continuum as Kaleb. Not as ruthless—she didn't think *anyone* was as ruthless as Kaleb Krychek—but a man who had walked long and alone in the darkness. The critical difference, of course, was that Judd had always been anchored to the world through his family, while Kaleb had been trained by a psychopath who'd murdered countless women.

"I'm in direct contact with more than one member of the squad." The SnowDancer lieutenant paused, his gaze shifting to Hawke.

At his alpha's slight nod, Judd added, "I'm also in direct touch with Kaleb, have been since long before the San Francisco op."

"I thought we weren't keeping secrets?" Lucas locked eyes with Hawke, alpha to alpha, dominant to dominant, his voice holding the edge of a growl.

Hawke folded his arms as Sascha put down her hot chocolate and patted her mate's chest to get his attention, his dark green T-shirt soft under her palm. Left alone in this kind of an aggressive mood, two changeling alphas would stare at one another until it ended in violence. "No fighting," she said to Lucas when he turned to scowl at her. "You know how cranky Hawke gets when his mate is out to lunch with a certain future leopard alpha."

Lucas's grin was very feline as he relaxed.

"Yeah," Mercy murmured, shoulders shaking, "be kind to the poor wolfie." She squeaked as her own wolf mate did something to her the rest of them couldn't see.

Growling low in his throat, Hawke bared his teeth. "We passed on the data," he said, "just not where it came from. Krychek's been Judd's connection for several operations—including the one that netted us Alice Eldridge."

Sascha sucked in a breath at the mention of the human scientist who'd completed what was possibly the most detailed sociological and anthropological study on E-Psy ever done. That research had been meticulously wiped after Silence, with only a rare few copies of Alice's seminal work—*The Mysterious E Designation: Empathic Gifts & Shadows*—surviving in the world of underground collectors. Alice herself had been put into a cryonic sleep, only to wake mere months ago with her memories in pieces.

"So," Sascha murmured, "Krychek wants easy access not only to me, but to Alice." Even with her problematic memory, the human scientist remained an invaluable resource. Alice's surviving published work might not have focused on how empaths did what they did, but no one knew what knowledge she held in her brain.

"Yes." Judd drank some of his coffee. "But he's aware of the state of her memories, so I think he's far more interested in you. Regardless, he won't harm a single individual in either pack."

Riley stretched his arm along the back of Mercy's chair. "Why do you sound so certain?" he asked, cutting to the heart of the matter as always.

"DarkRiver considers SnowDancer family, and Sahara considers DarkRiver family."

That much was inarguable. Not only had Kaleb's mate sought the protection of the pack for a time after she'd first been rescued from a hellish captivity, but she had blood ties to another member of the pack, not to mention her growing friendship with Mercy.

"Kaleb is no different from any of the men in this room," Judd said. "Hurting the packs would hurt his mate, and he'd never consciously do anything to distress her. DarkRiver and SnowDancer are safe. I'd go so far as to say that, in all probability, he'd actively stand with us against an enemy should we ever make the request."

Sascha couldn't imagine Kaleb Krychek, cold and powerful, loving anyone enough to sheathe his psychic claws. "I need to meet him," she said into the somewhat dubious silence that followed Judd's words. "While he's with Sahara." Not only so they could gauge if he could be trusted in pack territory, but to check on Sahara's welfare; seeing the younger woman safe with their own eyes was a far different thing to hearing her say the same on the comm.

Lucas looked at Sascha, the panther prowling to life in his eyes. "Sahara *is* family," he said, his tone that of the alpha he was. "I don't like the fact I've never seen the two of them together." A grim line to his jaw. "I want to make sure she's still okay with him before we make any kind of a decision."

"Say we accept Krychek's bona fides"—Riley refilled Mercy's mug with milk rather than coffee, to her unimpressed snarl—"that still leaves the others who'll be in our territory if we say yes to his proposal."

"The Es should be no problem." Stretching out in his chair, Hawke grinned as Mercy gulped down the milk as if it was medicine. "Long as Sascha confirms they are Es. Your designation has a problem with violence."

"The pain of the victim rebounds back on us." Though there were more subtle, long-term ways an empath could attack another living being, things that had shocked Sascha the first time she'd read *Empathic Gifts & Shadows*.

"Don't, however, make the mistake of thinking all Es are trustworthy," Lucas said on the heels of Sascha's thoughts. "Kitten, tell them what it said in Alice's book."

Conscious that a lack of awareness as to the threat posed by Es could be as dangerous as placing blind trust in Kaleb Krychek, Sascha shared the repugnant truth. "In the past, a minority of empaths were known to have consciously manipulated the emotions of others." Her skin crawled at the act that went against everything she stood for as an E. "One E wanted everyone to be 'good,' while others did it for money, revenge, power . . ."

Judd's mug hit the wood of the table with a dull sound. "A truly gifted and subtle empath wouldn't need mind control," he said, clearly seeing the weaponized potential of such an ability.

"There'd also be no painful rebound effect"—Hawke's hand curled into a fist on the tabletop—"because the victim wouldn't even know it was happening."

That was the most evil aspect of it; an empath could effectively take away an individual's right to choose. "The good news," Sascha said, fighting her nausea, "is that such manipulation apparently requires prolonged contact with the intended victim and a high level of skill." Newly awakened empaths would be stumbling in the dark in comparison.

Mercy tapped her fingers on the table. "So it's not a danger we have to worry about immediately, but it needs to be part of the briefing given to any member of either DarkRiver or SnowDancer who might come in contact with an E."

No one had any arguments with that suggestion.

"That leaves the guards." Riley angled his head toward Judd. "You have a line on who they're likely to be?"

"Arrows. I'll vouch for them, though I don't think that'll be necessary—Vasic's heading the security team."

Mercy's gaze sharpened. "He's the one who brought in the medic when Dorian was shot," she said, naming a fellow DarkRiver sentinel.

"Yes. He also helped Ashaya"—Dorian's mate—"escape the Net. He's not interested in picking a fight." Tone altering on those last words, Judd said, "He's a man I trust to the bone—if he says this is a straight-up op, then it is."

Hawke and Lucas both nodded, Judd having long ago earned the trust of both alphas.

"Location's going to be critical if we agree to this." Rising, Mercy found a map of the area and spread it out on the table, the slight outward curve of her belly the only sign of her pregnancy. "Anyone have suggestions?"

Hawke used his finger to circle a low-lying section. "This was the site of the hyena attack awhile back. It's on the edges of both our territories, bracketed by DarkRiver on one side, SnowDancer on the other."

"It can be isolated within a secure perimeter without problem," Lucas murmured, eyes on the map. "And the area's open enough that satellite surveillance is a viable security option."

For the next hour, the others discussed exactly how the site could be secured, while Sascha sat and listened, the ebb and flow of their voices a rough, familiar music. It had taken her only a short time after her defection to understand that an empath was as social a creature as a pack-minded changeling—it had hurt her to be deprived of that sense of community, of family in the Net, though she hadn't understood the dull gnawing pain at the time.

Because it had been constant, a second heartbeat.

"Sascha." Lucas's voice, pitched for her ears alone as he lifted their clasped hands to his mouth to brush a kiss over her knuckles. "Whatever happens, we won't abandon the other Es."

Adoring him beyond reason for understanding the forces tearing her apart, she leaned her head against his shoulder. "I want them to have this life," she whispered. "I want them to know what it is to live without being suffocated every minute of every day. I want them to know freedom."

Chapter 5

Loyalty is not a trait limited to the E designation, but over the course of this study, it has become clear that once an empath chooses to give his or her loyalty, the bond is not one the E will ever easily sever—even when that bond threatens to cause the E in question mortal harm.

Excerpted from *The Mysterious E Designation:*
Empathic Gifts & Shadows by Alice Eldridge

IVY TURNED TO head back to her cabin as soon as Vasic left, the teleport so fast she had the breath-stealing realization that he wasn't an ordinary telekinetic, but a Tk-V. A Traveler, someone for whom teleporting was as easy as breathing, and who could go from one end of the world to the other in a heartbeat.

That wasn't the scary part.

It was that there were no distinctive structures or natural formations in the part of the orchard to which he'd teleported. Which meant he'd done so by using her face as a lock . . . but he'd come in a little distance from her. So either he could 'port to within a certain radius of the target, or there *was* something in the orchard he'd been able to use as a focus. How then would he have obtained the image of the specific area in the first place?

She rubbed her forehead. Not that it mattered. If an Arrow wanted to find her, she'd be found. The fact Vasic was most probably a teleporter who could lock onto people only hammered home that inescapable truth.

"Ivy!"

Almost to the cabin, she saw her mother running toward her. Having thrown on a jacket over the simple khaki cargo pants and old sweatshirt that was her usual work wear when she wasn't handling her honeybees, Gwen Jane had longer legs than her daughter and made it to her side in seconds.

"I'm fine," Ivy said at once, kicking herself for not having telepathed that the instant it became clear Vasic didn't intend to do her harm. Her only excuse was stunned shock. "He only came to deliver a message." Her fingers pressed into the thick paper of the envelope he'd given her before he left.

"The settlement went into lockdown the instant we received your telepathic alarm." Gwen's chest rose and fell as she caught her breath, her pale skin flushed. "I couldn't stop your father from heading out to cover you with a weapon, however."

"I know." She'd felt her father's telepathic touch. And while she couldn't prove it, her gut told her Vasic, too, had been aware of her father the entire time.

Gwen's eyes shifted over Ivy's left shoulder just as Rabbit "woofed" and ran to greet Ivy's father. Turning her attention back to Ivy, her mother said, "I assume we need to talk?"

Ivy wasn't the least disconcerted by her mother's lack of an emotive response. Gwen wasn't maternal in any obvious way, but that said nothing; Ivy's mother had changed her entire life so that her child could heal, and she'd done it without ever making that child feel at fault.

As had her father.

Where Gwen was taller than many men, her hair the soft black she'd bequeathed Ivy, Carter Hirsch was a stocky man of medium height, his eyes a clear copper ringed with gold. Ivy had always loved the fact she was so clearly an amalgam of the two most important people in her life. Though the genetics had worked out to leave her the shortest in the family, she had not only Gwen's hair, but the fineness of her mother's bones, while her golden skin tone echoed her father's part-Algerian heritage.

Right this instant, Carter held his weapon at his side, his elbows and the front of his clothing wet, dirty. He must've been flat on the ground with a bead on Vasic the entire time, this man who had always been there for her, though she'd been meant to be nothing more than the completion of a simple fertilization contract.

The love and respect she felt for her parents was a hugeness in her heart she could never properly explain. "The settlement can come out of lockdown," she said, voice husky, and led them toward the cabin that had become her own the day she took responsibility for the fruit orchard that supplied the families who lived here, the majority of their crops far more prosaic grains.

Rabbit padded along in front, and it was such a familiar sight that the knots in her stomach began to unravel a fraction. "The Arrow—Vasic—came specifically for me."

"They don't send Arrows after fractured Psy," her father said, always the more phlegmatic of her parents, despite the fact her mother appeared the more practical at first glance. "Especially Gradient 3.2 telepaths."

"No." Ivy pushed through the door to her home. "I'll get you a blanket, Father. You really shouldn't stay in those wet clothes."

"I'm fine." He took off his jacket to reveal that his heavy work shirt was dry.

Seeing that he'd made up his mind, but aware his pants remained wet, she turned up the heat, then handed him the letter wrinkled from her grip. "According to Vasic"—she tugged off her gloves to put them on the counter, shrugged off her jacket—"I'm not a telepath. Or rather, that's not my main designation."

Her parents sat down at her small kitchen table and read the letter together.

It was her mother who broke the silence. "Well, it makes sense." Gwen stared down at the floor, her eyes crinkled at the corners and her arms wrapped around herself. "When you were a fetus," she murmured, "I had a serious problem maintaining Silence. The obstetrician sent me to a specialized M-Psy who did a complete workup, then told me it was simply an unusually severe but known side effect of pregnancy." Her shoulders grew stiff. "He must've known, kept me in the dark."

"I've never heard of an E designation. How can we be certain it's as the Arrow says?" her father said with his usual practicality.

Ivy had asked the same question. "Vasic told me to contact Sascha Duncan for confirmation." Former Councilor Nikita Duncan's daughter was famous for her defection to a changeling leopard pack . . . and for being a cardinal derided as weak and flawed for most of her lifetime.

The parallel was a difficult one to avoid. As was the dangerous hope that came with it. "I don't think she'd have any reason to lie, do you?"

Gwen nodded, but it was Carter who spoke, his words unexpected. "When your mother and I made the decision to take you in for reconditioning, we thought we were helping you."

"Father, I know," Ivy began, distressed he'd think otherwise.

"Ivy, let me speak." When she nodded, biting back her words, he said, "I don't judge us for making that decision. It was all we knew to do to help our child. You were in excruciating pain, and had we done nothing, you would've been forcibly rehabilitated."

Ivy couldn't keep quiet any longer. "I know," she whispered again. "I *know*."

But her father hadn't finished. "It wasn't until afterward that we realized we'd made a terrible error and that the price might well be our Ivy."

Ivy's eyes burned at the love embodied in those uninflected words.

"You were a ghost." Gwen stared off into the distance.

Rabbit immediately scampered over to stand with his paws on the tops of Gwen's scuffed boots, whining in his throat until she bent to pet him.

"The Ivy we'd nurtured from birth seemed erased"—Gwen's hand clenched on Rabbit's coat—"and while Carter might not judge us for the decision we made, I'll never forgive myself for handing my child over to be violated."

Ivy knelt in front of her mother. "I *wanted* to go," she reminded them both. "I thought it would help, too, and it did in one way. I don't think I'd be alive now without the reconditioning, no matter how bad it turned out to be." Her mind had literally been crushing itself.

"Our daughter is correct." Carter shifted to face Gwen, holding her gaze with his own until Gwen gave a slight nod.

Ivy glanced away, feeling as if she'd intruded on a private moment. She didn't know what her parents' relationship was beyond a joint commitment to her, but Carter was the only one who had the ability to get Gwen to change her mind. It made Ivy hope that they'd discovered a fragment of joy in the darkness.

"The reason I brought up that day," her father said into the silence, his skin pulled taut over solid bones, "is that whatever was done to you during the reconditioning brutally harmed an integral part of you." He pushed back sandy hair glinting with more strands of silver than there should be on a man his age.

Ivy's reconditioning had marked them all.

"This may be your opportunity to undo that harm," he said, "to find out who you're capable of being without the cage of Silence."

"But the decision must be yours." Gwen's voice was unflinching, her gaze steady. "If you need to run, get away from the Arrow, we're with you."

Ivy had a feeling there was no way to run from Vasic. Dark and dangerous and with an ice to him that made her want to brush her fingertips over the sharp edges of his cheekbones, see if he was cold to the touch, he was a hunter no one could escape . . . but Ivy had had enough of being prey.

"No more running," she said to her parents, her stomach tight and a strange exhilaration in her blood. "It's time I made my stand." Even if it meant going up against an Arrow with eyes of winter frost.

HAVING informed Aden of his decision to accept responsibility for the protection detail on the empaths, Vasic teleported that night to a man who had never been an Arrow but was a member of the squad in ways an outsider would never understand.

Those like Vasic were taught how to snap necks or garrote in shadowy quiet, how to build covert bombs and effect subtle sabotage as needed. They weren't taught how to set up businesses or invest money. The irony was that while Arrows were paid commensurate to their lethal skills and the danger so often inherent in their ops, over the past century, most had died without spending any but a tiny fraction of it.

Since Arrows were legally expunged from their family groups upon entry into the squad, that money had gone directly into an Arrow fund

set up by Zaid Adelaja. The first Arrow had fought to make certain the
Council would never have any right to a lost Arrow's assets. It was Aden
who'd realized a decade ago that the processes were now so automated
that everyone in power had *forgotten* about the fund in the interim.

It meant the squad had millions upon millions to work with as they
sought to save those of their own destined for cold, quiet executions
because the Arrows in question were too broken to any longer be the
perfect killing machines. But first, they'd needed someone who understood money, who could help them create a solid financial network of
properties and investments that no one could trace back to the squad.
Most of all, it had to be someone who could be trusted with the lives of
men and women who had earned their peace.

Now, the elderly man looked up from the book he had open on his
blanket-covered lap as he sat on the partially glassed-in deck of his home
beside Lake Tahoe. The small reading light he'd clipped to the arm of his
chair bathed the pages in a warm yellow light, the world beyond draped
in night. "Vasic," he said, and though there was no smile, no hint of
emotion, the word held welcome.

Going down on one knee on the wood of the deck, Vasic bowed his
head. "Hello, Grandfather." Many people called Zie Zen "Grandfather,"
using it as an honorific, for in his lifetime, he'd helped an unknown
number of people across the world. However, for Vasic it was a biological
truth—one generation removed.

Zie Zen was not his grandfather, but his great-grandfather.

No one could've guessed at the relationship from their physical appearance, a fact the two of them had used to their advantage. Zie Zen's looks
inclined strongly toward his Chinese father, his eyes dark brown and
slanted, his bone structure sharp, elegant. By the time the genes reached
Vasic, the genetic drift had come to full fruition.

He had the gray eyes of his great-grandmother, his features echoing
his own mother's half-Croatian heritage. His six-feet-four-inch height,
muscular build, even the softer texture of his black hair, was courtesy of
the Caucasian American male who had provided sperm for his conception.
That was where the relationship began and ended.

None of it mattered. Regardless of the fact his legal last name was Duvnjak rather than Zen, Vasic acknowledged only one being on the planet as family, and it was the man who now touched his hand to Vasic's shoulder in a silent request that he rise. Getting up, he took a seat on the edge of the deck that overlooked the vast quiet of the lake, his feet on the winter-hard and snowy ground, his forearms braced on his thighs, the rippling dark water his focus.

Zie Zen understood the value of quiet, of peace, and he said nothing, turning a page in a rasping whisper of sound that merged seamlessly into the night. This land, Vasic thought, kissed the edge of DarkRiver territory. It was possible a leopard changeling, its lashes lowered to conceal the night-glow brilliance of its eyes, watched him from the edge of the lake even now. Vasic couldn't imagine what it must be like to be a being of two forms, to have such primal wildness within. The "half-feral child" he'd once been, as noted in his training log, was long gone.

"We are to wake the empaths," he said to Zie Zen much later, the moon high over the lake, a spotlight on a world draped in pure white.

"Ah." The sound of skin rustling against paper. "I had wondered if that might be the next step."

Vasic told the older man everything he knew of the project. Aden would've done the same had he been here—Zie Zen had earned their loyalty long ago, while Kaleb Krychek remained an unknown. Then Vasic waited for his great-grandfather to speak, knowing the other man had far more knowledge inside him than most; at a sharp hundred and twenty, Zie Zen was one of the rare few individuals in the Net who had been old enough at the dawn of Silence to remember the past with adult clarity.

"I was eight years old when the debate first began." It was a murmur as soft as the night. "A child, uncaring of the worries of my elders, happy in my play." Coughing into his hand, he cleared his throat. "We played then, as freely as the changelings and the humans."

To Vasic, the idea was so wholly foreign that it took him several seconds to process it.

"The decision was made to embrace the Protocol the day I turned eighteen. My parents' generation and those just a few years older than me . . . they were too old to adapt to Silence, though they tried. Most died at obscenely young ages."

"I didn't know that." Vasic had, however, often wondered why the Net didn't have more elders like Zie Zen, the ones from before Silence.

"Some say the men and women of this lost generation were murdered for being too disruptive to the new regime, but I think the truth is much more simple. They died because their hearts were broken." Zie Zen's breathing was harsh, choppy, but nothing to comment on, given his age.

"Those long-ago Psy had to learn to live in a world where the children for whom they'd embraced an emotionless existence looked at mother and father both with cold eyes, and where their grandchildren were creatures they could not understand." Another cough, paper rustling again. "It was too alien an environment, one that stole the breath from the lungs of those who should've been my peers in this twilight."

Vasic watched the water ripple in to shore, the moon whispering over each silken undulation, and he listened.

"The empaths . . . the empaths died the fastest." A long silence pierced with the echoes of a past that to Vasic may as well have been a fever dream, and yet that Zie Zen had lived. "A small number did defect with those we now call the Forgotten, but the vast majority stayed, believing they could help their people. Instead, Silence eventually crushed the life out of the Es, until many simply didn't wake up one morning."

Vasic didn't feel, but that didn't mean he couldn't comprehend the nuances in another's voice. That skill was part of what made him such a good assassin, such a good soldier. "You speak from experience, Grandfather?"

Chapter 6

Dear Z²,

Yes I am mad at you, thank you very much. I can't believe you didn't wake me. I'm fine. Don't worry.

xoxo,
Sunny

p.s. Love you (still mad though).
p.p.s. I know we're not supposed to acknowledge emotions now, so burn this after you read it.

HIS GREAT-GRANDFATHER DIDN'T immediately answer Vasic's question, the quiet broken only by the faraway echo of a wolf's howl, as if a SnowDancer ran tonight in the territory of its leopard allies. If Krychek managed to obtain the approval of the two packs, Vasic knew he'd hear wolf song at far closer range.

"My growing up years," Zie Zen said long after the howl had faded, "were consumed with the discussion on Silence. You cannot imagine the world as it was then, the chaos and terror of it, our race on the brink of cannibalizing itself. We debated the Protocol at school, at the dinner table, in every corner of the PsyNet, on television, in newspapers . . .

"Trillions of words were spoken, written, thought, until Silence was the defining memory of youth for many of my generation. But . . . it is not mine." A rasping breath. "My youth can be encompassed in a single word: Sunny." This quiet was deeper, heavier, not to be interrupted. "Her legal name was Samantha, but no one called her that. She was my neighbor, and my friend, and when we were sixteen, she became my lover."

Vasic turned at last, bracing his back against one of the posts that bracketed the steps to his left. "A true lover?" he asked, looking into his grandfather's dark eyes. "Skin contact?" Rather than the financial and scientific dance that was the current mating ritual of his race, genetic and psychic profiles compared before an egg was fertilized at the point of a needle.

Zie Zen's expression was distant, his mind clearly in that strange long-ago world. "Yes, skin to skin." He touched his fingers to his jaw in an action Vasic had never previously seen him make, before dropping that hand back on the open pages of his book.

"I wanted to defect at the dawn of Silence," he said, and it was an unexpected admission, "but Sunny was an E, a powerful one. She wouldn't leave, said there was so much stress and panic in the Net that it would be the same as a doctor walking out of an ER bursting at the seams with trauma victims. So we stayed."

Vasic didn't know too much about the beginnings of Silence, but he did know that established couples hadn't been forcibly separated—instead each couple had been directed to live a chaste, distant life in order to set the correct example for any offspring. That left only one reason why Zie Zen had not had a child with his Sunny, Vasic's genetic history including no one named Samantha. "When did she die?"

"Five years after the inception of the Protocol," was the stark answer. "Only twenty-three and worn-out, worn-down. So many needed the help of an E after Silence, hundreds of thousands in agony because they had to sever ties of love and replace them with everything that was frigidly rational. Worse was the unrelenting pressure on the Es to stop *being*."

A quiet shake of Zie Zen's head, but his hand clamped down so hard on the arm of his chair that Vasic could count his great-grandfather's bones. "It would be akin to my asking you to stop breathing, for empaths then weren't the smothered, broken shells of today. Sunny was joyous, vibrant in her ability, her heart open to the world . . . and that world kicked her until she bled in ways I couldn't stem, couldn't fix."

The older man fell quiet for so long that Vasic was certain Zie Zen's time of talking was done for this night, but then he said, "Watch over your Sunny as I wasn't able to watch over mine."

The Silent answer would've been to say that Ivy wasn't his, was just another task. However on this moonlit night when his great-grandfather had told him of a woman named Sunny who Vasic would never meet—but who he now realized had shaped Zie Zen's entire existence, there was only one correct answer. "I will, Grandfather."

Zie Zen closed his book, his hands steady and his jaw a firm line. "You must make certain the Es aren't sacrificed as they were then, aren't broken under the weight of the burden that is this new world." His gaze locked with Vasic's. "They will walk into any hell; with very few exceptions, it's how they're made. Of stubborn courage and little to no ability to be selfish. This new chaos will annihilate them unless there is a stronger force that will put the Es first."

Vasic had made a vow to protect, and he would do it until his dying breath, but—"That is a task for a better man, a man like Aden." Strong and intelligent and without fractures in every corner of his being. Vasic's self was held together by countless jagged stitches that tore him bloody night and day.

"I'm a brute weapon and an expendable shield," he said as the night wind cut across his exposed face, "my task to stand in the way of any violence directed toward the Es." He'd do so without flinching. "I'm not strong enough to last the time the empaths will need their protector to last." Into untold decades to come.

Zie Zen shook his head again. "No, Vasic. This isn't your choice. It is a matter of honor—mine and yours." Another shaky breath. "You are the son of my heart, my truest descendent. You may have lost faith, but you will never give up, regardless of what you believe at this instant. You will do what must be done."

Vasic said nothing. Zie Zen's word was law as far as he was concerned, but there was no doubt in his mind that he would disappoint his great-grandfather this one time. Zie Zen was right—Vasic would never give up, but there would come a time when he'd simply stop working, his body and mind shutting down as a malfunctioning machine might do.

After all, that was what he was: a machine trained to mete out death.

Standing after another half hour of silence, he gave a respectful bow of his head before walking to the water's edge, the snow soft and the pebbles small and smooth beneath the heavy tread of his combat boots. Zie Zen was growing frailer, the hand he'd placed on his cane as Vasic turned away trembling a little, but Vasic had known better than to offer his assistance. His great-grandfather would've considered that an insult of the highest magnitude.

I'll need your help soon enough. When it is time, I will ask.

Reaching a hundred and thirty years of age was not unheard of in their world, with a limited few living beyond that, but Vasic didn't think his great-grandfather would make it. He saw the same tiredness in Zie Zen's eyes that he felt in his soul, and after what he'd heard tonight, he understood that Zie Zen had suffered blows that had left grievous wounds. And still he continued on.

You are the son of my heart, my truest descendent . . . You will do what must be done.

As Vasic once again considered his great-grandfather's life, he thought of Ivy with her too-perceptive eyes that showed her every thought and her scrappy dog that thought it was a mastiff. Yet there was a fierce strength there, strength that had led her to seek to protect those who were her own even if it meant facing down an Arrow.

. . . it's how they're made. Of stubborn courage and little to no ability to be selfish.

If Ivy followed that pattern, she'd be eaten alive by the monsters that prowled the Net. The world was an even harder place now than that which had claimed Zie Zen's Sunny. Too many people had had their sense of empathy worn away to nothing, become cold inside in a way that couldn't be ameliorated. Sociopaths reigned supreme in many areas of life—from business, to education, to medicine.

It would take decades to fix that imbalance.

Others were so used to being told what to do that they were finding it difficult to function under the current regime. Total freedom would be their worst nightmare. Voracious in their need, these hungry individuals would ask for more and more and still more from the empaths, until an E had nothing left.

Until she lay down to sleep one day and never again woke.

That realization uppermost on Vasic's mind, he walked for near to an hour along the rim of the lake. When he saw the large spotted cat watching him from the trees, he didn't make any sudden moves. Instead, he inclined his head in quiet acknowledgment. The leopard—or perhaps it was a jaguar—did the same, then whispered away into the trees, two predators passing in the night.

UNABLE to sleep, Ivy sat in her doorway wrapped up in a thick throw, and stared at the star-studded sky. A drowsy Rabbit had pulled and pushed his cushioned basket to her side with annoyed huffs, and now lay snoring beside her. A normal night, the sky holding a hard-edged clarity that came only on the coldest nights . . . except that her life would never again be normal.

Ivy's lips twisted. Her life hadn't ever been normal, not as the Psy understood it. Even before her collapse at sixteen, she'd known she was different. She'd tried so hard to be like her fellow students at school, increasingly rational and remote with every year of growth and training, but Silence had always been a coat so ill-fitting it exhausted her to wear it.

Mother, why can't I do it right? The teacher says I'm flawed.

She'd been sobbing as she asked that question, a nine-year-old girl who'd failed her Silence evaluation for the second time. Ivy would never forget what her mother had said.

Flaws make us who we are, Ivy. Without them, we might as well be made of plas, featureless and indistinct. Never ever be ashamed of your flaws.

Then her parents had worked together to figure out a way she could pass the evaluations, though inside, her conditioning was as bad as always. Now an Arrow named Vasic had given her the answer why, and it destroyed everything she thought she knew about the world, her mind turbulent with the need to *believe*.

A shooting star fell across the sky in a splinter of light at that instant . . . and her nose began to bleed.

Ivy had already made her choice. This, she thought as she used tissues from the pocket of her robe to deal with the blood, was simply the coda on that decision. If the E designation did indeed exist and Ivy carried the ability, she wanted to explore it with every ounce of her being. The fact it would likely stop her brain from crushing itself was a bonus—

Her breath caught in her throat, her hand falling to her side, fisted on the bloody tissues. "You're early," she whispered to the man who'd appeared in front of the cabin.

"I'm not here for your decision." Winter gray eyes scanned the area.

Rabbit jerked awake on a growl just as the Arrow disappeared around the side of the house. Heart thudding, Ivy could almost think she'd imagined the whole surreal experience, but he appeared around the other side of the cabin not long afterward. "You expected a threat?" she managed to ask, one hand on Rabbit's rigid back.

"No." His face an unreadable silhouette against the night sky, his shoulders outlined by starlight, he added, "A simple security sweep." Ivy was now under Vasic's protection, even if she hadn't accepted the contract.

A startled spark in eyes that were dangerously expressive even in the low light. "Oh." Continuing to pet her dog, she said, "Would you like something hot to drink?" A frown. "You must be cold if you're doing security sweeps at this time of night."

Vasic paused. She was afraid of him, the instinctive response an intelligent one. And yet she'd offered him sustenance. His great-grandfather was right—empaths did not appear to have the best sense of self-preservation. "No," he said. "Why are you sitting here?" Talking to her hadn't been on the agenda.

"I like the quiet." Her face softened, the husky thread in her voice more apparent. "There's a kind of secrecy in the world at this time of night, as if I'm allowed to see mysteries hidden in daylight."

Vasic thought of the deserts and isolated mountain outlooks where he went in an effort to find peace from the shades of those he had erased, considered if Ivy Jane would see mysteries in those locations, too. "You should go inside." His thoughts were immaterial because Ivy would never experience the places in question. "My readings tell me the temperature will drop considerably in the next fifteen minutes."

Getting to her feet, the throw bulky around her, Ivy nodded. "I think you're right. I can taste more snow in the air."

It was a sensual way to describe a meteorological function, another sign that Ivy Jane was in no way Silent. Not that he needed the confirmation—her presence was sandpaper against his senses, harsh and abrasive. It didn't matter. As Aden had pointed out, the sensation might be uncomfortable, but it wasn't debilitating.

And Vasic had made a promise.

So long as he drew breath, he would protect her.

Chapter 7

Sahara Kyriakus has simply been sucked into the gravitational pull of Kaleb Krychek's power. We should be considering how to rescue her, not peering in fascination at a bond that is a prison.

Letter to the Editor from "Concerned Citizen," *PsyNet Beacon*

KALEB AGREED TO meet Lucas Hunter and Sascha Duncan only because the alpha pair had been blunt in their request. "We need to see that Sahara is happy, content," Lucas had stated.

"Some men would take that as an insult."

The DarkRiver alpha had given an unconcerned shrug in response to Kaleb's reply. "Not in a pack, he wouldn't. We look after our own."

Kaleb was feral in his possessiveness when it came to Sahara, but he understood that such a connection to a powerful pack was a good thing for her to have in her arsenal.

"Sometimes, my gorgeous man," Sahara said when he stated that, "it isn't about strategy but about family." Her fingers in his hair, nails lightly grazing his scalp. "If DarkRiver and SnowDancer permit the empathic compound in their territory, it won't be because of politics, but because of ties of family."

"An unsound way to make a security decision," he pointed out, while the most scarred, most violent part of him stretched out lazily under her caresses.

"Is it?" Rising on tiptoe, she pressed kisses along his jaw. "Would you ever cause either pack harm when I call them family? Together, they are, after all, a dangerous aggressive force."

Realizing he'd lost this battle, he decided to be seduced instead. Later that day, when they arrived at the meeting, he was ready for Sascha Duncan to ask him and Sahara to lower their surface shields. He'd have drawn the line at that—no one had the right to intrude on his and Sahara's bond.

As it was, the cardinal empath asked nothing of the kind, yet her smile made it clear she'd sensed enough to ease her concerns. It gave Kaleb an acute insight into how deeply integrated an empath's abilities were to her ordinary senses. "Any team with an E on their side has a tactical advantage in a negotiation," he said to Sahara when they returned home. "Political, social, or business."

Sahara frowned. "I never considered that an E might work in a business capacity, but it makes perfect sense. If both sides have an E at the table, it balances out the negotiation." Kissing him with an affection that was still a surprise, she smoothed her hands down the black of his suit jacket. "But we can talk about that later. You don't want to be late for this next meeting, and I have a paper to write."

A minute and a much more thorough kiss later, Kaleb teleported onto the roof of a New York skyscraper to talk to a man who might hold the secret to the Psy race's future survival. "I appreciate you responding so quickly to my request."

Turning to face Kaleb, the city at his back and the wind tugging at the rich brown of the tailored coat he wore over a business suit, Devraj Santos raised an eyebrow. "It's not every day the most powerful telekinetic in the PsyNet asks to speak to one of the Forgotten."

Not simply *one* of the Forgotten. Dev Santos was the leader of the people who had once been Psy but were now something else, having defected from the Net at the dawn of Silence and intermingled heavily with the human and changeling populations. As a result, their psychic abilities ranged from zero to potent—and according to Kaleb's sources, for those Forgotten who did carry psychic abilities, the biofeedback from a neural network remained a necessity for survival.

"The PsyNet," he said to the dark-haired male, "is undergoing certain changes."

Santos slid his hands into the pockets of his open coat, an amused glint in his eyes. "That may be the understatement of the century." Not waiting for a response, he continued, "You want to know how we survived without Silence."

"Yes." The ShadowNet, as the Forgotten apparently called their network, was the most analogous construct to the PsyNet in the world. Yet, as far as Kaleb had been able to determine, the Forgotten network carried no infection. Furthermore, the percentage of serial killers among Santos' people was comparable to that of the humans and changelings, far less than that in the Psy population pre- or *post*-Silence. "I need to know why you survived, and are now thriving."

Expression darkening, Santos said, "We didn't. Not at first." He shifted to face the city, his gaze on the skyscrapers piercing the snow-heavy sky and beyond them, the turbulent water of the East River.

Kaleb joined him, waited.

"My ancestors," the other man said into the quiet, "formed the Shadow-Net in desperation when it became clear the only way to escape Silence was to defect, but they brought with them the problems that led the rest of the Psy to choose the Protocol.

"We had foreseers who fell into their visions and never returned, telepaths whose shields splintered until they couldn't block out the noise, telekinetics who broke the necks of the people they loved when their abilities spiraled out of control."

Kaleb attempted to imagine what it must've been like for the defectors, alone and cut off from the vast resources of the PsyNet. "Yet the Shadow-Net is producing individuals with unheard-of abilities"—the reason another Councilor had once attempted to hunt them—"while the PsyNet remains problematic."

"Will you accept a 'pathed image?"

Kaleb inclined his head at the inquiry, and Santos sent him the image. It was of a chaos of multihued lines, intersecting and parallel, numerous threads coming in from opposing directions, curving below and above, often smashing into a knot no one could ever untangle, only to spread out in new directions on the other side.

"This is the ShadowNet?" It was the most anarchic mental landscape he'd ever seen.

A nod from Santos. "We're connected to one another through multiple bonds of emotion. Friendship, love, even hate—negative emotions can create bonds as powerful as positive."

Kaleb had never before considered that, but of course the other man was right. Kaleb had spent most of his adult life searching for a way to destroy the Council, his focus relentless. A vicious connection, but a connection nonetheless. "Emotion alone can't be the key, or Silence would've never been necessary."

"There is another element, but it's not one you can replicate," the other man answered. "The ShadowNet is smaller than the PsyNet by a magnitude of hundreds." He turned to face Kaleb once again. "We keep a close eye on one another, notice the symptoms of any disintegration quickly, act even quicker. My personal, unscientific view is that the compactness of the ShadowNet also offers a certain level of automatic stability."

Kaleb thought of the vast spaces between minds in the Net. "Akin to a village where trouble is easily spotted, in comparison to a city where an individual may walk alone amongst thousands."

"Exactly. Consider the fact the changelings have been shown to have the lowest rates of psychopathy and mental illness of all the races. They almost always live in comparatively small, tightly linked pack groups."

If Kaleb were to follow that logic, it would mean breaking the PsyNet into manifold pieces. "Your levels of insanity?" he asked, exploring another path. "I was unable to access any hard data." His aide had compiled the information about the propensity for serial killing in this population by painstakingly tracking known members of the Forgotten in the prison system, then extrapolating that data using a statistical program.

"Attempting to break our encryptions?" There was unvarnished steel in Santos's tone. "Don't bother. We learned to protect ourselves a long time ago."

Kaleb had come to the same conclusion when his best hackers failed to get into the Forgotten's databases. "The data is less necessary than any coping mechanisms your people have discovered that can be adapted for use in the PsyNet." He could and would execute the predators as soon as each was identified, but that wouldn't fix the underlying problem.

The monsters would continue to spawn.

"Our elders," said the leader of the Forgotten, "think we should keep our distance from your problems. The original adult defectors have all passed on, but many of the current elders were youths at that time, can remember the turbulence and pain of it. They say we shouldn't get involved in your troubles."

"What do you say?"

"I'm not a dictator, Krychek. I listen to my people." He went silent as an airjet passed overhead, his expression giving nothing away. "But I listen to them all—including the ones who say that in working with you we may find answers to the problems that continue to haunt us." Golden brown skin pulled taut over his cheekbones. "We have our mad still; people we simply cannot reach."

"It's been said the broken ones are the price our race pays for violent psychic abilities," Kaleb pointed out. "We are our minds."

"I'm not willing to give up on any of my people. Are you?"

Kaleb wasn't used to thinking in such a way. The only person who mattered to him was Sahara. Everyone else was irrelevant . . . except that Sahara had asked him to save them. "I never give up on anything." With that he asked another critical question, "Your empaths have been active throughout, and yet you continue to have problematic rates of mental illness?"

Santos's answer was unexpected. "The Forgotten didn't have many powerful empaths to begin with." Face shadowed by the clouds that had moved in directly overhead, he said, "My great-grandmother says it's because the Es thought the defectors would be all right. We had a strong mind-set, were brutally organized, while the Net was in chaos.

"So, despite the fact Silence was anathema to their very being, the vast majority of Es stayed behind." He thrust a hand through his hair. "It meant our first generation was unbalanced enough that we never quite made up the numbers. Today, we have no high-level empaths as you'd judge them, but our mentally ill are far calmer and more productive in comparison to what I've heard of those in the Net." A questioning look.

"Rehabilitation was the usual response under Silence," Kaleb told him. "The more lucrative were locked up and made use of in their cogent moments."

Santos's mouth thinned. "We don't just erase those who break. And some *have* made recoveries to the extent that they can pick up the threads of their lives."

Rocking back on his heels, he answered Kaleb's next question before it was asked. "From what one of our elder empaths has told me of her sessions with Sascha Duncan, Psy empaths and Forgotten empaths have diverged to a degree that while we can offer some advice and direction, we can't train your people. Our minds no longer function quite the same way when it comes to psychic abilities." A faint smile. "Too much mixed blood."

Kaleb wondered what unique abilities that mixed blood had bequeathed Devraj Santos, the fact one Kaleb had been unable to unearth. "Regardless of our differences," he said, "having an open line of communication between my people and yours could prove beneficial to both."

Santos held his gaze, the world beyond sketched in gray. "Are you declaring a cease-fire between the Psy and the Forgotten?"

"No," Kaleb said. "I'm declaring peace." He held out his hand as the snow began to fall in a hush of white. Touch wasn't something he enjoyed with anyone aside from Sahara, but he could meet the Forgotten leader halfway. "I have no quarrel with the Forgotten." Kaleb's vengeance had always been focused on the corrupt within his own race.

Santos took a long moment before accepting Kaleb's hand. "Peace."

Chapter 8

The irony, of course, is that E-Psy are often treated as a vulnerable segment of the population. While this may be true in certain circumstances (as discussed in depth in chapter 3), such a simplistic understanding obfuscates the day-to-day reality of their existence.

Excerpted from *The Mysterious E Designation: Empathic Gifts & Shadows* by Alice Eldridge

LYING IN BED as the birds began to wake on the third day after an Arrow appeared in her life, Ivy thought of what Sascha Duncan had shared when she'd contacted the cardinal for confirmation of the E designation. *We heal the mind and the heart. Sorrow, fear, pain, we help people navigate their way out of darkness.*

The idea of it had made her chest ache, a painful pricking inside her . . . as if a numbed limb was stretching awake. Yet she had to face the fact that she was a patchwork creature, glued together through sheer stubborn will after the reconditioning that had almost erased her. Who was she to think she could heal anyone else?

We're strong, Ivy, stronger than you might imagine right now. We have to be, to take the pain of others and make it something better.

Claws clicking on the wooden floor, Rabbit tumbled out from his basket to come stand beside the bed, eyes huge in entreaty. "You're not meant to sleep on the bed." She tried for stern, but it was difficult with Rabbit.

He gave her a mournful look before he collapsed with his head on his front paws, a pitiful sight.

"You big ham," she said with a soft laugh and patted the mattress.

Sadness evaporating into mist, he jumped up and padded around before deciding on his favorite spot near the foot of the bed, diagonally across from her. Ivy smiled at his sigh of contentment, but her smile faded too soon, her thoughts tangled skeins. If she wasn't careful, her PsyNet shields would begin to crack, exposing her and the others to outsiders.

Her nails cut into her palms.

Made up of fractured Psy and their families, the settlement was safe only because the tiny population had learned to interlink their shields. It had taken months of trial and error, sheer desperation the juggernaut that powered them, until finally the group had learned to form the connections that allowed each person to remain private while bolstering the shields of the group as a whole.

However, even their enhanced shields could only take a certain amount of pressure, and Ivy had been responsible for a significant portion of it in the preceding two months. Pushing up into a sitting position on that thought, she closed her eyes, her intention to do a simple mental exercise meant to effect calm. She had to—

"Woof!"

Eyes flicking open, she was startled to see Rabbit standing right in front of her. "You know you're not supposed to interrupt me when I meditate," she chided gently.

He barked again, and this time she heard the worried whine underneath. "I'm fi—"

That was when she felt it, the trickle of wet from her nose. "Damn it!" Swinging her legs over the side of the bed, Rabbit bounding out beside her, she walked into the bathroom and turned on the light to confirm what she already knew.

She was bleeding from the nose. Not only that, but one of her eyes was bloodshot in the left corner, as if the capillaries had burst. Hands trembling and skin hot, she grabbed a wad of tissue to wipe away the thin trickle of viscous red, squeezing the bridge of her nose until the bleeding stopped. It didn't take long, this incident minor.

Cleaning up afterward, she went down into a crouch to cradle Rabbit's face. "I'm okay," she reassured him, rubbing at his ears until he stopped whining low in his throat and butted her chest with his small head. "Let's go have something to eat."

Once in the kitchen, having pulled on a thick cardigan over the camisole she wore with flannel pajama pants, she gave him one of the special dog treats she bought from the general store in the nearest township. The human farmers who ran the shops there minded their own business the same way the settlement minded its own, their relationship cordial. Two years ago, after a severe storm damaged the township, Ivy's group had helped in the cleanup and repair; a year later the favor had been returned when one of their barns needed to be rebuilt.

Other than that, the two groups didn't mingle, and Ivy knew it was the settlement at fault. Trust was a rare commodity for those who called these sprawling acres home, the majority of them having ended up here after violently traumatic experiences. It was as safe a place as they could make it, one she couldn't bear to leave . . . and that was why it was imperative she did.

"No more chains," she whispered, hands cupped around the mug of green tea she'd made herself, "especially not ones created by fear."

Rabbit wagged his tail in her peripheral vision, chewing deliriously on his treat.

It made her want to laugh, but she controlled the response, conscious once more of the strain she'd been placing on the settlement's interlinked shields. No one had said anything. No one would, because this place was about pooling their resources to survive, but Ivy had never wanted to be a burden. Even when she'd been little more than the shell of a person, she'd pulled her weight.

Her mother had once told her that her stubborn refusal to simply sit at home, even when she'd been so grievously violated, had given Gwen hope that somewhere beyond her teenage daughter's blank surface remained the girl who'd once passed a physics exam with honors after a teacher told her she was pathetic at the subject.

"You didn't even like physics," Gwen had said that day, as Ivy helped her transfer seedlings from the settlement greenhouse to the vegetable garden the group maintained to balance out their diet. "But you refused to change subjects, not until you'd made your point."

Knowing she'd need that stubborn streak even more in the weeks to come, Ivy opened the back door, pulled on her snow boots, and stepped out into the gray light of early morning. It was bitingly cold, the snow thick enough to mute sound, but she liked the freshness, the skeletal bareness of the apple trees stretching out in front of her, branches piercing the fog. Beyond them lay peach and plum trees, a row of fruiting cherry trees, even a trellis for the myriad berries Ivy managed to coax to life each spring.

All of it was bedded down or barren in the winter cold, but the landscape was no less beautiful for being so stark. Walking toward the trees, mug of tea in hand, she was unsurprised when Rabbit came after her, an aggrieved look on his face at having been forced to abandon his treat in order to escort her.

"I'm sorry," she whispered, her affection for her small friend a warmth inside her.

"Grr."

Muscles tensing at that snarling sound from a suddenly stiff Rabbit, she looked out into the mist and saw the man. Part of her was expecting Vasic, waiting for him, but it wasn't the Arrow. This man was running at her, face contorted and hand held out in front of him in a way that shouted of a weapon.

Ivy reacted on instinct.

Throwing her still-hot tea and mug into his face, to his howl of rage, Ivy turned and ran. "Go, Rabbit!"

They zigzagged through the trees to throw off the attacker's line of sight. Ivy didn't look back as she hit the cabin, slamming the door shut behind her and Rabbit just as something thudded into it on the other side.

The stranger was using a projectile weapon.

Shooting home the dead bolt, she urged a bristling Rabbit away from the door and crouch-walked to the kitchen cabinets to retrieve a gun her father had placed there. Her skin turned clammy at the idea of using it, of harming a living being, but when another bullet shattered the window above her head, she knew it was either that or die herself. Shaking off the slivers of glass to the sound of Rabbit's angry barking, she telepathed her parents and neighbors . . . but then the front door was shot open while bullets pounded into the back, and she knew she was out of time.

There were two of them.

She set her jaw and flicked off the safety on the gun. "No, you do *not* get to steal my life. Not again." Squeezing herself into a corner so no one could come at her from the back, Rabbit beside her, she waited for the intruder to come into view. While her angry determination to survive didn't eliminate the nausea in her stomach, she didn't allow it to affect her grip on the weapon.

A second later, she heard the intruder's feet hit the wood of the living room, followed by a loud thud, the gun at the back door falling silent soon afterward. Not sure what had happened, she was deciding whether to move or stay when Rabbit wiggled out and ran into the living room, cleverly avoiding the broken glass on the floor.

"Rabbit," she hissed over the pounding of her heart, but followed him out.

Her front door was busted, doorjamb in splinters, muddy boot prints on the floor and on the door itself. Swallowing to wet a dry throat, her pulse a thudding echo in her ears, she carefully walked outside and around to the back door to find it peppered with bullets. The damage had her releasing a shuddering breath. She hadn't imagined the assailants in a mental fugue—they'd simply disappeared into thin air in the space of three breaths.

A shiver raced over her skin.

It was no surprise to turn and find Vasic behind her; Rabbit was startled into an annoyed bark at his abrupt appearance. "How did you know?" she asked the man who had, in all probability, just killed two people for her.

His cold gray eyes scanned her from head to toe with the same clinical precision she'd noted on his first visit. "Are you injured?"

"What? No." Tremors threatened to shake her frame. Gritting her teeth to fight them, she repeated her earlier question. "How did you know?"

"The squad received intelligence just prior to the attack that a certain segment of the population has chosen to blame the empaths for the fall of Silence."

"That makes no sense." She didn't fight when—ignoring Rabbit's growling body between them—he eased the gun from her white-knuckled grip and flicked the safety back on. If she never had to touch the thing again, it would be far too soon. Rubbing her hands on the worn flannel of her pajama pants to get rid of the feel of the rigid black plas, she said, "E-Psy have been suppressed for over a hundred years."

"People are not rational at present."

"Did they follow you? To find me?" Ivy herself hadn't known of her empathic skill set until Vasic's visit.

A shake of his head, the deep black strands of his hair slightly wet, as if they'd been dusted by snow that had since melted. "It's random chance the two events coincided. The group behind the attack hacked into the database of the rehabilitation and reconditioning center where you were treated; at 9.3 on the Gradient you were undeniably the strongest of those who came in and as such were the first target."

9.3? That was a staggering level of power—and it had been forcibly trapped inside her. "My God," she whispered. "It's a miracle I haven't suffered a severe brain bleed."

He propped the gun against the side of the house, and she suddenly realized how physically dangerous he was. There was just something so contained about Vasic that she'd focused on the threat posed by his telekinetic abilities, but he could cause serious damage without recourse to his Tk. He was taller than her by a good foot, with wide shoulders and biceps shaped with taut muscle, strong thighs pressing against the black fabric of his combat uniform when he moved.

Not big. That wasn't the right word.

No, he was like the gun. A sleek weapon honed to ruthless perfection.

"The centers do have certain techniques to lessen the risk of a neural bleed," he said, eyes on his gauntlet as the small screen embedded in it flowed with data, "but your reconditioning, as we're both aware, was incompetent at best."

Shoving her fingers through her hair, she wrenched her eyes off the deadly purity of him and shrugged off the past. It was done. Finished. It no longer had any claim on her. Her focus had to be on the future—about which fate had sent her a flashing neon sign this morning, should she have needed one. "The others who were reconditioned at the same center?"

"In the process of being transferred to safe houses." His head lifted, the force of his attention a blade. "Do you wish a transfer?"

Ivy shook her head. "I should be safe here—this area is so remote it's unlikely any group has *two* teleporters who can find a way to 'port in." And the settlement was well guarded against more physical means of infiltration.

Vasic shook his head. "Neither one of them was a teleport-capable Tk." He tapped his gauntlet. "According to my sources, a small private plane flew over the orchard a minute prior to the attack. They likely parachuted in."

"Oh." Ivy folded her arms, having not even considered that option. "I don't think we have any defenses against attack from the air." Her parents and Ivy, the others, ran the farm at a deliberate middling profit so as not to attract unwelcome attention, but it meant they didn't have a lot of money to spend on expensive surveillance.

"The squad's tech team has already added the settlement to their aerial watch list," Vasic answered. "There will be no further surprises from that direction."

"Thank you." Biting down hard on her lower lip, she forced herself to ask the other question, the one she didn't want to ask. "Are the two people who . . . Are they dead?"

"No."

Ivy pressed a hand against the cold outer wall of the house as her knees went weak, breath rushing out of her lungs, but Vasic wasn't finished.

"We need to interrogate the two to discover if this was an ill-thought-out attack prompted by fear, or if they're part of a larger, more organized cell." Legs slightly spread, he slid his hands behind his back, a soldier at rest. "It's possible the fragmented remnants of Pure Psy," he added, naming the group behind a slew of horrifying violence prior to the fall of Silence, "may have had a hand in it."

"Ivy!"

Shifting on her heel at her father's yell, she called back, "I'm not hurt!"

A change in the air and she knew Vasic was gone before she saw the empty space where he'd been standing a second ago.

"Coincidence?" was her father's suspicious response when she shared Vasic's explanation for the attack. "Or a setup to make you more amenable to Krychek's offer?"

"I don't think Vasic would lie." The words spilled past her lips, born in a part of her she didn't consciously understand.

"He's an Arrow, serves another master." Flint hard, her mother's tone made Gwen Jane's view of the situation clear.

"You're wrong. I don't think he serves anyone." There was a sense of piercing aloneness around the Arrow with eyes of winter frost. "And Mother, if this was about scaring me into agreeing, all he had to do was teleport me over the edge of a cliff."

"But now you're grateful," her father pointed out. "You see him as your savior."

Aware her parents' words made sense and unable to articulate a rational reason for her desire to trust a man who made no attempt to hide his lethal nature, she spread her hands. "None of that matters—my decision was always going to be the same." She looked at her mother and father in turn. "I need to find out who I am."

Even if that meant trusting herself to an Arrow who was a weapon more deadly than any gun.

Chapter 9

The protection of Silence is the mandate of every Arrow. Execution of those who would challenge the Protocol will, at times, be necessary. Do not hesitate to take terminal action, for in so doing you protect our people from annihilation.

First Code of Arrows

VASIC 'PORTED INTO the cell where he'd thrown one of Ivy's attackers, the other in the cell opposite. Located in the bowels of Arrow Central Command, the cell was a solid square block with no door, teleportation the only way to enter or exit. Regardless of the fact that neither assailant was teleport-capable, Vasic had used a squad mental trick to temporarily leash their psychic abilities; it ensured they couldn't 'path for assistance or use the PsyNet to send a message.

He hadn't lied to Ivy. Neither was dead.

"Help me!" screamed the one whose arms Vasic had broken, his face heavily bruised from being smashed into the wall.

"You won't die of those injuries," Vasic said, just as Abbot teleported in with Aden.

A nod from Aden and Abbot left them alone.

You need to leave, too. Aden's voice in Vasic's head as the other man took over the psychic leash. *Go.*

Ivy is at risk.

I'll get you the information. Your task is to keep her safe.

Again, Aden was attempting to put Vasic on soft duty.

Having never shifted his gaze from the assailant who'd smashed open Ivy's door, Vasic went down on his haunches in front of the injured male. "Stop," he said quietly, and the man went silent, terror a slick sheen in his eyes.

A predictable response. This coward might wish to reinstate Silence, but his was a desire driven by a craven fear of the unknown.

"I'm capable of torturing you until you don't have a single unbroken bone left from here"—he indicated the male's breastbone—"to here." He pointed to the man's toes. "You'd resemble a piece of meat pounded with a mallet by the time I was done."

The threat was the absolute truth. He'd taken responsibility for Ivy's safety, and there was nothing he wouldn't do in pursuit of that goal. "I'm a Tk, can make you feel each individual break without lifting a hand."

He snapped the tiniest bone of the man's smallest finger as an illustration. Waiting for the screams to die down to snuffling sobs, Vasic said, "I can use the same tiny breaks to dismantle your torso, breaking your ribs into splinters, then cracking open your breastplate.

"Fracturing your collarbone into inch-long segments would take considerable time and skill, but I have both." He lowered his voice so the prisoner had to strain to hear. "I'm also patient. By the time I reach your toes, your fingers will have healed, and I can start the whole process all over again. You don't want me to stay in this room."

The man's entire body began to shake.

"Answer my questions," Vasic continued in the same even tone he'd used throughout, "and I'll leave."

Ten minutes later, the prisoner had given them everything he knew. It wasn't much. His partner knew even less, but the pieces led to a single answer: the attack had been orchestrated by one of the few remaining Pure Psy lieutenants. *Stupid*. If Vasic had been in the lieutenant's position, he'd have gone under and stayed there until he had the opportunity to strike at the heart of the new regime.

"I'll update Krychek," Aden told Vasic after they left the cells for the squad's common area, "and undertake the hunt for the lieutenant."

Vasic had no argument with that, the cleanup of Pure Psy far less important than protecting the Es. "What will you do with the two males?"

Aden was quiet for a long time, his eyes on the greenery beyond the glass, the ferns thick and curling on the lower part of the window. "Part of the problem with the Council was that everything was done in the shadows, 'justice' meted out on an arbitrary basis. We need to return to an open system, where men like this can be tried and punished according to our laws."

"The Net's not ready for that yet."

"No." Aden clasped his hands behind his back. "But it will be one day. Until then, I'll dump them in a maximum security prison, complete with a paper trail that'll guarantee they stay there for a long time."

"Their abilities?"

"It's not advertised, but any Psy who goes into the prison system has his or her abilities restrained by a self-sustaining leash. PsyNet access is restricted to a controlled area. I'll organize it."

Vasic thought of Aden's words about justice as he returned to the snow-covered orchard and to Ivy. The other Arrow was right in one sense, but the violence of the abilities possessed by their race meant there would always be some monsters so horrific they needed to be hunted down and executed, terrors no justice system could handle. When that time came, it was an Arrow who'd do the hunting, darkness pitted against darkness.

Scanning the area around Ivy's cabin in the muted morning light, he crossed over to the rucked-up snow beside it. Her small pet spotted him first, barking out a sharp warning from where he stood on guard in the back doorway. Ivy appeared a second later, a broom in hand and her curls held back by a purple and white scarf. "I knew it was you," she said with a slight smile. "You've now been downgraded from 'deadly threat' to 'irritation that won't go away' in Rabbit's bark vocabulary."

He thought perhaps there was a correct way to reply to that statement, to the wary softness of her, but he didn't have that knowledge. "Why are you on your own?" He'd left only because he'd seen her parents and others on the way, armed and ready to protect.

"I'm not." A quick glance over her shoulder before she lowered her voice to a whisper. "My mother, however, hasn't yet realized you're here. Do you want to meet her?"

"If you believe it'll assist her in accepting the parameters of your proposed contract."

"Probably not." A slight wince, her expression so open he knew she wouldn't have been able to fake Silence in the outside world. "She'll probably take one look at you and pull out a gun."

"If I'd meant to kill you," he pointed out, "you'd be long dead, your body disposed of in a crematorium incinerator."

Blinking, Ivy stared at him with those unusual eyes that made him feel stripped to the bone. "Maybe it's better if you don't meet my mother."

"I disagree." A taller woman, her body rangy, appeared in view a second after that pronouncement. "At least," she added, "he's honest."

Handing her own broom to an Ivy who was looking increasingly doubtful about the situation, the woman Vasic identified as Gwen Jane from Ivy's biographical data, said, "Your father's about a minute away with the materials to repair the window and doors." She stepped out to Vasic. "Let's take a walk."

The next ten minutes were . . . interesting. In the twenty-seven years since he'd been drafted into the squad, Vasic had experienced many things, but never had he found himself being interrogated by a mother concerned for her child. Gwen Jane might appear Silent on the surface, he thought, but in her ferocious protectiveness, he glimpsed the truth—and while he had no experience of maternal love, he understood it to be a formidable force.

"I'll make certain she comes to no harm," he told her. "Krychek's priority might be the Net as a whole, but mine is the safety of the empaths, with Ivy my particular assignment."

An intent look. "How can you promise that when you work for Krychek?"

"A common misapprehension." One the squad permitted because it gave the Arrows freedom to stay below the radar. "We choose to side with him because his current stance benefits the PsyNet and the populace. Should that change, he knows not to expect our support."

"Not tame dogs but wild wolves who've decided he's an ally for the moment?"

"Except we aren't wild." To be an Arrow was to live a tightly regimented life. It wasn't a choice but a necessity. Because there was always a reason an Arrow was an Arrow, and each and every one of those reasons was deadly.

"There are different kinds of wildness," Gwen said as they came within sight of the cabin once again.

He could see supplies for the window repair laid out against the outside wall—wood for the new frame, the old one having been cracked by the barrage of bullets, as well as a sheet of glass designed to click in. From the sounds echoing over the sunlit snow, Ivy and her father were working on the front door. It only took him a short time to take care of the window, his telekinesis at 7.9 on the Gradient. He didn't have to pound in nails, simply push with his mind; they went through the wood as if it was butter.

The skill required was of subtlety. Push too hard and the nail would exit out the other side. Working with a thick plank and hundreds of nails had been one of his easier and more fun exercises as a child—back when he'd lived with his "father." The same man had later dropped him off at an Arrow training facility and never looked back.

Not even once.

Vasic knew because the scared four-year-old he'd been had stood in the entryway of the training facility and watched his father's vehicle getting smaller and smaller and smaller. According to his memories, he'd cried, but he could no longer access the emotion that had led to the response.

"Well," Gwen murmured, this woman who'd proven willing to go toe-to-toe with an Arrow to protect her child, "that's useful."

"Yes." People had found Vasic useful his entire life, but it didn't usually have to do with anything as harmless or as oddly satisfying as fixing a window. "I assume from your earlier questions that Ivy has decided to accept the contract."

"I'll let her answer that." Leaving him with that statement, Gwen went around to the front door.

Ivy came over soon afterward. The sleeves of her faded denim shirt were now rolled up to the elbows to reveal the white of a long-sleeved tee, her scarf having slipped a fraction to set several curling tendrils free. Rabbit, of course, was at her heels. He bared his teeth at first sight of Vasic.

"I'll agree to the contract," Ivy said without prelude, "but Rabbit comes with me." Tipping up her chin, she folded her arms. "Where I go, he goes."

"He'll have to be taught to stay within the boundaries," Vasic said, wondering if Ivy was as loyal to everyone who belonged to her. "I'm certain the changelings would do nothing to harm him, but there are natural wolves and lynxes in the area, too."

Ivy's arms dropped to her side, eyes huge. "We're going to be near changeling territory?" It was a hoarse whisper that brushed over his skin like a tactile sensation.

"Inside it." Neither Vasic nor Aden had expected the changelings to agree to Krychek's request, but it was official as of the previous night. "DarkRiver-SnowDancer territory."

Ivy turned her attention to her growling pet. "Hear that, Rabbit? Don't go around snarling at our hosts or they might decide to eat you for lunch." There was a flush of quiet pink on her cheeks when she looked back up. "Sorry, I'm used to talking to him."

"Do you find it therapeutic?" Vasic had never had a pet, didn't understand the concept.

Ivy didn't know how to answer Vasic's question without saying too much . . . but what was the use of hiding things? He already knew her most perilous secrets. On that realization came a wave of freedom. "He was a stray," she began, "crawled into the orchard bedraggled, skinny, and broken up from a fight . . . while I was still . . . wrong." Not real, nothing but a shade of the girl she'd once been, her mind brutalized and her soul battered, chilling screams at night the only sound she made all day.

"I fed him because I didn't know what else to do, then carried him to the vet. No one would say anything, but I could tell the adults thought he was going to die." It had been a moment of acute insight, slicing through the fog in which she existed. "I wanted to tell them they were all wrong, that I could see his will to live in his eyes, but I didn't have the words then.

"Instead, I took him home with me after the vet cast his broken leg, fed him by hand, and made sure his wounds stayed clean." Her parents had found her curled up with Rabbit in the barn the first night, and carried them both into the family cabin. "It was maybe five days later that he staggered up and started trying to walk.

"A week after that, he fell into a muddy patch of field, and I found myself washing him." Laughter chased out the lingering echoes of horror. "I had to chase him around with a hose." Her pet had been so fast, even with the cast on one leg. "By the end, I was drenched head to toe myself."

Ivy met Vasic's gaze, tried to make him understand. "Caring for Rabbit was the first time in seven months I'd done anything except follow simple instructions." She'd been a living, breathing automaton, the only sign of conscious life her desire to help her parents do chores—even when it was clear her brain wasn't sending the right signals to her limbs.

Vasic considered her snarling dog. "He was a wounded living creature, and you are an empath. He spoke to the most immutable aspect of your nature."

Ivy didn't care about the technicalities of how or why. She just knew Rabbit had saved her as she'd saved him. Skinny but stubborn, he'd wriggle his way under her hand when she sat staring out into nothingness, nudge at her until she gave in and petted his then-ratty coat. When her fingers kept spasming open to drop the apples she was attempting to collect, he'd used his teeth to pick them up and put them in her basket. His determination had given her the impetus to bite back her tearful frustration and try again and again and again.

And again.

Somewhere along the way, her brain began to rewire itself, finding pathways around sections so badly bruised, Ivy's head had pulsed with the excruciating pain of it for three years after her reconditioning.

"I relearned to run because Rabbit wanted to play," she said through the knot in her throat. "He was so small and skinny, but he never gave up, so I couldn't, either." It had taken time for her pet to put on weight, for his coat to become shiny and healthy, the transformation echoed in her own healing mind.

When he'd collapsed in exhaustion, she'd picked him up in her arms. And when she'd fallen because her body refused to do what it should, he'd nudged and barked encouragement at her until she dragged herself back up. "Three months after he arrived, I spoke for the first time. A month after that, I asked for brain therapy."

The intense sessions with a settlement medic had slowly helped her reclaim the final pieces of her mind. "It was hard." Comparable to the agonizing physical therapy sometimes necessary after severe injuries to the body. "But each time I thought I'd reached my limit, I'd remember watching Rabbit crawl into the orchard even when he was so broken, and I'd find another store of willpower."

The wind riffled through Vasic's hair in the silence that followed her story. "I'll take care when 'porting him," he said at last. "Though perhaps I should be the one concerned for my safety."

Startled into a smile by that cool statement, she blinked away the burning in her eyes and reached down to pick up her teeth-baring pet. "He'll behave, won't you?" She turned Rabbit's face toward Vasic. "Hold out your hand so he can sniff it."

Vasic did so, but Rabbit refused to look at it, fascinated by everything in view *but* the Arrow's hand. Ivy attempted to get him to turn, only to be forced to concede defeat. "I'm sorry." She placed Rabbit back on the ground—and he immediately took position in front of her, canines flashing. "Maybe after he gets to know you a little more."

Vasic didn't appear put out by the rejection. Then again, he'd been as icily calm after handling the two intruders earlier. Ivy had the disconcerting sense that nothing could penetrate the cold black armor of an Arrow . . . and for some reason, she wanted to do exactly that, fascinated by the tiny glimpse of a personality beyond the ice.

"The experiment," Vasic now said, "is to begin as soon as the security perimeter around the site is complete. You should be packed and ready to depart at short notice."

"Will you comm me?" She fought the growing temptation to touch the frost of him, convince herself he was real and not a winter illusion sent to tell her fantastical things.

"Yes."

Ten seconds later, she stood alone, the only evidence of Vasic's presence boot prints in the snow . . . and a single perfectly repaired window.

Chapter 10

This world was once a true triumvirate, but we now exist as disparate pieces. Humans in their insular enclaves, Psy in steel and glass high-rises armed against intrusion, changelings in packs generally closed to outsiders. This cannot be a viable long-term existence. Change is inevitable.

Excerpted from an essay by Keelie Schaeffer, PhD (December 2073)

VASIC CALLED A meeting of his security team two hours after retrieving the parachutes used by Ivy's assailants and assigning a covert guard to watch over her. He'd already made the decision that the ratio of Arrows to empaths at the compound would be one-to-one, with each Arrow being paired with a specific E. Security had to be high and it had to be tight; Pure Psy wasn't the only group that might see the empaths as a threat.

The six males and three females he'd personally chosen for this duty stood in front him in the glade situated near the back of the subterranean green space at Central Command. All were dressed in identical black uniforms embellished only with a single silver star on one shoulder. "The empaths," he said to them now, "are our priority. Anything that places them at risk is to be eliminated."

"If we receive orders that contradict that directive?" asked a female operative trained as a combat telepath.

"You're under my direct command," Vasic responded. "Designation: Arrow Unit E1. If anyone else attempts to give you an order, you come straight to me." Krychek wasn't stupid enough to attempt to subvert Arrow leadership in that fashion, but the ragged remnants of Pure Psy weren't as intelligent.

Not that Vasic believed any of these men or women would be disloyal.

Some had been tempted by the idea of psychic peace espoused by the fanatical group, but any such leanings had died a quick death with the group's first violent act. "If you believe yourself unsuitable for this task," he said, because the Es would push them all to their limits with their simple proximity, "speak to me afterward."

There will, he added telepathically, *be no negative repercussions should you wish to withdraw from the team.* During Ming LeBon's leadership of the squad, the former Councilor had crushed any attempt at defiance or disagreement, to the extent of dosing Arrows with Jax, a drug designed to amplify their abilities as it turned them into ruthless assassins with no ability to distinguish right from wrong.

Vasic knew the team in front of him trusted him not to do the same, but he always made it a point to reiterate the message, remind his squadmates of their right to choose. Never again would anyone treat an Arrow as a disposable tool.

One of the males in the back row spoke up. "Will it cause problems if we request a transfer after the start of the operation?"

It was an astute question. None of the others had as yet spent any real time with an E, couldn't know how he or she might react. "No," Vasic said. "I've factored that into my plans." He had a backup list of five substitutes. "Alert me to any issues as early as possible, however."

Seeing there were no further questions, he used his gauntlet to bring up a holo-map and projected it to the left of his body. "We've been given access to a section of DarkRiver-SnowDancer territory." The map delineated an area the wolves and leopards had described as "small" but that to Psy eyes was an expansive landscape.

Vasic preferred open spaces over the more contained areas favored by most of his race, but he could function in either. "The instant we move beyond the marked perimeter we'll be considered hostiles and eliminated. The perimeter will also be rigged to cause injury or death."

Abbot stirred. "If there is an exigent risk to the Es and the teleporters in the unit are inaccessible or out of commission?"

There were three Tks in E1—Vasic, Abbot, and Nerida, the latter one of the extremely limited number of strong female Tks in the Net.

Telekinesis had been statistically shown to express more heavily in the male gender; Vasic had always considered it unusual that there was no counterbalance in the female population.

That mystery had been solved with the data coming in about the dormant empaths, the females outnumbering the males by a significant percentage.

Shelving that fact for the moment, he said, "I'll arrange for an emergency code to be embedded into your wrist units that'll link you directly to the changeling security team." He and Aden had a meeting with the DarkRiver-SnowDancer team in an hour to discuss the finer aspects of the operation. "Study the details of your assigned assets, alert me of any security threats."

Dismissing the team soon afterward, with none of the nine asking to be taken off the protection detail, he downloaded the files on the other Es. As the leader of the team, he had to have a complete profile of the situation. Paying specific attention to the images, he confirmed a fact he'd already suspected—it was only Ivy Jane's copper gaze that made him feel stripped to the bone.

Aden found Vasic when it was time to 'port to the meeting with the changelings, the image he needed to anchor the transfer having been forwarded five minutes prior. "It's an unknown situation," he said to Aden. "I should do a reconnaissance." Even Vasic wasn't fast enough to avoid a bullet shot at him from point-blank range directly after a teleport, but it would be one death rather than two.

However, his partner shook his head, his stick-straight black hair having outgrown its severe military cut enough for the strands to slide against one another. "The changelings have never shown a tendency to pick a fight, and this situation is a delicate one. We should meet them halfway—not for Krychek, but because the squad needs to build alliances of its own."

Aden, Vasic realized, was thinking years ahead as he always did, this time into a future where an Arrow might need friends outside the squad. "In two. One . . . two."

They arrived in front of a sturdy log cabin surrounded by open land that merged into dark green firs set far enough apart that there was plenty of light on the ground. That ground was coated in snow that glittered in the sun burning from a crystalline winter sky, the sound of water flowing over rocks in the distance.

Standing with their backs to the cabin were the DarkRiver alpha, the SnowDancer alpha, and two others. Vasic didn't know the tall female with the black hair and vivid indigo eyes who stood next to the wolf alpha, but he recognized the white-blond male beside the feline alpha. Dorian Christensen, the changeling who'd spoken to Vasic over the body of a young woman whose life and death Vasic had been sent to erase.

A dark-haired male who walked with the deadly grace of an assassin appeared from the side of the house at that instant. Judd Lauren, Arrow and member of the SnowDancer pack. There was no split loyalty; Judd had made it patent his primary loyalty was to the pack that had become his home. That didn't mean he wouldn't do everything in his power to assist the squad, so long as that assistance did no harm to SnowDancer or its allies.

Family comes first. Words Judd had spoken to Vasic in the deserted backyard of a Second Reformation church. *But the squad is family, too. I won't ever betray you unless you betray me by seeking to hurt those I love.*

Love was a concept of which Vasic had no comprehension, though he knew how to recognize the signs of it in others. Learning the subtle physical cues that betrayed emotional bonds had been part of his training, intended to give him tools he could use to exploit targets from the emotional races. He didn't, however, actually *understand* what it was any more than a trained animal understood the words spoken to it.

He could ask Judd to explain it to him, but he suspected he simply didn't have the correct emotional foundations to comprehend the explanation.

"You have the final details of the security measures?" Aden's voice cut through the sounds of the forest, the silence that disquieted many Psy nowhere in evidence—water, birds, wind, the hint of a wolf's howl in the distance, it was a natural symphony.

Hawke raised an eyebrow. "I guess the pleasantries are over then." Despite the wolf alpha's lazy words, the pale blue of his gaze was that of a predator. Focused. Unblinking. "Judd's got the schematics."

The other Arrow pinned the hard-copy map to the side of the cabin using his Tk. "The inner perimeter"—he tapped a border marked in yellow—"is set with underground sensors that'll detect any movement. No way to access them. They're buried deep and in large numbers."

Vasic had no intention of attempting to subvert the packs' security, but Judd knew how Arrow minds worked, and the precaution was a good one. "Outer perimeter?" Marked in orange, it was some distance from the inner one, creating a significant buffer zone.

"Laser line. Set to incapacitate immediately."

"You should set it to kill." An Arrow needed only the slimmest margin to alter the balance of power.

No surprise in Judd's expression. "That'll be taken care of by the security measures in the red zone."

"Are all the areas marked?" Aden broke in, attention on the map. "We'll have civilians with us."

Judd nodded. "Even a child couldn't miss the boundary lines. Anyone who manages to survive the red zone will be tracked and eliminated in a far messier fashion." A glint in the gold-flecked dark brown of his eyes that Vasic translated as humor. "Trust me, you don't want to be torn apart by wolf or leopard claws."

Vasic scanned the map into his gauntlet as a backup to the file Judd would no doubt send him. "That leaves teleportation."

Holding his gaze, Judd said, "Do you intend to use a facial lock to breach the perimeter and enter Pack lands?"

"Not unless it's an emergency where I have no other option." A vow, Arrow to Arrow, one that was accepted without further discussion; if Judd had had doubts, they wouldn't be standing here.

"The others can only 'port to a visual reference," Judd pointed out, "and the entire area beyond the outer perimeter is heavily patrolled. Subtle light barriers will ensure any attempt at taking long-range photographs will produce a distorted image."

Making them useless to an ordinary teleporter.

He's always had one of the most inventive minds in the squad.

Vasic agreed with Aden's telepathic statement. It was Judd after all who'd worked out a way to wean himself—and as a result, other Tks—off Jax, without sending up a red flag. Aden and Vasic had been working on the same problem for months when it became clear Judd Lauren had succeeded and that all they needed to do was quietly reinforce the changes he'd set in motion.

It's a pity we didn't realize he was one of us until after his defection, Aden said, referring to the other Arrow's rebel tendencies. *I almost approached him after the Jax maneuver, but he was such a "perfect" Arrow in every other way that the risk outweighed my instincts.*

Vasic wasn't so certain that had been a mistake. *If we'd brought Judd in, he may have made different choices, and he wouldn't be who he is now.* An Arrow who hadn't only survived, but who *lived.* It was a sharp distinction. Judd had a mate, a family, a real life that, unbeknownst to him, was a beacon to every splintered member of the squad.

Kaleb Krychek might be like them, but Judd *was* one of them.

In the ensuing minutes, the other man explained the remaining security protocols, the majority involving satellite surveillance. The trees in this area were spaced widely enough that the packs could and would keep a remote eye on the Psy in the compound—but the changelings promised to keep the surveillance at a general level as long as those in the compound made no aggressive or suspicious moves.

"We have no desire to spy on your lives," Lucas Hunter said bluntly, his arms folded loosely across his chest as he leaned against the cabin in a manner that struck Vasic as lazily feline. "But we'll come down hard the instant it appears you're using the compound as a base for aggression."

Any issues? Aden asked Vasic.

No. Their precautions are impressive. Vasic did have another geographic— as opposed to facial—lock in this territory, but it was not one with any military value. That hadn't been the point. *The Es will be safe here.* Ivy and her pet would be safe here. *The protections may be designed to keep us in, but they will also keep aggressors out.*

"We agree to all the specifications," Aden said aloud. "However, we do have a request." He stated the need for an emergency safe-passage protocol.

A quick discussion later, Vasic's proposed solution of an SOS code was accepted.

"Is Sascha Duncan willing to work with the Es?"

Lucas Hunter's green eyes took on a feral glow at Aden's query. "Yeah. But we'll talk about that after your people are in."

"We can build the remaining cabins," Vasic began, but the changelings waved away the offer, preferring to do it themselves in order to minimize the impact on the natural environment.

Vasic made a note to sweep the dwellings for surveillance equipment before moving in his Arrows and the Es. The changelings didn't appear interested in such intensive and invasive surveillance, but Vasic took nothing on trust. It made it much harder for people to betray him.

AFTER the two Arrows left the clearing, Hawke looked to where his and Lucas's people stood talking a short distance away. Indigo grinned and shook her head at something Dorian had said. A second later, Judd replied—to Dorian's sharp grin and quick retort.

"Could you have imagined this scene five years ago?" Lucas said at the same instant. "Not just leopard and wolf and Psy together, but the situation with the Arrows and the empaths."

"Five years ago, SnowDancer as a pack was isolated and content with it." The past had scarred Hawke's men and women, hardened them to anyone who wasn't their own. "We had no idea what we could be. *I* had no idea who I could be." Not simply an alpha who would bleed for his pack, but a man who'd savage the world for his mate.

It was clear Lucas sensed the primal protectiveness that lived in Hawke, his next question directly related to Sienna. "You still planning to mount an assault on Ming in a month?"

Hawke's wolf snarled inside him, lips peeled back to showcase its fangs. As long as Ming LeBon lived, he'd be a threat to Hawke's mate, and that was unacceptable. "This"—he nodded at the compound—"is throwing a spanner in the works."

He couldn't leave his territory with so many Psy in the vicinity, and the operation couldn't be moved forward. Ming was a combat-grade telepath with significant forces. They'd only get one shot at him, so all of the pieces had to be in place.

Lucas's cat-green eyes held Hawke's. "DarkRiver will help keep your pack safe." It was the promise of one alpha to another, the blood bond between them set in stone. "Ming threatens all of us. You told me Judd's contacts say he may have supported Pure Psy." The leopard alpha's jaw tightened at the mention of the violent force that had attacked DarkRiver and SnowDancer both.

Hawke had never trusted anyone with his pack, never truly would. That was part of what made him a good alpha—he took responsibility for each and every member of SnowDancer. However, if his and Sienna's plan went as intended, he'd only be gone for a day at most, and not only were his lieutenants eminently capable of covering his absence, Lucas had earned his trust. "I'll keep you updated."

Indigo waved them over right then, and the two of them walked across to the stump the others were using as a table. "We've decided on a further nine one-bedroom cabins," the lieutenant stated, "along with a larger cabin for the Arrows, since they'll be sleeping in shifts."

They discussed the placement of the cabins and the teams needed to get them up as fast as possible. Since DarkRiver was in construction, the leopards would take charge, with the wolves providing labor as needed.

"I know it makes humanitarian sense," Indigo said, rolling up the map to carry back, "and Judd you know I trust your judgment to the core—"

"But your wolf's still prickly at the idea of so many assassins in our territory," Judd completed. "I'm the same. This is our home," he said simply. "It's instinct."

Yes, Hawke thought, it was instinct of the deepest, most primal kind. Hawke's wolf, too, was on aggressive alert, claws pushing against the insides of his skin. The Psy had savaged SnowDancer once, brutalized them to agonizing pain, and no wolf in the den would ever forget that—but his mate, his fucking heartbeat, had also come from the Psy. Sienna had saved life after life in a battle meant to annihilate the pack, with no care for her own. As had Judd. His brother had protected their young. No wolf would ever forget that, either.

So, they would give the Psy race this one chance.

Whether it ended in trust or in blood-soaked battle was up to them.

Chapter 11

The child isn't psychologically suited either to the squad's training methods or to its mandate. Normally, I'd recommend he be removed from the program, but as the usefulness of his ability makes that a nonviable option, I suggest the immediate and repeated application of physical pain interspersed with psychological punishment to break him down. Only then can he be molded into an Arrow.

Private PsyMed report on Arrow Trainee Vasic Duvnjak,
age 4 years 2 months

SEVEN DAYS AFTER the attack, Ivy went to heft her pack when the weight of it was simply gone. Startled, she spun around to see Vasic standing a foot away, near a snow-heavy apple tree.

"I've sent it ahead to the location," he said, as if it was a perfectly reasonable thing to do.

Heart thudding, she realized it was for him. "Right. Of course." She looked at Rabbit, her pet staring fixedly at where the pack had been. "Don't do the same to Rabbit, okay?"

"No, he goes with you. I understand."

For some reason that cool response made her want to smile through the nerves that had created a tight knot in her chest. Turning to her parents, she went to say good-bye, then thought to hell with it and hugged them one at a time. She didn't expect much of a physical response, but they squeezed her tight, their unspoken love a vivid pulse against her skin.

Her breath caught at the idea of not having them within telepathic reach. She hadn't *ever* been that alone. Now she wasn't only about to leave her home and family, she'd disengaged her shields from the others in the settlement. It was the first time in seven years she'd been adrift in the Net on her own.

Take care, Ivy. The back of her father's hand grazed her mother's as he telepathed Ivy.

I will, she said, achingly conscious of her mother looking at her with an intensity that said Gwen was storing the sight for later recall. *I'll call, I promise.* Now more than ever she'd need their steady, grounding advice. *I'll miss you both so much.*

Gwen Jane's modulated breathing didn't alter, her expression didn't change, but her words held her heart. *If you ever feel unsafe, we'll come. Day or night, snow or rain, we'll find you.*

I know. Swallowing past the lump in her throat, Ivy picked up Rabbit. She knew he had to be kept under control during the teleport, but he disliked leashes and she didn't subject him to one unless there was no other way; she knew too well what it was like to be strapped in with no way to escape.

"We're ready," she said to the Arrow with eyes of clear, beautiful winter frost, his lethally honed body a powerful presence by her side.

She wasn't sure if he touched her, if he needed to, but there was a slight moment of disorientation . . . and then her parents no longer stood in front of her. Instead, she faced several small cabins set against a backdrop of dark green firs and snowcapped mountains under a stunning blue sky, the air holding a distinct bite and the area blanketed with fresh-fallen snow. Though it wasn't the orchard that was her home, the beauty of it hurt her heart.

A black-haired male with sea blue eyes moved out of the trees to her immediate right an instant later, nodded at Vasic, and teleported out.

Ivy was too startled to be scared. "He was wearing the same uniform as you," she said to Vasic after putting Rabbit on the ground. Her pet looked suspiciously around before deigning to sniff the snow. "Was he a member of your squad?"

A nod. "His name is Abbot. I stationed him here as a guard after I confirmed the area was secure." He indicated the cabin to their left. "I placed your pack inside, but as we're the first to arrive, you can choose another cabin if you wish."

"No, this is perfect." Located at one end of the rough semicircle of cabins, it wasn't far from the trees where she knew Rabbit would love to play.

Inside, the simple wooden structure proved much like her home. The kitchen nook was to her left as she walked in, a small table with two chairs to her right, the bed at the back with a private annex for the facilities. Her backpack was sitting neatly at the foot of the bed, beside a folded up screen she could use to block off the bedroom area from the kitchen.

"Where are you and your people going to sleep?" she asked Vasic, who'd remained in the doorway, his wide shoulders blocking out the light.

"We have cots stacked in the larger cabin situated at the center of the semicircle." Vasic's eyes followed Rabbit as her pet looked longingly at the bed. "Does he sleep with you?"

"Drat." Ivy lightly slapped her forehead. "I forgot his basket."

"I'll get it."

"Oh, thank you. It's just inside the back d—" And she was talking to air. "That could get extremely annoying extremely quickly." Her scowling mutter had barely cleared the air when he was back.

Vasic placed the basket near the kitchen nook. "There's food for him in one of the cupboards." Rising to his feet, he held out a small package of canine treats Ivy must've inadvertently left on her kitchen counter. "I guessed you might want these." He was absorbed by the idea that she spoiled her pet.

Ivy's narrow-eyed frown dissolved into panic. "Hide it before he sees," she ordered in a choked whisper, as if afraid Rabbit would understand.

Vasic 'ported the package into the same cupboard as the dog food he'd brought in for her pet.

Hand on her chest, Ivy shook her head. "You cannot *ever* show him the whole package," she told him in a tone as solemn as a church. "I made that mistake the first time, and he was like a junkie, standing in front of the cupboard salivating all day, every day."

Vasic didn't understand her. At all. She didn't act as a Psy was meant to act and so incited responses from him that were outside the norm. "Do you purchase treats for yourself as well?" he found himself asking, though why the knowledge mattered to him, he couldn't articulate.

Ivy bit down on the plump flesh of her lower lip, her eyes lit from within. "When I was eighteen and a half," she whispered, stepping so close that her exasperated dog forced his body between them, his furry coat pressed against Vasic's combat boots, "I went into the township's general store for the first time."

Not backing off, Ivy continued to speak in a low, private tone, as if she was sharing a secret.

He found himself bending toward her.

"I had money I'd earned from helping on the farm," she told him, "and I intended to buy useful supplies. Then the woman who runs the store with her husband offered me a sweet because I was 'too skinny by half.'" Her eyes drifted shut, her sigh long . . . and he thought perhaps she'd forgotten she was standing defenseless in front of a trained killer.

He stayed motionless, unwilling to fracture the strange, inexplicable moment.

"It was soft and sweet enough to incite sugar shock," she murmured, "and the most astonishingly delicious thing I'd ever tasted." Her lashes flicked up to reveal those perceptive, expressive eyes of copper and gold. "She told me it was called a Turkish Delight. I bought an entire box and gorged myself. Then I went back the next day and bought another box."

Glowing with a joy that saturated the air, she leaned in even closer and said, "I felt guilty so I bought Rabbit extra treats as well." Tiny lines formed at the corners of her eyes, bracketed the curve of her lips. "Alas, that was the end of my money, so we both had to wait another whole month before I could get more."

Vasic stared at her, wishing he had the capacity to comprehend her. Deep in the back of his mind, in the crumbled ruins of who he might've once been, he had the piercing thought that she was a rare, beautiful gift. And such a gift, came the ice-cold reminder from the core of his nature, would only end up crushed and bloody and defiled should he attempt to handle it.

Stepping away from her so suddenly that she swayed a little, he turned to walk to the door. "The others will be here soon."

Ivy stared at his shoulders, the raw intensity of his gray eyes burned into her retinas, her body missing the powerful presence of his own. He'd watched her as if she was the only thing in the entire universe, as if she was *his* version of a Turkish Delight. As if he wanted to devour her whole. Shaking her head to rid it of the foolish, impossible thought, she followed him to the porch.

Rabbit quivered by her side until she bent to pet him and whisper, "Go, explore. I'll stay in sight so you can still protect me." A happy lick, a "woof," and Rabbit scampered out to sniff at the rocks and the grass that poked up through the snow near the trees.

A few steps out, he froze, then started again, froze. Again and again.

Concerned, she spoke to Vasic without looking at him, unsettled after . . . whatever it was that had happened between them. "He's never behaved like that. Do you think he might be sensing contaminati—"

"He's picking up the scents of the wolves and leopards who built the cabins."

Oh. Ivy rose slightly on her toes, uplifted by the bubbles of excitement in her blood. "Will we see the changelings?" She'd never been near any big predator—discounting Vasic. He could've easily been a wolf, pure black with eyes of stunning frost.

"Highly probable."

Unable to resist, she turned her eyes to his profile. It was clean, pure. Hard.

"The experiment can't begin until your minds have relocated to this region of the PsyNet."

It took Ivy several seconds to wrench her thoughts back from the image that had formed in her mind between one heartbeat and the next—not of a black wolf after all, but of a warrior-priest from eons past. Strong and unwavering in the face of evil, and with a courage that defied comprehension.

"Yes," she managed to say, stunned by the force and potency of the image. Yet, was it a true insight born of instincts of which she wasn't consciously aware, or was she seeing such qualities in Vasic because she *needed* to see them, needed to think of him as a protector rather than the opposite?

"It shouldn't take long," he said into the heavy silence.

Rubbing her hands over her arms, her sweater suddenly too thin, Ivy simply nodded. Academics attempted to claim knowledge, but no one understood all the rules of the psychic plane. Minds were usually anchored in one place by a biofeedback link, but individuals could go anywhere in the Net, even travel physically to another continent with no change in their psychic location. However, if a person *wanted* to reanchor, as Ivy did, the process could take as little as twenty-four hours.

Hearing voices, she realized someone else had arrived. Curious but also a little shy, she turned to Vasic. "Shall we go meet them?"

He walked down the single step to the ground in response, the black silk of his hair kissing his collar. It couldn't be regulation length, and she liked the fact that despite first appearances, he *wasn't* the perfect soldier . . . was perhaps her warrior-priest after all.

The first meeting went well, Chang a personable cardinal not much taller than Ivy. "I'm a scientist in my ordinary life," he told her, before they parted so he could claim a cabin.

His Arrow was far more remote.

The others arrived in short order. Seated on her little porch only one step up from the ground, she drank a cup of tea and watched everyone settle in, while Rabbit ran around and sniffed at the newcomers, ecstatic at this adventure. Odd as it was, he didn't bristle at any other Arrow. Only Vasic.

Either her pet's instincts were diametrically opposed to her own . . . or he was jealous. And what, Ivy thought, did that say about her own response to an Arrow who remained a black-clad stranger—one who'd taken the time to make certain her cabin was stocked with food suitable for Rabbit.

Calling her pet back when his curiosity seemed to discomfort a small blonde who'd been the last to arrive, she promised him they'd play later. Satisfied, he drank from his water bowl, then sat panting beside her.

As it had so many times over the past two hours, Ivy found her gaze drifting toward Vasic. He was standing in the center of the clearing talking to several other Arrows. The presence of other members of his squad did nothing to mute her fascination with him—none drew her as he did, the quiet, dangerous mystery of him quickly becoming her new addiction.

Reaching out with her mind before she could second-guess herself, she "knocked" against his, her shoulders tensed in anticipation of a rejection. No doubt Arrows limited mental contact to those they trusted.

Do you have a question, Ivy? His telepathic voice was as cool as his physical one.

The hairs rose on her arms, born of a visceral reaction she couldn't define, but knew wasn't fear. *What are you doing?* It felt unutterably intimate to be speaking to him on the psychic level while the world moved around them, unaware of the connection.

Discussing security protocols. Would you like the information? The data flowed into her mind on the heels of his question.

Hmm, interesting, she said, though she couldn't make heads or tails of the complex diagrams. *I'm going to explore.*

You're free to do so. The perimeter is at some distance and clearly marked.

Rabbit rose the instant she did, his eyes bright. Smiling at him because it was impossible not to, she put her mug safely next to a porch post, then tapped her thigh, and they headed away from the cabins. "Be good," she said, though she wasn't worried her little white shadow would race too far.

Vasic? she said again.

Yes, Ivy?

It was strange how quickly his mental touch had become familiar. *Can you tell the changelings about Rabbit in case he accidentally breaches the perimeter?*

I've already done so. They have promised to herd him back if he does.

A deep warmth uncurling in her abdomen, she said, *Thank you.*

No response, no polite words. "Because he only says what is necessary." And, she reminded herself in an effort to fight the temptation to draw him out further, he was working. "Come on, Rabbit. Let's go find that stream we can hear."

Tail wagging happily, Rabbit padded beside her through the sun-dappled spaces between the trees. His first winter with her, she'd tried to keep him inside, but her pet had made it clear he loved the snow. Now it was only on the coldest days that she left him snug inside their home.

A couple of minutes of easy walking later, the two of them stood beside a stream that looked like a picture she'd once seen in a children's story-book, the water creating a quiet music as it ran over smooth pebbles as large as her palm.

Hearing the crackle of fallen branches underfoot behind her, she turned to see Chang. "Hello."

The distinctive night-sky eyes of a cardinal, white stars on black, focused on Rabbit. "Is that a pet?"

"Yes." Ivy had made a decision to own her new life, no matter where it led. No lies, no half-truths. Not even from herself. "My Silence is frac-tured to the point of being nonexistent." And no one, she decided at that instant beside a sunlit stream, would ever make her feel lesser for it; she wouldn't permit it.

Ivy?

Yes, Vasic? she said in a deliberate echo of the way he'd answered her earlier . . . and it felt like the beginnings of a secret language.

Are you at ease being alone with Chang? I saw him head in the same direc-tion as you.

Something twisted in her heart. *Yes. Thank you for checking.*

Your safety is my priority.

Chapter 12

Empaths thrive in communities. Extended periods of solitude are known to be damaging to their mental well-being.

Excerpted from *The Mysterious E Designation: Empathic Gifts & Shadows* by Alice Eldridge

AN HOUR AFTER she'd met Chang by the stream, Ivy found herself seated on one of the large rocks at the open end of the clearing, the sun having warmed the stone. Around her sat the other empaths, the ten of them having gravitated toward one another.

Three men and six women, they ranged in age and geographic localities. Chang had come in from a research station in Kenya, while the blonde woman who wasn't comfortable with Rabbit—Concetta—helped run a family business in Paraguay. Petite Lianne hailed from Kuala Lumpur, Teri from Houston, and Jaya from an atoll in the Maldives. Tibet born and raised Dechen sat next to Scottish Penn, the two of them across from Brigitte, a German based in Amsterdam. The final male, Isaiah, was from the tiny island nation of Niue.

Chang and Brigitte, both on the cusp of forty, were the oldest. "Apparently," Chang had said to Ivy as they walked back from the stream, "anyone older is apt to find it more difficult to become active within the necessarily truncated timeline."

That made sense to Ivy, as did the fact that there was no one younger than Jaya at twenty-one. A younger empath could well be too erratic—because while Silence was a terrible cage, it also taught strict mental discipline. Ivy's conditioning might not have held, but she'd used the skills she'd learned under Silence to shield herself and to exert control in situations where betraying a fracture could've led to dangerous consequences.

"Woof!"

Glancing down at Rabbit, Ivy said, "Shh," but his excitement made her smile. Her pet had investigated every corner of the compound by now, sniffed at everyone—even the Arrows—but remained full of energy.

"Your conditioning"—Isaiah's dark eyes zeroed in on her smile—"it's totally fragmented?"

Ivy was trying very hard not to dislike the male near her own age, but there was just something so smugly superior about him that it was near impossible. Now his question sounded like an accusation—but Ivy wasn't about to apologize for who she was. "Yes." It was true enough, given that the malfunctioning lock on her abilities, the source of her nosebleeds, was scheduled to be removed tomorrow.

It would leave her free of mental restraint for the first time in her life.

"My Silence, too," Jaya said softly, her dark brown skin glowing in the sunlight, "is close to complete failure." The pretty young woman, tall and with a quiet elegance that belied her years, petted Rabbit when he wandered over. "I was certain I'd be forced into a deep reconditioning . . . then Councilor Krychek mandated the fall of Silence."

"I'm here because I'm being paid to be here." Isaiah stared at the Arrows visible on the other side of the clearing, his hands clasped loosely between his knees. "I don't believe in a hidden E designation. It seems pointless."

Ivy couldn't understand his attitude. "Did you talk to Sascha Duncan?"

"No." Muscles worked in his jaw. "Councilor Duncan's daughter has deluded herself into thinking she has some kind of an ability when she's nothing but a flawed cardinal."

Since Isaiah's Silence was cracking like an eggshell to anyone who had eyes, Ivy decided to leave him to his theories and directed her words to the rest of the group. "*I* believe." She spread the fingers of one hand over her heart, thinking of how she'd never, *not once* questioned her parents' love or commitment, not even during her early childhood—when Gwen and Carter had adhered more strictly to the tenets of Silence. "Looking back, I know I've sensed emotion my entire life."

Big-boned, her hair a tumble of dark blonde, and her skin pale cream, gorgeous Brigitte spoke with a distinctive, raspy voice. "Two months before I was contacted for this," she said now, her accent that of a woman who'd lived all over Europe, "I witnessed a car accident. It was on a largely untraveled road through the Pyrénées, and I was the only one nearby to offer assistance."

No one spoke when she paused, her throat moving.

"After calling the authorities"—she tugged her white shawl snug around her shoulders—"I ran down the bank to where the car had come to a violent stop against a large tree, and managed to open the driver's-side door. The man inside was covered in blood and trapped by the way the car had crumpled around him." A long, deep breath, air releasing softly from her nostrils.

"He was human, and he was so *scared* that it felt like nails being driven into my flesh." Vivid, brutal, the image hit hard. "When he grabbed my hand, I didn't retract it, and I thought that if only he wasn't *so afraid*, his heart rate would calm, his breathing would even, and he'd have a higher chance of survival."

"What happened?" Ivy whispered when the other woman stopped to stare at the ground, as if once more alone with a dying man on a lonely mountain road.

Cornflower blue eyes met Ivy's. "The terror, *his* terror . . . it drained away . . . then it was inside me, choking me with a panic that blinded." She shook her head. "I excused the experience as being brought on by the stress of the situation. But a week after the accident, the hospital forwarded me a note from the injured man." She twisted her interlinked hands. "He thanked me for being there, for taking his fear."

A whispering quiet, the trees waving in the breeze.

Bearded Penn was the one who broke it, his big body throwing a shadow across the ground. "I haven't had a comparable experience, but the idea of a mind healer makes rational sense to me. We're a race defined by our minds—it would be illogical *not* to have a designation focused on psychic injuries."

Isaiah's biceps bulged beneath the thin fabric of his thermal pullover as he gripped his left wrist with his right hand, but even he had no words to refute Penn's statement.

"I've felt the darkness," Concetta blurted into the quiet. "The rot in the Net."

Everyone focused on the amber-eyed woman.

Her skin flushed. Ducking her head, she whispered, "It's licking at the Net not far from the town where my family makes its home. I didn't go near it, but it 'tasted' malignant even from a distance." Fingers trembling, she picked at the fabric of her black pants. "How does anyone expect us to deal with such malevolence?" she asked, voice cracking on the last word. "What gives Kaleb Krychek and his pet assassins the right to force us into this?"

Ivy bristled at the derogatory description of Vasic and the rest of the squad. "Were you coerced?"

"I may as well have been." Lip thrust forward in a pout that made the twenty-five-year-old appear younger than Jaya, Concetta wrapped her arms around herself. "The head of my family unit ordered me to accept—the contract fee, he said, was too generous to reject."

Ivy kept her silence during the ensuing discussion, but she was disturbed by the realization that the other Es weren't all a hundred percent committed to the success of this project.

Her nails dug into her palm.

Whatever Concetta and her ilk did or did not do, Ivy intended to see this through to the end. Her choice was both selfish and not—she wanted to help the innocents in the Net, but she also wanted to be more than the glued-together shards of the broken teenage girl who'd come out of the reconditioning chamber. She wanted to be the promise that had been stifled inside her for a lifetime. Good or bad, weak or strong, resilient or fragile, she needed to know who Ivy Jane was beyond the cage of Silence.

She found herself searching for Vasic on the heels of that passionate thought.

Four years old.

His life must've been brutally regimented, countless choices taken from him, his cage a punishing Arrow black. Would he ever choose to step out of the dark, or would he always stand as a lethal sentinel on the border? Protecting, shielding . . . but never being part of the world.

THE secondary security sweep complete, Vasic looked to where Ivy sat with the other Es. She appeared involved in an intense discussion with Jaya, while Rabbit drowsed at her feet.

"An idyllic image," said the man who'd just 'ported in a short distance from Vasic, his black on black suit a stark contrast to the combat uniforms worn by the squad. "If we don't consider the deadly infection they've been brought here to combat."

Vasic had known Krychek would appear sooner or later. "Have you channeled the infection to this part of the Net?"

"I was able to nudge it in this direction." Krychek's cardinal gaze lingered on the empaths. "At its current rate of spread, it'll take approximately twenty-four hours to intrude on this location."

"Will we be surrounded?" He had to make certain their exit strategy remained viable.

"No. Indications are it'll come in from one side in a creeping wave, then extrude tendrils inward."

A safer state of affairs, relatively speaking.

Krychek slid his hands into the pockets of his suit pants. "Are there any obvious problems?"

"It's highly likely that Concetta Galeano's family coerced her into accepting the contract." The Arrow in charge of the female E had reported his reading of the situation to Vasic an hour ago.

"Suggested course of action?"

"Give her another twenty-four hours," Vasic said, noting that Ivy's hair was beginning to come loose from her ponytail. "If Ms. Galeano's mind doesn't reanchor to this region"—thus proving the depth of her reluctance—"I'll return her to her family."

"Should that happen, I'll pay her a quiet visit to reiterate the importance of the confidentiality clause."

Vasic was unsurprised by the decision. The last thing Krychek wanted, or the Net needed, was a leak about this experiment. Pure Psy might be in pieces, but as evidenced by the attack on Ivy, even if the fanatical group no longer posed a threat to the Net as a whole, the last remaining Pure Psy faithful were still dangerous on an individual level.

The more problematic and potentially lethal threat, however, came from those in the general population who were having difficulty adapting to a life beyond Silence—to them the empaths would be the enemy, a direct risk to the way of life they sought to cling to with increasing desperation.

"Anything else I should know?"

"No." Vasic saw Ivy glance toward him, see Kaleb Krychek at his side. Shoulders going stiff, her copper-colored gaze swung back to him. It was odd, but he could almost imagine she was concerned about him.

Impossible.

Then he felt her mind brush his, her telepathic touch so gentle it was unlike any he'd ever before experienced. *Vasic, be careful.*

He thought he should tell her he was as capable of deadly force as Krychek, that they'd been formed in, if not the same, then analogous bloody crucibles. But now that he'd tasted Ivy's smile, now that he'd felt her psychic touch, he didn't want to see fear chill her skin again when she looked at him.

So all he said was, *I am safe, Ivy.*

And he thought perhaps if he had met her a lifetime ago, he would've been better than he was . . . but he hadn't. Now it was too late, his soul pitted and shredded, his hands instruments of death. Still, he could do one thing, he thought, his eyes dropping to the gauntlet that was an outward reminder of his inhumanity.

He could protect her to the last beat of his heart.

Chapter 13

Authorization not recognized. Any further attempt at access will be met with terminal action.

Automated security system response to Ming LeBon's final bid to reenter Arrow Central Command

MING LEBON HAD lost the Arrows. He'd accepted that, accepted too that it had been a mistake to treat them as ordinary grunts who would come to heel at his command. The Arrows were not the least ordinary, each operative having gone through rigorous psychological testing before being inducted into the squad. The majority were also acutely intelligent.

There was one loss, however, that he was unwilling to accept: Vasic.

The sole known true teleporter in the PsyNet was a critical asset. He'd saved Ming's life more than once by 'porting him out in the split second before terminal impact. No other Tk on the planet could do it as fast, and Ming had no intention of losing access to Vasic's ability. Vasic, however, was loyal to the squad and to Aden.

That left a single viable way for Ming to secure the teleporter's abilities. "You have the Jax?" he asked the medic who was the only one who knew of his plans.

The other man nodded at Ming's reference to the drug that, used as Ming planned to use it, could turn an Arrow into a weapon that could be pointed in any direction wished by its master. "Prepped and ready at the correct dosage."

That dosage wasn't calibrated for a temporary reset, but a permanent one, because Ming didn't want Vasic's brain, only his ability. He'd believed the teleporter's brain had already permanently reset years ago, but recent events had made that seem a premature conclusion.

"You're certain the problem that led to the Arrows being weaned off the drug was manufactured?" He'd initiated the inquiry after discovering that Judd Lauren wasn't only alive, but a defector who'd joined the Snow-Dancer wolves.

The rebel Arrow was the first Tk who'd shown signs of impaired physical and mental ability while on Jax, a side effect that had then spread subtly through the ranks, leading to dangerously erratic behavior. Given that Arrows were meant to be shadows, subtle and invisible, Ming had authorized the discontinuance of the Jax regime.

Judd Lauren's apparent mental health, however, argued for a far different interpretation.

"Yes," the medic answered. "I've run multiple controlled tests on the assigned unit of your soldiers."

Soldiers, who, Ming thought, had no idea they were being dosed with Jax and thus couldn't doctor their responses.

"It appears," the M-Psy continued, "the Arrows collaborated to get off the drug."

It was another indication of how little Ming had understood the men and women he sought to lead, a critical flaw in his strategic thinking. Ming didn't accept or tolerate flaws, so he would fix this. "Keep the Jax prepped at all times." It would take considerable planning, but Ming would find a way to enslave Vasic.

Chapter 14

Empaths can endure a lack of tactile contact, but those of designation E find such a lack difficult at best. When asked to describe the sensation, most simply said that it "hurt." What is impossible to put into words is the profound pain embodied in that single word.

Excerpted from *The Mysterious E Designation: Empathic Gifts & Shadows* by Alice Eldridge

DINNER WAS A quiet affair for Ivy, she and the other Es having decided they needed space to consider everything that had been discussed. First, she spoke to her parents on the comm; she'd messaged them after her arrival at the compound, and now she reiterated that she was safe and excited about this new phase in her life.

Then, ignoring the nutrition bars and drinks in the pantry, she put together a simple meal, akin to what she'd have at home. That, of course, was only possible because of the fresh ingredients stocked in the kitchen.

Would you like to have dinner? she asked the man who'd no doubt arranged the supplies. The quiet, intense compulsion he aroused within her continued to grow unabated. She'd watched him organize his unit with military efficiency in the past hours, deal undaunted with the most lethal predator in the Net, handle multiple questions from the Arrows and empaths both. Through it all, he'd been a solid wall.

No, she frowned, that was the wrong analogy. Vasic was stable, but in the way the sea was stable on a day without a breeze, his depths hidden beneath a reflective surface that was an impenetrable shield.

His voice slid into her mind like ice-kissed water on the heels of that thought. Almost too cold . . . and yet delicious to a parched throat. She shivered, her nipples tightening in a confusing physical response that left her breathless.

I've had the nutrition bars I need.

His response was a jolting reminder that her awareness of him was most-assuredly one-sided. To Vasic, she was simply a task, his job to keep her alive for the duration of this experiment. It might be that the winter-frost eyes in which she saw haunting mysteries, were instead nothing but remote gray: flat and without depth.

Disturbed at the idea, she took the salad she'd prepared and—leaving the fish to grill—went to sit on the edge of her little porch, her booted feet on the hard-packed snow below. When Rabbit ran out to join her with a reproachful look, she got up with a laugh and carried out his food and water bowls so he could eat with her under the night sky. She could've turned on the porch light, but she liked the silver caress of the moon, the way the glow from the cabin windows around her painted the air in hazy warmth.

Two seconds later, the hairs rose on the back of her neck and Rabbit growled.

"Is there a problem with your cabin?" Vasic asked.

Stomach clenching, she looked up at where he stood silhouetted against the night, tall and distant and every inch a soldier. "I just wanted to sit out here." Her breath was puffs of white, her pulse a rapid flutter in her throat

"The temperature is continuing to drop."

"I'm wearing warm clothes, and it's nowhere near as cold as the orchard." She ate a little of her salad in an effort to ease the sudden nervous tension that had her muscles taut, and decided to follow instinct. "Why don't you sit?" If he'd wanted solitude, he could've left as soon as she'd confirmed she was happy out here. "Keep me company."

When he took a seat on the porch, a foot of distance between them, she had to bite back an exhilarated cry. No, Vasic was no flat mirage. Never would be. He was an intelligent, complex, *fascinating* male who made her body and mind respond in a way with which she had no experience . . . but she knew she didn't want it to stop. "Are you sure you don't want anything?" she asked, feeling a deep need to give him something. "A drink?"

"No." Forearms braced on his thighs, he stared out into the darkness, his profile ascetic in its purity and his shoulders broad. "What are your views on the other Es?"

"Why?" Teeth sinking into her lower lip, Ivy fought the urge to trace the clean lines of him. "Are you making a report?"

No movement; even his breathing was strictly controlled. "If you'd rather I didn't utilize your answers in any official report, I won't."

"I'd rather." Forcing her eyes off the stark, dangerous beauty of him, she ate another bite of salad.

Vasic didn't rush her, just waited. He was, she realized, comfortable with quiet in a way very few people ever became. Again, she thought of a warrior-priest, relentless and devoted . . . but she no longer liked the idea of a man dedicated to an ideal. A warrior-priest was untouchable, and Ivy was beginning to understand that she very much wanted to touch Vasic.

All her life, she'd made physical contact with her parents. As a child, it had been instinct. As she grew older, she'd realized how lucky she was that they never rejected her touch as other Silent parents might. Tactile contact, she'd long ago comprehended, helped her feel centered . . . happy, but not just anyone would do. Aside from her parents, she'd exchanged hugs with only two others in the settlement, both close women friends.

Her pulse rocketed at the idea of such intimacy with the deadly male who sat beside her. Self-protective instincts should've shut that thought down before it took form, but it continued to grow in her abdomen, a tight ball of warmth and nerves and foolishness. Because Vasic hadn't given her a single sign that he'd welcome any physical contact. He was an Arrow, as inaccessible as the cold splendor of the stars.

Unfortunately, Ivy's body and mind refused to listen to reason.

"I talk a lot," she said, keeping a firm hold on her bowl and fork so she wouldn't yield to the compulsion to run her fingertips over his skin. "To Rabbit mostly, but I'll probably talk to you too if you're around." It came out too fast, his proximity continuing to do strange things to her. "Do you mind?"

Vasic's lashes, straight and dark, came down, lifted again. "No."

Deciding to take the one-syllable answer at face value, she hauled her wandering thoughts back in line with teeth-gritted concentration. "I like the majority of the other empaths," she said in answer to his original question. "A couple get on my nerves, and I think I'll become good friends with Jaya." The two of them had clicked at once. "All pretty normal."

"Yet you sound . . . disappointed." The last word was chosen with care, as if he'd taken in her words, considered her tone of voice, then run it against a mental database of emotional expressions.

Wondering if he'd tell her, she said, "How did you judge my emotional response? Do you have a specific process?"

"Yes," Vasic said, turning to look at the copper-eyed woman who didn't seem to comprehend that he was a monster. "Does the analysis have less value for being done consciously?" It was a serious question, her answer important to him in a way he couldn't articulate.

"No," she said at once. "People who live with emotion do it instinctively, but the process is the same."

It affected him to realize she saw him as a man, not as something lesser, but he couldn't permit her to believe a lie. "The empathic connection is missing." He didn't feel an echo of her emotions or think back to a time when he'd felt the same. "It's a wholly remote calculation."

Her fork making a clinking noise against the bowl as she abandoned her salad to one side, Ivy braced one hand against the wood of the porch and angled herself to face him. "I've never been truly Silent," she admitted as her pet wriggled under her arm to sit tucked up against her. "Not even when I thought I was." A sudden tightness to her jaw, her lips pressed to a thin line, and her spine rigid.

"Once, when I was fourteen," she said as he recognized the signs of cold fury, "I saw an older Psy boy using a sharp branch to stab at a cat trapped in a culvert. I told him to stop, and he said he was running an experiment."

Vasic went motionless. "That wasn't Silence." He knew because he'd seen men and women like that boy too many times—and a large number were in positions of power in the PsyNet. "It was a sign of the psychopathy Silence makes it easy to hide."

"Yes." Ivy shifted to run her hand over Rabbit's back, petting the dog to heavy-eyed somnolence. "But back then I couldn't think that clearly. I was so *angry* at him that I found another stick and began to poke him in the neck and the face until he lost his balance and fell." A tremor shook her frame, and her hand fisted on Rabbit's coat.

The memory, Vasic understood, still incited the same rage.

"He said I was being irrational and he'd report me"—the copper of her eyes glittered—"and I said go ahead."

Vasic catalogued the expression in a private mental folder in which he'd begun to collect even the tiniest details about Ivy. It was a small madness, and one of which no one need be aware. "He didn't, did he?" Cowards who attacked the defenseless and the vulnerable did not last long against Ivy's kind of honest strength.

"No," she confirmed, her voice steeped in disgust. "He knew what he was doing was wrong, and I knew never to be caught alone with him." Cuddling Rabbit, she shot Vasic a fierce grin. "The cat was fine—and it scratched him hard across the cheek before it ran off."

Vasic watched the vivid play of emotions on her face in a vain attempt to know every nuance of her. When color touched her cheekbones, her lashes coming down to veil her eyes, he realized he'd stared for too long, but he didn't shift his gaze. "Why are you disappointed with your reactions to the other empaths?"

"It's just . . . I don't know." Her shoulders slumped beneath the autumn orange of her cardigan. "I guess I thought there'd be an instant connection between us all."

"Telepaths, telekinetics, none of us feel any kind of an immediate connection with one another." Vasic handled a telepathic security check-in by his sentries even as he spoke. "Why should it be different for empaths?"

She made a face, brow heavy. "I didn't say it was logical," she muttered, as her pet jumped off the porch to walk to the center of the snowy clearing.

A small beep came from inside the cabin a second later to indicate the cooking cycle was complete on whatever meal Ivy was making, the machine now in the process of turning itself off. Ignoring it, she said, "You know something else?"

Adding another mental image to his private file of Ivy, who he did not understand and whose actions he couldn't predict, he said, "What?"

"I made a decision to go forward, to not be chained by the past." Her shoulders grew stiff. "A sensible choice, good for my mental health."

"And now you find you feel anger." There was no way to mistake the violence of emotion that was white lines around her mouth, rigid tendons on her neck, a barely controlled vibration in her voice.

"Rage," Ivy said, "that's what I feel when I think of what they did to me in that reconditioning room." Jaw clenched so tight that Ivy could hear her bones grinding against one another, she spoke through the brutal roar in her ears. "They *hurt* me. Not the pain, though that was bad, but what they did to who I was. I'll never again be the same Ivy who walked into that torture chamber."

Vasic's gaze—intense, unwavering, opaque—continued to hold hers. "You were once a girl who fought off a bully with a branch. Now you're a woman about to fight for the survival of your race. What did you lose?"

Ivy stared at him. Then, picking up some salad in her hand, she threw it at his head. It froze in midair to float gently back into her bowl. His control further infuriated her. "What did I *lose?*" she said through gritted teeth. "I used to be *happy*, to see the world as a good place. I lost that innocence."

Vasic took his time answering. "An innocent could not be here, could not attempt to do what you must. For this, the Net needs a warrior."

Her pulsing anger didn't lessen, too huge and too old a thing. It needed a target, but the people who'd hurt her weren't here and this infuriating Arrow had just called her a warrior by implication. "I don't understand you," she said an instant before hot pokers lanced through her brain.

"There's noth—" Vasic's head snapped up at the tiny cry of pain that escaped her lips. "Ivy, what is it?" *Ivy.*

Vision blurring, she gripped the sides of her viciously pounding head.

Something's wrong. Her mouth couldn't shape the words, her tongue thick and her heart a freight train. *I can't . . .*

Vasic scented iron, rich and wet, before he saw the crimson-black droplets roll down Ivy's neck. She was bleeding from one ear. *Drop your shields.* Blood began to trickle like tears over her cheeks. *I need to see what's happening.*

No argument, her shields going down in an act of trust so staggering, Vasic couldn't think about it if he was to function. Having already thrown his own shields around her, he scanned the surface of her mind to see countless ruptures, the mental landscape akin to a landmass ravaged by a major quake. "I'll be back in seconds," he said to her, so she'd know he wasn't abandoning her, then made himself go.

Ivy was hunched over shaking when he returned with Aden. Rabbit, having run back to the porch, nudged at her with his nose, a low whine escaping the dog's throat. "I need entry," Aden said to Vasic, after evaluating the situation in a single glance.

Vasic slid open the shield he'd slammed around Ivy's otherwise naked mind only long enough for Aden to slip in, then crouched down in front of her. Though physical contact wasn't something with which he was comfortable, he gripped her chin, forcing her to meet his gaze. So close, he couldn't miss that her eyes were bloodshot, her pupils hugely dilated.

Aden is the medic I told you about, he telepathed. *The lock placed on you during the reconditioning has collapsed. Aden is removing the broken shards.* Those shards were shoving into her brain itself, could cause irreversible damage if not extracted at once—and with extreme care.

Uncontrolled. It was a faint telepathic sound as her bloody tears dripped to the fists she'd braced on her thighs.

Yes. Ivy's scheduled operation had been meant to head off exactly this type of vicious, unpredictable fragmentation. *Don't be concerned. Aden is gifted at such delicate work.*

Ivy's hand closed around his wrist, slippery with blood. *I'm scared.*

Vasic hadn't experienced fear since he was a child, the emotional resonance long since faded. Now, however, he could physically sense Ivy's fear in the stutter of her pulse, the shallowness of her breath, the shaken tone of her mental voice, and it tore at things long dead inside him. *Aden will cause you no harm.*

An instant of startling clarity in the crimson copper. *He's your brother. Not genetically, but yes.*

Her head dropped, her hand spasming to fall off his wrist.

Having caught her instinctively with his telekinesis so she wouldn't wrench her neck, he shifted close enough that her cheek could rest against his shoulder. *Aden.* The speed with which she'd lost consciousness was not a good sign.

There are multiple fine shards already embedded in her brain.

Chapter 15

KEEPING HIS SILENCE while his partner worked with meticulous patience, Vasic didn't move so as not to cause any inadvertent damage. Part of him knew he could've achieved the same aim using telekinesis, but he chose to ignore that voice in favor of feeling Ivy's determination to live in the soft, warm air against his neck that was her breath.

"It's done," Aden said an hour later, pushing back his sweat-damp hair from his face. "You'll need to shield her until she's conscious and capable of doing it herself."

"Prognosis?" Vasic would accept only one answer—no one this rare and vivid was meant to die.

Aden shook his head. "Hard to predict. If she wakes, she'll have come through the worst of it. Whether she wakes will depend on her own internal strength."

"Then she'll live." Ivy had come back once from far worse. She'd do it again.

This time Vasic did use Tk to lift her, not wanting to risk jarring her brain. Placing her gently on her bed, he found a washcloth and wiped away the blood on her face and her hands. Rabbit didn't growl at him, simply watched until he was done, then jumped on the bed. Pulling a blanket over Ivy's body, her skin cool to the touch when he checked her pulse, Vasic left her with her pet curled up beside her.

"Will there be any side effects?" he asked Aden once he was outside, the sight of Ivy's deserted bowl of salad causing him inexplicable discomfort until he gave in and teleported it away.

Aden didn't reiterate his earlier cautious prognosis. "Unless she reacts in an unforeseen fashion," he said, "there should be none other than headaches caused by residual bruising. Those should pass within forty-eight hours." A pause. "I should say no side effects beyond the obvious."

Ivy's E ability, Vasic thought, was now wide open. "We'll need Sascha Duncan's assistance earlier th—"

A scream tore through the compound.

"Go," Aden said to him. "I'll keep watch on Ivy."

Vasic 'ported to the origin of the scream—the cabin belonging to the empath Lianne—but didn't step inside. *Stay at your posts*, he ordered his team, and attempted to contact Cristabel, the Arrow assigned to Lianne.

No response.

Listening with all of his senses, he heard only the rasping, unsteady breath of someone who was badly injured. *I'm entering the cabin*, he told Aden automatically, all Arrows trained to alert backup if it was available.

Lianne lay slumped at the table where she'd been eating her dinner. Cristabel was on the floor, blood pooling below her shoulder and head, while an unknown male of medium height and slight build lay against the opposite wall. A small round hole indicative of a precision laser shot marred the center of his forehead, his eyes staring in death.

Lianne's skin was clammy, but she didn't seem in any imminent danger. Cristabel's pulse, however, was thready at best. It was her breathing he'd heard, a faint rattling in her lungs that told him they could lose her. *Aden, in here.* He switched telepathic channels. *Abbot, cover Ivy as well as your charge.*

Sir.

He continued to monitor Ivy on the telepathic level even as he gave those orders. Aden ran into the cabin the second after Abbot's response. Aden took one look at Cristabel and said, "Clinic."

Ready, Vasic took them directly to the private medical facility Aden had set up after it became clear that the Council medics' orders included getting rid of "broken" or "under performing" members of the squad. All three of the highly trained staff at this clinic were alive because an Arrow hadn't carried out an assassination order while making it appear otherwise. Each was blood-loyal to the squad.

Leaving Aden to supervise the medical procedures—because regardless of their trust in the staff, no Arrow would leave an injured comrade at the mercy of anyone who wasn't a member of the squad—Vasic returned to Lianne's cabin to find her stirring. He transferred her to the Arrow cabin, setting up a cot and putting her on it before she opened her eyes.

Then he turned on the light.

Blinking, she squinted as if it hurt her eyes. "Ray?"

"Who is Ray?" Vasic asked, not concerned with the ethics of interrogating her while she was disoriented. He needed to know how anyone, even a teleporter, had managed to get inside the compound and into her cabin.

Lianne curled into a fetal position on the camouflage green of the cot. "My cousin," she said, her voice a little slurred. "Why is he here?"

That was the question.

Initiating a medical program on his gauntlet, he scanned the dazed empath and detected a mild concussion, possibly from having her head slammed against the top of the table where he'd found her. Sending Aden the data so his partner could evaluate her condition, Vasic waited for a reply to come in before he left to return to the scene. He'd record it later using his gauntlet in case a re-creation was necessary, and take blood samples, but his military-trained mind told him exactly what had happened.

That theory was confirmed when he stepped outside and made use of his connection with Judd to ask if the SnowDancer-DarkRiver satellite surveillance had picked up an extra body in the vicinity in the past hour.

"No. The last new entry came in with you a little earlier—I'm judging that from the speed of the 'port noted in the file."

That would've been Aden. Hanging up without thanking Judd for the information because such was understood among members of the squad, he considered what he'd found in Lianne's cabin. Ray had teleported directly *inside*, which meant he was either part of the rare telekinetic subset that could lock onto people as well as places, or he'd had an image file to use as a lock. Vasic's bet was on an image leak. Teleporters who could lock onto people were extremely rare and Vasic knew—or knew of—most of them.

Aden's reply came in at that instant, the message showing up directly on the gauntlet's small screen: *She doesn't need medical attention. Just keep an eye on her and alert me if she exhibits any of the following symptoms.* Below was a concise list.

Assigning the task to another Arrow, Vasic returned to Lianne's cabin. A scan indicated no computronic devices other than the wall-set comm and Lianne's sleek personal phone. He judged that if the empath had broken the rules, she'd have done it via her private device; picking it up, he circumvented the security key using a simple algorithm sent through his gauntlet.

It took him under ten seconds to discover that Lianne had been uploading hourly updates to a private family server. Not only a breach of confidentiality, but also of safety—because she'd uploaded photos. Scanning the images, he realized the exterior of the compound was now of higher priority than the interior of Lianne's cabin.

Stepping outside after smashing the kitchen area with a telekinetic blow to change its basic shape, he alerted his people to the coming disruption and the reason for it, then ripped up a tree by the roots and laid it in the middle of the rough circle of rocks the empaths had used as their meeting spot. To make the image lock useless now or later, he crushed three of the rocks, his base telekinetic ability more powerful than most people realized, given that it was his teleportation that normally grabbed attention.

The rapid-fire actions kicked his heart into high gear, his breath coming in shorter but no less controlled bursts. Not slowing down, he snapped several of the pine trees behind the cabins in half, so the background couldn't be used. The mountains weren't visible in any of Lianne's photographs, which eliminated a major risk factor, but Vasic would have to neutralize a number of others.

When his phone buzzed a few seconds later, he saw it was Judd.

"You suddenly have something against trees?" the other male asked.

"Image leak."

"Shit. Want some help?"

"Yes." He could complete the task himself, but he'd be tired at the end of it when he needed to remain alert. "As fast as possible."

Judd 'ported in a minute later, and together they surgically removed the porches from three of the cabins. Two more trees were sacrificed to alter the skyline directly behind the cabins, and then they dismantled the porches they'd removed, stacking the resulting planks beside several of the cabins.

"It's enough." To make certain, Vasic had Judd leave the area, then attempt to use the images to come back in.

"Couldn't do it," the other man told him when he returned, expression hard and hair as sweaty as Vasic's own. "How the hell did this happen? You've only been here a day."

Vasic led Judd into Lianne's cabin and to the body crumpled on the floor. Going down beside it, Vasic pressed one of the dead man's fingers onto the screen of the gauntlet and initiated a print search. "Rayland Faison," he said, rising to his feet as the data came in. "Resident of San Francisco. Listed as belonging to the same extended family unit as the empath who had this cabin." Another piece of information caught his attention. "Faison's Gradient level doesn't give him enough juice to make the 'port from the city."

"Send me the plate number of his vehicle—he probably abandoned it somewhere between here and San Francisco." Judd stared at the dead man. "Who took the shot? It's so pristinely centered, I'd say Cristabel if I had to guess."

"Yes." In her late thirties, the other Arrow was an expert markswoman. "She's in surgery. Prognosis unknown."

"Damn—Cris taught me how to shoot." Thrusting a hand through his hair, Judd met Vasic's gaze. "She was the most patient, most meticulous trainer I had."

The words described the fallen Arrow well. "I'll keep you updated on her condition." Vasic, too, had learned to shoot under Cristabel. She was the only trainer he'd had who had never punished him with pain—Cris's version of a reprimand was to make her students practice for an extra hour.

"I'd appreciate it." Judd returned his attention to Faison's corpse. "Why would Lianne's family want to assassinate her?"

"I'll be asking them that question myself." Ivy was still deeply asleep and unlikely to need Vasic, and this breach had to be handled—or the next time Ivy went walking in the woods with her pet, she might not come back. "We'll be two down if I leave," he told Judd. "Can you remain?"

An immediate nod. "Long as you need me."

Vasic left with Faison's body without further delay, his target the large home shared by those of Lianne's family based in Kuala Lampur, the internal image one he had in his master file on the empath. A loud crash to his left alerted him to the fact he'd startled a uniformed member of the house staff into dropping a vase. Water ran along the polished wood of the floor, creamy pink and yellow plumeria blooms lying amidst the glazed blue shards.

"I require the head of the family," he said to the woman, whose eyes had fixated on the body that floated next to Vasic.

Her head jerked up, her light brown skin so pale her pink lips appeared badly misplaced. "Y-yes." Flowers abandoned, she didn't look back as she ran past the windows that spilled the early afternoon light of this region into the hallway.

A woman of about fifty, with the stiff, regal bearing that marked her as Dara Faison, the matriarch of the family group, entered the hallway by a side entrance a minute later. She took in the body with no visible change in her expression but didn't speak at once, the silence no doubt a power play calculated to gain mastery of the situation.

Vasic didn't have time for games. "This is Rayland Faison. Records state him to be a member of your family unit. Is this correct?"

"Yes." Folding her hands in front of her black knee-length dress, the cut as severe as the bun into which she'd scraped back her dark hair, Dara Faison said, "Why was my nephew killed?"

"He attempted to assassinate Lianne." He caught the tiny flicker at the corners of her eyes, extrapolated that she wasn't as surprised as she should've been. "Did you order this assassination?"

"No."

"You'll be required to submit to a telepathic scan to confirm that."

Her shoulders went rigid. "I'm sure that won't be necessary. My nephew had . . . certain leanings. Fanatically pro-Silence. It's why we locked him out of the part of the system that held the data about Lianne's ability and contract."

"A good precaution—except for the fact your nephew worked in computronic security." Vasic had retrieved that data during the minute he waited for Dara. "Telepathic scans will be mandatory for all members of the family unit." If there was even a chance Rayland Faison hadn't been alone in his radical beliefs, Vasic had to unearth that information as fast as possible. "The scans will be carried out by a specialist telepath."

To her credit, Dara held firm, the taut oval of her face carved in stone. "You have no authorization to order such a violation of our privacy."

"You gave me that authorization when you instructed Lianne to breach her contract." Dara's complicity in Lianne's actions had been obvious from the messages he'd read. It had been a stupid move, one driven by an arrogance he knew the matriarch would profess not to possess.

"Lianne will be transferred here tomorrow." He eased his Tk until Rayland Faison's body lay on the floor. "Should there be any further leaks traced to your family, you will be terminated." Vasic would permit no one to harm those he'd promised to protect. "All data about the project is already in the process of being scrubbed from your systems."

Dara Faison hadn't moved since the instant he'd made it clear the telepathic scans *would* happen, as if finally comprehending that she'd attempted to play in a pool where she was so out of her depth, death was a real possibility. Now she glanced at the body of her nephew and said, "There will be no leaks."

Returning to Lianne's cabin without further words, Vasic took visual scans and collected blood samples that he sent back to Central Command, then began to clean up the blood molecule by molecule. It took time and concentration. Most telekinetics couldn't work on this level, their power too violent.

Can you take blood out of carpet? he asked the only Tk he knew who worked on an even more minute level, that of the cells of the body itself.

No, not like you, Judd replied. *Ironically, given what I was ordered to use it for under Ming, my ability seems to function best with living tissue.*

While Vasic's came in useful in death . . . and apparently in fixing broken windows. The odd reminder slid unexpectedly through his mind as he added more blood to the large floating globule where he was collecting the biomatter. He was slower than usual at the detail-oriented task, his resources depleted by the demands of the day to this point.

As a result, dawn was a soft glow on the horizon when he teleported the biomatter directly into a medical incinerator.

"If I hadn't just seen you do that," came a feminine whisper from the doorway, "I'd say it was impossible."

Chapter 16

VASIC HAD SENSED Ivy's presence, had expected horror at the sight of the liquid mass of blood floating in midair, but her voice held a kind of shocked awe. "You should be resting."

"My head feels stuffy from too much sleep."

"Headache?"

"A dull throb. Nothing too bad." Ivy ran her hands through her curls, aware of the steel black shields that had protected her when she couldn't protect herself, sliding quietly away. "Thank you."

"For what?"

"Shielding me."

Not responding, he walked over to physically right a fallen chair.

Her breath caught, an ache in her chest. He hadn't expected thanks, didn't know how to handle it. Did anyone *ever* thank an Arrow for doing what no one else would? "Anyway," she said past the fist squeezing her heart, "Rabbit was curious—and so was I after I saw the way the compound had been redecorated."

Taking a step into the room where she'd seen Vasic draw up blood droplet by droplet into an eerie liquid globule, before he vanished the whole thing out of existence, she looked for any remaining evidence that might tell her what had taken place, saw only the damaged kitchen area. "What happened?"

Vasic faced her, his expression inscrutable. "Cristabel foiled an assassination attempt on Lianne. She was seriously wounded in the process, the assassin killed."

Ivy's hand rose to her mouth as she recognized the name as belonging to the elfin brunette Arrow who'd been unfazed by Rabbit's inquisitiveness yesterday afternoon. "Is Cristabel . . ."

"Out of critical danger as of thirty minutes ago." Shifting the table several feet to the left, he used raw muscle to rip off a shelf on the far wall.

"And Lianne?" The quiet, somewhat shy woman had to be in shock.

"About to be transported out of the compound." He moved past Ivy to place the remains of the shelf on a stack of wood beside the cabin. "I decided not to move her until she was more stable."

Scowling at his back, she folded her arms as Rabbit "helped" Vasic by adding a stick he'd found to the woodpile. "Why? It's not her fault some fanatic came after her. I was in the same situation, remember?"

"The situations are not analogous." He began to walk toward the Arrow cabin. "Lianne breached her contract by sharing classified data with her family, including the names of every E in this compound."

"Wait, what?" Her mind struggled with the implication of his words. "Someone from Lianne's *family* tried to kill her?" Family was protection, safety, freedom, not hurt. "She must be devastated."

Vasic's response was as gut-wrenching as the realization that Lianne had been betrayed by someone she should've been able to trust. Turning in the doorway of the Arrow cabin so fast she almost ran into the leashed power of him, he said, "Your family is not how most families in the Net operate."

He stepped inside before she could recover enough to reply.

Feeling odd—scared of him in a way that just felt wrong—Ivy followed with Rabbit to see Lianne sitting on the edge of a cot that was literally just a taut piece of canvas stretched over metal. The black-haired, small-boned empath's eyes were red-rimmed, her shoulders hunched inward as she clutched at the edge of the cot with a brutal tightness that had to hurt. And her fear of Vasic . . . it was a sweat-soaked animal that smashed into Ivy and dug in its claws.

Staggering, she gripped the doorjamb.

Ivy? Eyes of silver frost locked with her own, her body stabilized by a phantom telekinetic touch.

Last night, what did Aden do to me? She had only vague, pain-filled memories.

He extracted the detritus of the block on your ability. Your empathic senses are now wide open.

Yes. Breathing was an effort. *Too wide.* Most Psy were taught how to filter input from a young age. As a telepath couldn't hear everything and stay sane, Ivy now understood an empath couldn't feel everything and not collapse under the overload.

Vasic closed the distance between them, his gauntlet flickering with lights as a cool blue beam swept over her. *You're not getting enough oxygen and your blood pressure is rising.*

Ivy attempted to regulate her shallow breaths, calm her pulse.

I don't know how to help you—Vasic stood as strong and stable as a deep-rooted oak as she steadied herself with one hand on his chest, his lightweight armor absorbing any sign of mortal warmth—*but I can get you to someone who can.*

No. Lips quivering and eyes wet as she looked at Ivy, Lianne appeared a forlorn child. Ivy couldn't abandon her. *It's all right.*

Forcing herself to break contact with the rock-solid strength of him, she began to walk through the thick syrup of nauseating fear. It clutched bony fingers around her throat, twisted her stomach into a knot that felt as if it would never unravel, and made her skin creep at the idea of Vasic at her back.

Ivy shook her head to dislodge the sensation. The response wasn't hers. *She* wanted to curl into his protective strength. No, this came from Lianne, the pungent emotional response clawing into Ivy's unprotected senses to bewilder and confuse.

The throb at the back of her head now a pounding, she forced her mouth to shape words. "Don't be afraid." She nudged Rabbit up beside the distressed empath.

Lianne's eyes flicked from Ivy to Vasic, then back. "I broke the rules." Shaking, Lianne clung to Ivy's hand when Ivy came down on the cot beside her. "I'll be punished."

It was difficult for Ivy to think with Lianne's fear threatening to suffocate her, so it took her several seconds to process the meaning of the other woman's words. *She thinks you're going to kill her,* she telepathed Vasic. *There's a good chance she'll calm down if you step outside.*

Vasic didn't move from his position by the doorway. *Lianne is now a known security risk. I won't leave you alone with her.* He switched from telepathic to verbal speech, his words directed at Lianne, before Ivy could argue with his stance. "You won't be executed so long as you keep your silence about this project from now on."

Ivy stared at him. *Are you serious? You would've killed her if you thought she might publicize what she knows?*

No. He turned his attention to her, the gray of his irises so cold, it made the hairs rise on the back of her neck . . . and this time, she didn't know if the response was her own or Lianne's. *I'd have simply had her memories locked down,* he continued. *Execution would be an overreaction, as this experiment will either succeed, in which case it will go public, or it will fail, in which case decisions will be made about the information to be shared.*

Is that what you'll do if I break the rules? she asked through the miasma of panic and fear fogging her mind. *Erase me?*

An infinitesimal pause. *That situation will never arise. You and your family don't want attention, won't do anything to draw it. Lianne's, on the other hand, is hungry for power.*

Ivy wanted to push at him until he gave her a real answer, but he was so scary she couldn't—

Lianne, she reminded herself with teeth-clenched concentration, this was *Lianne's* fear. Ivy might've momentarily doubted her own emotions under the influence of it, but while she accepted that, objectively speaking, Vasic *was* scary, she wasn't scared of him . . . would never be again. Because the one thing she remembered from the previous night was his strong-boned wrist under her fingers, this cold-as-ice Arrow allowing her to hold on to him, his voice—

Stabbing pain in her stomach, her mouth full of bile.

Conscious Lianne's increasing panic could soon paralyze them both,

Ivy twisted to face her. "Breathe, Lianne," she ordered, modulating her own inhales and exhales until the other woman fell into the same pattern. "The Arrows aren't planning to execute you."

It was over seven minutes of repetition later, Ivy's empathic senses raw, that Lianne calmed down enough to follow Ivy's request to shield her emotions.

Peace.

Ivy couldn't hold back the shudder that rippled through her.

Lianne, cheeks red, whispered, "I would've been exposed on the Net." Her hand spread on Rabbit's head where the dog was sprawled across her lap.

Ivy understood the other woman's worry. Silence might have fallen, but the change was too new to be trusted. Ivy herself had discarded her veneer of Silence now that she was safely away from the settlement, but that didn't mean she wasn't worried about the consequences of her actions. Even now, she maintained her PsyNet shields so her emotions wouldn't leak out and betray her to strangers who might wish her harm.

"I ensured you weren't."

Vasic's voice was an icy balm on Ivy's ragged senses . . . until she realized she couldn't sense him. At all. Even a shielded Lianne continued to register on her empathic senses, but Vasic was missing. If she hadn't been able to see him, she'd never have known he was in the room.

Her breath hitched as she understood the crushing depth of his control for the first time.

"It's time for you to leave the compound."

Lianne went rigid at Vasic's statement. Turning to offer comfort, Ivy found herself facing thin air. Vasic had initiated the teleport—after transferring Rabbit from Lianne's lap to beside Ivy.

Blinking, she shook her head as her poor, confused dog stood up and did the same. "Yes," she muttered, rubbing at her temples. "That is *definitely* starting to annoy me."

Rabbit woofed in agreement and bounded down to the floor while she continued to sit on the cot. Uncomfortable thing. And this was where

Vasic would sleep when he was off shift. Frowning, she wondered if he'd had any rest the previous night.

Then there he was, walking over to crouch in front of her. "Your headache is worse, isn't it?" His eyes focused totally on her, his hair black silk she wanted to feel against her skin. "Aden said they should pass within forty-eight hours."

He was so beautiful, she thought. All hard lines and strength and a strange, unexpected vulnerability. Of the latter she had no evidence, and yet her instincts insisted. Foolish Ivy. "Lianne?" she asked, drinking in the sight of him as if she'd been thirsty for a lifetime.

"Safe with those family members I've confirmed have no fanatical pro-Silence leanings. I have an Arrow keeping a discreet eye on her to make certain," he said. "Your headache?"

She hadn't expected him to care about Lianne's safety after the other woman's betrayal. That he did . . . "Yes," she murmured. "It's worse."

"Do you have the training to ease it?"

He had such solid shoulders, wide enough to block out the world. She wanted to smooth her hands over the breadth of them, tear off his armor, touch the living heat of him. Visceral, the need knotted her gut, made her hurt.

"Ivy?"

Fingers curling into her hands, she forced herself not to take advantage of his nearness to indulge her need. It would hurt worse if he started keeping his distance because she couldn't follow the unspoken rules. "Yes." All Psy children were taught how to manage pain, since pain medication had an unpredictable effect on psychic abilities. "But I haven't used it a lot," she admitted, and it wasn't quite a lie. "I'm rusty."

The truth was, she didn't want him to go.

"I'll talk you through it," he said, before switching to telepathic communication to do exactly that.

I like your voice, she said afterward, luxuriating in the icy strength of it.

Good, since you'll hear it throughout this contract.

Laughter sparkled in her veins. *Yes, I suppose so.* Unable to touch, she ran her gaze over the nonregulation-length hair that hinted so tantalizingly of a man behind the frost. *Hopefully, you don't find mine irritating.*

No.

"No." Biting the inside of her cheek, she tried for a solemn tone. "You're very verbose, you know that? I don't know how I'll stand your chattering."

No smile in his eyes, but when he rose to his feet, he said, "I don't see your bodyguard."

Hope exploded like confetti in her heart. That hadn't been an Arrow comment. It had been a *Vasic* comment. "I think Rabbit's starting to thaw where you're concerned," she said, fighting not to betray the strength of her response. "Still, it must've been something really exciting to draw him away while you were so close to me." She had no idea how right she was until they left the cabin.

A squeak escaped her.

Chapter 17

HER VERY SMALL dog was sitting at quivering attention in front of a huge wolf with a coat of silver-gold. A beautiful, scary wolf who could eat Rabbit in one bite, and who appeared to be listening to an unfamiliar male clad in jeans and a black sweater with the sleeves shoved up to his elbows. Not an Arrow, given his clothing, but there was something about him that said he wasn't much different.

From him, she sensed very little, but from the wolf came a whiplash of primal wildness and dangerous focus.

"Rabbit," she called, patting her thigh.

Instead of running straight to her, he glanced over his shoulder then looked back at the wolf, only racing over when the wolf inclined its head. Heart in her throat, she knelt down to pet him as Vasic strode over to speak to the visitors. A few minutes later, both the wolf—the changeling—and the unknown male headed into the trees.

Who was that? she asked Vasic, scowling at Rabbit when he tried to race off after the departing pair.

The SnowDancer alpha and one of his lieutenants.

Kissing Rabbit's sulky face, she continued to keep hold of him lest he be overcome by the urge to join a wolf pack. *The dark-haired man, he looked like an Arrow.*

Vasic gave her a considering look. *Judd defected from the PsyNet three and a half years ago, but yes, he is an Arrow.*

The pieces clicked. *Is he the one the reporters said was deflecting missiles using telekinesis?* Astonishing and riveting, the reports had come in during

Pure Psy's attempted invasion of this region the previous year. *A member of the missing Lauren family?*

Yes. He turned toward Abbot when the other Arrow walked over from Jaya's cabin. *You need to eat breakfast.*

Chancing relaxing her grip on Rabbit, she tried not to read too much into the fact that Vasic had made it a point to remind her to replenish her strength, and headed to her cabin. Rabbit, apparently over his starstruck reaction to the wolf alpha, kept her company—at least until he'd finished his own breakfast. Then he took off to explore, and she crossed her fingers the changelings would nudge him back if he attempted to follow the wolf's trail. Not that she could blame her pet for his dangerous fascination.

Look at her.

Can you do that? she asked Vasic, unable to control the urge to connect with him even when she knew he was busy with the shift change. *Throw missiles around?*

VASIC had never had a voice like Ivy's in his head. There was no restraint to it, the tone an iridescent kaleidoscope that hinted a thousand other things lay beneath. *Yes,* he said in reply to her query, considering what she'd do if he told her he could also initiate missile strikes through his gauntlet.

There goes that verbosity.

Filtering her comment through what he'd observed of human interaction, he confirmed his earlier suspicions that she was teasing him. No one had ever teased him. He didn't know the correct response.

I know you haven't had breakfast, she said while he was still working on the question of whether teasing required a response. *Come eat with me.*

He should've taken the chance to catch a couple of hours' rest, but he'd spent days awake at a time. One night was nothing. Not compared to a woman who teased him. That was unusual enough to require further exploration.

She smiled when he stepped up to her doorway, her curls tousled around her face and her blue cable-knit sweater too big for her frame. "Thanks for leaving me my porch."

"It wasn't in any of Lianne's photographs."

A delighted laugh that felt like a tactile stroke over his cheek. "Right." She mixed up a nutrient drink with hot water rather than the cold he always used, then took several meal bars out of the cupboard. "Here. You must've burned a lot of energy last night and this morning."

First she teased him, then she fed him. Neither action was one he could've predicted. Taking the food, he stepped back outside.

Ivy's face fell. "Are you going already?"

It was almost as if she was disappointed to lose his company. "No," he said, adding another inexplicable act to his private Ivy file. "Your table is small."

"Oh, you're right. You'd probably have to fold yourself in half." Eyes lit from within, she pulled on her boots and picking up her cereal, followed him out to take a seat on the edge of the porch.

He came down beside her, the distance between them approximately eight inches.

And though she'd warned him she liked to talk, they sat in silence for long minutes, the compound quiet now that the shift change was complete, the morning sunlight pale. Despite the silence, the experience wasn't like eating with another Arrow; there was a subtext to it he struggled to unravel.

The last time he'd eaten with anyone unconnected to the squad was the day he'd been permanently excised from the family unit. He could still remember that final meal with his biological father, though he'd lost the emotions of the child. What he remembered boiled down to the Silent space between him and the man who'd given him half his genetic material.

"Hey." A smile so open, he knew the world would savage her if she wasn't protected. "You're thinking too hard. Eat." Having finished her own meal, she put aside her bowl and peeled open the wrapper of one of the nutrition bars he'd set between them.

When she held it out, he realized it was for him. "Thank you."

"I think I'd better talk to Sascha," she said, taking the wrappers of the two bars he'd already eaten to drop them into her empty bowl.

"I put in the request earlier."

"Was that what you were discussing with Judd Lauren and the wolf alpha?"

Vasic nodded, eating the nutrition bar in methodical bites.

"Stop that." A narrow-eyed look as she held up the drink he hadn't touched. "I didn't make this hot so you could let it go cold."

Unpredictable, she was more unpredictable than a rogue missile. "Temperature doesn't alter the nutritional value of it," he said, drinking half a glass.

"I know that. It's to warm you up."

He thought about pointing out that his combat uniform insulated him against the temperature, but decided to keep his mouth shut for reasons he couldn't articulate. Perhaps it was because of the way she looked at him . . . as if concerned.

"I wonder what it's like for Judd"—her gaze shifted to the trees through which the other male had walked away—"living in a changeling pack."

"I can't hope to understand," he said, when he realized Ivy was waiting for an answer, though she hadn't asked a question.

"Of course you do. You're part of one yourself."

"The squad functions differently from a pack."

"No, it doesn't." She broke off a bit of his last bar to nibble on before giving him the rest. "They're as tasteless as I remember." Swallowing the bite with a shudder, she turned to face him, one foot on the ground, the other leg folded up on the porch, her hands on her calf.

"I admit I don't know too much about changeling packs," she said, the sun at her back, "but from what I understand, loyalty is the glue that holds a pack together. Isn't it the same with the squad?"

"Yes." It was often the only loyalty an Arrow had or would ever know. "Changelings, however, live in close proximity, bonded on a physical as well as emotional level." Two packmates near one another would touch sooner or later—a handshake, a hug, a kiss, it depended on the relationships involved—but touch was a constant in every changeling interaction Vasic had ever witnessed.

Which was why he had trouble comprehending Judd's life. Because unlike those in a pack—"Arrows are designed to function alone."

Ivy's sweater slipped off her left shoulder when she leaned forward, baring skin of golden cream to the morning sunlight. "Okay, I get that." She didn't notice when he nudged the sweater back in place with Tk, the temperature too cold for her to be so exposed. "But while you may be designed to function alone, that doesn't mean you're not as tight a family." Passionate words, with no echo of a Silence that had always been an ill-fitting coat. "Like Aden and you, you said you're brothers."

Vasic didn't talk about his childhood, but then he didn't normally say this many words in a day or eat breakfast with a woman who kept reaching out as if to touch him before she caught herself, her fingers curling into her palm.

Today was not a normal day.

"We grew up together," he said at last. "While I wasn't placed into full Arrow training till I was four, I had military-level instructors almost from the cradle." He sometimes considered how his unprotected mind might have been molded. What saved his sanity was the memory of his later childhood, when he'd been no model pupil. "Designation Tk-V is rare enough that the Council was notified at once of my birth."

Ivy leaned farther toward him, one hand pressed to the wood of the porch and her eyes dark with an emotion he couldn't identify. "How did they know your subdesignation so fast?" Her sweater slipped again and he nudged it back. "It usually takes time to be certain, even with genetic markers."

"I teleported out of the womb."

Ivy's mouth dropped open. "No, really?"

"That's what I was told when I was old enough to understand. The records I accessed as an adult bear out the story. According to the notes of the attending M-Psy, she almost dropped me."

Ivy shifted close enough that her knee brushed his thigh, the soft scent of her whispering across his senses. "How did you know where to 'port?"

"It was put down to the telepathic connection I had with the woman who gave birth to me." After which she'd severed all ties as per her conception and fertilization agreement with his biological father. "That's probably the correct answer."

Ivy looked at him for long minutes, and he had the sense he'd said something that distressed her, but he couldn't identify what when he backtracked through his words.

"You were telling me about Aden," she said at last, so close that he could've easily reached out and gripped the vulnerable arch of her neck.

Looking away, he stared at the hands that had ended more than one life. "He was assigned as my telepathic sparring partner." He and Aden had bonded as only scared children could do, long before their capacity to bond had been tortured out of them. "We've known one another for most of our lifetimes."

Ivy's fingers brushed his arm before she jerked her hand guiltily back. "See? You're family," she said, her pulse a rapid flutter in her throat. "And what's a pack but a great big family?"

Vasic glanced at her shoulder, nudged the sweater back up. This time, she noticed, color on her cheeks as her hand went up to the spot. "How many times?"

"Five." He got to his feet before he could make it six. "I need to rest."

Frown dark, she rose, too. "I've been keeping you. You should've said." Folding her arms, she angled her head toward her cabin. "You can use my bed. It's much more comfortable than one of those cots."

That bed would smell of green apples, taking the scent from her hair and skin courtesy of the changeling-stocked bath items in the cabins meant for the empaths. And . . . it would smell of Ivy. "No."

Her eyebrows drew together over her eyes. "We'll argue about that later," she told him. "After you've rested."

Walking to the Arrow cabin where two others lay sleeping, he'd opened up a cot and was removing his thin but effective chest armor when Ivy's iridescent secret of a voice kissed his mind. *Don't forget to take off your boots.*

All at once, he realized he didn't have to process her words. He understood that mental tone now, knew she was teasing him again. This time, he had an answer for her. *Arrows sleep in full uniform,* he said, setting the armor aside.

A pause. *Are you teasing me?*

Tugging off his boots, he put them under the cot. They were designed to allow him to slam his feet into them in two seconds flat in an emergency. *Where would an Arrow learn to tease?* he responded as he removed his belt and placed it with the armor.

From me, came the suspicious response. *You're very smart. Don't think I haven't noticed.*

Having decided to strip off his long-sleeved black uniform top since it wouldn't protect his upper half from attack anyway, and needed to be washed, he rolled it up to use as a pillow as he lay down dressed only in his uniform pants. He should've showered, but giving his body time to restore itself was a higher priority. *I'm going to sleep now, Ivy.*

Have a good rest.

Her voice was the last thing he heard before he shut himself down like the lethal living machine that he was.

Chapter 18

What gives Kaleb Krychek the right to decide the future of our entire race? What of those of us who do not wish to live in his new world? Will he now eliminate our voices as he is rumored to have eliminated his rivals?

Opinion piece from Ida Mill, *PsyNet Beacon*

KALEB STOOD IN the living room of his and Sahara's home, his eyes on the wall-mounted comm-screen. The feed was of placard-waving protestors walking in a circle below his Moscow HQ chanting pro-Silence slogans into the early evening foot traffic in the square directly adjacent.

"Do they not realize I could crush their skulls with a single thought?"

Glancing up from where she was curled up on the couch, translating a document for him, Sahara looked at the screen. "The protestors and Ms. Mill feel passionately enough to die for their cause."

"More would-be martyrs." Kaleb slid his hands into the pockets of his slate gray suit pants, the cuffs of his white shirt rolled up to bare his forearms. "I'm considering giving them their wish." He had to focus on rebuilding the very foundations of the Net after eradicating the infection, not on people who couldn't embrace change.

"Stop being big, bad Kaleb Krychek and come sit with me."

He only took orders from one person. Sitting down to her left, he wrapped an arm around the front of her shoulders as she leaned back against him. "They call themselves Silent Voices," she told him, tapping the laser pen she'd been using against her lip. "And they've made it a point to say they are nonviolent and unassociated with Pure Psy."

"A small sign of intelligence." Kaleb had promised to execute anyone who attempted to revive the genocidal group of fanatics. "They're disruptive."

Sahara patted his arm. "A common occurrence in a normal political system."

"We're not in a normal political system. This is a dictatorship." Nothing else would work with the Net on the brink of cataclysm.

Sahara turned her head to press a kiss to his upper arm through the fine cotton of his shirt, long strands of silken hair sliding over his forearm. "The Council would've shut them down, ended their lives for daring to challenge the status quo."

It was a gentle reminder that Kaleb had spent *his* life bringing down that corrupt structure. Considering the protestors for another minute, he turned off the screen. "They can protest so long as they don't threaten the stability of the Net."

"I think we need disparate voices." Sahara sat up and twisted to face him after putting her datapad and pen on the carpet, expression thoughtful. "Attempting to create a homogenous society is what got us into this situation in the first place."

Kaleb didn't see the world as Sahara did; his priority was to give her a safe, stable life. No matter what it took. "Ms. Mill and her merry band may get their Silent enclave if I'm forced to excise sections of the Net to stem the tide of infection."

Dark blue eyes locking with his own. "Is it worse?"

"Yes, and increasing in virulence by the day." While the empaths remained locked in their dormant state.

Chapter 19

Please reupload all technical data about the performance of the gauntlet for the previous thirty-four days. Our current data is leading to conclusions well outside the anticipated and may have been corrupted during one of the weekly uploads.

Message from Dr. Edgard Bashir to Vasic

SASCHA DIDN'T ARGUE with the security measures Lucas put in place for her visit to the E compound early afternoon on the second day of the empaths' residence in the area. The other Es might not be able to do her direct harm without it rebounding back on them, but there were Arrows in that compound, and regardless of how much she trusted Judd, the squad wasn't homogenous.

"Neither are empaths," Lucas reminded her when she vocalized her thoughts after they stepped out of the car on the edge of the yellow zone.

Cupping her face in strong, warm hands, he bent his knees slightly to meet her eyes. "Don't forget that. They've already had an internal security breach."

"I won't," she promised, and cuddled into the wild heat of his body, drawing in his scent until her own cells were drunk with it. "I feel like such a fraud, pretending to have expertise in the E designation." When all she had was a store of cobbled-together knowledge that might or might not help.

Lucas tugged on her braid. "An expert is simply someone who knows more than those she's teaching. That's you." A feline kiss, licks and flicks and persuasion that melted her bones. "As for the rest"—he wrapped her scarf around her neck—"you'll learn with them."

Centered by his touch, his faith in her, she petted his chest through the fine merino wool of his charcoal sweater. Like most changelings, he didn't feel the cold the same way as a human or Psy, but he was a cat, too, enjoyed such textures against his skin. Not that he'd ever bother to take the time to buy things like this for himself.

But he loved it when she did—and the small, domestic act gave her intense pleasure. As feeding her chocolate habit gave him. It wasn't only emotion, raw and real, that Silence had stolen from her race, she thought, but the myriad quiet intimacies that colored the intricate tapestry of life. "Okay," she said, after another nuzzling kiss from her panther. "I'm ready."

Having decided to walk in the rest of the way, other pack soldiers spreading out behind them, they stepped through the trees of the compound a half hour later. Vasic was waiting for them, a petite but curvy woman with softly curling black hair by his side. She wore a thick cowlneck sweater in white and jeans tucked into snow boots, her stunning eyes lit from within.

"Ivy." Sascha felt her lips curve, recognizing the empath from their comm conversation. "It's lovely to meet you in person."

Ivy's returning smile was infectious. "I've been so excited since Vasic said you were coming." She made to step forward and embrace Sascha, caught herself midstep to glance at Vasic, as if she'd received a telepathic warning.

Conscious the Arrow was playing by the known rules when it came to approaching a predatory changeling's mate, Sascha completed the hug herself, then introduced Lucas to Ivy, Vasic and Lucas having already acknowledged each other.

"Would you like to sit on my porch?" Ivy asked afterward. "It's so nice and sunny out."

"That's perfect." Sascha had been instructed to remain in sight of Lucas and the rest of the security team, and Ivy's suggestion removed any awkwardness from the situation.

Nodding, Ivy led her to the porch, the wood warm from the sun. Then, to Sascha's surprise, the younger empath whispered, "Are there guns pointed at me?"

Sascha gave a small laugh, knowing that no matter what happened with the other Es, Ivy Jane would become a friend. "What do you think?"

"I read that changelings are highly protective of their mates." Smile fading, the other woman's copper gaze shifted to linger on Vasic where the Arrow stood speaking to Lucas. "Do you think," she murmured, "that a person who's been Silent for almost the entirety of his life can learn to feel?"

It didn't take being an empath to guess at the reason for Ivy's question. "I think," Sascha said gently, "the Psy race has been kidding itself about Silence for a long time."

Ivy seemed to forcibly turn her attention back to Sascha. "In what way?"

Sascha paused to admire a little white dog, its breed unclear, that scampered up to the porch. Sniffing at Sascha's hand when she held it out, it wagged its tail, then went to sit at Ivy's side. "No one sane has ever successfully eliminated their emotions," she said. "It's simply a case of how deeply they've been buried."

Ivy petted the adorable little dog with absent affection. "And if there's a winter of the soul?" Troubled eyes met Sascha's. "If the ice is so integrated that even when there's a fracture, it seals itself as soon as he closes his eyes?"

"I don't know," Sascha said honestly. "There are probably some in the Net who've been intensely conditioned to the extent that they come as close to Silence without sociopathy as possible." The Arrows, she thought, fell into that category.

"These people," she added with care for Ivy's heart, "probably embraced Silence on such a deep level for a reason." Vicious psychic abilities, the threat of madness, a family history of violence. "They may not wish to shatter it."

The day I feel is the day I die.

Ivy's fingers stilled on Rabbit's coat as Vasic's words rang in her skull, as harsh as Sascha's had been kind. Ivy had been so happy this morning. He'd teased her, even if he wouldn't admit it, but when he'd woken three hours later, it was as if they'd never had that conversation, never started to weave the fragile threads of a bond she couldn't name but that she knew she wanted. So much.

"Ivy." Sascha's fingers brushing her cheek.

Seeing the gentle sympathy in the cardinal's starlit gaze, Ivy felt her eyes burn. She blinked the sandpaper of it away and consciously put aside her thoughts about the Arrow who made her want to take a sledgehammer to the ice he might need to survive.

"Can you teach me how to shield?" she asked Sascha. "I'm picking up every emotion in the compound—including your mate's feral protectiveness." One wrong move toward Sascha and Ivy knew she'd have claws buried in her throat. Even now, she could feel the changeling alpha's wild green eyes on her, though he stood several meters away.

Ivy—a caress of ice-cold water in her mind—*you're afraid of Lucas Hunter.*

Her fingers curled into her palms, her breath catching at the dark, beautiful sound of him. *Reading my mind?*

No, just your body language and facial cues.

Ivy wanted to tease him but couldn't find the heart for it, Sascha's words having made her realize Vasic's Silence could be a survival mechanism.

Then he said, *Don't be afraid. I won't let him hurt you.*

Ivy felt as if she'd been wrapped in his arms. Giving in, she looked across the compound to meet the eyes of clear gray that watched her. *I know.*

"Before I teach you to shield," Sascha said at that instant, voice thoughtful, "I'll say one more thing on our earlier subject."

Ivy broke the intimacy of the eye contact with Vasic to see the cardinal empath was watching him, too. "What?"

"I know two men who were once as remote as your Arrow."

"Judd Lauren," she guessed, not bothering to protest Sascha's description of Vasic. He *was* Ivy's Arrow. She'd claimed him. "And?"

"Kaleb Krychek."

Ivy shivered, tugging the sleeves of her sweater over her hands. "He's still . . ."

"Yes." Sascha nodded. "Except when it comes to his mate. If you succeed in cracking the ice, you have to be prepared to deal with a male as devoted and as violently protective as any changeling."

Ivy didn't know anything of men or of relationships, but the idea of having Vasic look at her as Lucas Hunter looked at Sascha . . . it made every cell in her body vibrate with a need so deep, it felt as if she'd been born with it.

"As for Judd," Sascha said. "A week ago, I saw him go down under a tumble of pups who decided to 'force' him to play tag with them." She closed her hand over one of Ivy's, squeezed. "I saw him *laugh*, Ivy"—the cardinal's eyes shone wet—"and never could I have imagined that when I first met him."

Inside Ivy the confetti whispered up on a soft breeze.

VASIC noted the ease with which Ivy accepted Sascha's embrace at the end of their two-hour session, and instinctively checked her PsyNet shields. The fractures were visible, jagged cracks that threatened to expose her emotional existence on the PsyNet. *Ivy*, he said as soon as the Dark-River couple had left the compound.

Her mind touched his in a familiar intimacy, the telepathic pathway private. *Yes?*

Will you accept my assistance in shielding you on the PsyNet? If she said no, he'd have to find another way to protect her. He would not compel or coerce, would not tie her down as she'd been tied down in that reconditioning chamber—the same way he'd been restrained so many times as a child.

Ivy hesitated in the doorway to her cabin. *Not yet*, she said at last. *I can seal the fractures for now.* She sought his gaze. *Having your shield over mine blinds me, and I need to be able to see the infection.*

It was almost as if she was explaining so as not to hurt his feelings, when she knew he had no feelings. No, he didn't understand Ivy at all. *I'll work with the other Arrows to firewall this section of the Net instead*, he said. *It'll give you freedom to work on the infection without scrutiny from unwanted sources.*

Shifting on her heel, she came to join him where he stood near the pines closest to her cabin. "That sounds perfect. I don't think the Net is ready for us."

Ivy always smiled with some part of her body, but there was no light in her eyes now, no curve to her lips. "The session didn't go well?"

"Oh no, it was incredible." She rubbed at one temple, and he knew her head continued to bother her. "Sascha taught me how to create an internal shield, so I won't get overwhelmed again like I did with Lianne—though from her experience, it looks like we can't completely turn off our ability."

Vasic had begun to suspect that. "Your empathy functions like an extra sense, analogous to sight or hearing." The same way his teleporting might as well have been another limb, it was so integrated into his body.

"Yes." Thrusting her hands into the front pockets of her jeans, she stared down at the ground. "I just . . . I thought this would be a better world, Vasic."

An indefinable sensation inside him caused by the sound of his name on her lips. "How?"

Ivy rubbed at her temple again.

Raising his hands, he said, "Stay still," and began a scalp and neck massage he'd learned after an injury of his own.

Ivy was so stunned at the skin-to-skin contact that it took several seconds for the pleasure of what he was doing to penetrate her nerve endings. Groaning, she allowed her head to drop forward, her palms braced against his chest. God, but she was starting to hate the stupid uniform that so effectively segregated the heat and strength of him from her touch.

But his fingers, his hands . . .

"Ivy."

"Hmm." Eyes closed, she focused only on the feel of those strong fingers taking away her hurt and turning her bones to jelly in the process. *More, more,* she wanted to demand, shameless in her tactile hunger for him.

"Why did you think the world would be better?"

Ivy had forgotten what she'd been talking about, had to dredge her pleasure-drunk brain to unearth the thread of their conversation. "After the fall of Silence," she murmured, eyes still closed. "If and when I ever permitted myself to imagine it"—she moaned again as he shifted his hands to the back of her neck—"I always thought it would be a halcyon environment." A twist of her lips. "But no matter what, people are still going to try to hurt one another."

"The attack on Lianne is on your mind." Ivy's skin was delicate against the rough pads of Vasic's fingers, but she inched closer instead of pulling away.

Her proximity increased the abrasive sensation inside his skin, a silent reminder that he should not be touching her, but he didn't break contact. It was his job to take care of her, and it was clear this was easing her pain.

"A member of Lianne's own family turned against her," she said after almost a minute. "It makes me worry about what will happen when the rest of the E designation begins to go active. How many of us will die?"

Vasic looked at her downbent head, the soft black curls shining in the light that fell through the leaves above, and knew the harsh answers he had would hurt her. So all he said was, "Even the best foreseer in the world can't predict the future with a hundred percent certainty."

Ivy lifted up her head, her smile lopsided. "You're saying I'm borrowing trouble." Not waiting for a response, she looked him straight in the eye. "Maybe I am, but I just can't seem to stop."

He had the inexplicable sense they were no longer speaking about empaths.

IN the days that followed, the compound settled into a quiet, familiar rhythm. The eighteen people within it slowly stopped being individuals and started to become a community, and like any community, they had their subgroups. Of the empaths, Ivy was closest to Chang and Jaya, though Penn quite often joined their discussions. The Scottish male tended to speak about as much as an Arrow, but was concise and penetrating in his comments when he did.

The others all had different relationships with one another, as was natural, with Chang being friendly with Brigitte, while Ivy couldn't seem to penetrate the older woman's reserve. Isaiah remained abrasive, but calm Penn was able to tolerate him, and so it went. No one was isolated or alone, which was the main thing.

The Arrows, of course, stuck to their own, but she'd noticed that several spent time with their Es when they could've as easily kept their distance. Abbot, in particular, was never far from Jaya's side.

As for her, she'd managed to talk Vasic into eating with her more often than not. He hadn't touched her again after those exquisite minutes that had turned her blood to honey, but she was already an addict. It was torture to sit so close and not demand a repeat, but being with him was worth it . . . though she did cheat every so often by wearing the sweater that kept sliding off her shoulder. When he fixed it—and he *always* noticed and did so without a word—it felt as if he'd stroked her.

"Here you go," she said on the fourth day after Sascha's visit, passing him several nutrition bars before she came down beside him on the porch, her now-favorite sweater warm around her. "Your daily, super-delicious breakfast." He'd already carried out the drink she'd mixed for him, along with her bowl of cereal and milk.

Vasic, his forearms braced on muscled thighs, ate one before replying. "You eat the same cereal every day."

"Yes, but it has tasty dried fruits and berries, as well as a mix of grains. Your bars are blandness personified." That was the point after all. "Here." She scooped up a spoonful of her breakfast. "Taste."

What happened next had her staring.

He actually leaned forward and accepted her offer. "There are too many flavors," was his cool conclusion.

Ivy's toes curled at that voice of his, so intense and contained it made her wonder what he'd sound like if he ever lost control. Eating a spoonful of cereal to give herself time to think, she realized her lips were moving over the same warm metal his had touched an instant ago. Skin flushing at the small intimacy, she said, "Sorry, but you don't get a vote. Not when you only eat nutrition bars and drink the same stuff in liquefied form."

Vasic didn't understand why he'd done what he'd done. All he knew was that Ivy was extraordinary. Though she'd entered the compound with the most severe mental and psychic wounds, she'd quietly shown herself to be one of the strongest people here.

That included the Arrows.

While Vasic and the others dealt with the dramatic shift in the PsyNet by attempting to stick rigidly to their conditioning, Ivy rode the wave. Every time she hit a wall, she stopped, thought about the problem with a determined concentration that caused two tiny vertical lines to form between her eyebrows, then found a way around it.

His mind wasn't as flexible as hers, but it had done an odd, unexpected thing in the past three days. While the other Es continued to scrape against his senses, Ivy no longer did, though she was exploring her abilities in depth. It was as if his mind had created a special category for this empath whose telepathic voice was one he was now so accustomed to hearing, it felt too quiet inside his skull when she was sleeping and he was on night watch.

His body, too, responded to her own in ways so alien that he had no experience with handling the reaction.

Now she ate another spoonful of cereal, and he saw the golden cream that was the exposed slope of her shoulder.

Reaching out, he physically tugged her sweater back into place.

Chapter 20

IVY ALMOST DROPPED her bowl.

Steadying it telekinetically, he returned his hand to its previous position, his eyes on two Arrows going through a martial arts routine at the other end of the compound. "Do you feel in better control of your abilities?" he asked into the tautly stretched silence.

"Not in control," she said at last, her voice a little breathy. "That implies too much conscious decision-making on my part. But it's getting easier to handle the instinct." Her bowl made a dull sound against the wood of the porch as she put it aside. "Does that make sense?"

"Arrows don't acknowledge instinct, but it's inarguable that our reaction times in certain situations are so fast they might be categorized as such."

Turning toward him, Ivy folded one leg up on the porch in that way she had, a bare inch between her knee and his thigh. "What do you call it then?"

"Repetition and training until the knowledge of how to react to problematic situations is burned into our cells."

"How?" A low whisper. "How do they teach you?"

He thought of having his arm broken over and over as a child until he stopped crying, of being trapped in a suffocating box for hours until he learned to psychically regulate his body temperature, of being thrown into sensory deprivation chambers until he could endure nothingness, and then he looked at Ivy. "Mundane, routine repetition."

Those eyes of copper that saw too much didn't stray from his. "You're lying to me, Vasic."

"There are some things that shouldn't be in your head."

The quiet words broke Ivy's heart. Taking courage from his earlier startling act, she grazed her fingertips over his gauntlet. It was a hard, cold carapace, but it was part of him. "Trust me."

He didn't break the violently intimate eye contact. "It's too late for me, Ivy. Focus your energies on the ones you can save."

Ivy didn't say anything when he rose, her fingers sliding off the gauntlet. He left without another word, tall and strong and alone as he walked across the clearing. He'd saved her life, was the heart of the psychic shield that protected every E here, would act as a living physical shield for any one of them in a split second.

Yet he expected nothing from her, from the world.

She didn't know how to get through to him, to tell him he had every right. Because if what she suspected was correct, then the Arrows weren't only the assassins they so often painted themselves to be, but the last line of defense against the infinite darkness that licked at the edges of the Psy race—might always lick at it.

That instinctive awareness was borne out by the historical psycho-medical records she'd downloaded from the PsyNet over the past three days, Vasic having gained her access to a secure database. It catalogued the *true* rates of mental illness in the Psy race across the spectrum, including cases of suspected or proven criminal insanity.

"I've gone back two hundred years," she said to Sascha later that day, the two of them walking in the trees after the cardinal finished her session with Penn. "The results are near identical. A percentage of our population always goes mad, and it's always a higher percentage than the other races."

"The price of our gifts?" The leaves of the evergreens in this region threw lacy shadows on the other empath's face. "Silence, from everything we've discovered, didn't change that. It simply made it easier for the true psychopaths to hide, while the ones who needed help were quietly eliminated."

Sascha turned her gaze toward the Arrows visible in the compound.

"Whatever they've done," Ivy said, stomach tight and voice fierce, "they did it believing they were helping their people." She saw that truth in Vasic's relentless protectiveness, in Cristabel's injuries, in Abbot's intensity on watch. "We can't blame them." Ivy would allow no one to hurt the Arrows that way.

"I don't," Sascha said softly, "but I think they blame themselves."

Ivy took a breath of the biting cold air, icicles hanging off the branches in front of her in beautiful, dangerous shards. "Yes," she whispered. "It's not fair, when they do so much to keep the Net safe."

The records she'd downloaded didn't state that outright, didn't even refer to the Arrows, but it was impossible to miss the stark difference in certain grim statistics before and after the formation of the squad, the date for which she'd received from Vasic. He hadn't realized what he was giving her, how it clarified the data she'd begun to piece together.

"No one ever talks about the serial murderers who suddenly stop killing." Far too many to be explained away by any statistical model, the percentage so much higher than before the squad's formation that it was obvious they'd dramatically altered the playing field. "Who else but the Arrows would take care of that dirty job year after year, decade after decade?" Because the monsters kept being born, kept creating horror. "Certainly not Enforcement."

Sascha, her eyes without stars, bent down to pick up a pinecone half-buried in the snow. Dusting off the frosty white, she played her fingertips over the edges as she rose to her full height. "I agree with you. The Arrows act as the only real control on the darkest elements of our race."

A pause before the cardinal continued. "I think when the squad was first formed, it was about doing whatever was necessary to keep Silence from falling. Even though I might not agree with the actions of those first Arrows, I can understand it came from a desire to protect the Psy race."

"And now that they know Silence wasn't the answer," Ivy said, forgiving those first Arrows for their undoubted part in suffocating and burying the E designation, "the Arrows from this generation are trying to redress the balance. I know Vasic would take a bullet for me without flinching."

"Yes," Sascha said at once. "The protective core has always been there, even if turned in the wrong direction . . . and I have a feeling the squad might've been manipulated into certain actions by some in power."

Hugging her arms around herself, Ivy said, "Do you know if they've been with Kaleb Krychek for long?" The cardinal Tk was said to be the most ruthless man in the Net, but from what she'd glimpsed during Krychek's fleeting visits to the compound, Vasic seemed to deal with him as an equal.

Sascha shook her head. "My contacts are light when it comes to information about the squad, but Judd did say Ming LeBon was their acknowledged leader for two decades. As an ex-Arrow himself, I'd say he was deeply trusted."

Dropping the pinecone, the other empath thrust her hands into the pockets of her winter coat, the color a rich aquamarine. "I don't have any proof, but given what I know of Ming's tendencies, paired with the squad switching its allegiance to Kaleb, I think Ming tried to turn them into his personal assassination squad."

Ivy stopped walking. "They believed in him and he used them." The betrayal would've struck at the heart of the loyalty that bonded Arrow to Arrow—the *one* thing on which, it was obvious, every single member of the squad relied.

Including Vasic.

He'd been abandoned as a child, tortured, then used. He'd never say any of that to her, but Ivy listened. So she'd made the connection between a child who'd started training at four years of age, and a man who called his parents "the woman who gave birth to me" and "my biological father."

There are some things that shouldn't be in your head.

No one became so encased in ice by being treated with kindness. He'd been hurt. Over and over. Then, in what must've been a final, staggering blow, he'd learned that the terrible things he'd been asked to do for the good of his race had instead been done so Ming LeBon could bloat himself with power.

Every muscle in her body locked tight. She wanted to destroy the system that had allowed this to happen. "It doesn't seem fair, Sascha, that he—that any Arrow—should have to walk alone and thankless in the darkness."

Slipping her arm through Ivy's, Sascha began to lead her back to the compound. "Do you remember what I told you about Alice Eldridge?"

It took Ivy a second to speak past her fury. "Of course." Ivy had hurt for the scholar who Sascha told her had been put forcibly into cryonic suspension for over a century.

"Well, in Alice's book—which she's given me permission to copy for all of you—she has a bit in the middle that's full of quotes by the friends and lovers of empaths." The stars returning to her eyes, Sascha smiled at Ivy, and the expression held a vein of unexpected mischief. "The most common word in that entire section is 'stubborn.' Apparently, Es have a problem with giving up on anyone. I'd say your Arrow doesn't stand a chance."

Ivy's responding smile was shaky. "No," she said, "he doesn't."

It wouldn't be easy, and there was a high chance she'd fail in her quest to shatter her Arrow's defenses, but Ivy hadn't survived a brutal reconditioning by being a shrinking violet. If Vasic needed Silence to survive, that was one thing—and agonizing as it would be to recognize that she could never truly know him, she'd accept it, because to do otherwise would hurt him.

But, if her warrior-priest was using the isolation of the conditioning to punish himself for the crimes of another man, one who'd sacrificed the hearts of good men and women on the altar of power, then no, Ivy wasn't about to let that slide. Not now. Not ever.

VASIC checked the PsyNet late that night to discover the infection, its tendrils a malignant darkness, had well and truly invaded the compound, though it wasn't yet touching any of the minds inside. It went against his every instinct to leave Ivy and the others in the infection's path, but to remove them would be to deny their nature.

Dropping out of the psychic network after taking one final look, he scanned the area. It was swathed in the pitch-black of a moonless night, the cabins quiet and the only movement that of the Arrows on sentry duty.

One, however, wasn't where he was supposed to be. *Abbot. Report.*

Sir. I'm with Jaya. She experienced a nightmare and requested I stay within her sight.

Does she need medical attention?

No. I believe she is . . . afraid.

Vasic considered whether or not to pull Abbot from the detail. He'd chosen the younger Arrow for his unit not because Abbot's Silence was flawless, but because it was cracking in an erratic and possibly dangerous fashion—the squad needed to know if their more damaged members could work with empaths going into the future. As a result of Abbot's mental state, Vasic and another senior member of the unit had kept a close eye on the male throughout.

It had soon become clear that he was stabilizing in an unanticipated way, his presence more ordered and calm than it had been for months, his concentration acute. The problem was that he appeared to have attached himself too deeply to his empath.

Vasic? A light going on in Ivy's cabin.

He caught the tremor in her voice, turned immediately to head to her. *What is it?*

I just . . .

He was on the porch pushing open her door before she finished. When she came directly to him, curling up against his chest while Rabbit leaned against her leg, he did what he'd seen humans and changelings do to offer comfort, and closed his arms around her upper body. And he knew Abbot wasn't the only Arrow who'd attached himself too deeply to his empath.

Holding her to him with his gauntleted arm, Vasic cupped the back of her head with his other hand, her curls a warm tumble around his fingers. The fabric of her pajama pants was green and white flannel, but her top half was clad only in a thin, strappy top. When she continued to shiver and attempt to get closer, her arms tucked up between them, he used his Tk to alter the air molecules around her to generate heat, at the same time that he tightened his hold, and widened his stance to allow her to tuck her feet between his booted ones.

It seemed to work, Ivy's skin warming under his fingertips where they grazed the edge of her face, and under his palm where it curved over her arm. Every other part of him was shielded from her, his combat uniform designed to protect . . . but now it was a barrier that stopped him from feeling the slight weight of her fist against his heart or the pulse that fluttered under the flushed gold of her skin.

He didn't understand why that mattered, but it did.

"You made it warm." She stayed curled up against him despite her words, the radiance from the kitchen light pouring past them to the porch.

He moved them fully inside by doing a minute teleport and shut the door. Ivy was open about many things, but she also had a private side, and this . . . it was private.

Hand flexing on his chest, a movement he saw but didn't feel, she said, "Did you just 'port us?"

"Yes."

She looked up with a wobbly smile. "Do you ever think about how amazing it is that you can do that?"

"No." For him, it was the reason he'd spent his childhood in excruciating pain.

"You can go anywhere you want to, anytime you want." Putting her head back down against his chest, she said, "Can we go somewhere tonight?" A tremor ran through her frame. "Just for a little while?"

Vasic evaluated the security situation, connected with his Arrows—to receive the same report. Each and every one of his men and women was awake, even those meant to be off shift. "Not tonight," he said. "I'll take you another day."

"Why not today?" Lifting her hand to her temple, she rubbed. "No, wait, I can feel it now . . . the empaths, we're leaking fear . . ." Her eyes, those big, penetrating eyes, stared up at him, the rim of gold vivid against the copper. "*All* of us had nightmares?"

"The majority." He forced himself to release her now that she was stable. "Isaiah, Brigitte, and Penn appear to have been immune to the precipitating event but were woken by the reactions of the others."

Shoving her hands through her hair, Ivy said, "Okay, okay, let me think." A decisive nod. "I need to be in the PsyNet."

Following her, he saw the same thing she did.

Chapter 21

"PENN, BRIGITTE, AND Isaiah," he said when they dropped back out, "are the most distant from the infection in terms of their location in the compound." While Ivy and Jaya were on the leading edge.

"I'm going to touch base with the others." Closing her eyes, she did so telepathically, and he took the chance to just look at her. Her skin was delicate, her collarbones fine, but there was a lushness to Ivy that was diametrically opposed to his own body. No hard edges, only soft curves. Everything about her promised the opposite of pain.

When a strap slid off one shoulder as she thrust her hand through her hair again, he didn't slide it back up, fascinated by the smooth line of her shoulder, the creamy plumpness of the exposed upper slope of her breast. It would, he calculated, take the barest telekinetic nudge to push the silky fine fabric farther down, exposing her fully.

Embers low down in his body flared to glowing life . . . and Ivy's skin flushed a deep peach.

Tugging the strap up with a trembling finger, she said, "Jaya was the most shaken. Having Abbot around seems to have calmed her." Her breath came fast and shallow. "He's playing cards with her."

As far as Vasic knew, the younger Arrow didn't know how to play cards. "Is he losing?" he asked, conscious he'd crossed a line in looking at Ivy as he had.

"Badly," she said rather than asking him to leave, "but Jaya says he's catching on fast. We're corrupting all your Arrows."

He thought of the warmth of her scalp against his palm, the featherlight caress of her curls, the sweet curves that would flow like honey under his hand. She was the softest, most beautiful creature he'd ever touched, and he wanted to experience her again, wanted to indulge in this tactile contact that had nothing to do with pain or training or a cold medical checkup.

"Perhaps," he said, watching her color deepen as he continued to look at her in a way he knew was sexual. He should've apologized. He didn't. "But," he said instead, "the corruption doesn't appear to be doing harm." A lie. Ivy was breaking things down in him that couldn't be broken down for his own sanity. Even now he found himself wondering about the texture of her skin at the dip of her breastbone, his fingers curling into his hand.

It was the hand attached to the arm on which the gauntlet was grafted. A gauntlet that could function on many levels. One of which was to control weapons that could annihilate hundreds in a single strike. The hands he wanted to put on Ivy were of a killer.

Ice doused the glowing embers. "I need to check the compound."

Ivy grabbed a thick orange cardigan she must've forgotten on a chair when she went to bed, and shrugged into it. "I'll come with you."

"You should remain safe in the cabin."

She stepped up to him, jaw set. "If there's a threat outside, you can 'port me out before I so much as see the threat. I don't want to be alone." A glance down at Rabbit. "Not that you're not wonderful," she reassured her pet.

He saw the quiver of her lip before she bit down on it and realized the level to which she'd sublimated her own fear to check on the others. "It's a cold night. You should wear this." Bringing in a heavy jacket he used when he had to go into bitterly cold environments and didn't want to waste energy maintaining his body temperature, he helped her into it. It swallowed her up, the zipped-up collar coming past her mouth and the sleeves swamping her arms until he folded them up.

That done, he nudged her to the kitchen counter. "Make your favorite tea." He knew the taste gave her comfort. "I can wait."

When they stepped out into the starry night five minutes later, Ivy with her hands cupped around the mug of tea and her feet in snow boots,

Rabbit scampered out after them. Giving Vasic her tea to hold, Ivy petted and cuddled the dog before carrying him back to his little bed. "Stay here, Rabbit. It's too cold outside for you," he heard her murmur gently, the sound carrying in the stillness of the night.

She was with him again soon afterward. Tugging the hood of the jacket up over her head, he stepped out to begin patrolling the compound. *Nerida, get some rest*, he said to one of the sentries. *I'll take over.*

The other Tk sent back a quick confirmation.

"How do you measure harm to your Arrows?" Ivy's voice was familiar in the darkness a quarter of an hour later. "Is it a breakdown in their Silence or something else?"

"It's different for each member of the squad."

She paused with him in the night shadow of the trees. "Some of them," she said, tone solemn, "they'll never break Silence, will they?"

They. As if he wasn't on that list.

"A few are physiologically incapable of doing so." He thought about how much to reveal, not because he didn't trust Ivy, but because certain knowledge would put her at risk. "Part of our training used to involve a drug that can reset neural pathways if used too long. It intensifies natural psychic ability but eventually leaves the Arrow with no sense of self."

"That's so sad." Stark pain in her expression, her empty mug hanging from one finger; she didn't seem to notice when he teleported it away. "Are the victims conscious of what's been done to them?"

"No." That, Vasic thought, was the only mercy. "They remain members of the squad, and we'll make certain they live out their lives at the optimal level possible." It wouldn't be anything those in the outside world would consider a good life, but it would be a hundred times better than anything Ming LeBon would've permitted.

Their former leader would've simply used up those men and women, then ordered their executions at the hands of medics who had promised to heal. Patton, the only other Tk-V Vasic had ever met, had been put down like a dog when he became so dependent on instruction that he was useless in the field.

An unfortunate error in his Jax regime, had been the note on the medical file Vasic had hacked into when he was old enough. *The regime is being modified to ensure this type of extreme compliance does not reoccur. Vasic should be useful far beyond the usual age of termination of Arrows.*

"And you?" Ivy asked, touching her hand to his gauntlet as she'd already done once before. "Did they use the drug on you?"

Vasic considered the delicate fingers on the machinery that encased him. "Aren't you repelled by the gauntlet?"

"What?" She glanced down, frowned. "No, and stop avoiding the question."

He thought he should tell her everything he'd done, so she'd understand who it was she touched, but then she'd be afraid of him . . . and he didn't want Ivy afraid. "When I was younger, yes," he said in answer to her question about Jax. "Later, thanks to a subterfuge by Judd, all Arrows were taken off it."

"And you were fine?"

"I'm much, much better at delicate 'ports than anyone realizes." They should have, after watching him deal with blood until not even a single fine droplet of it remained in carpet, but no one had ever made the connection.

Ivy's eyes widened. "You 'ported out the drug while it was still in the delivery system." A whisper that held a passionate emotion he couldn't pinpoint. "That's incredible."

"Unfortunately, it took me time to learn the trick." He'd been forced to work under the influence of the drug for dozens of missions and whenever Ming LeBon required his teleportation skills. As a result of the latter, he'd had more Jax in his system as a teenager than most experienced members of the squad.

He'd escaped a permanent reset by three injections at most.

"I couldn't do the same for the others, except on random occasions when I was in the room while they were being injected." He'd tried, but he couldn't risk giving away the fact that the squad wasn't as under Ming LeBon's control as the former Councilor had believed.

He hadn't needed Aden to tell him that those they lost to the drug, if given the choice, would've chosen that fate rather than jeopardize their brothers-in-arms. That made the losses weigh no less heavily on Vasic's heart, adding to the other bodies that lay on it, until the organ had gone permanently numb.

Ivy's hand tightened on the gauntlet. He could feel the pressure of her touch through the sensors that linked every single square millimeter of the hard black surface that protected the delicate computronics beneath to living nerve tissue. But he couldn't feel *her*. And for the first time, he began to question his choice to allow himself to be used as the guinea pig for the experimental fusion.

That was when he became aware of the sheen of wetness in her eyes. "Ivy? You're in distress."

"You carry so much guilt, Vasic." Raw, her voice sounded as if it hurt. "A crushing weight of it."

Vasic thought of the deaths he'd meted out in darkness, the lives he'd erased, and shook his head. "No, Ivy. I can never carry enough." Never do anything to balance the scales.

IVY wanted to pound against the armor that insulated Vasic, smash apart the gauntlet on his arm, though she knew her anger was misdirected. It wasn't the outer shell that mattered. She could batter it to pieces and still never breach the ice that encased him.

He held me today.

Her body ached at the memory of his strength against her, his hand so tender and gentle on the back of her head. It was nothing he would've done at the start of this operation. And . . . and he'd caressed her with his gaze, the silver of his eyes molten. Melting at the memory, she counseled herself to be patient.

"Did you and Aden ever play together?" she asked, cuddling into the coat that smelled comfortingly of him. Clean soap and a warm male scent that was distinctly his. Last time Sascha had visited, Ivy had seen the cardinal empath nuzzle her mate's throat as they walked away. Ivy wanted to do that with Vasic, draw in his scent directly from his throat.

He gave me his coat.

She smiled. Expert teleporter that he was, he could've no doubt called in something that was a better fit. He hadn't.

"Not ordinary games," he said into the hush of the night. "We didn't have the time, or the freedom."

"I'm sorry." And *angry*, so angry. No one had the right to steal a childhood.

"We did, however," he added, "find ways to keep ourselves busy during the rare instances we somehow escaped supervision. Once we managed to paint zebra stripes on every wall of a training room."

Delight cut through her anger. "How did you manage that?"

"Aden and I stole the paint from work elsewhere in the facility. Then," he said, "he created a distraction while I painted as fast as I could. Afterward, I hauled myself into the ceiling with the paint and the brushes, and crawled my way out. No one ever discovered it was the two of us that did it, since we left no clues and the head of the training center vetoed large-scale telepathic scans."

"Why didn't you teleport out for your escape?" Ivy asked with a laugh.

Vasic took so long to reply that her smile faded, dread growing in her abdomen. "I had a psychic leash on my personal 'porting ability as a child," he said at last. "It was the only way anyone could keep me where they wanted me."

Ignoring everything else he'd said, she focused only on the most important, most terrible part. "They created a lock on you like I had on my mind?" Except where she'd been unaware of what she was losing, he'd been fully conscious of it. It must've felt like having a limb hacked off.

"That doesn't work for subdesignation V. Our ability is too deeply integrated into our minds."

"Like breathing," she said, her horror growing.

"Yes. Not fully autonomous, but close enough. The only way to control me was to use another Tk-V to do it." He stilled as a wolf's haunting howl rose on the air in the distance, followed by another a moment later, then another, until it was a wild symphony.

Hairs rising on the back of her neck and breath frosting the air, she turned toward the sound. "I wish we were allowed to go farther, to interact with the changelings."

"They're protecting their vulnerable."

"Yes." The fact this compound existed at all was a huge trust on the part of DarkRiver and SnowDancer, the biggest step in the relationship between the Psy and the changeling races for over a century. "The other Tk-V," she said when the wolf song died down, leaving only a lingering sensory echo of its primal beauty. "He was an Arrow, too?"

Vasic nodded.

She waited for him to say something, but he'd answered her question, and as she'd already learned, he wasn't a man who talked more than he had to. The snow crunched under her boots as they walked on, the sky a deep midnight dotted with stars. She didn't interrupt his silence this time, her thoughts of a boy who'd grown up in a cage, taught to become a tool his captors could use . . . of the man who'd survived that with the will to protect a flame inside his heart.

Chapter 22

Kaleb Krychek may have mandated the fall of Silence, but he gives us no answers for who we are without the Protocol. He leaves us to drown.

Anonymous PsyNet posting

COMFORTABLY ENSCONCED IN the sun-drenched breakfast nook, Sahara completed the lesson she'd downloaded and considered the question asked by the lecturer. "What is the meaning of good governance?"

Kaleb looked up from the counter where he'd just finished preparing two nutrient drinks. Drinking from the glass he passed her, she blew him a kiss. "I love you."

"You only say that because of my cherry flavoring."

She almost splurted the drink out of her nose. "And to think people say you have no sense of humor."

Having finished his drink, Kaleb did up a cuff link. Sahara's stomach heated as it always did when she watched him dress or undress.

"Why are you studying politics when you're living it?"

She walked over to finish buttoning his shirt and do up his tie, the strip of deep blue, almost black silk lying around his neck in readiness for her touch. "Because," she said, delighting in this small ritual that had quietly become a part of their lives, "people who think they know everything end up becoming despots."

Kaleb's hands on her hips, his thumbs brushing over her skin after he nudged up her knit top as he had a way of doing. "Good governance," he said, "is acting for your people rather than for your own gain."

Her fingers stilled on his tie. "Yes," she whispered to the man she adored, a man who'd been brutally scarred by "leaders" acting for their own selfish interest.

"That is your definition." His fingers squeezed her hips. "Mine is to do nothing that would make you ashamed to be mine."

Sometimes, he broke her heart. "Never will I be ashamed to be yours."

Kaleb bent his head toward her, his eyes a moonless night. "Don't say things like that, Sahara. What will I become if I don't fear losing you through my actions?"

"You'll always be mine." She cupped his face, his jaw smooth. "And I won't let you cross those lines."

He said he had no conscience, but he loved her with a wild devotion that made her feel safe, feel whole, feel *cherished*. In that love she saw hope for who they'd become together.

His kiss was raw, sexual, his hands lifting to place her on the counter. Standing between her spread thighs, his shoulders beautifully muscled under the fine fabric of his black shirt, he kissed her as if she was his air. She thrust one hand in the damp strands of his hair, cupped his nape with the other, and kissed him back with the same hunger. They'd both been deprived of touch for so long, and now they denied themselves nothing.

When he tugged up her top, she lifted her arms to allow him to pull it off. Wrapping those arms around his neck afterward, she luxuriated in the feel of his hands on her skin. "I thought you had a meeting," she said, kissing his jaw, the line of his throat, the masculine scent of him overlaid by the clean bite of his aftershave.

"I've told Silver to postpone it."

Leaning back, she simply looked at him, her dangerous lover who always put her first. "We'll beat it," she said, conscious the infection was a problem about which he never quite stopped thinking. "With the empaths and the Arrows and our race's will to survive."

Kissing the upper curve of her breast, Kaleb bracketed her rib cage with his hands. "The Arrows and the empaths—perhaps. But you have more faith in our race than I do. Right now most are burying their heads in the sand, hoping I'll tell them who to be, what to become. They're sheep."

She tugged up his head with a hand fisted in his hair. "If they are, it's because they've been trained to be that way for a century. A good leader will lead them to true independence. You'll lead them to freedom."

Kaleb might not be a white knight, but he was the knight the Psy race needed. Strong, fearless, and willing to make the hard decisions. And he was *hers*. Wrapping her thighs around him, she sank into the kiss, into him.

Chapter 23

There have always been unsubstantiated rumors of a hidden designation in the PsyNet. Sascha Duncan's defection brought those rumors to the surface, only for them to be thoroughly quashed by the Council at the time. Now, however, new whispers are coming to the fore—and the Ruling Coalition has yet to make a statement to either confirm or deny their veracity.

PsyNet Beacon

ADEN MET WITH Vasic close to dawn the next morning, the two of them standing near the trees looking out over the mist-licked peace of the compound.

"Nightmares," the other man said, referencing the telepathic conversation they'd had the previous night.

"Ivy was unable to give me any specifics." Vasic had asked toward the end of their walk, when she'd seemed more centered, no longer afraid. "She described it as a feeling of suffocating darkness."

"Was she discouraged by the incident?"

"No."

The single word answer was characteristic of Vasic, yet the depth of confidence in it intrigued Aden. Vasic had stopped getting to know people in tandem with his increasing remoteness when it came to the world. Even with new members of the squad, he made no effort beyond what was necessary for him to function as part of the team. And *still*, he was one of the first ports of call for any Arrow in trouble. Not because he was a Tk-V, but because he inspired trust on a visceral level.

Vasic simply did not let people down.

"The other empaths?" Aden asked, remembering how he'd felt that same trust as a boy. It had never altered.

"I haven't had a chance to assess them, or to speak in depth with their Arrows, but it's possible we may lose one or two."

Empaths, Aden had learned from Vasic, weren't all the same. Rationally, Aden had already known that, but the mystery of the E designation was such that he'd lumped them into a single mental category.

"The recent episodes of violence in the Net"—Vasic put his arms behind his back—"seem erratic and small scale."

"The agitators tend to be individuals who are finding it difficult to adapt to the fall of Silence, but in one case at least, it was a surviving Pure Psy sublieutenant." Aden looked down at the small white dog that had appeared out of the mist to sit at his feet, its shining black eyes trained on him.

The canine belonged to Ivy Jane, he remembered. "We were able to eliminate the sublieutenant and his attendant cell," he told Vasic. "The cell was planning a larger-scale event that had no chance of success, though they were too wrapped up in their fanatical ideology to see that." Pure Psy didn't have the necessary independence of thought to function efficiently without their leader. And that leader was dead.

"Krychek?"

"He's left the Pure Psy cleanup to us and is concentrating on ensuring the Net remains stable." The latter couldn't be done by brute force alone, but Krychek was far more than that, the former Councilor's intelligence a blade, his connections labyrinthine.

"We don't need you on the team handling the cleanup," he said, to head off any offer Vasic might've made. "Your skills are better served here."

Vasic's gray eyes were penetrating when they met Aden's. "I can't leave the Es, not given the security leak we had with Lianne and the proximity of the infection." A glance at his gauntlet to check incoming data before he turned back to Aden. "That doesn't mean I'm not cognizant of your attempts to shield me from overt violence."

"I've never done anything behind your back." Aden had only ever had one true friend, someone he knew would fight for him and with him regardless of whether he held any power or not. The others in the squad he trusted, but Vasic occupied an entirely different place in his life, until it was as if their blood was the same. Aden would do whatever was necessary to make sure the other man made it, though he knew it might well be an impossible task.

The reason he and Vasic had become friends as children, the reason the others in the squad looked to him instinctively, was the same reason Vasic had never been meant to be an Arrow. He felt too deeply, was too much the protector. As an angry, scared eight-year-old boy when he and Aden first met, he should've been focused only on himself—yet he'd sensed Aden's continual and crushing fear for his Arrow parents.

Instead of resenting Aden for having parents who'd cared enough about him to fight to keep him with them through his enrollment in the squad's training program, Vasic had come up with distractions to help Aden cope. Later, Vasic had risked severe punishment to help Aden break into the control room so Aden could read the files on his parents' missions.

That part of Vasic had been buried beneath the weight of the life he'd been forced to live, but it existed. It had always existed. And it would destroy him if Aden couldn't find a way to redirect his self-hatred and guilt.

"It appears you've captured Rabbit's interest," Vasic said into the comfortable silence between them, and it was an unexpected comment.

Aden glanced down at the canine that was still sitting on its rump, eyes locked on him. "Perhaps he's weighing the pros or cons of biting me."

Vasic didn't answer, his head angled toward one of the cabins to their left.

Ivy Jane appeared on the porch a second later, a large Arrow jacket engulfing her small body and two steaming mugs in her hands. "Here," she said when she reached Aden and Vasic, the shadows under her eyes smudges of purple. "Hot nutrient drinks."

Aden recognized the jacket from a small tear on the upper left sleeve. It had happened during a brutal mission in Alaska, Vasic left alone in a ghost town full of corpses. Aden hadn't been able to prevent that, and Vasic had asked him not to try. To have done so would've put their entire plan to oust Ming LeBon in jeopardy. So Vasic had spent hours teleporting out the dead, the inhabitants of the remote science station having fallen victim to the infection in what was the first known outbreak.

The squad hadn't been aware of that fact at the time, however; Ming LeBon had withheld the information as he'd withheld so much from the men and women who'd trusted him because he'd once been an active member of the squad. It had taken them too long to realize that while the latter might've been true, Ming had never been one of them. He'd always been an "I," his personal political aspirations trumping any other loyalty.

The Alaska incident, Aden realized, was also the last time he'd seen Vasic wearing that jacket. The other man had used it in the interim, of course, but Aden hadn't been with him during those operations.

To see it now in such a different context was . . . interesting.

"Thank you," he said, taking the drink Ivy had prepared. Arrows never ate or drank anything from an unfamiliar source, but taking his cue from Vasic, Aden took a sip of the drink. *Why is it hot?*

Ivy doesn't want us to feel the cold.

From which, Aden deduced that Vasic hadn't told her about the weatherproof properties of the combat uniforms. He immediately understood why. It was strange to be cared for in this fashion, and the strangeness was so unlike everything else in the life of an Arrow that he could find no motivation to clarify the situation for Ivy, either.

He drank a little more, as the empath, her hair braided but curling tendrils falling around her face, looked pointedly at Vasic.

An instant later, the other Arrow said, "Ivy, meet Aden."

"Hi." The empath's smile was open. "It's nice to meet you when I'm not about to fall unconscious. Thank you for saving my life."

Before Aden could respond, Vasic spoke again. "You should still be asleep."

Ivy's shoulders rose then fell. "I tried but couldn't. I'll catch a nap later." Bending, she petted the little dog with unhidden affection. "My stubborn Rabbit will need a rest, too. He was wide awake and waiting for me when I got back from our walk last night."

Our walk.

Zeroing in on the words, Aden found himself thinking about the possible unintended side effects of being around the empaths for an Arrow. It was something he'd begun to research when Vasic reported Abbot's new stability, but the post-Silence Council had done what appeared to be an immaculate job of scrubbing the Net clean of data about the Es. Even non-Net databases had been cleared, printed books taken off shelves and incinerated. Rare copies were rumored to remain but were proving near impossible to track down. As soon as a merchant got even a whiff of Psy interest in the subject, the listing disappeared.

As a result, Aden still had no frame of reference for an empath's impact on an Arrow, but there was one thing he could judge with accuracy, and that was Vasic's psychological state. Seeing his partner interact with Ivy made Aden realize Vasic was no longer on the lethal edge where Aden needed to keep an eye on him at all times. Such a result had been his best-case scenario when he'd given Vasic the one task to which his partner had always been suited: protection.

With that best-case scenario already a reality, the future was now an unpredictable road. "We were discussing the impact of last night's events on your fellow Es," he said to Ivy Jane when she rose back to her full height. "Do you think any will ask to leave?"

Ivy thrust her hands into the pockets of the coat, her forehead furrowed. "We only touched base for a minute last night," she said, "but I had the feeling that while people were scared, they were also . . . invigorated."

"A surprising response."

"Not really if you think about it." Skin stretching tight over her jawline, she said, "We've been in a cage all our lives; most of us have been told we're defective. Now, finally, it's clear we're not—there's an enemy out there, and we can not only sense it, we may be able to fight it."

A purpose, Aden understood, could alter everything.

Ivy looked down when her pet swiveled its head to bark at the mist. "That's not his alarm bark," she said, glancing around all the same.

Aden scanned the area telepathically in case the dog had scented something they hadn't sensed, aware of Vasic doing a scan for unknown heat signatures using his gauntlet at the same time, but there were no intruders. When Rabbit took off a second later, Aden heard Vasic say, "I believe Rabbit is after one of his namesakes."

Ivy's shoulders relaxed. "Oh, that's all right. He never actually goes near them when he's about to catch one." Lowering her voice, she whispered, "We don't speak about it, but I'm pretty sure Rabbit is a little scared of rabbits."

Aden's eyes were on Ivy, his attention on Vasic. So he saw the way her face glowed when she spoke to Vasic, noted the very slight movement of Vasic's head as the other Arrow bent toward her.

Never, not once, had he thought his friend might possess the capacity to bond with a woman. Not even when Kaleb Krychek had bonded with Sahara Kyriakus, throwing open the idea that such a connection was possible for members of the squad. Aden had believed Vasic too damaged, had fought only to save the other man's life.

Now . . .

He looked again at the two of them silhouetted against the mist and felt a new respect for the empath. She'd somehow hauled Vasic out of the numb nothingness that was his self-imposed purgatory. The question was—was she strong enough to go the distance, to walk in Vasic's darkness?

If she wasn't, the damage would be permanent.

Chapter 24

Vasic, I appreciate you're on an active mission, but according to the data you sent through, I need to calibrate the gauntlet to offset a minor overload. To prepare, I'll also have to run an internal diagnostic while you're connected to our systems. I estimate the entire procedure will take under two hours.

Message from Dr. Edgard Bashir

IVY FINISHED THE comm conversation with her parents and went out to wait for Jaya on the porch, Vasic's jacket draped over her thighs and legs. It was a sad substitute for being held in his arms, but it made her feel warm and safe nonetheless.

Ivy, Aden said you asked after me.

A crowd of butterflies took flight in her abdomen at the sound of Vasic's telepathic voice, her nipples going painfully tight in a response that left her breathless. Intellectually, she'd known about sexual attraction—but no one had ever told her that all it would take was the sound of a certain male voice to make her lower body clench, her breasts aching and swelling as her pulse rate rocketed.

She thought of how he'd looked at her the previous night, pure Arrow concentration and ruthless focus, and bit down hard on her lower lip as her mind whispered that she should've pushed the strap down instead of pulling it up. Maybe then, he'd have put those strong fingers on her needy flesh.

I just missed you, she said through the sensual storm, unable to see him in the compound.

It was a simple errand, he said after a long pause, *and a good time to take care of it with Aden free to cover me. I'm walking in from the sentry line.*

Heart skipping a beat at the fact her Arrow had actually explained himself to her, as if she had the right to question his movements, she flexed and unflexed her fingers atop his jacket . . . and then she did something either very brave or so stupid she'd never live down the humiliation. She sent him the erotic visual her mind had created, of her peeling down both straps of her camisole to reveal her breasts.

The silence echoed.

Groaning, she hid her flaming face in her hands. What had possessed her to, to— "Oh, God."

Ivy . . . I may have caught an accidental image from your mind.

He was giving her an out. Chest heaving as her blood scalded her skin from the inside out, she grabbed some snow and pressed it to her cheeks. *It wasn't an accident,* she admitted before the knots in her stomach tied her up into an incoherent ball. *It was for you.*

VASIC remained on his knees in the snow where he'd fallen when the picture of Ivy had slammed into his mind. It might as well have been a roundhouse punch to the jaw, his head was spinning so hard, his heartbeat erratic and a roar of blood in his ears.

It was for you.

No one had ever just *given* him something he wanted so much. Even though he knew he should erase the image from his mind, that it went against every one of the rules that helped him stay sane, stay stable, he opened it again. This time, the punch hit him directly in the solar plexus.

She was all shy smile and a peach-colored blush as she tugged down the straps of her top to reveal plump breasts topped with dusky pink nipples. The flesh of her breasts was a creamier shade than the skin of her shoulders, and he knew it'd mark easily. Unable to resist, he ran a mental finger over one of those nipples, felt his rigid penis throb. The line of her neck drew his gaze, the curve of her shoulder, the slenderness of her arms.

The lush softness of her lips.

Overwhelmed and incapable of processing the sensory input, he did the only thing he could: He shut it all down with jaw-clenched focus, sense by sense. It took several minutes, but he had both body and mind under control when he rose to his feet—after using a handful of clean snow to wash the sweat off his face and the back of his neck.

Then, instead of reprimanding Ivy for doing something that had cut his legs out from under him, he said, *Thank you.* He wasn't going to erase that image. Not now, not ever. It was his.

No one could take it from him now, steal the piece of herself she'd handed him. He would keep it in his private mental file of all things Ivy Jane, and he'd look at it any time he needed an instant of beauty in the darkness.

TOES curling inside her boots, Ivy swallowed. *Jaya and I are going to explore the infection.* The Es had decided as a group that no one should undertake the task alone the first time. *The others will be doing the same throughout the day, in pairs.* Her own partner—her friend—had arrived half a minute ago, taken one look at Ivy's scarlet face, and demanded an explanation.

Ivy had stuttered that it was nothing, but Jaya, her elegant features shadowed by the hood she'd pulled over her head, wasn't convinced. The other E might be quiet and composed, but she was also relentless. Now she nudged at Ivy with an elbow. "You had such a guilty expression in your eyes, I know you did something. Even Rabbit knows it—look at his face."

"Hush," Ivy muttered with her best attempt at a glare. "I'm telling Vasic what we're planning."

I'll keep an eye on you, Vasic said at that instant, *pull you out if I see any signs of distress.*

Wrapping his words around her like a shield, she nodded at Jaya, and the two of them entered the vast psychic sprawl of the PsyNet. Each mind within it was represented by a cold white star, the darkness between streaming with data. It was a creation of painful beauty, and of necessity.

No Psy could survive without the biofeedback provided by a neural network, but now, the biofeedback itself had turned toxic. Ivy flinched at what she saw directly in front of her—the viscous, fetid blackness that denoted the infection, its tongue licking out at the eighteen minds located within the compound.

"Hunger . . . such hunger." Chilled horror in Jaya's tone, all traces of teasing wiped away. "It's starving and it wants us all. Every cell, every limb, every breath."

Ivy rubbed her abdomen in a futile effort to ease the gnawing ache that had eaten up the knots and spilled out scraping pain. Tears dripped down her face, caught in her throat. "It's so lonely. It hurts." As if it was a sentient thing, not a mindless disease.

"Yes." Jaya's voice held a sob. "It knows it's unwanted."

They stared at the oil-slick black that *wasn't* sentient, and yet . . . and yet . . .

All the air rushed out of Ivy's body. The infection was changing, becoming a woman of absolute, endless darkness. She reached out toward Ivy and Jaya with her hands, a pulsing malevolence to her that made them stumble back. It took but a heartbeat for Ivy and Jaya both to stop and reverse direction, compelled to ease that piercing, haunting loneliness, but they were too late. The woman collapsed out of existence, and the infection was once more a mindless disease without emotion or thought.

Opening her eyes to the crystal-clear air, Ivy wiped away her tears.

"What was that?" Jaya whispered wetly.

"I don't know." That was when Ivy realized the sun was in a different position in the sky from when she and Jaya had begun. *Who is she?* Ivy asked the gray-eyed Arrow who now stood only three feet away. *The dark woman in the Net?*

The DarkMind. According to Kaleb Krychek, she is created of all the emotions our race sought not to feel and attempted to suppress out of existence. He believes the infection was born from the same festering soup.

Does the DarkMind control the infection?

No, but it is impervious to it.

Ivy shivered and shared the information with Jaya, wanting the protective strength of Vasic's arms around her, but he was already turning to walk away, his expression distant. It was as if they'd never had their earlier conversation, never found themselves entangled in her inappropriate fantasy. Her heart ached. Every time she thought she'd made a crack in the ice, she was forced to confront the fact that a lifetime spent in the shadows couldn't be so painlessly navigated.

"It's hard, isn't it?" Jaya lay her head on Ivy's shoulder. "I'm falling for my Arrow, too."

"Do you think," Ivy said, "it's just the proximity?" Even as she spoke, she knew it wasn't; she'd felt a dangerous tug toward Vasic the first time they'd met, in the apple orchard as he, a man encased in winter, crouched in front of her.

"No." Raising her head, Jaya pushed back her hood to reveal a neat braid. "The others get along with their Arrows, but it's not like me with Abbot or you with Vasic." A trembling sigh, her eyes on where Vasic had halted to talk to Abbot. "Maybe the others . . . maybe they're the smart ones."

Jaya was right. It would, in all probability, be smarter to walk away, to try to build a bond with a different man, a man who hadn't grown up an Arrow, but—"I don't want to live a safe, smart life, Jaya. I want passion and fury and Vasic."

Jaya's lips curved in a tremulous smile. "Me, too," she whispered, the deep brown of her skin glowing in the sunshine. "Only I don't want your Vasic. No offense, but he has nothing on my Abbot."

Ivy looked at the other woman, said, "Come closer," in a solemn tone of voice. "I need to examine your eyes . . . since you're obviously going blind."

Having fallen for Ivy's first words, Jaya pushed at her shoulders, and then they were laughing, their fingers tightly intertwined.

VASIC was held motionless by the sound of Ivy's laughter, so rich and warm and vibrant. *Tell me why you laugh,* he demanded, wanting to understand it, understand her.

Tilting her head to the side, she shook it. *That's between me and Jaya.*

Her words drew his attention to the woman beside her. He became aware at the same instant that Abbot, too, was focused on the porch.

Having already made the decision to leave the younger Arrow with his empath, Vasic didn't comment.

If there was a chance Abbot could forge a better life for himself, then Vasic wouldn't steal that chance from him. Neither would Vasic permit the E to savage Abbot. *Your friend,* he said to the woman with tousled curls who watched him from the porch, *must understand that Abbot may not catch emotional nuances. If she's merely using him to explore her emotions, she needs to stop.*

Ivy hugged Jaya, both women now on their feet. Only when her fellow E had begun to walk toward her cabin did Ivy say, *Come over here and talk to me.* The demand held more than a hint of challenge, her arms folded defiantly across her chest.

Glancing at Abbot to see the other male was staring after Jaya, he said, "We'll continue this discussion later."

Abbot left without further words, his course set to intersect with Jaya's. Striding across to his own E, Vasic stopped a foot from her. "Did my statement about your friend offend you?"

Arms still folded, Ivy narrowed her eyes. "You ever think about the fact that maybe it's Jaya taking all the risks?" she demanded. "For all she knows, Abbot could turn around and say it's too late for him."

He heard the echo of his own words, knew it had been deliberate. "Abbot and I," he said, "are not the same."

"Why? You're both telekinetics, went through the same training—"

"No." Ivy had to understand that what she sought to see in him was simply not there. It was his fault—he'd been selfish, withheld the truth from her and stolen time, allowing things to go so far that she thought his hands were clean enough to touch her. "Abbot," he said, "wasn't inducted into the training program till he was ten."

Frowning, she unfolded her arms. "But he's a very strong Tk."

"Abbot's father was the same, and he not only took responsibility for his son, he held enough power to enforce his decision. It was only after his death that Abbot was claimed for the squad." That had always been part of the problem—unlike many Arrows, Abbot had known what it was to be valued as an individual before he was thrust into a world where their leadership saw them as interchangeable pieces. Under Ming, an Arrow was valuable because of his training, but only until he began to malfunction.

"At ten," he continued before Ivy could interrupt, "Abbot already had excellent psychic control. His father had made certain of that." There was no question the younger Arrow had suffered considerable physical and psychological pain in the intervening years, but he hadn't been tortured as a child.

The sudden contrast was one of the reasons why Abbot was so unstable. The shock of it had left jagged fractures in his psyche. "Abbot did eventually adjust to the change in his life," he told Ivy, "and he's an Arrow I would have at my back in a heartbeat, but he's also fragile on a certain level. Jaya is the first person with whom he's bonded emotionally since he lost his father."

Copper-colored eyes watched him with a near-painful clarity. "Jaya is falling for him and she's just as scared." A lopsided smile. "You don't have to worry about his heart."

Vasic didn't know anything about the heart, but Abbot was his responsibility. "Do you understand, Ivy?" he asked into the air filled with birdsong.

Abbot was damaged, but he'd had a foundation once, had been loved, even if only in the cold way of Silence. That fact had shaped his life . . . the same way Vasic's total abandonment by his own father had shaped his. "I'm not like Abbot." He'd been too young to fight the torture, and it had broken him. "I didn't survive my childhood."

Ivy stubbornly shook her head. "You can't push me away, so stop trying."

Catching the fisted hand she touched to his chest, he battled the desire to surrender to her will. If he acknowledged the nascent bond between them, she'd use up her very life force in an attempt to heal him—and the abyss of numbness that existed deep inside him would suck her in, suck her dry.

Watch over your Sunny as I wasn't able to watch over mine.

His honor might be in shreds, but this one good thing he would do—he would keep Ivy Jane safe from her own too-generous heart, so she wouldn't end up dust long before her time.

Chapter 25

"THANK YOU FOR making me feel alive for the first time in a decade," he told her as he fought and failed to release her wrist. "If I could alter time, I'd make myself into a man who could walk by your side, but I'm meant for the shadows." Meant to live in the cold dark with the other monsters. "It's where I intend to stay."

Ripping away her hand to leave him forsaken, Ivy said, "Inside," in a voice that shook. "I have something to say to you, and I won't do it out here."

He shouldn't have gone behind closed doors with her, but he teleported them into her cabin. Pacing to the kitchen counter then back, Ivy slapped both her hands against his chest and pushed. "You don't get to *do* that, Vasic! You don't get to just give up!"

He gripped her wrists again, the feel of her skin against his own water to ground so parched he knew it had no hope of recovery. "I'll never give up." Peace, dark and quiet, had long been the beacon that kept him moving along the numb road of his life, but he could never find it by leaving her to face the world alone. "I will protect you until the day I die." *No one* would ever hurt Ivy, ever bruise the bright hope of her. "I'm tainted, Ivy. There's so much ugliness on me it can never be washed away."

Ivy's chest heaved as she tried to gasp in air. "You think that makes me happy?" Her hands attempting to push against him again. "To know you intend to spend the rest of your life at the periphery of mine, alone in the darkness?"

"It's who I am." The pattern had been set long ago. "I can't change." Could never erase the horror of all he'd done.

"Or you *won't* change!" Her body trembling, she tugged at her wrists again, this time with far less force.

And he had to set her free, the warmth of her leaving a sensory tattoo against his palms even as ice formed in his bones. Ignoring the pain, he gathered up the echoes of sensation and placed them carefully in his private mental vault, though he knew memory would never do justice to all the facets of her. The green apple scent of her hair, the lush softness that was simply Ivy, the silken fragility of her skin, the angry flutter of her pulse beneath his thumb . . . he couldn't hope to capture Ivy Jane in any box.

"Wear the jacket." A snapped-out command as he headed for the door. "It's started to snow."

He obeyed the order, stepped out into the cold. However, when it was time for him to go off shift, he returned to her night-dark cabin ostensibly to leave the jacket for her. Hearing her calm, steady breathing beyond the screen that hid her bed, he hung up the jacket on a kitchen chair, then stretched out on the floor. Comfort was meaningless, his body trained to find rest where it could . . . but at least here, he was close to her.

His hands were too stained with blood to touch her, but he could use those same brutal hands to keep her safe, protect her from harm.

A whisper of clothing against skin followed by the sound of feet on the floor.

Vasic kept his eyes shut, felt a blanket being placed over him, Ivy's palm cupping his cheek for a single instant before she broke contact to slide a pillow under his head with a gentle touch. "I am so mad at you," she whispered, then tugged up the blanket and pressed a kiss to his temple that smashed an ice pick through his defenses, green apples and Ivy in his every breath. "And this is ridiculous, sleeping on the floor. Stubborn man."

Opening his eyes after she left, he stared into the darkness as he fought to ride out the dissonance for the thousandth time since he'd met her. At its basest level, Silence worked by linking pain to emotion until the mind learned to avoid that which caused it hurt.

The brutality of the punishment was multiplied tenfold for Arrows:

Vasic hadn't only had his leg broken when he'd asked to go home as a child. He'd been deliberately burned then healed, not once, not twice, but over and over; had suffered electrical shocks; had been locked naked in an icy room until his extremities froze, only for him to then be put into overwhelming heat that made his nerve endings scream awake.

All before he was eight years old.

The worst thing was that it had been done by people he'd initially thought he could trust. His mentor, Patton, had doled out many of the worst punishments, his years on Jax having erased any empathic center he may have once had. A few of the other Arrows had tried to ameliorate the viciousness of Vasic's training, but they'd been limited in what they could do, the rebellion that had begun to simmer in the ranks not yet strong enough to emerge from the shadows.

Vasic's brain was now hardwired to equate emotion with pain and to strengthen the message with further punishment, agony spearing down into his spine. A perfect loop that had been programmed to end in death should the subject continue to defy the conditioning. It was fortunate, therefore, that he didn't have the physiological triggers in his mind that backed up the psychological coercion.

The dissonance could not kill him.

He had no idea how Judd had broken those deeply embedded telepathic controls without suffering severe brain damage. Vasic wouldn't have been able to do so without Aden, his own telepathy lacking the required delicacy. The other Arrow's expertise had been hard-won, the cost paid in agonizing convulsions that could've left him brain-dead.

Now only a single critical tripwire remained in Vasic's mind—one that would give him a sharp, pointed warning should his telekinesis threaten to rage out of control. Vasic didn't know how many other Arrows Aden had helped escape the vise around their minds, but it wasn't a small number—and it included Abbot. What Aden couldn't fix was the long-term psychological impact of the extreme dissonance on many of them. While Vasic could tell his mind emotion and sensation didn't mean pain, it had learned otherwise too early.

Learning the opposite would take time, but Vasic would rewire himself to accept the pleasure that was Ivy's lips on his skin, her skin against his. If that was all he'd ever have of her, he would experience the memories in all their glory. Exhaling in silence, he opened his mental Ivy file and located the one of her whispering to him about Turkish Delight. He'd researched the candy during a night shift, found a store in San Francisco that sold it, and now started to scroll through their online listings.

Stop, said the part of him that had made him confess his perfidy to her, forced him to show Ivy the hands so soaked in blood, the stain was permanent, *she isn't for you.*

Vasic ignored that voice. He'd torn himself to shreds today with what he'd done, but he'd hurt Ivy, too. That had never been his aim. This candy made her happy. So he'd order it now, pick it up tomorrow. Taking care of her was his reason for being.

THE world went to hell at eleven the next morning.

Ivy was stomping around in the woods with an equally grumpy Rabbit when Vasic blasted a message to everyone in the compound. *Shield and maintain until advised otherwise. Do not venture into the Net.*

Reaching for him, she touched blank nothingness, as if he'd gone too far for her telepathy to reach. It was tempting to jack into the Net, read the datastreams, but she knew Vasic. He wouldn't send a warning like that unless it was necessary. Leaving the woods, she walked to the center of the compound, the other Es already converging on the snow.

"Ivy," Isaiah said the instant she was within earshot. "He's your Arrow. What do you know?"

Yep, the guy was still an arrogant ass. "Nothing you don't." She hadn't even spoken to her obstinate male this morning—he'd been gone when she woke, and hadn't turned up for breakfast as he usually did. When she'd looked out the window to see if he was just avoiding her, having every intention of hunting him down, she'd seen him with his unit, the nine of them locked in a taut discussion.

An hour ago, she'd returned from a conversation with a couple of the other Es to find a box of Turkish Delight on the kitchen table. Ivy wanted to alternately throw it at his head and haul him down so she could share the taste with him, mouth to mouth.

Concetta raised a hesitant hand. "I was on the Net before the warning came." Lower lip trembling when everyone focused on her, the shy empath ducked her head.

Rabbit ran over to nuzzle at her leg in an attempt to help. Aware the other woman was afraid of her pet, Ivy went to call him back, but to her surprise, Concetta bent down to very carefully stroke Rabbit.

"Well?" one of the men urged.

"Can it, Chang." Isaiah walked over to crouch next to Concetta, his next words too low to carry.

Nodding, the tiny blonde allowed him to gently tug her to her feet. "I was looking at the infection, and"—she locked her fingers together, flexed, unflexed—"I saw the leading edge of a power wave smashing through the Net, like during the anchor collapse in Australia, but this was *worse*." Her amber eyes stark, she shook her head. "I expected to go down under it, but I haven't felt anything."

Neither had Ivy. It took a split second for her to guess why. *Oh God!*

"The Arrows," Jaya whispered as Ivy glanced frantically around the compound. "They must've protected us."

"Where are they?" she asked, unable to see a single black-clad figure. "Where are the Arrows?" *Vasic! Answer me!*

The others scattered in a rush of pounding boots over snow.

Abdomen twisting as she thought of the blank absence when she'd reached for Vasic, Ivy fought her nausea to bend down to her loyal pet. "Rabbit, where's Vasic? Find him. Find Vasic."

Her dog took off toward their cabin. Racing after him, she saw her Arrow seated against the far wall, his open eyes bleeding ruby tears, and his hands fisted so tight, she could count each tendon and bone. "Vasic!"

No answer.

Collapsing to her knees in front of him, she sucked in a breath. No iris, no pupil, his gaze was the pure black that denoted a massive use of power. A vein pulsed dangerously on his temple, drops of perspiration rolled down to his jaw, his breath ragged but present. When she touched her fingers to his wrist, she found his pulse was running so fast, she couldn't count the separate beats.

Dawning horror in her veins.

The incident, whatever it was, wasn't yet over. Vasic was holding the shield that had protected her and the other Es.

Jaya, have you found Abbot? she asked, telling herself she could give in to the clawing panic inside her after Vasic was safe. *Is he conscious?*

Yes, but I can't reach him, Jaya replied, her mental voice shaky. *Isaiah's Arrow was with Abbot, and he just lost consciousness. Isaiah's checking his vital signs.*

One hand on Vasic's rigid leg, his muscles strained to the breaking point, she touched base with the others. The news was not good. *Six Arrows are down,* she telepathed to the group once she'd heard back from everyone. *That leaves only Vasic, Abbot, and Mariko to hold the shield. I know Vasic told us to stay out of the Net, but we need to help them.*

Unanimous agreement.

Already on the PsyNet, Ivy ignored the ferocious turbulence beyond the transparent black of the Arrow shield, forced thoughts of her parents aside, and talked the others through how to merge shields. The resulting creation was ragged but effective.

It was also . . . different.

Where the Arrow shield was a hard dome, the one below it rippled with the kind of hazy color seen in a bubble of sunlit water, and appeared as thin and as fragile. Yet when part of the Arrow shield cracked, Abbot losing his battle with unconsciousness, the empathic shield didn't collapse under the strain. It simply flowed with the storm surge until there were no more waves, the PsyNet quiet.

And still Vasic's jaw remained clenched, his blood crimson against the gold of his skin.

VASIC telepathed Judd the instant the shock wave stopped pummeling their shield. *I need your pack and DarkRiver to make sure the empaths come to no harm. There's an emergency in the Net.*

The fallen Arrow responded at once. *We'll take care of it.*

Vasic was conscious of Ivy's worried voice, her touch—so soft against his jaw—but he couldn't sink into it, couldn't reassure her. Shooting through the disordered skies of the PsyNet, he came to a section of Alaska that had collapsed into gaping nothingness.

The PsyNet no longer existed beyond the point where he stood.

On the ground, there'd be carnage, people falling where they stood as their biofeedback link was severed, resulting in death—an agony that would be over in seconds for most. The toughest might last a minute. Unless . . . Vasic quickly married up this section of the Net with the physical region and realized it was centered on the abandoned Sunshine Station. Not only was the station uninhabited, there were no other outposts for miles in any direction.

That didn't mean there'd be no casualties—the psychic shock wave had been brutal.

He saw Kaleb and Aden working together to seal the breach before it could widen and swallow up further sections of the Net. Aden was being careful not to overtly showcase his strength, but anyone who thought about it afterward would realize he shouldn't have been able to work side by side with a cardinal without flagging.

Vasic had no doubt Krychek had the brute strength to stop the damage from spreading, but he couldn't do that and seal it up at the same time. Not with a wound this large. *Aden.*

Infection caused the sector to collapse, his partner replied. *Entire region is riddled with it.*

Vasic was almost expecting the news. Sunshine Station was the known site zero for the infection. What was surprising was that no one had spotted the virulence of the infection here, given that the region was under heavy watch. Krychek, the squad, Ming, all had placed observers here.

Vasic. Krychek's obsidian voice. *You need to head to Anchorage.* Images he could use for a teleport lock poured into his mind. *It's not in the collapse zone, but I'm picking up reports of sudden, inexplicable violence alongside the expected shock wave injuries. It may be an outbreak.*

Vasic opened his eyes to see Ivy in front of him, her hand holding a bloody towel she must've used to clean up his face. "I have to go," was all he had time to say before he left, taking with him the remembered sensation of Ivy's fingertips just brushing his own as he 'ported into carnage.

During the cleanup in Sunshine, he'd seen corpses with their brains bashed in, others who'd been stabbed over and over, still others who'd been beaten with whatever was nearby. So he wasn't surprised to find himself in the middle of a dead-end street overrun with the violent mad. He saw two other Arrows, both at the open end of the affected street. A Tk and a telepath, they were managing to stop the swarm from escaping to spread out over the rest of the city, but the tide was rising.

There was also a changeling—a predator—who must've been on the street when the world went insane in the space of a few seconds. He was protecting a group of roughly fifteen human and changeling schoolchildren behind him, his claws slicing at the mad as the terrified children huddled against the wall.

Another man, a human, was bleeding badly from a gut wound but trying to calm the children. A teacher, Vasic surmised.

Several bodies littered the street that had obviously been cleared of snow only a short time before.

Taking it all in a single glance, he began to telekinetically pick up and slam the crazed against the walls of the buildings around them, hard enough to slam them into unconsciousness. He tried not to use fatal force, but his priority had to be the children and the other noninfected he could see fighting off those who'd been driven insane by the disease.

He knew full well he might only be delaying the inevitable.

No one from Sunshine had been able to be saved.

"Behind you!"

Turning at the shouted cry from the injured teacher, he smashed back a middle-aged woman who'd been about to sink a butcher knife into his back. The knife flew out of her hand to land on the street with a thick clump, her neck snapping to loll her head forward as she hit the wall at the wrong angle. Then there was no more time to think.

Chapter 26

Breaking News Catastrophic damage across the Net as result of a recent unexplained shock wave. Casualties estimated to be in the tens of thousands. This feed will be updated as further news becomes available.

PsyNet Beacon

BY THE TIME it was all over, the street was littered with bodies, but the schoolchildren were safe, and Vasic had managed to disable but not kill most of the infected. A few had landed wrong the same way as the knife-wielding woman, and two others he'd immobilized had been set upon by other infected, but the majority were breathing. A number of noninfected had also lost their lives or been badly injured, the majority prior to his arrival.

Looking at the changeling male, his claws now bloodied and his eyes glowing a pale feline yellow that said he was probably a snow leopard, given the region, Vasic nodded toward the children.

The injured teacher—slumped on the ground—said, "Go" when his students hesitated at the changeling male's order to leave.

"Help is coming," Vasic said, the sirens filling the air getting louder by the second.

The changeling knelt by the teacher. "I'll make sure they get home safe," he said, his voice holding a growl, then he shepherded the children away.

Certain the children were in hands that would protect not harm, Vasic met up with the two other Arrows on the scene. Younger and less experienced, they looked to him for direction. "Separate the injured noninfected from the infected," he ordered. "The latter will need to be restrained if they don't slip into comas."

"Sir, triage?" the female Arrow asked.

"The noninfected are to be treated first." It was a ruthless but practical decision. "The infected rate of survival is currently zero, regardless of their physical health."

That done, he started to go over the scene. He tagged the dead so the medics wouldn't have to waste time searching through the bodies themselves, then he shifted the corpses to the back of the street. Behind him, the medics worked at rapid speed to assist the wounded.

Judging the situation was now under control, with the local authorities out in force, he was about to begin clearing the low-rise apartment buildings that dominated the street when he passed a narrow space between two street-facing buildings and heard a stifled sob. Pausing, he waited for his eyes to adapt to the darkness within. The boy huddled inside the snow that had collected there couldn't have been more than thirteen.

It's safe, he telepathed, instinct whispering the juvenile was Psy.

The boy's head jerked up, fear on every inch of his face.

Vasic crouched down to make himself appear less of a threat. "You're not in trouble."

"I cried," the boy whispered, knuckling away the tears that ran over his wide-cheeked face, his uptilted eyes swollen and red.

"Silence has fallen," Vasic said, and because he knew many people didn't yet believe the fall was real, added, "It was a traumatic and unusual situation. No one will remember your reaction in light of the other events that took place here today." The Net was in too much chaos to notice the fractured Silence of a child. "What's your name?"

Wiping his face on the sleeve of his winter jacket, the boy said, "Eben." Then it was as if he couldn't stop speaking, his words tumbling over one another. "I was walking to catch the jet-train to school. We had a late start today because the teachers had a meeting, and I passed the trippers—"

"Trippers?"

"The elementary school children," he said. "There's a museum that backs onto this street at the cul-de-sac end, and the school transports usually stop here, and then the trippers use a public pathway to get to the museum. It's faster than going all the way around, and one of the museum staff usually shovels away any snow in the morning."

Vasic had allowed the boy to ramble to ease his nerves, but now nudged his recollection back on track, "Go on. You'd passed the children."

"I was thinking of my science homework"—Eben swallowed—"and about a girl at school." His brown eyes, the pupils dilated, met Vasic's. "I was a few meters past the elementary school kids when they started screaming, and I turned to run back. I thought maybe there'd been an accident. I've had first aid training at school."

"Breathe." Vasic used the same tone he used on Arrow trainees who began to panic during simulations. "You did the right thing."

"I couldn't get to them." The boy's entire body shook, shivers wracking his gangly frame even as perspiration broke out over the pale brown of his skin. "There were people pouring out of the apartments on either side and coming at me with knives and other things." He began to rock back and forth. "I didn't want to, but I had to."

Vasic realized Eben was holding something by his side. "Give it to me."

Shaking, trembling, the teenager lifted a baseball bat wet with blood but couldn't seem to pass it across. "I have baseball practice today."

Vasic 'ported the bat away, so it wouldn't be in Eben's line of sight as the teen continued to speak.

"I didn't want to, but they wouldn't stop and I had to. The little kids were screaming and I couldn't help. I *tried*. I tried so hard!"

"You did everything you could." He considered how to handle the clearly traumatized child. "How far is your home?"

"Four buildings down."

Vasic froze . . . and that was when he became aware he was experiencing a dull version of the abrasive sensation he felt near all empaths but Ivy. From a Psy who lived in the center of the zone of infection and should, therefore, have gone insane along with his neighbors. "Were your parents home?" Their current location didn't matter, of course. Anyone resident on this street would've been anchored in the infected part of the PsyNet and would've gone insane the instant the infection reached critical mass. Considering the time of day, a large number would've been at work.

Eben looked at him blankly.

Standing up, Vasic walked to an ambulance and grabbed a thermal blanket. When he returned, he stepped into the space too narrow to be called an alley and wrapped the blanket around Eben before picking the child up in his arms, and at this moment, the boy *was* very much a child, despite his age. With no information on Eben's parents or next of kin, Vasic made the decision to bring the boy directly to Ivy's cabin.

Rabbit barked, scrabbling into the room from the porch. Ivy followed on his heels. One look at the boy in Vasic's arms, and she didn't ask questions, simply took control. Eben was tucked up in her bed with Rabbit sitting sentinel next to him within minutes. "I'll take care of him," she said when Vasic indicated he had to leave.

"I'm certain he's an E, so he shouldn't be violent"—the only reason Vasic was leaving the boy with her—"but be careful. I've alerted Judd and the conscious members of my unit to his presence."

Ivy spread her hand over her heart. "He's hurt inside," she said, the boy's anguish so deep and heartrending she'd sensed it even without lowering her empathic shields. "His family?" It was an instinctive question; she'd checked on her parents the instant after Vasic 'ported out, discovered the shock wave had been nowhere near as violent in their region. Everyone in the settlement was safe.

Vasic's response to her question was brief. "Unknown."

Releasing an unsteady breath, she shook her head. "There's a good chance one or both of them are dead, isn't there?"

"Yes." No expression on his face, no hint of care, but he'd wrapped the distressed teenager in a blanket and brought him here instead of leaving him to the medics on-site. That told Ivy everything she needed to know about the man who had quietly wound chains of stunning winter frost around her heart.

"You be careful, too," she said, and touched his arm.

Glancing down, he just barely brushed his fingertips over her own.

She curled her fingers into her palm when he was gone, holding on to the contact like a precious jewel.

. . .

ADEN sealed another part of the jagged tear in the fabric of the Net, conscious of the staggering depth of power that kept it closed so he could do what needed to be done. Kaleb Krychek's strength was beyond all known measurements.

Repair complete, he telepathed and moved to the next section.

Vasic, Kaleb said without warning. *Do you want to pull him out of Alaska? I can have a unit of my own men in the area within a half hour.*

The question betrayed an understanding of Vasic's psychological state that Aden had trouble believing came from the ruthless dual cardinal. Emotional intelligence had never been a weapon in Krychek's arsenal . . . but the other man was no longer working alone. The question and its attendant insight, Aden thought, was far more apt to have come from Sahara Kyriakus.

No, he replied. *Vasic won't leave, given the scale of the situation.* Aden couldn't order Vasic to do so, as he could the rest of the squad. That wasn't how their partnership worked.

I neither discard nor undervalue my people, Aden, was Krychek's response. *Vasic is too critical a piece of the squad to lose.*

That sounded more like the cardinal, the equation a calculated one—but beneath the calculation was the same capacity for loyalty that had first drawn the squad to him. Unlike Ming LeBon, Kaleb Krychek might be ruthless, but he did not sacrifice or betray those who kept faith with him.

He's stable at present, Aden said at last, unwilling to trust Krychek with the changes he'd sensed in Vasic—their alliance remained a new construct, with secrets on both sides.

I'll bow to your judgment on this point. Krychek caught a fraying edge, held it in an unyielding telepathic fist. *However, we need to talk about the gauntlet. I've accessed the latest reports, and it's clear the biofusion is becoming increasingly more unreliable.*

Surprise was an Arrow's enemy, but Kaleb Krychek had provoked it in Aden today. It wasn't the fact the dual cardinal had managed to get his hands on medical files that were technically private that disconcerted Aden. It was that he valued an individual Arrow enough to bother. Then again, Vasic was a very useful tool. *The biofusion team is continuing to work on stabilizing it. The threat of a further malfunction is minimal at present.*

They worked in silence for the next forty-five minutes, and again, it was Krychek who broke it. *Status on Cristabel Rodriguez?*

Healing and liable to be back to active duty within a month, Aden supplied. *The squad's strength has not been compromised—we have another shooter with the same level of accuracy as Cris.*

Kaleb's reply was another unexpected statement. *I'm aware of that. Cristabel, however, is a highly gifted trainer, according to the squad's own training records.*

Again, it was information the cardinal shouldn't have, but Aden didn't interrupt.

Losing her would have a ripple effect, Krychek continued. *Have you considered pulling her off active duty?*

Retiring under Ming LeBon had inevitably led to an execution disguised as an accident—because no Arrow was ever permitted to retire until he or she was so worn-out that mistakes were inevitable. *Yes,* he responded carefully, wanting to measure Krychek's response. *Cris has an affinity for teaching and is unlikely to oppose the transfer.* Aden had, in fact, discussed the possibility with the older Arrow. The E placement had been meant to be a quiet one intended to give her time to think.

Then do it, Krychek said. *You now have total control of the Arrow training program. Shape it to fit the needs of those who come to you.* A long pause. *I know how I was trained. I can guess how Vasic was trained. There has to be a better way, a way that doesn't threaten to turn children into monsters.*

Aden was silent for over an hour, not because he didn't agree with Krychek, but because he did. He'd already ousted the sociopaths and the sadists from the training program. Some had been Ming's men, others Arrows so far gone that they couldn't tell that what they were doing was wrong. Torture was no longer permitted on any level.

That had taken care of the short-term problem, but the larger one remained. Arrows were Arrows for a reason: their power was vicious and almost always deadly. *Yes,* he said at last. *There has to be a better way.* All he had to do was find it.

IVY checked in on Eben two hours after he'd fallen asleep to find the teenager sitting up in bed. Rabbit was butting his head against Eben's chest, the dog's tongue hanging out in ecstasy, while the boy scratched him behind his ears.

"Careful." Ivy kept her tone gentle, one hand on the screen she'd unfolded to block out the light from the open door and the kitchen window. "Rabbit's a scam artist, will have you doing that all day."

Eben had gone motionless at her first words, his eyes wild, but he jerked to movement again at Rabbit's demanding bark.

"See," Ivy said with a smile. "Would you like a hot drink?"

A hesitant nod.

Leaving the room, Ivy went to the kitchen and mixed up a nutrient drink, judging the boy would prefer the familiar. Traumatized on the deepest level, he had no control of his fear and pain, and it scraped against her every sense. The other empaths had felt it, too, offered to help, but she'd asked them to stay away for the time being, not sure Eben could handle any more strangers.

Footsteps on wood.

"Take a seat," she said without stopping what she was doing. "I'm Ivy."

Eben sprawled into a chair at the table in a way that was pure teenage boy, Rabbit hopping up onto his lap to shamelessly demand more scratches. "You're Psy." It was a blurted-out comment.

Placing the nutrient drink in front of him and bringing out a little pot for her tea, Ivy said, "So are you."

"But you smile."

"I was always a very bad Psy," she admitted. "You're safe, Eben. No one here will betray you."

Adam's apple suddenly prominent as he swallowed, he said, "I can't maintain my Net shields."

"I'm sure Vasic's already taken care of that." Her strong, protective, infuriating Arrow who thought he should be condemned to live in the shadows even as he fought to save countless others. "He's the teleporter who brought you here."

Eben's eyes unfocused for a second. "Yes." Shuddering, he seemed to crumple in on himself. "I hurt people." His agony almost brought Ivy to her knees. "I hit and I hit and I hit and there was blood and other wet things and it was on me and they wouldn't stop. I screamed at them to stop but they wouldn't! They wouldn't stop, Ivy. They wouldn't stop."

Throat thick, Ivy breathed past his pain and her own response, and managed to get herself into a chair across from him. "Will you let me help you?" She took his hand, understanding his nauseated disgust at what he'd been forced to do in a way only another empath could. The sole mercy was that he didn't seem to be suffering from the rebound effect, perhaps because he'd acted in self-defense, with no desire to cause harm. "Eben?"

His fingers grasped hers with bruising force, his eyes awash in tears. "Please."

This was far beyond anything she was trained to do, but there was no choice—Eben's psychological state was devolving by the second. Opening up her empathic senses, she tried to take the boy's pain into herself, where it would be neutralized.

She didn't know how long it took, but she was conscious of her own stomach threatening to revolt as her mind began to blur at the edges. Ivy stiffened her spine, clenched her jaw—she couldn't collapse in Eben's presence. That would undo any good she'd done . . . and when she looked at him, she thought maybe she had done some good. The strain on his face had faded, his eyes clear, his shoulders no longer hunched.

Fighting the nausea that shoved at her throat, a toxic obstruction of fear, grief, rage, and guilt, she released his hand with a small pat. "Feeling better?"

Eyes wide, the teenager nodded. "Yes."

Ivy could feel his need to ask questions, but she wasn't going to last much longer. "Would you mind doing me a favor?" She found a smile from somewhere and told a small lie. "I haven't taken Rabbit for his walk today."

His face lit up. "Oh, sure. I— Does he like fetch?" A shy question. "One of my human classmates has a dog, and I've seen them playing fetch."

"He'll love you forever if you play fetch with him." Tapping her thigh, she said, "Fetch, Rabbit."

Tail wagging quick and excited, her pet skidded to his basket and returned with a stick they'd found in the woods. "It's just right for throwing."

Rabbit lunged for the door with a hopeful look over his shoulder, and Eben followed, too involved with the dog to look back. Just as well because Ivy was doubled over, Eben's horror now her own.

Chapter 27

Intelligence and the capacity for independent thought are prerequisites for entry into the squad. An Arrow is a finely honed instrument capable of handling situations beyond the skill set of even the most well-trained black-ops soldier.

First Code of Arrows

IT ONLY TOOK Vasic minutes to ascertain that Eben's custodial parent, his father, was in a coma. His mother lived in another region and was uninfected, but it made no sense to send the boy to her in his current state—he was much better off with Ivy.

That task complete, he joined the other Arrows in their house-to-house search for further survivors. In view of the risk posed by the infected, many of whom had struck out wildly with their psychic abilities during the fighting, he'd informed the local authorities that no one would be allowed into the homes until the Arrows had cleared the area.

They found a number of dead victims in the first building. At first glance, they all appeared to have killed one another, but he was sure Aden would make the pathologists check for brain aneurysms such as that which had struck down Subject 8-91.

Reporting the locations of the bodies to the local authorities, Vasic and his small team continued inward, each taking a different floor as they entered the next building. The work required meticulous concentration and unremitting alertness. A small number of humans were hunkered down behind locked doors, and Vasic told them to stay there after verifying the fact they *were* human.

"We have injured," a young male told him, his voice shaking. "Is it safe to take them out?"

Seeing the extent of one woman's injuries when the youth opened the door fully, the wounded woman's hands pressed over her blood-soaked sweatshirt, Vasic said, "I'll 'port her out. Carry the others out quietly down the corridor and through the stairwell."

His team also found a scattering of uninfected Psy—people who had just moved into the area, guests from out of town, a university student who'd had to barricade herself in the bathroom when her study partner came after her with a broken glass bottle. As with the humans, Vasic 'ported out the most injured, while human neighbors helped the walking wounded out through cleared exit routes.

It was on the third floor of the final building that Vasic heard something from inside an apartment with an ominously open door. Warning the others to be on standby, he moved quietly down the corridor. The door bore a single bloody handprint, the body of a middle-aged brunette lying just inside—it appeared she'd been bashed over the head with a vase that was now in splinters around her.

A small barren table by the door bore the faint mark of a water ring that told Vasic the vase had been sitting there before it was turned into a weapon.

Vasic checked the victim's pulse, found her skin cold. Her heart had stopped pumping blood long ago; if he had to guess, he'd say at the start of the outbreak. She'd opened the door to a knock and found herself face-to-face with death. Noting the location of the body to pass on to the local authorities, he checked the other rooms. Bathroom, kitchen, first bedroom, they were all empty.

Looking into the final room, its walls pale yellow with a white trim, he saw a curtain waving in the breeze and disengaged the alert, guessing the fabric must've dislodged something from a nearby shelf. He'd just cleared the tall cupboard to the left when he heard wordless murmuring coming from the other side of the room.

There was only one thing there: a crib.

Muscles tensed against the horror he might discover, he crossed the cream-colored carpet . . . to find himself the cynosure of big brown eyes in a round-cheeked face. The baby's face broke out into a smile at the sight of him. Babbling incoherently, it kicked up its feet, grabbed its toes in tiny hands, then held out its arms.

Vasic had never been around anything this small and weak, but he couldn't bring himself to simply 'port the child into a waiting ambulance. That would scare her, and the child who'd surely just lost its custodial parent—a parent who had dressed her carefully in soft pink pants and a matching sweater emblazoned with the words "Girls rule" on the front— didn't need more pain. Her face scrunched up when he didn't move in fast enough, her lower lip quivering.

"Your Silence is terrible, little one," he said gently, lifting her from her crib to cradle her against his chest.

One tiny hand, her skin close to the color of fresh-fallen snow, spread open on his combat uniform, her good humor restored now that she was in his arms. He could feel her mind batting curiously against his as her hands patted at his chest—it appeared she'd had no training under the Protocol at all. Her parent or parents had either been bad at teaching her, or they'd read the currents of the Net right and realized their child didn't have to grow up Silent, or . . .

The abrasion against his mind was faint but familiar.

He was holding an empath.

Picking up the yellow blanket in her crib, he bundled her into it, then accessed property records to identify who paid the rent on this apartment. Cross-checking that against birth records gave him the name of the baby's mother, the custodial parent. He telepathically requested an updated list of the dead and the infected from the medical team, scanned it as he stepped outside.

The baby's mother wasn't on the list, but that meant nothing since not all of the dead had been identified as yet. Ten minutes later, just after an M-Psy confirmed she showed no signs of infection, the child in Vasic's arms began to burble happily, forgetting the tension that had made her hide her face against his chest during the M-Psy's examination

Turning carefully, Vasic watched the baby's face light up at the sight of the crowd behind the barricade. Vasic had already accessed the image of the mother on his gauntlet so he could identify her body. It didn't take him long to locate the distraught woman—tall, with bone-white skin strained over slashing cheekbones, she'd shoved through the crowd and was attempting to climb over the barricade.

She broke down in tears when she saw him walking toward her.

Placing the baby in her arms, he said, "Your child shows no signs of any trauma."

Frantically checking her child with gentle hands, the woman shuddered and cuddled her close. "My cousin, Miki?" Her voice shook. "She watches Marchelline while I'm at work."

"Brunette, small half-moon scar on her right hand?"

"Yes."

"I'm sorry, she's gone." It was pure luck the infected who'd attacked Miki hadn't found the baby—Vasic's gut roiled at the thought of what might have happened had the child cried out at the wrong instant.

In front of him, the woman's face almost crumpled again before she got it under control. "W-will you report us?" Terror in the big brown eyes that shouted her familial link to the child she held so protectively.

"No. Silence has fallen." And he'd just found a third empath, a third survivor.

KALEB had known from the start that Aden wasn't simply a low-level telepath and field medic, but the kind of power he'd seen from the Arrow today should have been impossible given Aden's noncardinal status.

"Factoring in that Sunshine Station was site zero," he said to the other man as they stood out of sight at the end of the affected street in Anchorage, "the majority of the Net is safe from collapse for the present." The fact the Sunshine collapse and this outbreak had occurred near-simultaneously was a grim coincidence; one hadn't initiated the other.

"The collapse does give us a timeline of decay," Aden said.

Yes, and that decay was far more virulent than anyone had guessed. A chunk of the Net had simply crumbled to nothing today, akin to fabric eaten away by insects until it was too fragile to bear any pressure. If they didn't find a way to ameliorate the damage, cure the infection, Kaleb *would* have to slice away the infected sections in order to save the pieces he could.

"The infection, however," Aden said, his eyes on the carnage on the street, "is going active in the victims faster than it's eroding the Net. Anchorage was clean as of two weeks ago."

"Most of it still is." Kaleb had called in reports from his men and women in the area. "This was concentrated on a single street."

"A subtle thread of infection we didn't spot and that could have been here for months." Aden nodded. "Makes it more dangerous than the larger, visible tendrils."

"We'll need a rapid response team that can liaise with the local authorities. They'll end up being first responders if we have multiple outbreaks in a single day."

"Agreed." Aden glanced at Kaleb, his dark eyes displaying such acute intelligence that Kaleb couldn't believe Ming hadn't regarded the male a threat. "An Arrow unit?"

"No, this has to be a unit that can deal with civilians of all races." The Arrows terrified most people. "We need a manager skilled at handling people and logistics."

Kaleb? Sahara's voice. *You realize you have that person working for you?*

He'd asked the woman who held his soul to sit in telepathically on this meeting and his earlier discussion with Aden, her insights invaluable when it came to the squad. *Silver is too useful to second.* His aide had a brilliant mind.

I think she'd enjoy the challenge.

Kaleb considered it. If he gave Silver this position, she'd understand it was one that indicated a deep level of trust. It would also increase her status—not in a way that would pose a threat to him, but that her family would appreciate. It would further cement their loyalty to him.

"Silver Mercant," he said to Aden. "Can you work with her to ensure Arrows are sent to the most critical incidents?"

"Mercants tend to be efficient, so I don't foresee a problem." Aden was silent for a minute, and when he did speak, it was on another topic. "The empaths. They're being asked to do the impossible—how can a designation that's been stifled and crushed for over a century hope to save our entire race?"

WHEN Kaleb repeated Aden's question to Sahara after returning home to Moscow, she frowned. Seated in bed with a datapad on her lap, the world draped in the darkness of very early morning on this side of the world, she was watching him undress. They both needed to catch some sleep. Before her, he would've stripped, showered, and slept in silence.

Now hers was the last voice he heard before he closed his eyes.

"The first public defection was an empath," she reminded him. "Then there's the fact that there are thousands and thousands of older Es in the Net—no one ever considers how strong they must be to have survived psychic imprisonment for decades." Setting aside the datapad, she shoved aside the blanket and got out. "I think the empaths are far more resilient and resourceful than anyone knows."

He let her remove his cuff links, unbutton his shirt. She was dressed only in the T-shirt he'd been wearing earlier. She always did that, always wore him close to her skin when he was apart from her. It was as much a caress as her fingers on him as she pushed off his shirt. "You'll have to make a statement."

Shrugging the shirt to the floor, he undid his belt and dropped it on top of the fabric. "I'll consider it. At this point, I can't promise a cure—the populace should get used to fear, if only for self-preservation."

"Silent Voices has already sent out a press release."

Kaleb ignored her.

Sahara laughed, well aware that *was* a response. Guilt threatened nearly at once as she remembered the losses of the day, but she refused to succumb to it. The world would never be a perfect place, and she and Kaleb had already spent too many years in the dark. Never would she willfully turn her back on happiness.

Wrapping her arms around his bare chest, she rose on tiptoe to kiss his jaw, his skin a little rough by this time of day. It made her nerve endings flare, the sensation exquisite. Smooth or rough, she loved the line of his jaw, loved too that she was the only woman who ever got to see him stripped of his obsidian control. There were no masks between her and Kaleb.

He pushed one hand into her hair. "Do you feel forced into assisting me with the political situation so I don't cross ethical lines?"

Startled at the question, she settled back flat on her feet. "No." He used her as his sounding board, so it wasn't as if she were ever in the dark about any of his decisions.

"I don't want to hold you back from exploring the options open to you." Cardinal eyes locked with her own. "Your intellect is in the highest percentile, meant for study and research."

"I am studying, remember?"

"Not as much as you could be if you weren't handling multiple things for me."

"I enjoy the variety of things I do behind the scenes for you." Like translating documents he could trust were verbatim to the original and being the contact person with DarkRiver. "But mostly, I just like being with you." Never did she feel as alive as when she was with Kaleb. He challenged her, loved her, made her think in innovative and exhilarating ways. "Do you mind?"

The stars disappeared to leave his eyes endless black. "*Sahara.*" His kiss was a branding, a reminder that he would've destroyed an entire civilization for her. *You could be with me every instant of every day and I would ask for more.*

Breaking the kiss to look into his face, she petted his nape with possessive hands. "Come to bed."

"Le—" He broke off his reply, paused, then said, "I have to handle a business matter—it appears a certain conglomerate has decided to flout my mandate for price stability in the current climate."

Sahara wished she could growl like the changelings. Throwing up her hands instead, she managed a good approximation of a snarl instead.

"Damn it! Idiots." Economic uncertainty could do as much damage as the infection, not only to the Psy, but to the entire world.

"Yes." Hands on his hips, Kaleb seemed to be listening to something. "I'll have to pay the CEO a personal visit. It shouldn't take long."

"Wait." She squeezed his shoulder, the muscle firm under her touch, his skin warm. "You've been working nonstop for the past twenty-one hours." And not only today. "Can you ask one of the squad to handle it?"

Kaleb stared at her. "Arrows don't normally deal with economic issues."

"This isn't an economic issue—this is about scaring the pants off an arrogant CEO who wants to destabilize the economy," she pointed out, tugging him down with one hand in his hair. "And you need to learn to delegate. Don't be like Ming and not use the Arrows to their full capacity."

A pulse along the bond that connected them. Irritation.

Her lips twitched. "Sorry I put you and Ming in the same sentence," she said with a kiss. "But you know I'm right. This is *exactly* the type of situation an Arrow could contain so you don't have to—they're highly trained operatives capable of subtlety."

Hands curving around either side of her rib cage, he said, "And in utilizing them in such a fashion, I show the Arrows I value them beyond their ability to kill."

God, but she loved him, ruthless political mind and all. "Yes," she agreed. "Words mean nothing after their betrayal at Ming's hand." From everything she and Kaleb knew, the former Councilor had attempted to destroy the very foundations of what it meant to be an Arrow.

"Aden says he has the perfect Arrow for the task," Kaleb responded a minute later. "It'll be done immediately."

"Good. Now, come to bed."

Chapter 28

I've reviewed the scans we took yesterday. It's imperative we speak at once.

Message from Dr. Edgard Bashir

VASIC TELEPORTED DIRECTLY inside Ivy's cabin to discover it silent, but he could sense her behind the screen that concealed her bed. Unwilling to venture into the private area without an invitation, he reached out with his mind. *Ivy?*

No response, not even a sleepy one.

He strode past the screen to find her curled up unconscious under a heavy blanket. Refusing to acknowledge the ice creeping into the edges of his mind, an ice that didn't numb but burned, he checked her vital signs.

Her skin was clammy, her pulse sluggish but present. His hand clenched convulsively on her wrist at the confirmation that she lived; he had to force himself to release her slender bones before he caused bruises.

"Oh."

Turning at the startled sound, he saw Jaya. "What happened?"

"She helped Eben," the other woman answered, her eyes shadowed with concern. "I called Sascha Duncan after Isaiah and I found her collapsed in the kitchen. She drove over immediately and said Ivy should come out of it on her own, that she simply overloaded her empathic senses, but that we should watch over her."

"Thank you."

"Isaiah's keeping Eben occupied. I've been sitting with her, just stepped out for a minute to return a call from my father. Shall I—"

"No," Vasic interrupted. "I'll take care of her now."

Jaya leaned down to brush her lips over Ivy's forehead, her fingers trembling as she stroked back the silky black curls that always made Vasic want to touch. "You'll tell me when she wakes?"

Nodding, Vasic said, "Stay a few more seconds." He thought of Aden and was beside his partner a split-second later, the other man in the midst of talking to the pathologists who'd already begun to conduct autopsies on the infected.

I need you to check Ivy. It wasn't that he didn't believe Sascha Duncan's assessment; he simply trusted his partner more.

Aden nodded and asked the medical staff to excuse him. *Go.*

Hand clasped around Ivy's, Jaya remained while Aden scanned Ivy using a small medical device, then a light telepathic touch. "She has the same signs as a classic flameout, should recover with rest," was his diagnosis. "I haven't had any experience with empathic minds, but Sascha's recommendation to keep an eye on her and allow her to recover naturally would be mine as well."

Teleporting Aden back to the morgue, Vasic returned to Ivy. Jaya left a few moments later, after once more making him promise to keep her updated. "Rabbit will probably run in soon," she told him as she slid her arms into her jacket. "He's been doing that the entire time—but he goes back to Eben before the boy can miss him and start to follow. It's almost as if he understands Eben can't see Ivy in this condition."

Eben, however, had clearly guessed more than anyone realized. The boy entered the cabin twenty minutes after Jaya's departure, his shoulders tense. "Did I hurt Ivy?" he asked in a ragged voice. "Please tell me the truth."

"No. She's simply resting after the power outlay."

Open relief. "Oh, I've done that before, when I stretched my telepathy too hard." He petted Rabbit when the dog came out from behind the screen after checking on Ivy. "We'll go hang with Isaiah and Penn so we don't disturb her. Come on, Rabbit."

It was sixty-seven minutes after that conversation, the world graying into evening outside, that Vasic finally heard a rustle.

Checking Ivy's pulse—strong and steady—he touched her mind again, and this time sensed the normal patterns of sleep. What he didn't expect was the sleepy, *Vasic?* that was Ivy's telepathic voice in his own mind.

I'm here. Rest.

Stretching out, then curling up again, blanket pulled to her neck, she smiled. He should've left now that she was stable, but he hesitated. And then he went down on his haunches by the bed and dared touch his hand to her hair, the silky strands snagging on the calluses that marked his palm.

TWO hours later, Vasic was in the trees at the inner perimeter, speaking with Judd, when he sensed Ivy's presence. Turning around, he found her walking toward him, her hands in the pockets of the jacket he'd given her and her unbound hair dusted with snow that must've fallen from a tree branch.

"There you are," she said with a deep smile before she noticed Judd. "Oh, I'm sorry. Am I interrupting?"

"No. I was giving Judd some details about Anchorage." The other man had asked in his position as a SnowDancer lieutenant, the pack wanting to ensure it was prepared in case there was a similar incident in any part of their sprawling territory. "You should still be resting."

Ivy's smile morphed into a scowl. "Says the man who sleeps less than anyone else in this compound."

I wouldn't. Judd's mental voice touched Vasic's mind when he would've pointed out that she'd experienced a major psychic strain today. *She's ready to be annoyed with you.*

Vasic met Judd's eyes. *How do you know?*

A faint amusement in the other man's expression. *I have a mate and two nieces. I also live in a wolf pack. Trust me when I say I know annoyed women.*

As the only women Vasic really knew aside from Ivy were the other Es and his fellow Arrows, he decided to take Judd's word for it. "Did you need something?" he asked Ivy.

Scowl fading, she said, "I wanted to ask about Anchorage, actually." Her tone was bleak. "I'm following several PsyNet news feeds, but all they're saying is that there was a mass psychotic outbreak, no other facts."

Vasic's instincts rebelled against dousing her in the ugliness of the death and madness he'd witnessed today.

Tell her. Judd's telepathic touch again.

She's had a traumatic day.

You'll be the one having a traumatic day soon. Strong women don't like being wrapped in cotton wool.

Vasic held his ground. *Were this your mate, would you tell her?*

Of course, was the immediate answer. *Mating is a partnership. It's not about keeping secrets or about one half of the pair bearing all the weight.*

"Do you two geniuses think I can't tell you're talking about me?" Eyes narrowed, Ivy folded her arms.

"Sorry." Judd coughed into his hand. "I'd better be heading off anyway." A glance at Vasic. "Think about what I said."

Ivy waited until the other man was gone before raising an eyebrow. "Well?"

He realized she was tapping her foot. For some reason, that tiny action fascinated him. "You suffered a major psychic burnout earlier," he said, disregarding Judd's advice in his need to protect Ivy.

"Empaths are built to handle turbulent emotion." She rubbed the heel of her hand over her breastbone as she stated that fact in an exasperated tone.

Zeroing in on the unconscious act, he said, "You're feeling the after-effects of working with Eben."

"Yes, like a bruise," she admitted. "And like any bruise, it'll fade." A piercing look. "Now talk to me—we can't work blind, Vasic."

She was right. Such blindness could be fatal. "It appears the infection is more stealthy than originally believed," he said, and gave her everything he had to this point. "I'll make sure to brief the rest of the Es, too."

"Thank you." She swallowed. "Were there any other Psy survivors?"

He knew she was talking about people anchored in the region, not visitors. "A mother and child. I'm certain they're empaths."

Ivy said nothing for a long time, and Vasic simply watched her. The top of her head just reached his breastbone and he could see the snow on her hair had melted to leave jeweled droplets of water on her curls. As he watched, a single droplet rolled stealthily down past her ear to disappear into the raised collar of his jacket.

He imagined it laying a wet path across her collarbone and over the creamy mound of her breast until it caught on the peak of a dusky pink nipple. The urge to tug down the zip on the jacket, push aside her other clothing, and undo the cruelty of the day with the soft, generous warmth of her was a violent storm surge in his blood. Holding it back with a bloodless grip, he told himself fantasies didn't count.

So long as he didn't put his hands on her flesh, he wouldn't taint her.

Another part of his mind grabbed on to that thought with hungry teeth. *Looking* wasn't touching, it whispered.

"That answers one question." Ivy's breath fogged the air as her voice merged with the voracious one in his head. "Empaths are immune to the infection."

Subtly altering the air molecules around her face so the air she inhaled was no longer so cold, he muted the sly voice that had found a loophole in his resolve. "Yes." Even if it could be argued that Eben and the baby's mother had somehow protected themselves, the same couldn't be said of the infant. "There may also be another empath among the wounded survivors."

"Three confirmed empaths in such a small area, possibly four." Ivy stepped close enough that the sleeve of her jacket brushed his arm. "It hints at exactly how many there must be in the Net."

"And the fact of their necessity." The PsyNet was alive in a way no one understood. It wouldn't have produced so many empaths in this generation unless they served a vital function.

Nodding, Ivy bit down on her lower lip as she had a habit of doing, her eyes focused on the ground and a vertical line between her eyebrows.

What are you thinking? he asked, though he had no right to know.

Give me a minute.

So close to him that he could reach out and embrace her, she—

He paused, worked through all the tiny details he knew about her. *Would you like me to hold you?* he asked, unsure he was correctly reading the subtle cues.

She turned into his body in answer. Wrapping his arms around her, he took care to make certain the gauntlet didn't dig into her, and cradled her head as he'd done when he'd held her after the nightmare. She seemed not to mind the hold, and he liked the feel of her hair, silky and warm against his skin.

This touch didn't count, either, that starving part of him whispered. Ivy needed this; to deny her the contact would be to hurt her. Cheek pressed to his chest and arms around him, she was a small weight he could feel through her jacket and his combat uniform. He preferred her dressed as she'd been the other time, her clothing thinner, less of a barrier. It made him consider how much more of her he'd feel if he, too, was dressed in light civilian clothing.

His mind jabbed a warning down his spinal cord, telling him sensation equaled pain. Fighting the psychological brainwashing, because there was *nothing* painful about holding Ivy, he lowered his head to speak to her, the words quiet in the intimate space between them. "Should I have been there when you woke?"

Ivy stroked his back, and he wanted the armor off, wanted to know what it felt like to be touched by someone who did it for no reason but that she *liked* him. "It's all right. I know you have a lot of duties." Continuing to pet him in the way he'd so often seen humans and changelings do with one another, she said, "Was it bad?"

Vasic knew he should break contact, not for his sake but for hers. But if he didn't hold her, protect her, who would? Yet the brutal fact was he had no right to even ask that question, have that thought.

"Not as bad as many other operations," he said, putting aside the cold truth for this stolen instant. "I found survivors this time." It hadn't only been blood and desolation.

"I'm glad you weren't hurt."

He didn't know what to say to that, so he just held her tighter.

"Thank you for holding me."

"It's what you need."

"What about you?" she asked, leaning back in his arms so she could look up into his face. "What do you need?"

"This." Having her so close, so trusting, was far more than he deserved.

Ivy shook her head a fraction. "I can sense you now. Just a hint every so often." The clear, penetrating copper of her eyes seemed to see right through him. "I felt your hunger before." A whisper that touched him in places she shouldn't have been able to reach. "You want something." Bracing her hands on his shoulders, she rose on tiptoe. "Tell me."

He could feel his pulse rate accelerating, her words threatening to unleash the selfish, hungry thing that lived in him. "Holding you," he said, because it was vital she understand, "it doesn't come with any strings attached."

Ivy's lips curved. "I know." Breath brushing his jaw as he leaned down a little to hear her quiet voice, she said, "You did it because you like taking care of me."

He couldn't dispute her conclusion.

"Well"—another whisper of air against his skin—"I like taking care of you, too. Let me give you what you want."

Vasic knew he shouldn't . . . but the news he'd received over the comm an hour ago appeared to have obliterated his defenses against his empath. "Send me another image," he said before he was aware of forming the words.

Ivy's eyes widened, her throat moved, and he knew he'd crossed a line, might just have lost the tiny part of her he'd permitted himself to have. A stabbing sensation in his gut, he went to withdraw his request when she said, "D-do you want to see me, rather than an image?"

Chapter 29

BLOOD A ROAR in his ears, Vasic wasn't conscious of teleporting them back to her cabin. It was lit by a lamp Ivy had left on beside the bed, the glow soft around the screen she hadn't folded up.

Breaking contact with him, Ivy took a step back. "Rabbit's usually home by now," she said after a quick glance at her pet's cushioned basket. "Eben?"

"Spending the night on a cot in Isaiah's cabin." And because he knew her, he told her the rest. "Isaiah has three younger brothers—he offered to take Eben to allow you to rest, and the boy appears to have bonded with him. Rabbit is with Eben."

"Oh, that's good." Her voice trembled, her skin flushed hot . . . but she raised her fingers to the zipper of his jacket.

"Don't," he said, hating himself for having asked, for having pushed. "I'll go."

Ivy reached out to grip his hand. "Stay." A whisper that wrapped steel chains around him. "I want to . . . I just—" Blowing out a shuddering breath, she gave him a nervous, coaxing smile. "I've never done anything like this before. Be patient with me."

Her words turned him to stone. He didn't move when she released his hand and began to tug down the zipper. There were so many things he would never do with Ivy Jane, but this one thing, this experience of erotic pleasure, it would always be a thing they had shared. Breathing ragged despite his attempts at control, he followed her every move as she took off the jacket and put it on the chair to her right.

She wore her heavy orange cardigan beneath, over a long-sleeved white top. He watched her fingers fall to the buttons, slide one after the other out of the holes until the garment was open. His rock-hard penis pulsing in time with the thumping beat of his heart, he clamped down on his Tk. Using it on her would be breaking the rules, would be touching when he'd been invited only to watch.

Making a quintessentially feminine move, Ivy shrugged the cardigan off over her shoulders to drop it on top of the jacket. The white top was a thin thermal knit, shaped her curves with gentle precision. When she crossed her arms in front of her, hands going to the bottom of the top, he had to close his eyes, his chest screaming for air. His lashes flicked up the next instant.

He didn't want to miss even a millisecond of this.

Ivy bit down on her lower lip, released the swollen flesh . . . and tugged the top off over her head. Raising one hand to pull back strands of her hair that had curled over her face, she didn't attempt to hide herself from him, the plump mounds of her breasts cupped by a confection of ivory satin and lace. "That's not Psy issue," he said, fighting every single cell in his body not to push the delicate fabric aside and look his fill.

Ivy's own breathing was unsteady, her breasts rising and falling as if in invitation. "No," she admitted in a husky tone. "I've always liked certain textures against my skin." Raising one hand, she pushed off a strap.

Desert winds rolled around them, the wood of the floor suddenly porous. Ivy made a startled noise, and he had her back in the cabin the next instant. "Sorry." It was proving nearly impossible to keep a handle on his ability with so much of her bared to his eyes, despite the painful psychological echo of dissonance.

"It's okay," she said, breathing even shallower. "Shall I keep going?"

The cabin could've collapsed around them at that instant, and it wouldn't have induced him to say no. "Yes."

Ivy pushed off the other strap, and though her cheeks were hot peach, her skin heated, she reached behind herself to undo the bra . . . and lowered her arms to allow it to drop to the floor. He was aware of her backing up until her shoulders hit the screen. It held, the black-painted wood framing her like an erotic artwork of golden cream flushed with life.

He was too close. He couldn't remember moving, but he was an arm's length from her. Gripping the top of the screen above her head, he looked down past her shyly lowered eyelashes, the soft curve of her cheek, the lush shape of her lips, the slope of the neck she'd angled to her right . . . lower.

The screen cracked under his hands.

She was made for his palms, promising to fill them to the brim, the dusky pink of her nipples tight little knots he wanted to touch, to feel, to know. Ignoring the sound of wood groaning under his hands, he looked and looked, her body separated from his by bare inches, the hard black of his Arrow uniform throwing the vulnerable softness of her into stark relief.

Hot desert winds as his ability slipped the leash again, Ivy grabbing on to him.

Back in the cabin, he said, "Please let go." He had to enunciate each word with extreme care, his mind not quite certain it remembered how to shape speech.

The tumble of her curls in his vision, Ivy released him . . . and he made himself back off before he teleported them somewhere less private. "Dress." The order came out harsh. "Please," he said, to ameliorate the roughness, and bent to pick up the scrap of satin and lace for her.

Not meeting his gaze, she took it and turned her back to him. The line of her spine was a thing of unutterable beauty, the flare of her hips making his hands itch to shape them. Hooking on the bra with quick movements, she pulled up the straps and turned. He'd thought he'd hurt or insulted her with his order, his entire body rejecting that unwanted coda to the gift she'd given him, but she shot him a nervous, wicked smile as she reached for her white top and pulled it on over her head.

Tugging her hair out from beneath, she said, "Next time, I'm asking you to strip."

It took Vasic's hazed mind at least a minute to process the words. "It'd be a paltry substitute." His body was nothing in comparison to hers.

"Oh, I don't think so." Leaving her cardigan and jacket on the chair, Ivy didn't close the space between her and Vasic. Her Arrow was on a razor-thin edge, his body rigidly controlled and his eyes pure black.

Ivy, too, realized she'd hit her limit . . . at least tonight. Pleasure was like a drug. She couldn't gobble it up, or her starved mind would overload.

Skirting around the only man with whom she could imagine taking the next bite and the next, she busied herself making drinks for them, her skin prickling at Vasic's presence. He hadn't laid a finger on her, but his eyes, those *eyes*. Swallowing at the memory of the heat in the silver before it turned to midnight, the dominant strength of his body as he trapped her against the screen, she almost spilled the sugar she was putting into her tea.

She could hear the sound of his boot moving on wood as he headed to the door.

Ivy turned, searching for a noninflammatory subject to keep him here for a little longer. "Your gauntlet," she blurted out as the light caught on the black gleam of it. "Will you tell me about it?"

Vasic went motionless, the lingering heat in his eyes doused as if she'd thrown a bucket of cold water over his head. "We should talk about the infection."

Ivy wasn't stupid. "What's wrong with the gauntlet?" she asked, her blood turning to ice.

"It would take too long to explain the complexities of the biofusion."

She strode over to him, her pulse in her mouth and all thoughts of passion buried under an incipient panic. "What's wrong with it?" she repeated through a throat gone bone-dry. "*Vasic.*"

"It's classified."

"You're scaring me."

He didn't flinch, but she had the sense the words had hit him like a blow. Glancing at the gauntlet, he said, "It's an experiment. There are significant glitches."

"How bad?" She gripped the hand of his gauntleted arm, held up the arm with her other hand under the smooth black carapace.

"When it was first integrated to my arm," he answered, not pulling away, "there was a twenty-five percent chance of an overload that could permanently short-circuit my central nervous system."

Death, she thought, horror uncurling in her gut, he was talking about a twenty-five percent chance of *death*. "And now? It's lower?" It'd be a terrible risk at any percentage, but the lower it was, the more time they had to find a solution.

Then his eyes met hers. "No."

The single word smashed her heart to pieces. "Don't make me ask," she whispered.

"Ivy, I volunteered for the experiment long before I knew you."

No, she thought, *no*. She couldn't have found her quiet, strong, protective Arrow only to have lost him before they'd ever exchanged a single word, a single touch. Eyes burning, she just stared at him.

"Seventy-two percent probability of a fatal overload."

A strangled, broken sound tore out of Ivy. "How could they . . ."

"The biofusion team believed they could use a living trial to work out the final glitches, but the technology is proving too complex and too unpredictable." None of that had mattered to Vasic until a woman with eyes of startling copper had looked at him and seen not a monster, but a man.

Just a man. Just Vasic.

"You have to get it removed," Ivy ordered, blinking rapidly. "Contact Aden right now and have him arrange it."

He wished he could do exactly that, turn back the clock on his self-destructive choice. "It's too late. The fusion is too advanced, the computronics integrated into my nervous system."

Ivy shook her head, jaw set in a stubborn line. "No."

Vasic went to touch her, but she stumbled back. "No, no, no!" She came at him a heartbeat later, slamming her fists against his chest. "How could you do that? How could you value yourself so little?"

He gripped her wrists, her skin delicate and warm against his palms. "Because I was already dead." A walking, functioning shell. "You brought me back to life. And seventy-two percent still means I'll likely have years."

Ivy's face twisted, tears rolling down her cheeks. "Find a way to get it off," she said, tugging at one hand until he released it. Dashing away her tears, she gave the order again. "You know the most powerful man in the Net. *Find a way.*"

The robotics expert who had designed the heart of the biofusion technology was gone, presumed dead, and the people on the current team were the best of the best, but Vasic had no intention of giving up. Not this time. "I'll fight, Ivy." He'd wage war against his own body, grip at life with bloodied nails and broken fingers. "I'll push for advancements in science and medicine, hunt down any individual who might possibly offer even a glimmer of an answer, hack into every secure database. I will *fight.*"

Ivy's breath was a sob. "Don't ever give up." Using her free hand to cup the hand he had around her wrist, she bent her head to press a kiss to his knuckles. "Promise me."

His entire body in shock at the sweet, hot caress, he nodded. For her, he'd conquer even the dark numbness that had been eating him alive for years. "I promise." He touched her hair. "Ivy, I was trying to protect you." He'd never intended this bond to form, never intended to cause her pain. "From the terrible things I've done, the destructive choices I've made, the broken mess inside me."

Ivy shook her head, her expression haunted. "It was too late the first day we met. You're inside me, and I'm inside you. It's done."

Rubbing her cheek against his hand, she broke contact. And though the knowledge was a starkness in her eyes, her next words had nothing to do with the gauntlet. "This experiment won't work." She waved her hand to encompass the compound in her statement. "It was good for training us in the basics, but we won't learn anything about how to fight the infection here—Es are immune and the Arrows are too well shielded. We need to be in an under-threat area surrounded by the normal population."

"This is a pure site," he argued, his mind full of the carnage he'd seen in Anchorage, and at Sunshine during the very first outbreak. Ivy didn't belong in the midst of the nightmare. "A clean canvas on which to test your theories."

"The infection is reacting oddly to us—you know that." Folding her arms, she shook her head. "I think it's because there are too many Es concentrated here, with only the Arrows to provide balance. That's still a one-to-one ratio."

Vasic wanted to disagree, but he'd seen the way the fetid blackness of the infection just sat on the edges of the compound, not coming closer, but not leaving either. The instant an E tried to get near it, it slid away, only to return once the E backed off. Vasic wasn't certain the Arrows were safe from the insidious contagion, even given their highly developed shields, but the theory couldn't be tested—not with the Es' immunity spilling over onto them.

"The risk will increase exponentially." Immunity wasn't everything; one of the infected could as easily crush an empath's skull with a blunt object. "You'll be exposed to the pro-Silence lobby for one." Sparks of color, that was what Ivy's mind looked like inside the firewall created by the Arrow unit, a diamond splintered with light.

Skin drawn over her cheekbones, Ivy said, "It'll be worth it if we manage to stop even a single outbreak."

He understood her well enough to guess the direction of her thoughts. "You couldn't have stopped today, Ivy," he said. "The amount of infection found in the cerebral cortex of the victims already autopsied shows long-term exposure—they were dead before I ever came to you in the orchard."

He only realized what he'd said when Ivy's eyes went huge with distress. This time, he didn't reject his instincts. Reaching out, he wrapped her in his arms, his cheek pressed to her temple. "I'll fight, Ivy," he vowed again as her own arms locked around him. "I'll *fight*."

Chapter 30

How much more can we take? Pure Psy murdered hundreds of thousands, and now we're cannibalizing ourselves in madness. Our race appears headed for extinction.

Letter to the Editor signed "Lost and Without Hope," *PsyNet Beacon*

KALEB MET WITH Vasic and Ivy Jane near eleven p.m. their time, having caught five hours of sleep in the interim. The empath was adamant about relocating to an infected zone, and Kaleb agreed with her logic. Leaving her and Vasic to canvas the other Es to see if they wanted to follow the same route, he teleported to Nikita Duncan's office in central San Francisco.

"I received your message," he said to both her and the male who stood looking out of the plate glass windows to the left of Nikita's desk.

Anthony Kyriakus turned, his dark hair silvered at the temples and his bearing that of a man at the head of one of the most influential families in the Net. "Anchorage?"

"Handled for now. I'll have Silver send you a report." While Kaleb didn't consider either of the ex-Councilors an ally in the sense that he trusted them, the three of them currently had the same end goals in mind. "Is there a problem?"

Nikita brought up a financial overview on a wall screen without rising from her desk, the glossy black of her liquid-straight hair brushing her shoulders. "Share prices for stock in Psy companies have dropped precipitously after the events in Alaska." Slanted eyes of deep brown focused on the screen as she used a remote to highlight several significant drops. "This could undermine the entire government structure."

Ruling Coalition aside, that government was truly more of a dictatorship at present, but Kaleb saw her point. He could only lead the PsyNet to where he wanted it to go if he had the support of the major corporations. "Options?" Nikita was a ruthless businesswoman—it'd be foolish not to take advantage of her skill set.

Leaning back in her chair, she steepled her hands in front of her. "If NightStar is willing," she said with a glance at Anthony, "I suggest we leak visions of a future when all is calm."

In other words, lie. Not a bad short-term solution.

"Anthony?" Kaleb turned to the man whose family line had produced more foreseers than any other; the most accurate and gifted F-Psy in the world was a Kyriakus. That same family line had produced the woman he'd left curled up warm and sleepy and sated in their bed, which technically made Anthony and Kaleb family.

The two of them had a silent understanding to ignore that awkward fact.

Now, Anthony said a curt, "No." When the older male's eyes met Nikita's, Kaleb had the feeling he'd walked into the middle of an argument.

Interesting.

"NightStar can't risk staining its reputation."

"In that case"—Nikita broke the intensity of the eye contact to face Kaleb—"I suggest we begin to buy up devalued stock and allow that to leak. It'll be assumed we know something the populace doesn't, that we might even be purposefully orchestrating the deaths for our own gain."

Which, Kaleb thought, would drive those prices right back up. "It'll work as a stopgap solution."

"We need to come up with a strong long-term financial strategy." The lights of San Francisco glittered behind Anthony as he continued to speak. "I assume you were responsible for the turnaround earlier today by a conglomerate that sought to gouge profits?"

"An Arrow," Kaleb told them and it was a deliberate reminder of the fourth part of this Ruling Coalition. "As for a long-term economic solution, I think Nikita's the most capable of drafting something workable. Nikita?"

A cool nod. "It'll involve one-to-one discussions with the most influential businessmen and women in the Net. Where they go, others will follow."

Sheep, Kaleb thought again, but admitted silently that that dangerous lack of independence was changing. Irritants or not, Silent Voices was also a sign of a society that was reclaiming itself. "I'll put the share buys in operation now."

It was as well that all three of them acted at once on their stopgap plan. When a lower Manhattan street erupted into an insane bloodbath five hours later, the share market wobbled, but didn't dive.

The casualties were minor in the scheme of things—forty-five dead with twenty in comas. It appeared another insidiously fine tendril of infection had just brushed one small section of the street, taking everyone in its path with it. The good news was that Kaleb and Aden's hypothesis about the infection being slower to eat away at the fabric of the Net—in comparison to the speed with which it moved in the brain—was proven correct. As with Anchorage, there'd been no Net rupture.

"We have to start thinking of containment," Kaleb said to Sahara an hour later, as the two of them went over every detail of both outbreaks in his study. "It's time to prepare for the worst-case scenario." The empaths had been awakened too late, were too raw and untrained, and Kaleb couldn't wait for them to find their feet.

Sahara sucked in a breath where she sat on the other side of his desk, dark blue eyes shadowed. "Cutting away the infected tissue to stop the gangrene from killing the entire Net." She hugged her knees to her chest. "The gossamer filaments of infection—we can't know how deep they've burrowed. Outwardly healthy sections could be petri jars of infection."

"That's the biggest problem." Before he started to make the surgical cuts that would rend the Net into an unknown number of segments, he needed to know how to identify the enemy.

"The DarkMind," Sahara began.

Kaleb shook his head. "It's having trouble distinguishing those fine tendrils from its own self-image." Born from the same self-hate that had driven an entire race to abandon its emotions, the infection and the Dark-Mind were kin. "But I'll keep trying to get it to focus."

Kaleb met the gaze of the woman Judd called Kaleb's mate. The humans called her his lover. Kaleb simply called her his. And he needed to know that she understood, that she was with him. "If the empaths find a solution before I figure out how to pinpoint the tendrils of infection, I'll back them every inch of the way." Because this wasn't about power or politics but the people Sahara had asked him to save.

Rising from her chair, she came to wrap her arms around his neck from behind, her cheek pressed to his. "How long can we give the empaths?"

"At this rate, maybe a month." After which, the PsyNet would cease to exist except as fragments scattered across the world. A few would survive, and possibly merge back into a larger unit at some stage, but the infected sections would eventually all erode and collapse, snuffing out the lives of millions.

The problem was, Kaleb was beginning to see signs that the majority of the Net was infected.

Chapter 31

The E designation has no official subdesignations. That doesn't mean those subdesignations don't exist.

Excerpted from *The Mysterious E Designation: Empathic Gifts & Shadows* by Alice Eldridge

MUCH AS IVY wished she could keep Eben with her, she was in no position to offer him a home. For now, the boy was better off with the paternal uncle who was his new legal guardian. "Once we've beaten this," she told him as they walked out of the cabin the next morning, "I want you to come back, undertake specialized training."

The lanky teenager's return gaze held a new maturity. "What shall I do for now?"

"Shield yourself as deeply as you can." According to Kaleb Krychek, the NetMind was protecting empathic minds from discovery—except for those such as Ivy who'd gone fully active—but no one knew if and when the neosentience's ability to do so might be compromised by the infection. "If you feel any kind of a threat, psychic or physical, contact me or Vasic, and we'll come get you."

"I will." Hugging her, he bent to pet Rabbit. "I hope you figure this out, Ivy."

"Me, too," she whispered.

Abbot waited until the teen had waved good-bye before teleporting him to his new home. Hoping he'd be safe, Ivy crossed the snow to the gathered knot of Es in the clearing in front of the cabins. She'd already told them her decision and the reason why, as well as the fact she could very well be wrong.

Now, Brigitte turned to her, a thick yellow scarf wrapped around her neck. "Our Arrows will go with us if we decide to follow your path?"

"Yes." As Vasic had pointed out, the threats they'd face wouldn't only come from the crawling rot of the infection.

"I think you're wrong in one sense," Chang said, eyebrows drawn together above narrowed eyes. "You should have an empathic partner, at least so you can test different methods."

Ivy hadn't wanted to pressure anyone by making that request, but now Jaya slipped her arm through Ivy's. "I planned to ask you if you'd mind some company." On the telepathic level, she added, *Abbot and I both believe in your theory.*

Ivy squeezed her friend's hand.

"I'm afraid," Concetta whispered, her amber eyes miserable in her heart-shaped face. "I wake up with nightmares of the oily, ugly evil, my breath choking in my throat."

"I don't think we can eliminate our awareness of the darkness." Ivy, too, had woken up slick with sweat more than once, her heart pounding so hard it was all she could hear.

"Yes, we can." Concetta wrapped her arms around herself, her wool coat a pale beige. "If we go back to sleep, go back to being normal!"

Beside her, Isaiah shoved his hands into the pockets of his jeans. "You can do that." His voice was toneless, his jaw rigid. "But it's not only the nightmares you'd be losing."

Face crumpling, Concetta raced off toward her cabin.

Jaya glanced after the other woman, a helpless expression on her face. "Shall I . . . ?"

"Leave it." Tone harsh, Isaiah resolutely didn't turn to look at where Concetta had gone. "We have to each make this decision on our own. If the Council and our families hadn't screwed us up as children, we wouldn't need to, but the bastards did fuck us up. I, for one, don't intend to be a coward hiding out in a cabin in the woods."

Ivy thought of the Eldridge book that Sascha had shared with the group. In the past, while some empaths had helped those with terrible mental illnesses, others had worked as school counselors or even in corporate offices. Es covered as wide a spectrum as any other designation.

It appeared Penn's mind had tracked the same path, because the big man stared at Isaiah, his accent heavy as he said, "Not everyone's meant to be a soldier. Doesn't mean what they have to offer isn't of value."

Shoulders tense, Isaiah didn't respond, but left a minute later. He returned with his hand holding Concetta's five minutes after that. In the end, the decision to leave the compound to head into infected zones was unanimous. It didn't take much longer to confirm partnerships. Penn ended up with Isaiah and Concetta, since Concetta was obviously not built to handle the infection directly. She'd instead focus on the victims, see if she could help ease their trauma.

"This'll be our last night together then," Chang said, after everything was settled. "I suggest we have dinner together. All of us, empaths and Arrows."

That was what they did, bringing extra chairs into the Arrow cabin. The Arrows were quiet, but no longer silent as they'd been at the start, all of them adding their thoughts to the intense discussion about possible tactics.

The Arrows' security responsibilities meant they rotated in and out, and whenever Vasic was outside, Ivy missed him until she couldn't breathe. *Jaya, Abbot, you, and I are to be stationed in New York,* she told him telepathically. *One of the others has family in Alaska and requested Anchorage.* That had originally been Ivy's intended destination.

I'll arrange apartments near the street that suffered the outbreak today.
Thank you.

It's my job, Ivy. There's no need to thank me.

Her nails pricked her palms. *Is that all I am to you? A job?*

Why would you ask me a question to which you already know the answer?

She thought of his arms around her, of the tender way he had of cradling the back of her head . . . and she allowed herself to think of the ugly thing she'd never forgotten. That the man who held her with such care had a ticking time bomb on his arm.

Ivy?

I'm mad at you, she said, panic and nausea twisting inside her. *Be quiet*.

When he rotated inside a half hour later, he attempted to catch her eye. Scared for and angry with him for having made a decision that could end them before they began, she kept her gaze stubbornly on the others. When the talk finally faded, she got up and headed to her cabin, Rabbit bounding up ahead and Vasic a silent shadow by her side.

"Don't be silly," she snapped when he went to take a watch position on the porch. "It's snowing." The sharp words dripped crimson with her own heartsblood, the sheer unfairness of the blade hanging over Vasic's neck making her want to rage and scream and throw things in useless fury.

He came into the kitchen, held up the wall while she stomped around packing up her belongings. It didn't take long, and then she could no longer avoid looking at the horrible thing on his arm, the thing that was killing him.

"If I can't undo this, will you be angry with me till the end?"

The quiet question broke her. "No," she whispered, throat raw. "I just need to be angry first." Before she sank into him, so deep that he'd leave a tattoo of himself on her cells, the memory one that would never fade.

"Would you like to go somewhere?"

She jerked up her head from where she was writing his name over and over on the counter with a fingertip. "What?"

"I'm off shift for the next six hours."

"Yes." Trying to think past the storm of anger and agony inside her, she looked down at her jeans and favorite white cowl-neck sweater, having taken off his jacket when she'd entered the cabin. "Am I dressed okay?"

"Yes." He stepped closer. "Would you like to bring Rabbit?"

God, how could this incredible man ever have thought himself so beyond redemption that he'd volunteered for an experiment that was a death sentence? Stifling the words because she didn't want to fight with him anymore, she said, "He'd enjoy the adventure." Bending down, she gathered her pet in her arms. "Ready."

"Close your eyes." A pause, his fingers rising to just barely graze her hair. "Please."

Charmed and heartbroken, she did so, felt the slight psychic shimmer of a teleport. When Vasic murmured, "Open," she lifted her lashes to find herself atop a sand dune, amidst a stunning sea of rolling sands spotlit by a huge silver moon.

A gasp escaped her, pure wonder in her blood. She'd never been anywhere near a desert except for those fleeting instants the previous night when Vasic had lost control. "It's cold!" she said as Rabbit jumped out of her arms.

"Temperatures drop steeply at night here."

Utterly mesmerized, she sat down on the fine, fine sand, while Rabbit sniffed suspiciously at the unfamiliar environment before racing down the dune. "I've never seen such an enormous moon." She could almost reach out and touch it, it sat so heavily in the sky.

Sitting down beside her, Vasic said, "I come here to think."

"I understand." It was peaceful without being barren. The silica glittered under the moonlight, a gentle breeze played with the rare clumps of grasses she could see in the distance, and the dunes threw smudged moon shadows that turned the landscape into an oil painting. "Thank you for showing me," she said, watching Rabbit chase imaginary prey below them.

They sat in silence for several minutes. It wasn't a comfortable silence, the haunting beauty of the night not enough to make Ivy forget what Vasic had done. It was stupid to feel betrayed, but she did. He should've known, should've waited for her to find him, cried a stubborn, irrational part of her.

"Are you still angry?"

Her anger crumbled. Leaning her head against his arm, she said, "I'm sorry for taking out my temper on you."

Vasic put his gauntleted arm around her shoulders. "I wish I'd met you ten years ago."

His words destroyed her, they carried such loss, such tightly held pain. What, she thought with a stab of fury, had her strong, wounded, beautiful man been forced to do in those ten years? She didn't ask, unwilling to contaminate his haven with such terrible memories. "Look," she said instead, "Rabbit's trying to climb up the dune." Her poor little dog kept sliding down, unable to figure out how to make the sand behave.

Face set in increasingly stubborn lines, Rabbit continued to try in an adorable display of will. "Come on," she said to her pet, "you can do it. You can do it, Rabbit."

And then he was scrambling up, slowly but surely. She slapped Vasic lightly on the chest. "You're helping him."

"It seems only fair since I brought him here."

Rabbit flopped down beside them seconds later, his eyes closed and tail wagging slowly as he rested from his labors. Ivy went to pet him when Vasic stood, slightly unbalancing her. She braced her hand on the sand, looked up. "Do we have to leave?"

He shook his head and came back down . . . except this time, he sat behind her, his legs on either side of her own and his chest a hard wall at her back. Wrapping his arms around her, he held her close. She didn't shy away from the gauntlet; the malfunctioning piece of technology was part of Vasic and as angry as it made her, never would she reject him in any way.

At this second, however, her focus wasn't on the hardware. Neither was it on the stunning landscape. Not with her body deliciously imprisoned by the muscled heat of his. Pulse racing as a fine sheen of perspiration broke out over her skin, she whispered, "Vasic."

His breath was hot against her neck as he leaned down . . . and then she felt his lips brushing over the place where her pulse jumped. Whimpering, she gripped at his thighs. The muscles in his forearm tightened in response, pushing up her breasts, but he didn't intensify the intimacy, didn't reach up to squeeze her needy flesh, tug at her nipples.

No, Vasic was patient. Excruciatingly patient. He explored her with an erotic attention to detail that made her squirm. But no matter how she begged and pleaded, he wouldn't allow her to turn. "I'll lose it," he said bluntly. "Let me be selfish."

"If this is you being selfish," she gasped, clenching her thighs together in a vain effort to ease the ache within, "I'll never survive your version of generous."

Ivy—another kiss—*let me.*

That was when Ivy realized she had a serious Achilles' heel when it came to negotiating with a certain Arrow. She couldn't say no to him. Shivering at the wetness as he opened his mouth as if tasting her, she melted into him and let him be as selfish as he wanted.

. . .

VASIC met Aden at dawn the next morning, deep in the woods surrounding the cabins. "The gauntlet," he said, "I need you to help me run down any possible solution, no matter how dangerous."

Aden, who'd opposed the procedure from the start, said, "I've been keeping up to date with the science since the day you volunteered. Edgard and the biofusion team have pushed their limits and are now at a dead end. The only person who might have an answer is the original inventor of the concept, but—"

"All indications are that Samuel Rain is dead." Vasic had attempted to 'port to the brilliant engineer, using his face as a lock, to no avail. The only other thing that could explain the 'port failure was a complex telepathic shield. However, given the fact that Samuel Rain had literally disappeared off the face of the planet, leaving projects half-finished when he was known to be meticulous and obsessive about his work, that was a slim possibility at best.

Now, his partner met his gaze. "After giving you the last report," Aden said, "Edgard received the cross-sectional scans of several components he hadn't considered a priority because they were designed to last a lifetime. The entire biofusion team worked through the night to recheck that data— he sent me the results twenty minutes ago."

The fact Edgard Bashir had wanted Aden to deliver the news told Vasic it would be bad even before his partner telepathed him the short report. According to it, the team had found severe and inexplicable degradation in a number of tiny internal components that interfaced the gauntlet computronics with his brain. Those pieces were why this was *bio*fusion; the connections allowed him to control the gauntlet with a thought, turning it from a grafted tool to simply another part of his body.

When the listed components fail, read the report, *it will ignite a power surge directly into his cerebral cortex. His chance of survival is zero. Should no other components degrade in the meantime, the gauntlet will cause the subject to suffer a fatal neurological event in eight weeks, factoring in a margin of error of one week on either side.*

Vasic stared out at the dawn as a cold, hard anger smashed through the numbness that only his emotions for Ivy had been able to penetrate thus far. 'Porting to the desert with Aden, he set it free in a roaring telekinetic storm that sucked the sand into violent tornados that howled across the landscape as far as the eye could see. If his mind attempted to tell him that emotion was pain, he didn't hear it, didn't feel it, the anger a consuming rage.

He didn't know how long it lasted, but when the wind fell, the landscape was no longer the same one Rabbit had played across only hours before, the dunes left in an unfamiliar pattern. Pulse slamming in his throat and eyes and mouth gritty with the fine sand, Vasic let the hot desert sun beat down on him and knew he'd keep fighting, keep searching for an answer. Never would he give up.

But . . . he wouldn't tell Ivy the truth of his current projected life span. He'd go against Judd's advice and keep a secret. He didn't want her sad and angry again, was thirsty for her smile, her soft sighs as she turned to honey under his touch. Even knowing what he was, what he'd done, she'd chosen him, allowed him to put his hands on her.

"Will you make sure she's safe after I'm gone?" Her heart would break; his loyal, beautiful Ivy who'd mourn for him.

Aden, his hair dusty from the sandstorm and his uniform the same, shot Vasic a look that was an answer in itself. The question didn't need to be asked.

"I won't forgive you," his partner said into the quiet. "Don't ask it."

Vasic accepted that. In volunteering for the gauntlet, he'd broken the trust formed between them when they'd been two scared boys who had no one else to turn to, a trust of brotherhood that said they'd fight together to the end. "I was weak," he said. "I'll be strong now."

Aden didn't look at him. "If you were weak, you'd have killed yourself years ago. It's your strength that doomed you—and your loyalty." Aden clenched his jaw so tight, the bone pushed white against his skin. "Take your chance at happiness, Vasic. Be with Ivy. It's little enough recompense for the lives you've saved."

"And the lives I've taken?"

"You gave yourself a death sentence."

Chapter 32

Reports of an oily black "nothingness" in the Net have been trickling in for weeks. Now there has been an unexplained outbreak of murderous insanity in Anchorage, followed by another in Manhattan. Something is clearly very, very wrong with the PsyNet.

PsyNet Beacon: Special Edition

HAWKE MET KALEB Krychek in the most remote section of the woods around the empathic compound. The other male wasn't dressed in his usual razor-sharp suit, but dark cargo pants, boots, and a camo-green T-shirt that exposed his arms to the cold, including an intricate tattoo of an eagle on his inner left forearm. His eyes, however, were the same. White stars on black. Cardinal and ruthless.

"Krychek," Hawke said, holding the other man's gaze.

"Hawke."

If someone had told Hawke six months ago that he'd be working in cooperation with Kaleb Krychek in any capacity, he'd have suggested the other person find a good mental health professional. But that was exactly what he was doing. Krychek had been the source that had confirmed Ming's location in Europe. More importantly, the cardinal had helped avert what could've been a catastrophic act of mass murder in San Francisco during Pure Psy's violent rampage.

"This is about Ming," Krychek said without further ado. "I'm requesting you delay your move against him."

Hawke's wolf snarled inside his chest. "The man is a threat to my mate." He folded his arms across his white T-shirt. Unlike Krychek, he wasn't a Tk, couldn't affect the air molecules around himself—his changeling body was simply far more resistant to the cold.

Now the cardinal gave a curt nod. "Understood."

Hawke knew that wasn't just a word. From everything he'd heard from Lucas, Krychek and Sahara Kyriakus were bonded in much the same way as changeling mates. "Then you know I can't delay."

"I had no intention of getting in your way—Ming is no ally of mine," Krychek said. "However, circumstances have changed."

His wolf's claws pricking against the insides of his skin, Hawke jerked his head to the trees up ahead. "Let's walk. I can't stand still and talk about that bastard."

"You've heard of the increasing instability of the Net." Krychek's movements were almost as silent as a changeling's.

"Yeah, hard not to." Hawke leaned down to run his hand through the fur of a wild wolf that had loped over to join them, its paws soundless on the snow. "You're saying Ming's death could make the situation worse?"

"The Council might no longer exist," Krychek said as they began walking again, "but Ming still has the largest personal military force of all the former Councilors. His numbers are even greater than mine, and he's doing a significant amount to maintain calm in Europe."

Hawke wanted to tear Ming apart with his bare hands for the hurt he'd caused Sienna, but he knew his mate would be the first to tell him that no vengeance was worth the life of even a single innocent. *Fuck.* "I'll discuss it with Sienna."

HAWKE ran in human form an hour after Krychek teleported out, the icy wind rippling through his hair and pasting his T-shirt to his chest. Five wild wolves ran with him, the trees sliding past in a blur of dark green and snowy white, the scent of pine thick in his nostrils as he instinctively navigated the forest that was his territory . . . as he followed the scent of autumn fire and a wild, nameless spice.

Sienna was laughing with another SnowDancer soldier when he tracked her to her sentry position on an overlook, but her head turned toward him even before he broke from the trees. It soothed the ragged edges inside him to see her, her love for him a rippling fire along the mating bond.

Exchanging greetings with the other soldier on the outlook, Hawke waited until the young male had continued on in his security sweep before opening his mouth to speak to Sienna. She beat him to it.

"What's the matter?" The cardinal starlight of her eyes scanned his face as her hands alighted on his chest. "You're tense enough to snap."

He undid the neat braid into which she'd tamed her hair.

"Hawke!" The admonition was more affectionate than sharp. "Don't lose the tie at least."

Coming into his arms after he'd freed the ruby red silk, she held him while he rubbed the side of his face against the softness, grounding himself in skin privileges with his mate. The wolf rubbed against the inside of his skin at the same time, craving her touch as much as the man. He allowed his claws to slice out of his fingers where he'd curled his hand around her nape, giving in to the animal's need enough to calm it.

Sienna didn't flinch. Closing her eyes instead, she leaned back into his hold. "Remember that night we danced in the forest?"

He growled. "You mean the night you decided to cause a riot in that damn club?" She'd been dancing on top of the bar when he arrived, dressed in fuck-you boots and jeans that might as well have been painted on, her shirt faithfully hugging every sweet feminine curve.

Rising up on tiptoe, her warm but lightweight winter jacket pressing against his chest, she nipped his chin. "I was just trying to get a certain stubborn wolf's attention." She played her fingers through his hair, petting him to calmness. "Talk to me."

And he did. Because she was his mate, who knew him to the core and who took no bullshit. "Krychek asked me to delay the strike against Ming."

Sienna narrowed her eyes as the wild wolves who'd run with him decided to prowl to the edge of the outlook. "Since we know he'd be more than happy to see Ming dead, I'm guessing it has to do with the infection Uncle Judd briefed us on?"

"Indirectly. Turns out Ming has the biggest personal military force in the Net."

"Really? I always assumed Kaleb had more offensive forces."

So had Hawke. "I guess it doesn't matter in terms of holding power when he's so damn strong himself, and when he has the cooperation of the Arrows." From what Hawke knew of them via Judd, the deadly operatives were so highly trained, each one was equal to a hundred ordinary soldiers.

"Judd," he said now, "was able to confirm what Krychek told me, that Ming's actually using his army to maintain calm in Europe." Though total panic hadn't yet set in, tensions were apparently rising at a stratospheric rate. "If we execute him, we risk throwing a large part of the continent into anarchy."

Sienna slid her arms around his waist, her fingers clenching in the back of his T-shirt. "That's the thing with Ming, you know. He's a predator, but he's not evil all the time." A twist of her lips. "I don't know if it's political self-expediency or if he actually feels responsibility for the population on some level, but he's stepped in like this before—when I was twelve, there was massive flooding in Ireland. Ming sent his troops in to distribute supplies, get the trapped out to safety."

Hawke figured Sienna was right with her first guess as to the telepath's motivations—political self-expediency. "Ming's probably doing this to strengthen his power base in Europe."

"It doesn't matter, does it?" Sienna tucked her hands under his T-shirt and against his skin. "We can't move. No vengeance or preemptive strike is worth sacrificing a single innocent life, much less hundreds of thousands."

Hawke wanted to bare his teeth, howl his defiance, but he knew his mate was right.

Rising up on her toes after shifting her hands into his hair to tug him down, she said, "It's all right, Hawke." A kiss of words, her lips soft against his. "I'm safe and Ming will keep."

He tugged her flush against his body and tumbled to his back on the snow with her sprawled over him. The wild wolves immediately flowed to sit around them, their fur brushing against his skin.

"And," Sienna added after shoving her hair out of her face and nuzzling playfully at him, "Ming isn't going to have time to come after me if he's busy in Europe."

"Yeah, but he's never going to forget the threat you pose." Sienna had bested the ex-Councilor in their last confrontation, and arrogance such as Ming's would never forgive that—even if the other man hadn't already decided that if he couldn't control Sienna and her breathtaking psychic ability, then she wouldn't be permitted to live.

Running her fingers through Hawke's hair when a snarl erupted from his throat, Sienna said, "We wait and we watch. Ming might not always be evil, but his core is rotten. He'll revert to it soon enough, and when he does, we'll be prepared to strike." There was a battle-ready light in her eyes, this woman who'd survived a monster when she'd been only a child.

He growled in pride, and gripping her nape, hauled her down for a kiss that had her moaning. He nipped and licked and played with her until she pushed at his shoulders, her breathing choppy and her lips plump, wet. "I'm on sentry duty," she admonished with a mock scowl, before escaping his hold to stand up again. "I can't have people saying I'm getting special favors because I'm the alpha's mate."

Having rolled to his feet when she did, Hawke slid his hand down to the curve of her butt, dipping his head to kiss her throat at the same time. "You can have all sorts of favors." He coaxed her into another long, deep kiss.

"We wait and we watch," he said afterward.

Ming LeBon was still marked for execution; only the date had been changed.

Chapter 33

In this chapter, I intend to focus not on the empaths, but on those who are in long-term relationships with them. As noted in the statistical breakdown on page 237, these individuals are from all walks of life. Some are in professional occupations, others in trade or in the arts. Yet my observation of these men and women leads me to state with categorical certainty that they all share a single common trait—that of being highly tactile.

Excerpted from *The Mysterious E Designation:*
Empathic Gifts & Shadows by Alice Eldridge

THE FRENETIC BUZZ of Manhattan was strange after the quiet that had been Ivy's life ever since her family's move to a rural existence in North Dakota. It took a short twenty-eight hours for her mind to reanchor, likely because she hadn't been in the compound for that long . . . or because the PsyNet knew she needed to be here. The psychic network, as they were all learning, was a living organism, albeit one none of them would ever truly understand.

Her and Vasic's apartment was on the top floor of a five-story building, the view from the windows of a busy street. Fully furnished in a clean, modern style, it had a large living area, a neat little kitchen, and two bedrooms separated by the living area. Each bedroom had its own en suite facilities.

Jaya and Abbot were in an identical apartment across the corridor, except their view was of a small park utilized by the residents in this section of the city.

The Arrows, of course, had arranged for the rest of the floor to be devoid of tenants. As for the elevator, Vasic and Abbot had rigged it so no one could accidentally or otherwise come to this floor, while the stairwell doors could only be opened via palm print.

Ivy had left her bedroom door open since they'd arrived, but Vasic hadn't touched her once after that frustrating, wonderful night in the desert when he'd taught her that her neck was an erogenous zone. At first, she'd put it down to the fact he was preoccupied with making sure the security was airtight here—she was accustomed to his protectiveness by now. It didn't annoy her; it was simply a part of Vasic.

"He can't shield me from the infection," she said to Rabbit as they stood in the living area, looking out through the window at the people passing below, scared but unaware of the insanity and death many already carried in their veins, "but he'll damn well shield me from everything else."

That protective urge, however, didn't explain the stiff distance he'd kept between them since the morning following the desert. Ivy might not know anything about intimacy except what she'd explored with Vasic—didn't *want* to learn with anyone else—but she trusted her instincts. Something was wrong, and her Arrow was holding it inside. He was so good at walling up his emotions behind icy control, but she was an empath.

It was anger she'd sensed in him the last time he'd come close. A ferocious contained storm so dark and black that it had made her stagger . . . but it didn't shock. She was angry, too.

The man she adored was dying, and there was nothing she could do.

Shoving away the jagged pain of it because she'd made a promise to herself that she wouldn't waste the time she had with Vasic on regret, she pulled on her ankle boots in preparation for their upcoming walk. The anguish wasn't so easy to exile, of course, the tight ball of it pulsing in her chest.

"Woof!"

Swallowing past the pain with a determined smile, she rubbed Rabbit's head. "Come on, we're going to explore." But for a short visit to the park behind the building so Rabbit could stretch his legs, she and Jaya had spent the previous day in psychic exploration. Now she needed to test whether she could sense the infected on the streets.

"And"—she scowled—"I think it's time I reminded my Arrow how to talk."

Getting to her feet, she rubbed her hands on the jeans she'd paired with her white sweater and a raspberry colored coat she'd brought from home and never worn because she preferred Vasic's jacket. Unfortunately, it would make her stick out here when she needed to blend in. That didn't mean she was giving it back to him.

A footstep at her bedroom door. "Are you ready?"

Ivy looked up . . . and her mouth fell open. She'd become used to seeing Vasic in his black combat uniform, hadn't really considered what he might look like in civilian clothing. The answer was that he looked luscious. "Hot," that was the word the other races used; he looked hot.

As hot as her skin at the sight of him.

Blue jeans over his combat boots, black T-shirt, a black leather-synth jacket with a high neck that he'd left open, he was . . . Ivy didn't have the words. She just knew she wanted to pounce on him.

No armor, she realized with a clenching of muscles low in her body. If she stroked her hands over his chest now, she'd be able to feel all that gorgeous, tensile muscle, the soft cotton of the T-shirt little barrier to her exploration. Especially since she could push it up, graze his abdomen with her fingertips.

"Is something wrong?" He stepped closer as Rabbit ran back from where he'd been nosing around in Vasic's room.

"No." Smiling, she stroked one hand down his jacket and thought only of hope, of an unknown future full of possible answers to the lethal question of the gauntlet. His death wasn't set in stone. So she would live with him, play with him, adore him. "You look gorgeous."

Vasic closed his hand over hers, and it was rain on her parched soul. "Civilian clothing seemed appropriate."

"Yes, very." Mouth curving at the fact he was utterly clueless of the impact of his masculine beauty, she dared brush her fingers over his shoulder just to touch him a little more. Her toes curled when he didn't protest her right to pet him . . . and the same audacious wickedness that had given her the courage to send him an erotic image, whispered another suggestion in her ear.

Heart pounding hard and urgent against her ribs, she rose on tiptoe. "Will you bend a little?"

"Why?"

She bit down on her lower lip, saw his eyes follow the action, the winter frost of his irises shaded by his lashes. It twisted her stomach into knots, the confetti and the butterflies trapped inside. "Because I asked."

A slight hesitation that almost made her want to smile, except that her blood was a surging roar in her ears, her skin prickling with a sensation she couldn't name. Then he dipped his head just enough that she could reach his mouth. Not giving herself time to lose her nerve, she curved her free hand over the warm strength of his nape and brushed her lips once, twice over his.

She didn't know how to kiss, had never before done it, but she'd seen humans and changelings kissing, had convinced herself it couldn't be too hard. It was . . . because this was Vasic, who made her neurons stop working and her body hunger. Going down flat on her feet after that slight contact that shot lightning through her body, her chest heaving, she waited, unable to meet his gaze.

When he didn't move, didn't speak, she lost her nerve at last, went to turn away.

Unyielding male fingers manacled her wrist. "Ivy, look at me."

His voice curled around her like a stroke. Taking a quick breath, she obeyed the order and felt her spirits dive. His face was drawn, his expression stark. "I did it wrong, didn't I?"

"I need to tell you something." He held her in place when she would've pulled away. "I was planning to lie to you, but I can't. Not when—"

Ivy felt her blood run cold as he cut himself off, suddenly realizing this had nothing to do with her bad kissing technique. "The gauntlet. It's worse."

Vasic didn't draw out the agonizing suspense. "Yes. Eight weeks, maybe less."

A keening cry broke from her lips. Shaking and still making that horrible sound she couldn't stop, she collapsed against his chest. His arms locked around her, one big hand cupping the back of her head. "Every Arrow in the squad is searching the Net for answers alongside me." His breath hot against her ear as she sobbed so hard, it felt as if her body were shattering like glass hit from within. "I am not giving up, not this time."

Somehow, she heard him through her anguish, heard what he was trying to tell her. Her Arrow who'd once placed no value on his life now understood that it had worth. It only made her sob harder. Vasic held her throughout, strong and warm and so breathtakingly alive that she couldn't imagine him any other way.

"Please, Ivy." He rubbed his cheek against her temple. "You are causing Rabbit distress."

Her breath hiccupped.

"And me." It was a rough murmur. "Don't cry."

His words splintered her already broken heart. She sucked in air, tried to temper her breathing. It took time, but eventually she could speak without her words fracturing, though her voice was hoarse. "Tell me the details."

Vasic gave Ivy a concise summary of the problem. He hated himself for savaging her so badly, but when she'd caressed him sweet and soft, her body open to his, he'd known he couldn't betray her with a lie, couldn't touch her on a false promise.

Now her jaw was set, her eyes red-rimmed but clear. "Together," she said. "We will handle this together—if you shut me out, I'll take a sledgehammer to the ice." Her hands fisted on his T-shirt, tugged him down. "I mean it."

No one had ever cared so passionately about him. "My fierce, courageous Ivy," he said, slipping his hand from her hair to her nape. "Will you kiss me again?"

Her lashes fluttered, her cheeks coloring, but she drew her eyebrows together in a severe vee. "Don't avoid the question."

"Was it a question?" Moving his thumb over her skin, he said, "Anything you want, you can have. I have no defenses against you."

Ivy's throat moved as she swallowed. Remembering how her skin had felt under his lips that night when he'd indulged himself so selfishly, he bent down and tasted her. Cream and salt and Ivy. He wet the flesh, sucked, felt her pulse kick.

Her pleasure intensified his, the psychological dissonance no match for the power of it. The brain was an elastic organ, and his had begun to learn that emotion wasn't the enemy. Especially when it brought with it such exquisite sensation.

"I want to explore every sensation with you," he said, taking another taste before he raised his head. "I want to crush the softness of your naked body under mine, want to learn how to touch you so you'll make tiny sounds of need, want to feel your fingers curling around my penis while I put my mouth on your nipples and suck."

Vasic's bluntly sexual statements made the place between Ivy's thighs liquid, heat uncoiling slumberously through her veins. "I"—she coughed to clear her throat, her breath shallow—"I want to do that, too. All of it."

He squeezed her nape. "Kiss me," he repeated.

Ivy licked her lips, slid her hands up to his shoulders, and confessed. "I don't know what I'm doing."

"Neither do I," he responded, the glittering silver of his eyes on her mouth. "Arrows learn by repetition and practice until the basic skill is honed, at which point we begin to specialize."

The words should've been dry, but they made her breasts swell, her nipples so plump and tight the lace of her bra became abrasive. Because he was talking about repetition and practice when it came to intimate contact. Kissing. Touching. Sex. Her lips parted and he lowered his head.

"Do it again, Ivy," he murmured, his breath mingling with her own. "Repetition—"

"And practice," she completed, and brushed her lips over his.

Again and again and again. It felt better each time. Especially since he was holding her so firmly against his body that her breasts were crushed against the hard muscle of his chest. Ivy inwardly cursed her sweater, her coat, even her bra.

Then Vasic said, "I think I understand the mechanics," and gripping her jaw with his free hand, angled her head, and placed his mouth over hers.

Her lips had been parted to ask him something—she didn't know what—and so the kiss began far more intimately than any of the others. And it only grew deeper from there. Vasic didn't hold back. No, her Arrow did as thorough a job of investigating kissing as he did of any other operation, his touch confident as he changed the angle by minute degrees to find the perfect fit.

Then he did, and it felt *wonderful*.

All hot and wet and delicious in a way she'd never imagined.

Making a needy, hungry sound, she wrapped her arms around his neck. The action made her nipples rasp against the lace of her bra, his hair raw silk in her grasp and his body a rigid wall that somehow fit perfectly against her own.

God, she liked kissing.

When Vasic broke contact, his forehead pressed against hers and his breath jagged, she caressed his cheek, kissed the clean-shaven smoothness of his jaw. Never had she felt so alive, so pleasured. But below that was a sexual hunger brutal in its ferocity, hard and dark . . . and then she knew. It wasn't her desire she was sensing. It was his.

Body melting even further, she kissed his jaw again. "I'm picking up your desire. Do you mind?"

"No." He kissed her again on the heels of that statement, one hand on her lower back, the other on the side of her neck.

Then he licked his tongue against hers.

Her brain exploded.

Ivy wasn't sure she had a rational thought in the hot, tangled minutes after that. She copied his action, found it made him crush her even closer, the hard ridges of his body digging into the softness of her own. Hot, ragged breaths, voracious mouths, strong male hands on her skin . . . Ivy became a creature of pure sensation.

It was the blare of a siren on the street that jerked them to their senses. Staring at Vasic, Ivy found the breath to say, "I want to try everything on your list." Only with her Arrow could she be this bold; only with him could she strip herself to the skin and feel utterly safe.

His hair a little tumbled from her touch, he took her hand. "We'll begin after the reconnaissance."

FIFTEEN minutes later and Ivy's heartbeat had calmed enough that she could take in the street around them. She couldn't help but feel a teensy bit smug—the first time she could recall feeling the emotion—at the glances they attracted from other women *and* the occasional man. Vasic got what she thought of as the "sigh" look, the one that indicated a melting in the bones, while Ivy was the recipient of pure narrow-eyed envy and good-natured grins that said she'd done well.

Yes, she thought, she had. And Vasic's looks had far less to do with that than the strong, loyal, courageous heart of the man hidden behind the Arrow.

Vasic wasn't the only male in the party who drew attention. Rabbit didn't like the leash he had to be on in the city, but he was well behaved, and when an elderly human lady stopped to gush over him, he took the praise as his due. Quite unlike the far larger male by Ivy's side, one who noted everything but seemed affected by none of it.

Vasic's battle readiness was a reminder that much as she wanted to pretend this was a date, as she'd read about in the novels she'd "accidentally" downloaded onto her reader back home, they were out here for a far bleaker reason.

Anchoring herself in the warmth of Vasic's hand clasped around her own, Ivy began to listen with her empathic "ear."

Tension dominated the air, understandable given what had happened in the neighboring street. Psy, human, changeling, the race didn't matter; the emotion was the same. She hadn't expected to find many changelings in such a compact city, but while they were a minority, there were enough. Of course, she was only guessing with her identification of them as changeling—but there was a wildness to their emotional scent that echoed that of Lucas Hunter.

"Do you know the species of changelings who live here?" she asked Vasic.

"Eagles are the apex predators." Releasing her hand as a large group exited out of a restaurant right in front of them, he put his own on her lower back and angled his body to take the accidental shoulder hit of one.

"Sorry!" the human male called back, before carrying on.

Tucked against Vasic's side, Ivy didn't try to keep her smile from her face—even as an influx of dark emotion battered her senses. Dread, sweat-soaked terror . . . and below that the taste of rot, of infection. A business-woman who passed them in a hurry of swift strides smelled so pungently of it that Ivy went to stop her.

Vasic caught Ivy's hand.

Chapter 34

"IT'S A DEATH sentence at present," he said when she began to argue.

Confirming it when she could offer no cure, Ivy realized, would do nothing but rob the woman of hope. And hope, cried Ivy's own bruised heart, was everything.

Tears in her throat, she turned back to continue walking and almost ran into an overalled man bearing the badge of a major comm company on his front pocket. "Oh, I'm sorry."

A curt nod at her apology and he was gone, the infection in him, too. Again and again and again, she tasted the fetid miasma of it, until her stomach began to churn. Yet when she glanced into the PsyNet, she saw nothing . . . nothing but Vasic right beside her. *Oh God.* Understanding crashed into her with the force of a freight train.

"You and Abbot"—she half turned into Vasic's body—"you're no longer safe." Arrows had been protected by default at the compound, the infection leery about approaching the heavy knot of high-Gradient empathic minds. Now, Vasic was open on multiple sides.

"Our shields are extensive. The infection has shown no signs of penetrating them."

Ivy shook her head, her hand on his gauntlet. "What about the microscopic filaments? We can't even see them!" It was horrifying to know that that ugliness could invade his brain, destroy what made him Vasic. "I need to tie my shields to yours."

We'll talk about this back at the apartment.

She brought up the subject again as soon as they walked out of the elevator door onto their floor. "You know I'm right." Having already unclipped Rabbit's leash, she dropped it onto the hallway table after Vasic entered the apartment first in order to clear it of threats.

"How can shields protect me if the infection comes in through the biofeedback link?" he asked.

She stared at his back, wide and strong. "You *knew*."

"The infection is in the Net," he said, striding over to check her bedroom, Rabbit trotting at his side. "That means we're all vulnerable to breathing in the poison if we come too close to it."

Yet he—the other Arrows—had all agreed to walk into an infection zone. And these men and women saw nothing heroic about themselves. "I can't tell you how I know," she whispered after he'd cleared his own bedroom, too, "but I *know* that linking my shield to yours will extend my immunity to you." The knowledge was a rapid stream of visuals in her head, as if she was being sent a message by a mind at once innocent and vast.

It should've scared her, but there was absolutely no harm in the sender. No, it felt like the touch of a child . . . an oddly wise one. "Vasic," she said when he didn't respond. "Let me do this." *Protect you this much at least,* she thought through the rain of tears inside her soul.

"My task is to shield you." He folded his arms. "Not the other way around."

Ivy wanted to shake him. Striding over until they stood toe-to-toe, she held the winter-frost gaze that had become the center of her existence. "You won't be able to protect me if the infection burrows into your cerebral cortex and turns you into a madman."

Vasic didn't want Ivy near his mind, didn't want to risk tainting her with the darkness that lived in him. However, he couldn't refute her point—should he become infected, he could turn on her, snuff out the luminous candle of her life. "The others should also connect to their Es." They might be separated, but he remained the leader of this unit.

"I've already telepathed Jaya." Ivy stroked her hands down the sides of his jacket.

He hadn't ever been touched as much. Raising one hand, he closed his fingers over the fragile bones of her wrist, holding her to him.

Not disputing his right to the contact, Ivy said, "We'll talk to everyone else the instant the merge is complete."

She closed her eyes, and ten heartbeats later, the flat black of his shielding became interwoven with the translucent color of hers. The increased visibility was anathema to an Arrow. Vasic would deal with it because hiding Ivy was impossible—and shouldn't be done. Any attempt to suffocate the wild beauty of an E, of *his* E, was a crime he'd punish with lethal efficiency.

He'd been handling the curious and dangerous attention she drew since the instant they relocated. He hadn't had to execute anyone yet, but he would the instant any individual posed a threat. He wasn't a good man, but she was something exceptional. He would protect her . . . till the day he died.

Unacceptable, said the grimly resolute core of him, his eyes on the gauntlet.

"Vasic?" Ivy's fingers curled into her palm. "I can feel you."

He could sense her as well, in a way that meant he'd be able to tell if she was hurt or in pain. "Good," he said, and used the technology that was killing him to send out a message to the unit about merging shields, while Ivy got on the comm and did the same with the Es.

She'd just finished the final call when he remembered something she'd seen in a shop window just before an elderly woman had stopped to admire Rabbit. "We forgot to buy the pastries you wanted to try."

Ivy blinked, laughed. "Next time."

And he wanted there to be a next and a next and a next. Cupping her face, he kissed her smile into his mouth. Her gasp was startled, her nails digging into his chest through his T-shirt a tiny bite of sensation.

Ivy's body rubbed against the hard ridge of his erection as she tried to become taller. It was, he thought with a surge of emotion in his heart that he couldn't categorize, an impossible task. She was small and perfectly formed, her curves made for his hands. When she broke the kiss to go down flat on her feet, he waited to see what she'd do.

This was an operation for which he had no training. The boundaries were unclear.

"If we keep doing that," she said a little breathlessly, "you'll get an awful crick in your neck."

"My neck isn't the part of my body that has my attention at this point."

Ivy's cheeks went bright red, her eyes dipping to his groin, then flying back up in a flustered flick. It was as if she'd gripped him in her hand, squeezed. He tightened his abdominal muscles, dead certain he was nowhere near ready to handle the feel of her slender fingers imprisoning his erection. "Should I not have said that?"

A shy look, her hands petting his chest in a way that was already familiar. "I think we should say whatever we want," she whispered, skin glowing gold as her blush faded.

Vasic decided to take her up on that. "I wasn't finished kissing you."

Her skin heated up again. "There." She pushed him gently back with her fingertips. "Sit in that armchair."

Vasic allowed himself to be nudged down and had his cooperation rewarded by Ivy's soft weight on him as she took off her coat and straddled his thighs, her knees on either side. "See?" It was a whisper.

"Very practical," he said, and slid one hand under her curls to her nape. He liked the delicate warmth of her skin there, liked how she always gave a little shiver when he surrendered to the urge to touch. But most of all he liked that the hold was perfect for gauging her reaction to his kiss.

Her pulse thudded hard and fast against his fingertips when he opened his mouth on hers, spiked when he played his tongue against hers. Vasic took note, repeated the act. Making small, impatient, feminine sounds, Ivy wrapped her arms around his neck and licked her tongue along the roof of his mouth.

Vasic's free hand clenched on her hip, his fingers brushing the curve of her backside. Firm and yielding both, it made him want to explore. He shifted his hand down, cupped one cheek, squeezed.

"Vasic." Shuddering, Ivy's head fell back, her pulse visible beneath her skin.

He put his mouth on it, sucked . . . just as something smashed to the floor. Telepathic senses having been set to an automatic security sweep, he moved with ruthless speed to lift Ivy off and shove her into the armchair out of harm's way as he stood in front of her.

There was no intruder.

There was, however, a mountain of fine sand on the carpet.

Ivy hooked her fingers into his waistband as she sat up on her knees behind him on the armchair and looked around his body. "There goes the security deposit."

He turned at the solemn statement to see her eyes sparkling. Shoulders shaking, she fell back into the armchair. Laughter escaped her in giggling bursts. Bright and beautiful and sexually addicting and *his*. No way in hell was he leaving her. No other man would ever have the right to touch Ivy Jane.

ZIE Zen was reading an old and faded note when he received a comm call from the son of his heart.

"Grandfather," Vasic said, his eyes steady and his voice calm, "I need your help."

Then, as Zie Zen listened, Vasic told him about the malfunctioning gauntlet and the death sentence he'd been given. "Amputation won't solve the problem," his great-grandson told him. "The most critical malfunctioning component is directly integrated into my brain stem."

Zie Zen thought of Vasic as he'd become in the past decade, remote and increasingly distant, as if he was already walking in the twilight lands. Zie Zen had tried to hold his great-grandson to the world and knew he had failed. Now, however, he saw that someone else had succeeded. "You fight to live," he said, something breaking inside the heart he'd walled up behind titanium shields an eon ago.

"Yes, Grandfather." Ice gray eyes met his. "I cannot leave my Ivy to the care of any other on this planet, not even Aden."

Zie Zen's hand clenched on the top of his cane, his thoughts suddenly full of a girl with sunshine in her smile who had teased him and laughed with him and left him notes all over the house.

Z^2—Eat this sandwich. I made it especially for you. xoxo Sunny

Dear Z^2, I hope you like the roses. I think men should get roses, too, don't you? Love you, Sunny

Z^2—Gone out to party till I drop with the bride. I promise not to run away with a stripper. Love, Sunny
p.s. I wouldn't say no to a private show from my man ;-)

Zie Zen, how dare you?! Samantha

That last was the note he held in his hand today. She'd been so angry that day, his magnificent Sunny. "Send me the complete file," he said to his great-grandson now. "I will find a solution for you. It is not your time to die."

His own death, he thought after the conversation ended, was coming. But not yet. Not until he'd seen this through. Then, he could finally close his eyes and see his Sunny again. She'd be angry with him for taking so long . . . and for many of the decisions he'd made, but she would love him. Always, she would love him.

As Vasic's Ivy would love his great-grandson. All Zie Zen had to do was unearth the answer to a seemingly impossible problem.

THREE hours after his conversation with his great-grandfather, Vasic was on night shift while Abbot caught some sleep, when his mind alerted him to a threat. As there were no intruders in the apartment, he checked the PsyNet.

There.

Vasic didn't warn the mind that was attempting to hack Ivy's open with brute force. He simply reached out with his own and crushed the attempt, tearing open the other man's shields in the process. *Abbot,* he said at the same time, *wake up and take over.*

I'm up, the other Arrow answered almost immediately.

Having gleaned the attacker's physical location by slamming in through his torn shields, Vasic used the image coming in through the man's visual cortex to teleport to a utilitarian room with brown carpeting. The attacker lay convulsing on the floor. Vasic came down on one knee beside the thin man in his forties and waited until he'd stopped convulsing to speak.

"Why did you attack?"

"She's an abomination." Zeal in his blue eyes, fanatical and furious, his ears and nose dripping blood. "Tainting the purity of the Net with her strange mind, like the others. They must all be destroy—" He began to convulse again, his teeth slamming together over his tongue.

Vasic used his Tk to stabilize the attacker's head as blood pulsed from the self-inflicted wound and his back arched, fists and feet pounding the carpet. When it stopped, he was dead.

Vasic contacted Aden using the mobile comm built into his gauntlet. "I shouldn't have hit his shields that hard," he said, after giving his partner the rundown on the situation. Vasic's control was legendary in the squad, but the dead male had been a threat to Ivy, Vasic's reaction arising from a primal instinct that awoke only for her. "We need to find out if he was part of a larger cell—I'll check his apartment for any physical indicators."

"I'll get our people to go through his life, track down his associates," Aden replied. "He might simply have been working on his own—we're seeing more and more incidents of people unable to cope with the fall of Silence. The Es are an easy, visible target."

"Tell me if they find anything pertinent." With that, Vasic began a meticulous and detailed search of the apartment. He discovered nothing obvious but dropped off several datapads at Central Command for further investigation before returning to New York. *I'll take over now,* he told Abbot. *Rest the full six hours. You need to recharge.*

Yes, sir.

The next voice he heard was softer, feminine . . . and one he did not want to hear while his hands were stained with death. "Vasic?"

Chapter 35

HE TURNED FROM the night-dark living room window to see Ivy in the doorway to her bedroom. Sleepy eyed, her body clad in a pair of what looked like pale pink flannel pants teamed with a strappy white top, she looked warm and vulnerable and touchable. He wanted her in his arms, wanted to sink into the softness of her.

"Go back to sleep," he said instead, his fingers curling into his palms. He hadn't used his hands to kill tonight, but he remained a killer nonetheless. That instinct had been trained into him, and it wasn't one he could ever erase. Nor would he even if he could—it was part of what made him capable of protecting Ivy.

It also put him permanently on the dark side of the line, while Ivy stood in the light.

His empath covered a yawn with one hand and rubbed her eyes with the other. "I felt something," she said, padding across the distance between them. "A pounding at my temples, but it was gone before it became truly painful."

Vasic used his Tk to nudge her slightly. "You can't be in the line of sight of the window." He'd made certain his body was angled so as not to give any assassin a target.

"Oh." Changing trajectory, she walked to stand in the corner beside him, walls at her back and side.

He couldn't keep from turning to face her, and the instant he did, he realized his mistake. The corner blocked her in, and when he shifted slightly, his body completed the shadowed, intimate cage. Ivy didn't recoil or look afraid. Her eyes no longer hazy with sleep, she touched her fingers to his jaw in that way she had—as if he was the fragile one.

"You took care of it, didn't you?"

"Yes."

Sliding her hand down his neck to his shoulder, the black fabric of his T-shirt little barrier to the lush heat of her, she said, "Did you have to kill?"

"I used too much force. Death was the outcome."

"One more death," she whispered, her eyes huge and dark. "It hurts you."

"No," he said. "I don't allow it to." Even as he spoke, he realized that the numbness that had protected him for so long was cracked in multiple places, shattered by this raw, powerful thing he felt for Ivy.

Her gaze searched his, her shoulders stiff. "Are you angry at me for it?"

The question was so unexpected that he couldn't work out what had prompted her to ask it. "No." Nothing could ever make him turn away from Ivy. "Do you sense anger?"

Ivy's gentle fingers traced his lips before she dropped her hand to his chest. "Yes. Deep and violent and so contained it's a gathering storm." She tugged him closer with her grip on his T-shirt. "And if the anger isn't directed at me, then it must be directed inward."

Vasic wasn't ready to talk about the violence inside him, might never be ready. But one thing he had to say, one choice he had to give her. "I shouldn't touch you with blood on my hands."

Lifting one of those hands with both of hers, she brought it to her cheek, turned her face into it. Her eyes were wet when her lashes lifted. "That blood is there because you protected me." A sweet, tender kiss pressed to his palm.

It stabbed him to the core. *"Ivy."* He fought not to close the final inches between them, to take the gift of her. "I've done terrible things," he told her, showing her the dark, hidden places in his soul. "I've ended the lives of innocents and erased the murders of others. I'm no knight."

Ivy's tears wet his palm. "You're mine," she said huskily, pressing two fingers to his lips when he would've spoken. "You were forced into a

certain shape by those who wanted to take advantage of your strength."
Her eyes glittered with unhidden fury as she continued to speak. "You
were drugged, and then you were betrayed by a leader you thought you
could trust. The instant you understood the truth, you began to do everything in your power to effect change."

"None of that excuses my actions." Vasic would carry the weight of
each drop of blood forever.

"No." Ivy rose on tiptoe to cup his face in both hands. "But now, *now* you
have a choice, Vasic. A real choice. What you do now is what matters."
Each word was honed in stone, her resolve absolute. "Don't you give those
who wanted to break you the satisfaction of allowing the past to hold you
back."

Shuddering, he braced himself with his palms on either side of her
head. "I can't pretend the past twenty-five years didn't exist."

"I'm not asking you to." Ivy's hands continued to hold him with near-
unbearable tenderness. "Those years will always be part of your history,
but they don't have to dictate the shape of your present or your future . . .
our future."

The words she spoke, the things she said, they made him want to
believe he could be a better man, could find redemption. Further cracks
in the numbness, the rage he'd contained for so long beginning to boil
over. He thrust it back down. Not yet. He didn't have that freedom yet,
couldn't afford to be compromised by a storm that could alter the bedrock
of how he dealt with the world.

"Vasic." Soft breath, Ivy's lips on his throat.

Fingers tightening into fists, he stood in place, his head bowed slightly
and his arms trapping her. Instead of fighting to escape, she kissed his
throat again, licked out with her tongue to taste him. It made every muscle in his body go tight, the tattered vestiges of the psychological brainwashing he'd survived attempting to overlay the pleasure with pain, but
he didn't move.

"Vasic," she whispered again, her kiss damp this time, the sensation
going straight to his rock-hard erection. "My Vasic."

No one had ever claimed him so completely. Enslaved, he wanted to bend his mouth to her skin, lick her up as she was doing him. But this . . . being adored by her, it was an addiction that kept him in place. "Stop," he forced himself to say, when he wanted the opposite. "I'm on watch. I can't be distracted." And he hadn't yet worked out how to control his teleporting when she put her hands on him.

A last, lingering kiss. "Good night."

"Good night."

Her lips curved. "You have to let me out."

He didn't move. "Don't go," he said, and it was the first time since his father had abandoned him that he'd asked anyone to stay with him.

Ivy's smile lit up the room. "Why don't I make us some coffee, and you can teach me how to keep watch like an Arrow?"

Shifting one hand down to the thin strap of her top, he tugged it, only his nail brushing her skin. "Did you get this in the township by the orchard?" It was delicate and lacy and not the least bit sensible.

"I ordered it from a catalogue," she whispered, as if confessing a secret. "I have a very bad habit of buying impractical items simply for the sensual pleasure of it." Nuzzling him, she said, "My favorite texture is that of your hand against my skin."

He closed his fingers around her nape, squeezed in a silent reprimand that had her laughing, the sound a quiet intimacy as she slid her arms around his waist and pressed a kiss to his chest. It was a perfect moment, one he wished he could encapsulate and live in forever. But time, he thought, his eyes landing on the gauntlet, continued its relentless march forward. It wouldn't stop for a disintegrating PsyNet, nor would it halt for an Arrow who had finally found a beautiful reason to live.

THE first major wave of protest marches took place in New York, Shanghai, and Jakarta, with more scheduled in Berlin and other world cities in the coming days.

Kaleb watched the news feeds from all three cities in his home study, taking in the banners that advocated a return to Silence, each emblazoned with the logo of Silent Voices. Unlike the small knot of placard-waving malcontents outside his Moscow office, hundreds marched in these groups, professional signs strung out between them.

His first instinct remained to crush and eliminate what he saw as a threat, but Sahara, her hand on his shoulder as she leaned over his chair to look at the feeds, had a different view. "Under eight hundred people," she said, her breath soft against his temple. "And that's across three huge cities. Their numbers are minuscule, but it's good the dissent is out in the open. Our people have festered in the darkness too long."

"Silent Voices isn't dissent—it's a symptom of the mind-set that paralyzes so many in the populace," he said, the truth a pitiless one.

"You're right." She wriggled into his lap, her legs hanging over the arm of his executive chair. "But we're attempting to change the course of an entire race. It's going to be chaotic and messy, and people will make mistakes."

Kaleb ran one hand down her thigh, his other arm around her waist. On the feeds, the protestors continued to chant, continued to irritate, but he ignored that to focus on the people on the sidewalks where the marches were taking place. Humans and changelings looked on curiously, but he also picked up faces that were clearly Psy. No one was joining in.

That would alter, he thought, as fear crippled more and more. But change had begun, and it was inevitable, as evidenced by the color-washed minds that had begun to appear in the Net. Silent Voices might want to erase that color, but many others looked on with wonder, astonished that such beauty could be born in the stark cold that had always been the psychic plane.

Kaleb fell into neither category. He was interested only in what the empaths could do to curb the infection—if those of the E designation could do anything at all. "I can only give the Es another two weeks at most." Then he'd have to begin to carve the Net into countless pieces.

Sahara's exhale was shaky. "There's still no way to detect the fine tendrils of infection?"

"No."

"But," Sahara said, her mind seeing what his already had, "if the Net is in pieces, there's a higher chance at least some parts of it will stay clean, survive." Where now the infection could crawl unchecked across every inch of the psychic fabric that connected their race.

"Have you considered a mass defection from the PsyNet?" Sahara asked, playing with the lapis lazuli pebble he'd had on his desk. "Everyone could drop out, create a new network, start fresh."

"We'd take the infection with us." A large number of people already carried the disease in their brain cells. "A small group, however, one made up of those immune to the infection and those who share their immunity, could work."

Sahara sucked in a breath. "Arrows and empaths," she said, the dark blue of her eyes vivid with realization. "Have you told them?"

"No. Everything I've observed about designation E tells me they won't go voluntarily. I'll tell the Arrows when necessary, and they'll force the Es out." Kaleb had noticed how protective the squad had become of the empaths, and it was a relationship he'd use without compunction to get what he wanted.

Sahara's fingers wove through his hair, her smile lopsided. "And will you do the same to me, Kaleb?"

"No—I'll make sure we're in the piece of the Net that holds your father." Parental love was a concept with which Kaleb had no personal experience, but he had no doubt that Leon Kyriakus loved his only daughter.

Never, not once in seven long years, had the older man given up hope of his lost daughter's return. For that, he had Kaleb's respect. "I will do everything in my power to keep him safe." Because Sahara's heart would shatter if her father died, and Kaleb would never permit that to happen.

Eyes wet, the woman who was Kaleb's own heart locked her arms around his neck and held on tight. "I hope," she whispered a long time later, as she lay curled up against him, "it doesn't come to that. I hope the Es find their wings and fly."

Chapter 36

To be an empath is to understand pain in all its myriad facets.

Excerpted from *The Mysterious E Designation: Empathic Gifts & Shadows* by Alice Eldridge

IVY WATCHED THE final part of the protest from the sidewalk outside the apartment, surprised it had been permitted to take place. She heard the same hushed astonishment from the others around her. Everyone—human, changeling, and Psy—had expected Kaleb Krychek to ruthlessly crush any hint of rebellion.

There had been so much fear in the protestors that Ivy's nerve endings were raw from sensing it, yet they'd exposed themselves with a courage she had to admire, even if their objective were at odds with her very existence.

"Do you think Kaleb will quietly execute them now that he knows who they are?" she asked Vasic.

Her Arrow, steely eyes continuing to scan the street as the crowd began to thin, took time to answer. "Krychek is no longer predictable in any sense because we can't predict Sahara Kyriakus. Her motives and views remain unknown."

"Have you seen their bond?" Ivy hadn't dared go close to it yet, but she'd heard the rumors, had trouble believing the deadly man she'd met would ever willingly tie himself to another: love, after all, was a soul-deep vulnerability.

"Yes. It's . . ." A shake of his head, the silken black strands of his hair gleaming in the midmorning sunlight. "You'll have to see it for yourself."

He touched her lower back when a passing male smiled at her. "I'll take you to it."

Delighted by his touch, by the quiet but unmistakable display of possessiveness, she said, "He doesn't shield it from view?"

"No, though getting close isn't recommended." A speaking glance. "Especially for too-curious empaths."

Ivy felt her stomach somersault, her breath catch. He kept doing that to her. Right when she thought she was used to the sheer potent masculinity of him, he'd look at her with those eyes of stunning winter frost, and she'd remember the things they'd done together, the things they planned to do.

Ivy. It was a gentle admonishment, the ice of his voice a shivering caress inside her. *You can't look at me like that on a public street.*

Flushing, she ducked her head. "I can't help it. You're—" Ivy froze, every tiny hair on her body rising to prickling alarm.

She turned on her heel, stared down the street.

"What do you sense?" Vasic asked, his jacked-up vigilance intense.

"It's happening." Her voice shook, blood curdling at the shriek of violent insanity surging to the surface about ten feet away. It was as if a line had been drawn in the sand. Those anchored beyond the line would go viciously insane, those on this side would be fine.

Ivy!

She jerked at the telepathic cry. *Jaya, where are you?*

In the apartment. I can feel it, Ivy, feel their twisted confusion, their compulsion to bludgeon and murder.

Ivy heard the first scream on the heels of Jaya's words, and all at once, a panicked horde ran wild-eyed in their direction. Bags were dropped, datapads abandoned, designer heels left on the tarmac. Ivy knew what she'd find behind the living mass of terror, but it was still a kick to the gut to see the infected armed with knives, blunt weapons, hands fashioned into claws. Blood rushed to burn Ivy's skin, her own terror visceral . . . but this was the battle for which she'd been born.

She didn't shrink from it, didn't run.

Vasic took position in front of her and slightly to her right. *Can you see?* he asked as he began to shove back the insane so the uninfected could escape.

Yes. Chaos continued to reign around them, but what Ivy saw within it gave her hope even in this darkness.

Screaming, crying children were scooped up by strangers when they stumbled, a frail older man was lifted up in the arms of a burly construction worker, two teenagers—a boy and a girl—stopped to haul a businessman to his feet when he fell, while a third grabbed the hand of a woman who'd gone motionless in shock and hauled her forward out of danger.

The teen looked at Ivy as he ran past, the whites of his eyes showing. "Run, lady! Those people are fucking out of it!"

"I'm fine!" Ivy cried out. "Go!" She took hold of the back of Vasic's leather-synth jacket with one hand to make sure they wouldn't be separated as more and more people streamed past.

Blocking out the hysteria using the shielding techniques Sascha had taught her, though she couldn't do the same with the chilling screams that filled the air, Ivy took a deep breath and reached out with her mind. But when she attempted to grab hold of the infected so she could calm them, her ability simply slid off, like water off slick plas. *Jaya, can you reach them?*

No, but I'll keep trying.

Ivy did the same, but as horrific violence broke out on the street, a number of uninfected caught in the midst of the carnage, she knew neither one of them was having any effect. "Go." She pushed at Vasic's back. "Go, help! You're more use than I am!"

He didn't budge an inch. "I won't leave you unprotected."

"I'll go inside that shop," she said, the grocer wide-eyed beyond the window. The elderly man, his hair snow-white against his mahogany skin, had locked the door, but when Ivy caught his attention, he motioned for her to come inside. "I'll be safe." While others died around her.

The bitter knowledge of her uselessness was bile in Ivy's throat.

"I thought you said never to give up."

Vasic's words might as well have been bullets, they wounded so much.

"I don't know *what to do*!" All her plans, her ideas, and she had no practical knowledge of how to put them into effect. "There's no manual, no training! Even Sascha—" Her mind cleared for a single, piercing instant. "Wait, wait."

Shuddering, she thought of the chapter in the Eldridge book that spoke of empaths controlling crowds, of the experiments Sascha had done with volunteers from her pack. Ivy had nowhere near the cardinal E's level of expertise, but what did she have to lose? She used Vasic as a focus and visualized the apple orchard in spring behind her closed eyelids, the bright green trees, the endless sky, the crisp, clean air.

Her mind rippled, settled, a tranquil sea.

Exhaling, she sent that feeling outward, as if she was snapping out a sheet to dry. She didn't know what she'd expected, but it wasn't what she saw in front of her. The infected looked up at the sky, and then, one by one, began to sit down.

It was beautiful and perfect, her body and mind flawlessly integrated into the empath she'd been born to be . . . for the ten seconds it lasted.

Ivy cried out as a vicious blade of pain rent the peace, sending blood dripping out of her nose and her body to her knees.

Screams filled the air once again, followed by the dull, wet thud of weapons and fists meeting unprotected flesh. Her vision blurred from the pulsing agony in her frontal lobe, Ivy tried to push up off the sidewalk so she could try again, but she was in the living room of their apartment the next instant, Rabbit beside her.

Vasic was gone almost before she realized what he'd done.

"Ivy!" Jaya ran in through the door short seconds later, and Ivy knew Vasic must've 'pathed her. Ducking into Ivy's bedroom, the younger woman returned with a small box of tissues and knelt down beside her. "What did you do?" Wonder in her intense, dark eyes. "It worked!"

Coughing, her chest filled with crushed rocks, Ivy leaned back against the wall and used the tissues to clean herself up. "Abbot?" It came out gritty, as if she'd been screaming.

"He's helping Vasic, can be back here in a heartbeat if we need him."

Jaya stroked back Ivy's hair. "It was perfect, Ivy, your peace." Her eyes sheened wet. "I wanted to wrap it around myself like a blanket and just sleep, content and happy."

Glass shattered outside, a car alarm went off. Rabbit barked and ran to jump up on the wide windowsill at agitated speed. He wanted to be out there, wanted to be with Vasic. So did Ivy, but right now she was a liability. Vasic couldn't help the uninfected if he was concentrating on shielding her.

Curling her hand into a fist, Ivy focused on Jaya. "It was too short." Disappointment was a leaden weight in her gut, though Sascha, too, had reported being unable to "control" her volunteer crowd for anything beyond a highly limited period.

"It's a start." Jaya sat back on her heels, her twin braids lying neat and tidy on her heavy green sweater. "Show me what you did. Maybe I can give Vasic and Abbot a little help."

The other woman walked to look out the window after Ivy shared her process. Placing her hand on Rabbit's neck, Jaya stroked him gently as she spoke. "It's bad. Abbot says he and Vasic have managed to get most of the uninfected out," she said, her lilting accent intensified by the stress of the situation, "but the infected are turning on one another."

Ivy's stomach knotted.

"Oh, my God." Jaya pressed her face to the glass. "There's a child wandering in the street! I don't think anyone's seen her!"

Now, Jaya, Ivy said urgently, alerting Vasic to the presence of the child at the same time.

Both hands dropping to grip the window ledge, Jaya stared down at the street. The peace lasted three short seconds, but it was enough to save the child's life.

I have her, Ivy.

Crawling over to Jaya's crumpled form as Vasic's voice touched her mind, Ivy checked the younger woman's pulse. It was thready but present beneath the clammy stickiness of her skin. *Jaya?* Using fresh tissues to soak up the blood trickling out of one of her friend's ears, she continued to try to wake her, deeply worried by the abruptness of her collapse. *Jaya, sweetheart, wake up.*

It took over five minutes for the other empath to rouse, her eyes cloudy with pain when she did so. "Why did I collapse so fast?" were the first words she spoke.

"I don't know." The Gradient difference between them was a mere .5, Jaya at 8.8. "Did you feel anything before you collapsed?"

"It was like my mind just shut down," she said, as Ivy pulled herself to the window. However, when she tried to assist Vasic with a particularly virulent knot of fighting, she couldn't even muster a single pulse of empathic power. Her mind was fried.

Jaya hauled herself up beside Ivy. "My God, Ivy." The helpless horror in the other empath's whispered exclamation echoed Ivy's own feelings.

Sirens pierced the air now, shots were fired. One woman fell the second after she sank her teeth into another woman's jugular, blood painting her face in a macabre red mask.

Ivy knew from Vasic that Kaleb Krychek's office had sent out instructions to all first responders on how best to deal with an outbreak should there be no or limited psychic assistance available, but the responders had clearly had no time to internalize those processes.

It was . . . bad.

By the time it ended, seventy-five people lay dead on the street, with fifty-one others critically injured. One hundred had been or would soon be placed into induced comas from which they would never awaken, the infection eating away at their brain. Allowing them to remain conscious was not an option—not only were the infected viciously violent, hurting themselves and others, the infection progressed at an accelerated pace in those who were awake and aware. A coma, at least, gave them a slightly higher chance of surviving long enough for a cure to be discovered.

Deciding to leave Rabbit safe in the apartment, Ivy and a still-hurting Jaya went down to sit on the top step of their apartment building, the street littered with blood and debris in front of them. Numb, her psychic senses dulled to fog, Ivy stared. The authorities had cordoned off the area, but it was simply too big to keep that way for long, and already some of the yellow caution tape was flapping in the wind.

"I thought I was ready but this . . ." Jaya hugged her arms around her knees. "Are we fooling ourselves that we have the ability to halt this?"

Ivy didn't have an answer, all her hopes of helping to save her people in ashes at her feet. Vasic, Abbot, the cops, and firemen, even the strangers who'd stopped to assist the vulnerable, they'd done *something*. While Ivy had collapsed after ten seconds. Incredible as those ten seconds had been, they would never win this gruesome war.

Unable to comprehend the scale of the death in front of her, she watched Vasic walk through the street to another Arrow. With his razorstraight black hair, slanted eyes, angular bone structure, and a more slender but still muscular build, she recognized Aden at once. He was a medic, she remembered. Of course he'd be here. Right now, he was using a handheld scanner to examine one of the dead.

Vasic crouched down beside his friend.

And she remembered how long Vasic had been fighting, how long he'd been walking in the darkness. "We should go check the bodies." Giving up was simply not an option, even if she felt bruised black-and-blue by her spectacular failure, her faith in her ability a hollow shell. If she did quit, then Vasic would have to do this over and over and over.

No, she thought, *just no.*

Her Arrow had earned a life that wasn't drenched always in blood and death, and if she had to try and try and try again until she figured out how to fix this so he wouldn't have to step back into the shadows, that was what she'd do.

When Jaya didn't rise with her, she reached down to squeeze her friend's shoulder. "There might be something we sense that they can't."

"What's the point?" Jaya's tone was flat, her face drawn. "They're dead. They're all dead."

"Hey"—Ivy changed position to stroke sweat-damp tendrils of hair off the other woman's elegant, lovely face—"you said it yourself; we did help, even if it was only a little." The reminder was as much for herself as for Jaya. "It's a start."

The younger empath didn't respond but followed when Ivy headed down the steps. A uniformed member of Enforcement would've stopped them from crossing the yellow tape, but Aden waved them in.

Skirting the blood that splattered the road, Ivy went to where Vasic and Aden hunkered beside the body. "Why this one?" she asked, not ready to look at the victim.

Aden was the one who responded, though Vasic curled his hand around her calf in an unexpected and welcome expression of support. A single contact, and already she felt more steady, despite the continued opacity of the fog in her brain.

"Her skull is still whole." It was a statement pitiless in its practicality. "She was stabbed through the gut and collapsed slowly rather than falling, so her brain wasn't damaged by a blunt-force collision with the ground. An examination of the tissue may give us more detailed answers as to the progression of the disease."

"I-I ca—" Sobbing into her hand, Jaya ran back the way they'd come, Abbot heading after her.

Ivy wanted to escape the carnage, too, but she focused on Vasic's touch, tensed her stomach muscles, and forced her eyes to what remained of a woman who appeared to have been in her early sixties. Her black winter coat was open, revealing a dress of simple blue wool over tights. It was rucked up around her knees and bloody and torn at her abdomen; the skin of her face was marked by deep gouges that said someone had come at her with their bare hands.

"Are you sure she was one of the infected?"

Vasic squeezed her calf. "Yes. I saw her while she was alive." *You're feeling better?*

It was all she could do not to throw herself in his arms and burrow into his strength. *Yes. Jaya had a much more debilitating response—I think she's still in quite severe pain.* Crouching down between the two men, she touched her fingers to either side of the woman's head, though she didn't hold much hope of sensing anything.

The dead, after all, didn't feel.

And yet . . . "I can *almost* sense something," she said, trying to push through the blank wall of nothingness.

Strong hands clamping on her wrists, jerking her away without warning. "You're bleeding again," Vasic said, touching the pad of one thumb to below her ear. It came away dark red.

A rustle sounded from behind Ivy at the same instant.

"Sorry for before." Jaya came down beside her on that husky whisper, her blue-eyed Arrow standing watch at her back. "I felt her death agonies, her confusion and shock, and it was like I was dying."

Biting back her questions, Ivy shifted to create some space, Aden steadying her with a hand on her back when she might've become unbalanced.

Beside her, Jaya tugged down the woman's dress with gentle hands, tears rolling down her cheeks. "She suffered terribly at the end." A statement so hoarse, it was barely recognizable as Jaya's voice. "The echoes of it are trapped in her brain, and the pain, it wasn't just from the stab wound, but from the horror inside her mind."

Ivy held her breath, unwilling to break the other empath's concentration.

"The darkness was trying to become part of her," the younger woman said. "But it didn't fit. There was no place for it, so it stole space, and it broke her." She fell back into a sitting position in a jerky move, sobbing into her hands. "It hurts to die from the infection. It *hurts* so much."

Chapter 37

My dear, gorgeous, scary smart Z²—I love you and will into eternity. I know you know that, but I wanted to write it down. Things . . . they're changing so much, and I never ever want you to wonder. Silence might quiet the whole world, but it will never quiet this heart that beats only for you.

And Z, promise me this—even if something bad happens, even if we're separated for some reason, you'll continue to fight for our people. We are better than this fearful cowardice, and I know you have the courage to show others that truth.

I'm sorry for sounding so melodramatic, but I just have a bad feeling deep inside me. It's so cold, my love.

You'll probably find this in the morning and tease me mercilessly for my theatrics, but for now, I'm going back to bed and to your arms. I intend to think up some brilliant rejoinders to the inevitable teasing as I warm myself against you. Perhaps I'll be terrible and wake you for a kiss, though I know you're tired, my strong, fearless Z.

I could watch you forever as you sleep, your lashes shadowing your cheekbones (it really is unfair that you have such beautiful ones you know), and your lips relaxed as they never are in life. I am definitely going to wake you.

—Your Sunny

ZIE ZEN HAD lived a long lifetime, and in that lifetime, he'd met countless people. Many of those people owed him favors. Some he'd never collect, his actions not undertaken for any personal gain, but because those actions spoke to the part of him that was and would always belong to Sunny.

Ashaya Aleine was one of the people he'd helped in Sunny's name. The gifted neuroscientist was also a trusted friend, despite the wide difference in their ages, and so he'd spoken to her about his great-grandson. "Can you or Amara do anything about the gauntlet?" he asked her over the comm now. Ashaya's twin was a true sociopath but for one thing—she loved Ashaya. For Ashaya alone, Amara would put her brilliant, broken mind to work on this complex problem.

Ashaya went as if to thrust a hand through her hair, then seemed to realize the electric mass was in a neat knot at the nape of her neck. She dropped the hand to her side, her forehead lined in thought and her distinctive blue-gray eyes striking against the deep brown of her skin. She'd never been so expressive when he'd known her in the Net.

"We've done a detailed first pass through the data you sent us last night," she said. "The technology is highly experimental." Folding her arms across a cardigan of pale gray, she shook her head. "It's a stunning construct on one level but lethal on another—even Amara admits we'll certainly kill Vasic if we attempt to remove it, and you know the razor-thin safety margins within which she operates."

Zie Zen heard pained frustration in her tone. "Every fragment of data will assist," he told this woman who had no genetic connection to him, but who he trusted more than any of his blood aside from Vasic. "Send through any and all information or theories you collect as you continue to explore possibilities."

Ashaya didn't argue with his request. "You're worried you'll need to move in an emergency situation."

"It's a ticking time bomb." Fused to the body of a son who should've had a century more of life to live.

"I'll forward you everything we have to this point and set up an automatic forward for any new material," Ashaya said, open compassion in her gaze. "I'm sorry. I never realized how much he meant to you."

"I did not allow anyone to realize. It was better that way." Permitting them both to work in the shadows with no one aware that they were two sides of the same coin, one older, one younger. "And you, Ashaya? Are you well?"

"Oh, yes." A deep poignancy to her expression, she said, "I sometimes feel as if I've been given too many gifts."

"You've earned every one." She'd saved the Psy race from the slavery of a hive mind, helped the humans develop a covert technology that appeared to protect them against psychic coercion, but most important of all, she'd fought for a child's right to live.

Ashaya went to respond when there was a sound offscreen, and she turned, her face wreathed in a smile so vibrant, it held purest joy. "Keenan, come here. Grandpa Zen is on the comm." Reaching down, she lifted her son into her arms, the boy's eyes the same distinctive blue-gray as Ashaya's, his skin the color of aged gold.

Keenan leaned forward excitedly. "Hi, Grandpa Zen!"

Zie Zen was listed as Keenan's father on this extraordinary child's birth certificate, but that was a fiction meant to preserve Keenan's life. Now, the boy had a real father in the leopard changeling who'd mated with Ashaya. Zie Zen had kept an eye on the family unit from afar, seen photographs of the changeling playing with Keenan—the dominant male, who was a gifted sniper, treated Keenan with the same discipline and affection as if the boy was his own natural cub.

Keenan's open smile, his hand pressed to the screen of the comm, was another reassurance that he was in good hands. Zie Zen caught not even a hint of the strained pain and fear that had so often been in his eyes at the start of his life. "Hello, Grandson," he said. "What are your plans for this day?"

"We're going to study the alphabet!" he cried, before lowering his voice. "I already know it, but some of my friends don't, so I help them."

"That is a good thing, Keenan." The boy, Zie Zen thought, was showing every sign that he'd one day become a strong, honorable man. And unlike another child Zie Zen had once known, he was being given the chance to grow into himself in an environment where that honor and strength would be nurtured rather than abused.

Zie Zen had often wondered what would've happened had he simply stepped in and removed Vasic from the Arrow training program. At the time, he hadn't done so because even he hadn't been immune to the deadly power of the Council, and to show his hand in such a way would have jeopardized a thousand other lives. So he'd made the ruthless decision to sacrifice one small boy for the good of many.

Vasic did not blame Zie Zen for his choice, but then, Vasic did not expect anything from anyone, even from the one person he accepted as family. The matter of the gauntlet was the only time he had ever asked for Zie Zen's help, even as he laid his own skills at Zie Zen's disposal.

"Why don't you recite the alphabet to me?" he said now to Keenan, knowing he would have to beg forgiveness for his crimes from Sunny when he crossed the threshold of this world, for she would've never made the same choice.

Each life, every life, is important. Even this incredibly terrifying insect with way too many legs. Take it outside, Z. Don't squash it!

Keenan's young voice intersected with the memory of Sunny's. The boy ran through the entire alphabet without hesitation, complete with examples for each letter. A smile of pride on her face, Ashaya cuddled her son before Keenan scrambled away with a cheerful good-bye.

"He's extremely intelligent," she said. "Far beyond his age level." In her face was the knowledge that Keenan's DNA held myriad secrets. "But he doesn't want to skip anything, wants to attend the same classes as all his friends."

"It is a happy thing for a child. To have friends." Vasic had only ever had one, but sometimes one was all that was needed to maintain a hold on reality, on the world. "You can always work with his teachers to make sure he has more challenging assignments as he matures."

"I'm already in touch with them," Ashaya said, before her lips curved. "And I wouldn't have him miss anything, either—I want him to be a child, to grow up at his own pace. He does finger painting and loves it just as much as any other child. And yesterday, he joined a cubs and pups baseball team that'll start practicing come spring. Dorian's coaching."

Zie Zen saw the softening in her expression as she spoke her mate's name, and he didn't admonish her for that tenderness of feeling. He'd once seen the same expression on his own face in the mirror, and he knew it did not weaken but rather, made one strong. He wanted to see the same on Vasic's face, wanted him to have the chance to grow into the love that had rooted itself in his heart.

I could not save the child, Sunny, he told the woman who had lived in his own heart through all the cold, lonely decades. *But I will save the man. I promise you this.*

Chapter 38

An Arrow trusts no one but another member of the squad. Any Arrow who breaches this rule must be placed under immediate probation and given corrective training.

First Code of Arrows

AN HOUR AFTER Jaya's unexpected, pained reaction on the street, the tall, elegant woman lay curled up on Ivy's bed. "I'm different from you."

"Yes." Sitting down beside her, Ivy stroked the lustrous hair Jaya had released from her braids. "That must be why you collapsed when you tried to calm the crowd. Your tolerance for that type of empathic act is lower than mine." Because, as had already become clear, empaths weren't all the same. "But I couldn't even penetrate the victim's mind. You saw everything."

"What use is it?" Jaya grasped a fistful of the sheet, crushed it, released the wrinked fabric, then repeated her actions. "To read the emotions of the dead?"

"Maybe it's not about the dead," Ivy said, having had a chance to consider it. "Remember that bit in the Eldridge book about the impact on Es of long-term critical-care work? We all assumed it had to do with conscious patients, but what if she was talking about—"

"People in comas." Jaya sat up, twisting to face Ivy, her pupils huge.

"Or those otherwise trapped in their bodies." Wonder burst inside Ivy at the miracle of Jaya's gift.

"I have to know." Jaya's hand shook as she thrust it through her hair. "I have to know, Ivy."

Ivy nodded—if Jaya did have the ability to help people trapped within their own minds, they couldn't waste a single minute in confirming it. "The nearest hospital isn't too far. We can walk." Ivy paused, considered the logistics. "We should probably have an escort though." Confirmed Es continued to be the targets of attempted violence and simmering unrest. "I'll ask Vasic."

Aden will go with you, he said in response to her telepathic query, and that was when she understood just how much he trusted the other Arrow. *There may be further outbreaks—Abbot and I should remain close to the scene.*

The ice in his tone was somehow harder, edgier. Ivy wished she could hold him, remind him that life wasn't only horror and pain. *We'll be down in a few minutes,* she said, as Jaya rose and motioned that she was going to get her coat.

No, Vasic replied. *Wait for Aden to reach you.*

All right. Going with instinct, Ivy blew him a telepathic kiss, unsure if he'd understand the message that held no words.

You have a bad habit of distracting me, Ivy Jane.

Ivy shivered, then smiled, because while the ice remained, it now held an undertone of tenderness she didn't think her Arrow was aware of, but that she heard often when he spoke to her. *I'll behave . . . for now. Take care of yourself—I'll be really, really angry if you get hurt.*

I would never disobey your orders.

Heart aching, she decided that, somehow, today hadn't done the damage she'd feared. Her Vasic was still her Vasic. It was difficult not to continue speaking to him, but he was right; he had to concentrate—and she had to put on her own coat and shoes.

"I'm sorry, Rabbit, but you have to stay here," she said to her pet when he jumped up at the sign that she was going out. "I have to go inside the hospital with Jaya, and I don't want to leave you tied up outside." She rubbed his furry head. "What would I do if someone stole you, hmm?"

Her dog didn't look impressed with that, but hopped up on his haunches on the sunny windowsill, eyes on the activity outside.

Vasic, she said on her way out, *I'm leaving Rabbit here. Could you or Abbot check in on him if we're gone long?*

Vasic didn't tell her he had far more important things to do. Instead, he said, *I'll pick him up once we've cleared all the buildings of threats. He can help me keep watch.*

He melted her from the inside out, her dangerous, beautiful Arrow, made her veins fill with a joy so incandescent, it was captured sunshine. *I adore you.*

Tell me again when we're alone.

IVY was still a little breathless from the rough sexual promise inherent in Vasic's last words when she walked into the hospital with Aden and Jaya. She didn't know what Aden said to the nurse in charge of the ward in question, but the trim Hispanic woman didn't dispute their right to be there.

In fact, she led them to a young male in a state-of-the-art monitoring bed. Though he was free of wires, his vital functions monitored by the bed itself and accessible through the panel at the end, he had at least three tubes feeding in and out of his body.

From what Ivy could see of his face and shoulders, his pallid white skin was clear of cuts and bruises.

"Vehicle accident resulting in severe head trauma," the nurse said, a subtle wildness to her emotional resonance that told Ivy she was changeling. "We've done all we can, but he's been in a coma for the past eight weeks."

That explained the lack of visible injuries.

"He's human," the nurse added. "That make a difference?"

"No, I don't think so." Jaya's shoulders rose then fell as she inhaled slowly, exhaled as slowly. "Is it all right if I touch him?"

"I'll monitor his vitals in case he has an adverse reaction."

Standing near the doorway with Aden while Jaya took a seat in the chair beside the bed, Ivy found herself examining him. At about five feet nine inches, he wasn't as tall as Vasic, and his features were Asian to Vasic's Slavic, but the two Arrows were cut from the same template regardless. Military bearing, eyes that saw everything, a face that gave nothing away.

"May I ask you a question?" she said softly, one eye on Jaya as the other empath placed her hand on the patient's forehead with conscious gentleness.

Aden nodded. *Telepathing will be easier if you don't wish to be overheard. Thank you. It's about Vasic.*

Aden's dark eyes—so rich a brown they were near black—held hers. *I know.*

I want to ask you to tell me the things he never will. Her Arrow was too protective, too uncaring of his own pain. *Teach me what I need to know.* Vasic and Aden were blood brothers, intertwined on a level that made them as close as twins. She couldn't get to know one without the cooperation of the other.

Aden was quiet for a long time. *I've lost him, too,* he said at last. *He's been walking toward the abyss since the first time he was injected with Jax and forced to take a life. I watched it happen, and I couldn't stop it.*

Nothing in his voice or his expression betrayed any hint of pain, but Ivy knew Arrows now. These men and women were too strong and too intelligent not to have the capacity to feel with wild fury. *You helped him stay stable.*

No, Ivy. I made sure he didn't go over the final edge, but that isn't enough. He maintained the intensity of the eye contact as he continued. *Deep within, Vasic doesn't believe he has the right to have a life. Do you understand?*

Pain stabbed the backs of her eyes at the confirmation of what she'd already suspected. *Yes. I've told him the future is his to make, that he can choose the path he takes.*

Aden put his hands behind his back, the fingers of one clasping the wrist of the other. *He may appear to accept that on the surface, but the wounds go deep. He's lived in his personal purgatory for years. You can't be complacent.*

I won't, she said, jaw tight. *I think if the ones who used him and hurt him stood in front of me, I'd happily forget I was an empath and do them serious damage.*

You'd have to wait your turn.

Ivy looked up at that lethally cold statement, her gaze on the clean angle of his profile. *Do you mind? That I'm trying to get him to bond with me?*

Even were you Nikita Duncan, Aden said, *I'd back you with every cell in my body, so long as you promised to haul Vasic into life.* A pause. *An empath though . . . he needs softness and kindness and care on the deepest level. And he needs it from someone strong enough to care for him even when the return seems negligible.* Again he turned to her. *Do you have that courage?*

The answer was easy. *It's never negligible, Aden. Vasic speaks with his eyes, with his touch, with the way he cares so deeply and truly that I've come to simply accept he'll be there when I need him.* Emotion burned her eyes, her telepathic voice impassioned. *He has a heart so huge, it's kept pumping, kept going long past endurance—even though life has bruised it to a pulp.*

Aden turned his body toward her . . . and then he did an unexpected thing for an Arrow. He reached out to cup her jaw, hold her face for a long, taut second, their eyes locked. *I think,* he said at last, *you are a worthy match for my friend, Ivy Jane. You see the greatness of him—and you see his vulnerability. Neither scares you.* A decisive nod as he broke contact. *Anything you need from me, you can have. You need only ask.*

Ivy blinked rapidly to swallow the scalding wet of her tears, conscious Jaya had just gasped and turned toward them. "I can sense him." A dazzling smile. "He's in there, and he's frustrated and angry that no one can hear him. I can *help* him find a way out." Jumping up, she tugged Ivy close with excited hands. "You try."

Ivy did, caught only the dull echo of emotion that told her the patient wasn't brain-dead. "I think this is your gift, Jaya," she whispered, hugging her friend in awe.

Aden didn't speak again until after Jaya had gone to talk to the nurse about the readings the nurse had picked up during the session. *It's a priceless gift,* he said, *but it isn't enough. There have been two further outbreaks in different parts of the world in the time we've been at this hospital. We are losing this war.*

Chapter 39

Alice was one of the most gifted graduate students I have ever had the pleasure to supervise. In truth, I had come to consider her a colleague long before she earned her doctorate. Alice saw the truth with an incisiveness that is rare in academia and, indeed, the world. She often asked me questions that made me take a second look at my conclusions, challenging me to dig deeper, uncover more.

What she accomplished in a short twenty-seven years is extraordinary. She leaves behind a legacy that will stand the test of countless decades. The consequences of the upheaval in the Net means there are few empaths in attendance today, but they stand for the many, and those many tell me that no one knew designation E as well as Alice. No one.

Excerpted from Professor George Kim's eulogy for Alice Eldridge, PhD

SASCHA'S MIND WAS full of her intense, frustrating discussions with the Es scattered around the world, when Lucas picked her up at the pack healer's home around two. Their destination was the Sierra Nevada wolf den. According to him, he had business with Hawke, but the truth was, he knew how much the news of the outbreaks had shaken her. So many dead and injured and it was only the tip of the iceberg.

As for their baby girl, she was being looked after by Kit and his best friend, Cory. The soldiers also had charge of Tamsyn's "twin terrors," the healer having gone to take care of an injured elder. Sascha would've been leery of leaving the two young males with a baby if she hadn't known all the juveniles in the pack grew up pulling babysitting duty—and as evidenced by Kit and Cory, most didn't mind pitching in even when older.

Her phone beeped right then, the screen filling with Kit's handsome face, a happy Naya cradled nonchalantly in one muscular arm. "Sascha, Naya wants the Toy That Shall Not Be Named. Did you forget to pack it?"

Sascha's lips twitched, the shadows lifting at the sight of the two of them. "In the side pocket of the bag. I put it in at the last minute."

Kit disappeared, then appeared with the fluffy little wolf in his free hand. Naya gurgled and reached for it with a squeal of delight before her attention was caught by seeing Sascha's face on the comm. Making "Mommy" noises at her baby, Sascha waited until Kit had distracted Naya with the plush toy before hanging up. "You're still growling," she pointed out to her green-eyed panther.

"Why?" Lucas snarled. "Of all the things in the world she could've become attached to, why did my otherwise brilliant daughter pick that damn wolf's stupid gift?"

"Careful," she said, voice husky with the knowledge of how lucky she was to have this life, this freedom, "or you'll start to need that knit cap Hawke gave you." According to the wolf alpha, it was for when Naya caused Lucas to pull out his hair.

"Grr." Managing the all-wheel-drive vehicle with ease, he reached out to grab her hand and bring it to his mouth for a playful bite. "You okay?"

"I just hate the unfairness of it all." She dropped her head back against the seat, choked by the unvarnished fury of her emotions. "All this death when, for the first time in a hundred years, life in the PsyNet might be something more, something better than cold Silence."

"Give yourself and the other Es time to figure things out," Lucas said, placing her hand on his thigh after a kiss to her knuckles. "I know exactly how tough empaths can be."

She curved her fingers over the firm muscle of him. Lucas purred. "Harder."

Digging her nails into him in a kneading motion, Sascha leaned across and grazed her teeth over the muted-gold skin of his throat. The purr intensified. "I'll pet you later," he promised, running his knuckles over her cheek.

Feeling petted and spoiled already, Sascha settled back into her seat but kept her hand on his thigh. The contact, Lucas's voice as they discussed pack matters, they centered her; she felt far more able to face the stark facts of the crisis in the Net when they walked into the SnowDancer den. Splitting at the entrance to the light-filled network of underground tunnels, they agreed to meet in two hours for the drive back.

When little Ben overheard Sascha asking the SnowDancer healer about Alice's whereabouts, the human scientist not in the quarters she'd been assigned after being released from the infirmary, he tugged on her hand. "I'll show you, Sascha darling. She's outside."

Bubbles of laughter in her blood, Sascha attempted to frown at the pup, his eyes a gorgeous rich brown and his fine silky hair so deep a mahogany it appeared black in this light, but it was a losing battle. "Where did you hear that?" she asked, knowing the culprits full well.

Ben gave her a cheeky smile as she scooped him up into her arms for a cuddle. "I guess I have a guide," she said to the SnowDancer healer, after hitching Ben on one hip. "Will he be warm enough dressed as he is?" It snowed heavily at this elevation.

The other woman ruffled Ben's hair. "He's a wolf," she said with a kiss to his cheek.

"Yeah." Ben lifted a hand, claws out, and made a fierce face. "I'm a wolf! Grr."

Pretend growling at him in turn, to his delighted laughter, Sascha carried him outside, one of his arms slung companionably around her neck. At least ten other pups near to Ben's age were already playing in the fine white powder that coated the area. When she glimpsed Judd's niece, Marlee, in the distance with a group of older children, she whispered, "Are you and Marlee still fighting?" The cause of the fight was a mystery to all as far as Sascha knew.

Ben smiled and waved at Marlee, but didn't wriggle down to run over and join his friend. "No," he said as Marlee waved back. "I 'pologized for messing up her girl party, and she said sorry for her friends calling me a dumb baby."

Sascha's curiosity won out. "How did you mess up her girl party?"

Sighing, Ben lay his head against her shoulder. "I shifted and jumped on their picnic blanket from a tree after Julian and Roman showed me how to climb, and I squished their cake and spilled stuff on their clothes."

Sascha had a hard time not bursting into laughter, the image of a cake-and-cream-covered little wolf pup bringing tears to her eyes. "Was the cake nice?"

Ben grinned, glee in his expression. "Yes. I ate it *all* since everyone except Marlee ran away."

Pressing a laughing kiss to his temple, she said, "I'm glad you two are friends again."

"Me, too." He pointed to the right. "Ally is over there. She likes to sit by the small waterfall pond. Sometimes I sit with her."

Putting him on the ground, she said, "Thank you for showing me."

A sweet smile. "I'm gonna go eat a cookie now. Mama said I could have one 'cause she's baking. Bye!"

Watching after him until he was safely back inside, she walked out to the "waterfall pond." It proved an apt description. Unlike the large waterfall a longer distance out from the den, this one was tiny, would barely create a splash as it poured into the pond in summer. Right now, it was a stunning piece of natural sculpture, the water frozen as it fell, the pond a mirror.

Alice sat on a sun-drenched boulder beside the sheet of ice, her eyes closed and face lifted up to the late-afternoon rays. That fine-boned face was no longer sallow, her brown skin holding a golden glow. Her hair, too, Sascha saw, had begun to grow, though it was only a delicate feathering on her scalp right now, the glorious curls that Sascha had seen in an old photograph not yet in evidence.

"Sascha." A quiet smile, a faded shadow of the huge grin Sascha had seen in that same photo. "Have you come to see if my cracked egg of a brain has any more information?"

Sascha made a rueful face. "Does it feel like that's the only reason I come to see you?" The truth was, she wanted desperately to help the other woman heal, but Alice wasn't ready yet.

First, I have to mourn, she'd said on Sascha's last visit. *I lost everyone I loved when I was put into that cryonic chamber. I don't know if my heart is strong enough to recover.*

Sascha believed differently. Alice had already shown her strength in waking from a sleep that should've consumed her; it might take time, but the scientist would put the pieces of her self back together. When she did, she would be extraordinary, of that Sascha had not a single doubt.

"No," Alice said in reply to her question. "It's me." Closing her eyes, she tilted her face up to the sun again. "I wish I could give you the answers you need." She exhaled, lashes lifting as her gaze turned to the frozen water. "I heard about what happened, the madness and the violence."

Taking a seat on a nearby boulder, Sascha told Alice what she knew. As a result of the relationships Sascha had formed with the Es in the compound, she'd heard from every one of them since their placements—it made her the one person who could see patterns within the individual experiences, mine answers that could help them all. The trouble was, the pattern was bleak.

"At least," she said, clinging to the single point of light in the darkness, "we now understand one of the unofficial subdesignations." Jaya did instinctively what it had taken Sascha considerable time and intense focus to accomplish. "An elderly Forgotten empath once told me only cardinals could stop riots," she said, thinking aloud. "Something to do with a terminal field. But Ivy can clearly tap into a similar ability—though neither one of us can maintain it for long."

Angling her face out of the sun, Alice frowned. "The Forgotten empath conflated two different elements, unsurprising given that the two are often used in concert. Only a cardinal can create a terminal field, but other high-level empaths can control crowds."

Sascha stared at Alice . . . who blinked and stared back. "Did that just come out of my mouth?" the other woman whispered, her eyes huge and luminescent in the indirect sunlight.

"You sounded like a professor." Sascha's heart thudded against her ribs. "As if I was a student who'd made a basic error."

Alice rubbed at her face with gloved hands. "It's gone now, but for that instant, it was as if I was the Alice of before, my mind tumbling with ideas and concepts and a thousand thoughts instead of this dullness I can't penetrate."

Sascha touched the other woman's shoulder, hope a golden surge in her blood. "It's okay, Alice. I think . . . I think you're coming back." Bringing with her the knowledge that might save an entire race.

Chapter 40

Aden—the surgical simulations you asked me to run all end in Vasic's death. Given the seriousness of the matter, I went outside my official authorization and liaised with other surgeons after telling them the problem was a hypothetical model. None were able to offer any suggestions I haven't already considered and ruled out.

Message from Dr. Edgard Bashir

IVY STOOD AT the window that night, looking out at the high-powered lights that illuminated the street below. The bodies were gone, but the authorities were still collecting evidence. She knew in her gut that if the outbreaks continued, such careful work would soon be considered a luxury.

Hearing a noise from Vasic's bedroom, she stepped through the open doorway to find him shrugging off his leather jacket, his boots already discarded. The last time she'd seen him, it had been for a fleeting instant when he dropped Rabbit back at the apartment. He'd been on watch outside for hours, not to mention the work he'd done to help clear away the bodies. She'd missed him with every breath . . . but the man who'd come back to her wasn't the same one who'd surprised her with a pastry that morning, before the world fractured in a hail of terror and madness.

"Getting ready to shower?" she asked, stomach tightening at the ice of him, his emotions walled up so effectively that the emptiness made her chest clench in pain.

A curt nod. "Excuse me." And he was no longer in the room.

Ivy stared at the space where he'd been as the shower came on after a minute in the attached bathroom, the words Aden had spoken to her at the hospital vivid in her mind. As the other Arrow had pointed out, Vasic's wounds ran bone deep. Those wounds had been drenched in death and violence anew over the past fourteen hours, were rubbed raw and bloody.

Understanding why he'd gone distant and cold didn't mean she was about to permit him to brood alone. That bad habit was one she intended to break, and break quickly. *You know,* she said telepathically, *it's extremely frustrating to try to have a conversation with a man who can simply teleport away.*

Hands on her hips when he didn't respond, she strode over to the open bathroom door—clearly her Arrow didn't appreciate her determination where he was concerned. Leaning against the doorjamb, she felt her breath leave her lungs in a pleasured rush at the blurry outline of his nude body behind the steamy glass of the shower enclosure.

It took serious effort to find words since her brain seemed to have forgotten the concept of language. "So"—she saw him freeze beyond the glass, his hands in his hair—"did the medics discover anything new about the infection?"

Lowering his hands, he said, *"Ivy."*

"Yes?" She didn't budge. "You were about to answer my question."

"I was about to ask you to leave."

"Sorry, I didn't hear you." Wickedness woke in her. "Where are you going to teleport naked?"

"I could go to my quarters in Arrow Central Command."

She stuck out her tongue at him. "That's cheating!"

Turning off the shower, Vasic slid open the shower door. Ivy was determined to stay . . . but lost her nerve at the last second. "Damn it." Twisting out of the door, she stood with her back against the wall beside it, her skin hot and breath short.

When he stepped out, a towel wrapped around his hips, she bit down on her lower lip. He was *beautiful.* All sleek muscle and strength, a finely honed blade of a man. Trickles of water from his hair trailed down his back, and she had to fight so hard not to reach out and touch. She wasn't sure he'd accept it. Not tonight. "You didn't dry your hair properly." It came out a husky whisper.

Turning toward her, he braced himself with his palms on either side of her head, his bare skin inches from her, the heat of him smashing against her hungry skin. And his fury . . . that was a stunning thing, the storm in his eyes molten silver.

"I can't give you what you want." It came out ice-cold, but those eyes, those eyes . . . "I thought—" He shook his head. "You can't change the core of a man, Ivy. You can't take a man christened in blood and make him into something better."

Ivy narrowed her eyes, furious at the way he continued to see himself. "I don't want you to change. Haven't I made that clear?" Rising on tiptoe, she fisted her hands in his hair. "I want *you*. All of you. Even the part that infuriates me."

Vasic could feel the numbness that had crawled over him in a defensive reaction to the carnage he'd seen, the bodies he'd handled, begin to crack. Jagged and sharp, each crack echoed through his mind, ice splintering across a frozen lake. "I handled the dead with my hands and my mind today," he said, and it was a brutal, inescapable truth. "Do you really want those hands on you?"

She released his hair . . . and something broke in him, only to heal even stronger when she tugged one of his hands off the wall and intertwined her fingers with it. "I've told you—I want your hands on every inch of me." Passion glittered in her eyes, was hot on her cheeks, and a large part of it, he realized too late, was anger. "You used these same hands, that same mind, to save lives today. Why don't you ever focus on that?"

Vasic set his jaw.

Gripping it in her slender fingers, Ivy forced him to meet her gaze. "No more, Vasic. You don't get to live in purgatory, and you certainly don't get to punish yourself by shutting out everyone who cares for you. If you want to brood, you do it with me so I can knock some sense into you."

Vasic couldn't take his eyes off the vibrant life of her, the numbness in a thousand pieces by now, no match for the force of Ivy's fury. "You," he whispered, "are the most beautiful thing I've ever had in my life."

Eyes afire, she shook her head. "No, you are not getting out of this fight that easily." A glare. "I want a promise."

His skin hurt with need for her, but he didn't close the distance between them, uncertain of Ivy's temper. "What do you want me to promise?"

Fingers still on his jaw, she pressed down. "That you will never again attempt to drive me away because you think I'd be better off without you." A hard, fast kiss that was a punch right to the gut. "That will *never* be true. I wake up excited to see you, Vasic. I dream of you. Your voice, your mind, your hands. I love every part of you. I imagine a future with you!" Face flushed and body tensed, she sounded angrier and angrier with each word. "Don't you dare try to tell me you're not worth it! Don't you dare!"

Vasic didn't have the will to repudiate her. He'd used it all up. If she didn't want to heed his warning, then he was going to be selfish and make his claim, accept hers. "I promise." It was a vow.

Chest heaving, Ivy stared at him, the suspicion on her face making something twist deep inside him, the strange emotion at once gentle and fierce. "Wait for me in your bedroom," he said, taking what he needed because Ivy had said he could have it. Have her.

Ivy had fought for his right to have her.

She never denied him, never punished him by withholding the touch he craved—*her* touch—and he planned to take terrible advantage. Now and always. "I need to make sure everything is secure before I join you." The mattress on his bed was hard, would discomfort her. "I want you under me, naked and aroused and mine."

Ivy's cheeks went a hot peach. Running a hand down his chest, she scowled. "I'm still mad at you . . . but don't take long."

Vasic didn't, but he was thorough nonetheless as he completed a security sweep of the floor after pulling on a pair of jeans and boots. Then, apartment door bolted behind him, he walked into Ivy's room. Kicking off his boots by the side of her bed, he just looked at her for a minute. She'd changed out of her earlier clothes into the flannel pants she liked and that lacy, strappy top that didn't cover much at all. The upper curves of her breasts were visible to his gaze, her nipples peaking below the fabric he could tear with a single tug, it was so ridiculously flimsy.

Ivy rubbed her feet on the sheet. "Why are you looking at me that way?"

"I'm thinking how easy it would be to tear off your clothes." It would leave her bared to the skin, the cream and gold of her open to his touch.

She shivered, and he'd had enough of looking. Getting into bed, he came over her and placed his gauntleted arm above her head, then gripped her jaw as she'd done his. "Open your mouth," he said. "I want to taste you."

Ivy's fingers clenched on his nape. "Vasic." Her lips parted.

Not hesitating, he placed his own over hers and indulged as he'd never indulged before Ivy. Her body was soft and silky underneath the hard weight of his, her taste lush, her welcome unhidden. He wanted more, took more, controlling the kiss with his grip on her jaw. Ivy didn't seem to mind, her free hand rising to wrap over his shoulder from behind as she held him to her.

The voluntary dissonance trip wire in his mind sparked a warning, but it was only a yellow alert, a reminder of the power he had to control. Ignoring it, he continued to keep Ivy trapped below his body as he smashed the rules of Silence to rubble and kissed her in unrestrained demand. Ivy wasn't very good at being angry with him—she gave him the wetness, the raw intimacy that he craved with a wild generosity that only made him hungrier.

Humans and changelings had hobbies, he thought in one corner of his mind. This would be his.

"Sex can't be a hobby," Ivy gasped, tiny nails digging into his flesh in a bite that made him want to demand more, and he realized he'd telepathed the words to her.

"Why not?" He reinitiated the kiss, having had nowhere near enough. *It's a physical act. All physical acts require practice if an individual wants to improve.* And Vasic intended to become an expert at making Ivy utter those small, soft, intrinsically female sounds that went straight to his already painfully erect penis.

"I don't think you need to improve." Ivy moaned when he slid his mouth down from her jaw to her neck and nipped at her, her body moving restlessly beneath his. "God . . . How . . . Where . . ."

I had to think about something good while I was on the street. I thought about what I wanted to do to you. The second the words were out, he wished he could recall them, not wanting the ugliness of the past hours in their bed.

But Ivy wrapped a leg around his waist, and said, "Excellent use of your time," and it was all right.

Sucking on the pulse in her neck because the rapid tattoo of it fascinated him, he felt her stiff little nipples rub against his chest. He wanted to suck on those, too, wanted to lick and bite and taste every naked inch of her, wanted to drown his parched soul in the pleasure that was Ivy Jane.

His Ivy Jane.

IVY was melting in Vasic's arms, her need at a keening pitch, the weight of his body pinning her down in a delicious prison . . . which was probably why it took her several seconds to realize she was no longer in bed. In fact, she was no longer in her bedroom. Breath ragged as their lips parted, she whispered, "I can feel sand underneath me."

Vasic ran the pad of his thumb over her lower lip. "We're in the desert," he said, and dipped his head again.

When he licked his tongue over hers, she licked back. She had no idea if they were doing this "right," but oh, it felt *goooood*. Sex was the best hobby, she decided, as Vasic began to lave his tongue over her collarbone after nudging aside the strap of her camisole. "I want to do that." She tugged at the raw silk of his hair.

He grazed the ball of her shoulder with his teeth. "Later."

Brain hazy at best, she decided she could wait her turn since his turn was making her blood transform to honey . . . until an icy chill penetrated her back. "Vasic!"

Lifting his head, he said, "Alaska," and then they were back in her bed, his hands braced on either side of her and his gorgeous chest rising and falling in harsh breaths above her.

She went to touch him, caught the shake of his head. It took almost a minute for her brain cells to start working again. "So," she gasped. "Slight technical glitch."

Silver-frost eyes locked with hers. A heartbeat later, they were kissing again, wet and hot and so good . . . until Ivy yelped, the earth hard and cold beneath her thinly clad form. At least it wasn't snow, she thought, looking around at the tall green grasses that created a cocoon around them. Then the first fat droplet of rain hit Vasic's naked shoulder.

The bed was below her the next second, the air warm.

Pushing away, Vasic fell onto his back beside her, his gauntleted arm above his head. She rose on her elbow, and though it took teeth-gritting control, didn't immediately pounce on the beautiful, *beautiful* man in bed with her. The one who'd just kissed and nibbled on her like she was the most delicious thing he'd ever tasted.

He could devour her as often as he liked.

"What about you?" A piercing gray-eyed glance. "Your shields?"

Not shifting her gaze from her very private, very gorgeous view, Ivy accessed her empathic senses. "My abilities seem heightened, but I'm not reading you, not consciously." She bit her kiss-swollen lower lip. "I suppose I could've been doing it subconsciously, but if I was, I was too in the moment to know it."

"I don't mind, Ivy," he said, clearly hearing her worry. "It's not as if my desires were unclear." He ran one hand over the erection pushing at his jeans.

Ivy's mouth dried up, her eyes locked on that spot even after he dropped his hand aside. "Why," she said, voice hoarse, "is that so erotic?"

"Is it?" His gaze dipped. "Touch one of your nipples for me."

As breathless as if she'd been running, Ivy lifted her hand, blushed, but bracketed the tight, pouting tip between her fingertips through the camisole. It was her own body, and she'd touched it thousands of times as she showered and dressed, but this time it was different—because Vasic was watching her, his eyes heavy-lidded.

Turning her lips inward to lick them wet, she rolled the taut nub between her fingertips . . . and almost fell when the bed turned to sand, her hand dropping to dig into the porous softness. The displacement only lasted a second, then the mattress was firm beneath them once more.

"Verdict?" she asked, playing her finger through a tiny river of sand caught in the sheet.

"Highly erotic." Vasic reached down to undo the top button of his jeans, lower the zipper a fraction.

Ivy whimpered when he stopped. "That's not going to ease the pressure," she said, her breasts pushing against the delicate fabric of the camisole.

Reaching out, Vasic just barely brushed the back of his hand over her swollen flesh. It shot a bolt of intense sensation right to her core, her panties beyond damp. Rubbing her thighs together only made the frustration worse. "The desert's nice," she began in a cajoling tone, creeping her hand toward him. "We—"

"Will probably end up in a Siberian prison the next time." Gripping her hand on that dark warning, he returned it to her side of the invisible line in the bed. "Do you know what I want?"

Ivy ran her foot over his jean-clad leg. "What?"

"To watch you touch yourself between your thighs as you tug on your nipples," he said, the frank sexual request ratcheting up her need to a fever, "but we'll have to wait until I have the 'slight technical glitch'"—a silver-eyed glance, his thumb stroking over her lip—"under control."

Ivy bit at the firm flesh, frustrated and playful both. "Your voice should be illegal." Sucking at his thumb when he didn't immediately withdraw it, she saw his lashes come down, his breathing alter . . . and sand all around them.

To her toe-curling delight, though he broke the intimate contact after they were back in the apartment, he began to twine one of her curls loosely around his finger. "I hope you really do like the desert. Because it looks like we'll be visiting it on a regular basis."

She giggled and snuggled a tiny bit closer. "I do."

"I have one advantage over other Tks." His abdomen flexed under her touch, but he didn't tell her to keep her distance this time. "My primary power is teleportation, and it appears that's what my brain defaults to when I lose control—otherwise, I might cause serious damage."

Ivy thought of the sand, the snow, the grasses. "Well, as long as your brain picks isolated locations, I don't care." All she cared about was being with him. "Though," she teased, "I think you should be on the bottom next time."

"We'll negotiate that after I can keep us in one place."

Ivy drew a design on his abdomen, her head nicely cushioned on his shoulder. "The places we went, you recognized them in a glance."

"They were all locations I choose to go to when I'm not on assignment." Releasing her hair, he tumbled her onto her back again, his expression altering to the cool remoteness she knew so well, but his hand, it gently collared her throat. "Are you sure, Ivy?"

It was a potent, quiet question, one for which she didn't need an explanation. "Yes," she answered without hesitation. "I'm sure."

Vasic nodded and returned them to their former positions, Ivy cradled against his chest. She released a shuddering breath. She was where she was meant to be, and she would fight to hold on to the wild beauty of it with everything she had.

"Woof!" Scrabbling paws, then a small weight jumping onto the bed.

"Rabbit," she chastised with a laugh.

Padding over, he looked at how she lay in Vasic's arms, huffed, then curled up on Vasic's other side. It made her smile. "I like that you two are friends now."

Vasic said nothing, but he cupped the back of her head with one hand and rubbed Rabbit's back with the other, the black sheen of his gauntlet gleaming in the light. It was a moment as perfect as it was heartbreaking.

Chapter 41

Silent Voices continues to be anything but silent. The Ruling Coalition has not yet made a public statement regarding their demands. More importantly, neither has Kaleb Krychek.

PsyNet Beacon

DEMOCRACY, AS THE humans understood it, didn't work in the PsyNet. It was populated by too many powerful minds that could career out of control if not kept in strict check—which meant the people at the helm had to be ruthless and powerful themselves. Orders were given and followed, any revolt dealt with quickly and quietly before it could impact the Net.

Which was why Kaleb found it surprising that he was about to have a meeting with the woman behind the formation of Silent Voices.

You know how to be charming, Sahara 'pathed as he teleported into the woman's home. *Charm. Smile. Don't make this a clash but a discussion.*

It fascinated Kaleb how Sahara saw him—he wasn't charming, and the smile he reserved for the world was a calculated, cold-blooded facsimile meant either to discomfort or to put the other party at ease. Of course, Sahara never saw that smile. *I'll attempt not to scare her witless at least.* Sahara could've ensured that by coming with him, but she'd made it clear she had no desire to be a political powerhouse.

"I'm your extremely private, highly personal advisor," she'd said to him when they'd discussed how visible she wanted to be. "Our bond needs to be viewable in the Net, but our life together will never be for display." Hauling him down with a grip on his tie, she'd sealed the promise with a kiss.

The memory making the dark heart of him stretch out like a cat in sunshine, he walked through the living area of the small apartment to find the head of Silent Voices in a tiny study. Ida Mill was seated with her back to the door, her eyes on a wall-mounted computer screen. "You really should face the door."

Spinning around so fast her chair slammed into the desk, she said, "Councilor Krychek."

It was to her credit that she'd kept her cool. "Just Krychek will do."

Dark eyes in a narrow, dark-skinned face met his, her hair steel gray and pulled into a neat knot at her nape. She was only forty-seven according to the file his aide had put together for him, but had gone totally gray by thirty-two. That early sign of aging was a genetic family trait that hadn't been bred out, likely because it gave the possessors a regal appearance, regardless of their chronological age.

Now, Ida Mill rose to her feet, a woman five feet eight inches tall, with perfect carriage and steely self-possession. "So," she said, "how long do I have?"

They are terribly melodramatic aren't they?

Kaleb didn't remind Sahara that if he'd had his way, the founder of Silent Voices would've been dead and buried by this point. "I've come to talk, Ms Mill." Stepping back, he returned to the living area.

The room was the stereotypical featureless Psy box, no art on the walls, not even a single photograph . . . such as the one Sahara had found on one of her old datapads, her father having thrown nothing of Sahara's away after she disappeared. It was of her and Kaleb, taken with the camera on the datapad. They'd been sitting on a tree branch, Sahara laughing as he used his telekinesis to float the datapad into the correct position to take the shot.

That photograph was now centered on the left wall of their living room, next to an image of Sahara with her father. Yesterday, he'd quietly added another one to the collection—of Sahara curled up on the couch, brow furrowed and teeth bared at something on the comm screen. She'd laughed when she'd seen it, promised revenge, and he knew that wall would fill over time with pieces of their lives.

"You aren't known for talking."

Hands casually in the pockets of his suit pants, he met Ida Mill's wary gaze. "It appears I'm turning over a new leaf."

The woman's skin blanched, just as Sahara said, *Kaleb.*

I think she should be a little scared, he replied, finding it interesting that Ida Mill's own Silence was nowhere near pristine. *I don't want her to start believing she can cross certain lines with impunity.*

A slight pause then, *You're right. Those lines need to stay in place for now.*

It was possible, Kaleb thought, that they would have to do so forever. Because the Psy weren't like the humans or the changelings, and each of those cultures had their own power structures. "You wish to reinitiate Silence."

The force behind Silent Voices, their effective leader, drew up her shoulders. "Pure Psy went off track, but they had a point. Without Silence, who would we be?"

"For one, we'd have had far fewer sociopaths in the Council super-structure."

Blinking, the woman stared at him. "A worthy trade-off to stop the insanity and serial killing that led us to this point."

Kaleb 'ported in a file and placed it on the small table by the window. "Read that. You might change your mind about just how many serial killers operated within the PsyNet during Silence."

"Records can be doctored."

"True. These aren't." He hadn't needed to do anything; the horror of Silence was laid out in black and white. "And that isn't the major issue; the infection, the details of which I'm sure you're fully aware, is rooted in Silence."

"You can't know that." Her skin pulled tight over her entire face, lines fanning out from the corners of her eyes. "It's the empaths who are the abominations—we should've eliminated them from the gene pool. They feed the infection."

I didn't expect that. Sahara's voice was quiet. *Rebellion, yes. But this is bigotry. This is what you anticipated though, isn't it?*

Yes, but for Sahara's sake, he'd hoped for a better outcome. *You're the one who told me fear comes from the unknown—and the empaths are the biggest unknown in the Net.* "So your solution is wholesale slaughter of the Es?"

Ida Mill immediately shook her head. "Of course not. No, we simply believe that the E gene should be spliced out of all future births."

"It's been tried before. It didn't end well."

"It wasn't done correctly," was the reply. "We have data from those times"—a quick glance as she admitted to illegal hacking—"and it appears the E removal was only attempted for a single decade. Hardly enough time for a true experiment."

"The fact the Net nearly collapsed in those ten years isn't data enough?"

"We would've recovered!" Folding her arms, the woman shook her head. "The plug was pulled too soon."

"And this is the central tenet of Silent Voices?"

"No, it's only an adjunct." Unfolding her arms, she said, "Without Silence, you yourself would be a lethal risk to society. That training is critical for certain members of our race."

"Such as your son." Ida Mill's child was a Tk, an eight-year-old boy who'd been drafted into the cadet academy that spawned black-ops soldiers—previously, it had been for the Council. Now, ironically, those men and women belonged to Kaleb. When it came to children like Ida Mill's son, he'd ordered a halt on all physical and mental torture, but he hadn't interfered with the psychic instruction, though it would need to be modified for a post-Silence world.

Lips thinning, she nodded. "What will he do without the Protocol?"

"The fact that Silence has fallen doesn't mean all the training associated with it is to be discarded." Every single Arrow he knew, including Judd, needed that training on some level.

"That's impossible." The leader of Silent Voices sliced her hand horizontally through the air. "There can be no control without Silence."

"An opinion without fact."

Her face set. "If it weren't fact, our ancestors would've never chosen Silence in the first place."

"We aren't who we were then; the decisions we make are our own." He 'ported out before she could answer, having heard enough. "Her thought patterns are set," he said to Sahara where she'd been working at his desk at the home office.

Sahara ran a hand through her hair, her expression pensive. "Is it possible she's terrified for her son and clinging to the only thing she knows might help him?"

"I have multiple groups working on how to modify Silence training for a non-Silent world—and I've made no attempts to keep those strategic sessions a secret." He'd sent out invitations to academics and medics, philosophers and more concrete thinkers across the globe. "Ida Mill chooses not to see any other option."

Sahara had to agree, having been telepathically linked to him throughout the meeting. "If the Es do find a solution to the infection and the Net stays whole, we'll have to come up with a way to deal with Silent Voices on a day-to-day basis. It's not as if we can corral these people off—"

"An excellent idea," Kaleb said. "They can set up a 'Silent' corner of the Net, and I'll make a generous offer to slice them away so they can have their own isolated little Silent community that'll soon be erased by the infection since they'll have no Es. Problem solved."

Having risen to walk over and join him where he was scanning the news headlines on the comm screen set on the wall, Sahara lightly slapped the chest of the man who was her heartbeat. "Stop it." The thing was, she knew he was perfectly serious, even as he tweaked her. Because Kaleb had a sense of humor, perhaps one only she ever saw, but it was there. It was also very dark. "We aren't consigning them to roped-off corners of the Net."

He turned and slid his hands under the waistband of the gray sweats she wore with a black tee in anticipation of the workout she'd planned to do after the meeting. Her body was strong and healthy now, and she intended to keep it that way.

Kaleb nuzzled a kiss to her throat. "It's a viable plan."

"Are you going to be serious?" She scowled.

"No. I'd rather cause an earthquake." Sliding one hand into the back of her panties, he stroked her already damply aroused flesh.

Sahara gasped. "You . . ." Unable to find the words, she began to undo his tie in an effort to fight fire with fire. "This is a serious political decision about the future of our race."

"There'll always be a serious political discussion," Kaleb pointed out, removing his sinful hand to push down her sweats and lift her out of them. "Into infinity."

Unfortunately, she couldn't argue with him on that point. As the most powerful Psy in the Net, Kaleb would always be at the top. The fact was, without him, no one would take any ruling body seriously—because he could change everything in a heartbeat.

Raising her arms to allow him to tug off her T-shirt, she dropped his tie to the floor and began to undo the buttons on his shirt. "You're right," she said, as he wrapped one arm around her neck and used his other hand to remove the cuff link on that sleeve. "Let's cause an earthquake."

The tremor registered forty-five minutes later with the increasingly confused seismologists at the Russian Seismic Agency. A half hour after that, Kaleb stroked Sahara's lazy-limbed body and said, "Information is power. Let's put a certain percentage of that power in the hands of the populace."

PSYNET BEACON: BREAKING NEWS
STATEMENT FROM THE OFFICE OF KALEB KRYCHEK

Silent Voices has styled itself a rebellion. It is nothing of the kind. It is instead a political party with a particular viewpoint. Such a political party has a right to exist in the PsyNet, as do groups representing other interests.

Designation E also has a right to exist. However, unlike Silent Voices, the empaths are critical to the survival of the Psy race. The previous Council hid this knowledge, but in light of the current situation, it is imperative that it be shared so that each individual can make an informed decision as to his or her personal viewpoint: *The PsyNet cannot survive without the Es.* This is not an ideological stance, but proven fact.

An attempt to eliminate the empaths from the gene pool was made at the dawn of Silence—it led to the deaths of tens of thousands and to an acute spike in cases of severe mental illness in the population, including criminal insanity. The proof of this fact is in the continued existence of the Es. Designation E would have otherwise been erased three-quarters of a century ago.

As a result of the above, any attack on an E will be seen as an attack on the foundations of the PsyNet. Should members of Silent Voices, or any other group, incite others to act against the Es, they will be dealt with as terrorists. Political disagreement is acceptable. Aggression that threatens to collapse the PsyNet is not.

—Kaleb Krychek

Chapter 42

Chaos Reigns.

PsyNet Beacon headline

IVY WAS DEEPLY asleep on the muscular pillow of Vasic's arm, the two of them having decided passive contact wouldn't activate his ability, when she physically jerked awake under a slamming punch of black panic. Her skin went clammy, dots sparking in front of her eyes.

"Vasic, they're dying," she gasped, screams echoing in her ears. "It's close, right on top of us."

Vasic was already out of bed, his feet in his boots in the next two seconds. "Grab a jacket. I'll get mine and confirm the location of the outbreak."

Ivy scrambled out of bed to slide her arms into her raspberry-colored coat, wrapping it over her pajamas and pulling on socks and her snow boots seconds before Vasic reappeared. He'd tugged on a dark gray T-shirt that was far too thin for the cold, thrown his leather-synth jacket over it, but there was no time to make him change.

"Rabbit, stay," she managed to get out before Vasic thrust a knit cap on her head and 'ported them into carnage.

This time, the majority of the screams came from inside the apartment buildings. A body flew out of a window, glass shattering. Vasic caught the male using his Tk, lowered him gently to the ground . . . where he got up, his body bleeding from countless cuts, and immediately ran to the wall in front of him. His head made a wet, ugly sound as it repeatedly hit the concrete.

Shocked, Ivy reached out to calm him. He fell to his knees. She couldn't hold the calm for long, but he remained on his knees regardless, rocking back and forth and making bloodcurdling animal sounds of pain. Deciding that was better than self-directed rage, she began to zero in on one mind at a time, while Vasic took care of the violent infected who had begun to spill out onto the street.

Two cabs that had turned into the street right at the wrong time screeched into reverse in an effort to escape. One backed into a parked car, the other was hit by oncoming traffic in a low-speed impact. Abandoning their vehicles, the drivers all scrambled out and ran.

Then there were just too many infected and Ivy's focus narrowed to those who seemed the most dangerous.

A few undirected telepathic strikes glanced off her without doing any damage. The telekinetic strike, however, would've crashed her into a wall if Vasic hadn't seen her take the blow and stabilized her.

Thanks, she telepathed, and they dived back into the fray.

She didn't know how many people she managed to soothe into a state less dangerous than mindless rage, but she lost strength far too soon for her level on the Gradient, her nose bleeding, her muscles jelly, and her head pounding so hard it felt as if it would split open if she made a single sound. Frustrated near to tears, she collapsed in the street, a kaleidoscope of horror around her.

Another scream, high-pitched and holding a terror that paralyzed.

Jerking up her head, Ivy felt her stomach lurch. No, not a child. *No!* Driven by protective anger, she found the strength to run toward the barefoot little girl who stood in the direct path of an adult wielding a heavy metal pipe. No real empathic power left in her, she lashed out with her low-Gradient telepathy and managed to distract the adult long enough to grab the child.

Ivy, I have your back, Vasic told her. *Go!*

Her faith in him absolute, Ivy ran, stopping only once she was over the defensive line set up by the local authorities. The officers, all armed with weapons designed to disable not kill, waved her behind them. She knelt on the asphalt and gulped in the cold night air as the little girl clung to her, sobbing.

Fear, pungent and blessedly normal, pulsed off her tiny frame.

Thank God. Murmuring comforting words to the traumatized child, Ivy got up again with the little girl in her arms, and jogged to the wall of Enforcement vehicles that formed a heavy barricade on this end of the street. Behind them were the ambulances. She guessed it was the same on the other end of the affected street.

Having scraped together just enough empathic ability to leech off the worst of her small charge's shock and panic, Ivy left the girl in the capable hands of a medic who promised not to let the girl out of her sight.

No one stopped Ivy when she returned to the fray afterward, the carnage on the street unbelievable. Vasic was using both his Tk and the laser built into his gauntlet to try to contain the insane without causing death, but each time he took one out of the equation, ten more seemed to appear out of nowhere. The sheer overwhelming number of infected wasn't the only problem.

In front of Ivy, two human Enforcement officers went down without warning, and she realized they'd fallen victim to one of the erratic telepathic strikes being thrown out by the infected. Checking the pulse of first one, then the other, she exhaled a breath she hadn't been aware of holding. Both were alive, but given that a powerful Tp could turn a human mind to soup, that was more luck than anything else. Weak as her telepathy was, she tried to do what she could to protect the men and women around her as the fighting continued.

A light touch on her shoulder. "I'll take over," Aden said, crouching by her side. "I'm a strong telepath."

Ceding the task to him, she accessed her empathic ability and discovered it had revived to a certain degree. Though she was barely able to slow the infected down, her efforts made it easier for Enforcement to stun them. A large group of humans who lived in the street had also joined the fight to control their psychotic neighbors, and were doing whatever they could to immobilize people without causing serious injuries.

When large predatory birds, their talons wickedly curved, swooped from the sky to take down a number of aggressive infected, Ivy thought she'd begun to hallucinate as a result of the pulsing in her brain. But the feather that floated down in front of her a minute later argued otherwise. Changeling eagles, she realized through her exhaustion.

Their help turned the tide, and the street was under control within the next forty minutes.

Tongue thick, mind fuzzy, and body not quite under control, Ivy forced herself to her feet. *Vasic?*

I'm helping to check the buildings. You're hurt.

The ice of his voice was balm on senses rubbed raw, as refreshing as the soft flakes of snow that kissed her upturned face. *Psychic strain,* she said as the vise around her head continued to tighten, the migraine vicious. *I'm going to talk to Jaya.* Her first stop, however, was to check on the little girl she'd rescued, but the child was gone, already claimed by her non-custodial parent.

"She was real happy to go with her mom," said the Enforcement uniform who'd handled the transfer. "I checked the mom's identification against the national database to make sure she wasn't some weirdo out to steal a kid, but the way the two of them were clinging to each other, it was pretty obvious they were mother and daughter." Blinking to dislodge a tiny snowflake caught on his lashes, he passed over a card. "Mother's details. I figured you'd want to know."

Ivy slipped it into a pocket, happy the child had a surviving parent who cared for her well-being. "Thank you."

"You're welcome." He reached into an open first aid box on the hood of a squad car, came out with a cotton pad meant to go under bandages. "Your nose is bleeding, and I think one of your ears, too."

Ivy cleaned up as best she could so as not to worry Jaya.

"Whatever you did," the other empath said when Ivy found her, "it's put some of the victims in a place I can reach." There was a tired but hopeful glow in her eyes, the hood of her fluffy jacket protecting her face from the snow. "But"—a haunted look shadowed the hope—"I don't know if I'm actually helping or just providing palliative care. Do you think I should keep going?"

Ivy nodded and hugged her friend. "Any victim you treat seems more at peace." She didn't tell Jaya of the report Vasic had received earlier that day that said a third of the infected survivors from the Alaskan outbreak were already dead. The victims had apparently convulsed in their hospital beds, strange blood clots breaking open in their brains.

It was clear the infection had mutated, become more virulent. But Jaya didn't need the pressure of that knowledge on her; if she could change the odds with the instinctive use of her gift, that was a different matter. "You're doing something good," she reassured the other empath.

Shoulders squared, Jaya nodded and returned to her work. Sensing she'd be okay, Ivy walked slowly back down the street littered with blood, shattered glass, feathers, weapons of opportunity, paramedics, Enforcement personnel . . . and bodies. Dead, immobilized, injured, slumped over against walls and flat on their backs, the horror and agony in the air was a crushing weight.

And over it all fell a delicate, pure snow.

Chapter 43

It is clear Samuel Rain is not amenable to a live trial of his cutting-edge innovation. Given his brilliance, I suggest we covertly co-opt his research and put a watch on his files, rather than using force. A trial can be run without his knowledge.

Recommendation from analyst in charge of evaluating
biofusion as a viable military tool

SAMUEL RAIN HAD disappeared so cleanly that most people assumed he was dead. Zie Zen wasn't most people. His contacts had unearthed rumors the man was alive but brain damaged. Depending on the depth of the latter, Rain might well be of no use, but Zie Zen wasn't about to assume anything. It had become increasingly clear that the man who had initially come up with the concept and underlying principles of biofusion was the only one who might have the solution to Vasic's deadly problem.

At the time of Rain's disappearance over a year ago, he had been residing in California. That meant nothing. He could've been transported anywhere in the world in the intervening period, but it was a starting point. Nikita Duncan and Anthony Kyriakus were the two most powerful Psy in the area, so Zie Zen would start with them. Nikita, he tabled for now. She might be ruthless, but she tended to be open about her financial interests—this type of long-term subterfuge didn't seem her style.

Anthony on the other hand . . . the head of the NightStar Group was used to dealing with damaged minds. Regardless of Silence, F-Psy still went insane more regularly than other sectors of the population. That meant NightStar had private facilities for the care of its damaged members, and according to everything Zie Zen had been able to unearth, the family *did* provide care, rather than simply executing or hiding away its malfunctioning elements.

Decision made, Zie Zen contacted Anthony on a private comm line known to a very few. It was late to call, but Zie Zen knew Anthony was often in his office long past midnight. The other man's interests had aligned with Zie Zen's on a number of occasions, and Zie Zen considered him a courteous ally of sorts.

The former Councilor's face appeared onscreen in seconds. "Zie Zen," Anthony Kyriakus said in welcome, the silver at the temples of his black hair glinting in the overhead light.

"Anthony." Zie Zen took in this man who understood family, who'd fought for his daughter's right to live with a cold ruthlessness that to many had seemed to spring from a mercenary motivation, and considered how much to reveal. "I'm calling in a marker."

"You're the only man to whom I can bear being beholden," Anthony said. "What can I do for you?"

"I need to know the whereabouts of Samuel Rain."

Anthony's expression gave nothing away. "He's rumored to be dead."

"Rumors mean little." In the end, it wasn't a difficult decision to lay talk of markers and debts aside and trust the other man with the truth. Zie Zen knew Anthony hadn't fought for his daughter because she was the most gifted and, therefore, most lucrative foreseer in the world. No, he'd fought for her out of the protective instincts of a father for his child. "I ask for Vasic."

This time Anthony did react, his eyes sharpening. "Is the gauntlet failing?"

"Yes."

Anthony's response was unanticipated. "The Net can't afford to lose him—no one truly knows how much he's done behind the scenes in the past decade, how many lives he's saved." An intent look. "I didn't realize he was one of yours."

Zie Zen could've let Anthony believe Vasic was simply another contact, but he didn't. He wanted to publicly own his relationship with the child who was his blood. "He's my great-grandson."

A blink. "A relationship no one in the Net suspects. Masterfully played, Grandfather."

Once, Zie Zen would've smiled at the honorific address, knowing it was both sincere and the rueful acknowledgment of an opponent who'd been bested. Today, he simply asked his question. "Do you know anything that will help me track down Samuel Rain?"

This time it was Anthony who caught Zie Zen unawares. "I have Rain," he said. "He's been in NightStar's care since an attempt at psychic manipulation left him with severe bleeding in the brain."

Unprepared for such immediate success, Zie Zen paused to gather his thoughts. "How?"

"You will find this apt; the SnowDancer wolves discovered him badly injured and I asked Vasic to pick him up after the leopards contacted me through my daughter."

"My grandson is unaware who it is he saved?" Zie Zen asked, thinking of all the myriad connections that had led to this instant.

Anthony nodded. "He was on an Arrow operation at the time and could literally only give me a minute. I sent him what he needed to complete the 'port, which he did in under five seconds—and I believe from a distance." The former Councilor's expression held respect for the level and precision of Vasic's skill; being born with an ability was only the start—what Vasic could do, it spoke of intense training, concentration, and intelligence.

"I'm not certain if he had any physical contact with Rain," Anthony continued. "Even if he did, he wouldn't have recognized the man. Rain's face was covered in blood and distorted by a rictus of pain." He paused, shook his head slightly. "And Vasic had no reason to follow up on it with me. He must've thought the man he rescued was another random victim, especially since Rain's disappearance wasn't reported until much later."

This time, the pause was longer, but Zie Zen didn't interrupt.

"Given the apparent success of the biofusion program," Anthony murmured, "I never considered that Vasic might need access to Rain."

Putting aside the ironic vagaries of fate, and the question of why a man who'd been an asset to those in power at the time had been targeted, Zie Zen said, "Rain's current status?"

"He is . . . damaged." Anthony clasped his hands behind his back. "I don't know if he's capable of assisting Vasic, but I also don't know if he isn't."

"I will send through the files—"

Anthony shook his head. "No, Rain isn't functional on that level. He can't seem to focus on data—Vasic must meet him in person if we are to get a true indication of whether the man has any capability to do what he once did."

Zie Zen understood the situation was grim, for Anthony wasn't a man to exaggerate things, but it was a chance, however slim. "I'll speak to Vasic, arrange a time." Looking into the other man's eyes, Zie Zen said, "Has it been worth it, Anthony? The choices you've made?" The ex-Councilor was considerably younger, but he was the patriarch of an influential and gifted family, had been faced with as many pitiless decisions as Zie Zen.

"I've lost a daughter," Anthony said at last, "seen another find freedom, have a son who chooses to align himself with me though he was raised by his mother, my foreseers are more content and less in pain, but their minds remain fragile . . . I don't know if it all balances out in the end, but I know I've done all I could. It is the only thing a man can do."

Absolute focus in the eyes that remained locked with Zie Zen's . . . before one of the most powerful men in the PsyNet bowed his head in an act of quiet honor. "Do not doubt yourself now, Grandfather," Anthony said when he looked up. "Without you, we wouldn't be standing in a time without Silence. You laid the foundations on which Krychek, Vasic, the empaths, my daughter, and I all stand."

It was, Zie Zen thought, an epitaph a man might be proud to call his own. Zie Zen wanted more. He wanted a life for his great-grandson, a real life, such as the one Zie Zen had lived for twenty-three short, wonderful years. *Sunny, I am alone without you.*

How can you be alone, Z? I'm here.

At that instant, he could almost touch her . . . and he knew his mortal time would come to an end very soon. *Not yet,* he whispered to her. *First I must save the son who is the best of both of us.* Vasic might not carry Sunny's blood, but he carried her heart.

Chapter 44

Only twenty-three and worn-out, worn-down. So many needed the help of an E after Silence, hundreds of thousands in agony . . .

Zie Zen to Vasic

IVY.

Having helped carry another stretcher to a waiting ambulance to free up a paramedic, Ivy looked up at Vasic's psychic call. *I'm here.*

There's a survivor. Not a child. Not an empath.

A spurt of energy from somewhere deep within. *Where?*

Number 24, apartment 5B.

Ivy stumbled and ran to the building as fast as her enervated and chilled body could take her, the snow a white lace curtain in front of her eyes and the hammer in her head a pounding drumbeat. When she entered the apartment, it was to find Vasic crouched in front of an open closet. He rose to walk to her, touched his fingers to her face. "The blood vessels have burst in your eyes."

Ivy hadn't even thought about that. "Let me wipe my face and wash out my eyes so I don't terrify the survivor." It'd help a little at least.

Vasic said nothing but shifted his hold to her nape and nudged her to a bathroom. "The surv—" she began, conscious of the air warming around her.

"I have a telepathic eye on him." Stopping inside the tiled enclosure, he waited as she washed out her eyes using tepid water. When she was done, he drew her close to pat her skin dry with tissues he'd grabbed from a nearby dispenser.

Though his face betrayed nothing, she had the sense he was furious. "Vasic." She curled her hand over the solid bones of his wrist.

"Do you think," he said in a quiet tone that raised every hair on her body, "you could attempt not to kill yourself in front of me?"

She flinched at the whip of words. "I was trying to help." It hadn't been much in the scheme of things, but neither had she been totally useless.

"How will a dead empath help anyone?" Throwing away the tissues he'd used, he undid her snow-wet coat and 'porting it away, brought in his Arrow jacket. Zipping her up in it, he said, "Do it again, and I'll have you back in the orchard so fast, you won't have time to draw breath."

Unadulterated anger had her ripping herself from his grasp. "Don't threaten me."

"I'm not threatening you. I'm taking care of you, since you seem incapable of doing it yourself." He went to step out of the bathroom with that harsh judgment.

Ivy grabbed his upper arm, seeing through his cool ferocity to a violent darkness beneath. "Talk to me." It was an order. "You're hurting."

No sign of a thaw. "We have a situation to handle."

Placing herself in front of him, she shook her head. "You're just as important." She cupped his face, held that icy gaze, and let him see her own determined fury. "You know I'm stubborn enough to stand here forever."

His jaw worked under her hand . . . and then he finally lowered his forehead to touch hers. "We found children," he said, voice raw. "Trapped with their maddened guardians, with no way out. Tiny limbs, tiny faces, fragile bones."

Eyes gritty, Ivy held him close, kissing his temple, his cheek, as she stroked his hair. "I'm so sorry." She knew he'd carry the images with him forever. That was who he was—a man who cared, who *remembered*. It made her heart hurt for him, for her Arrow who would not cry but who felt more deeply than anyone she'd ever before known.

"The little girl you helped me save?" she said, in an effort to ease a little of his pain. "Her name is Harriet, and she's safe and sound." Touching his mind, she 'pathed him an image Harriet's mother had sent to her phone after Ivy called the woman to ask how Harriet was doing. "See, she's warm and snuggled up in bed, her favorite toy beside her."

Allowing Ivy to hold him, comfort him, for another minute, Vasic raised his head and tucked a strand of her hair behind her ear. "Thank you for being mine, Ivy Jane."

"Always," she said, voice wet, then followed him out to the closet, where she crouched down to look into the tiny space within.

The thin man inside had to be in his late twenties, his teak-colored skin soaked in sweat. Having shoved himself totally to the back of the closet that appeared to hold neatly ironed shirts and pants, he whimpered at the sight of her. She wanted to absorb his fear, his hurt, but aware of Vasic barely leashed behind her, she controlled the instinct. As evidenced by the headache that hadn't decreased in intensity over the past hour, her senses were too battered to take more . . . and she had no desire to end up in the orchard.

Because her Arrow would carry out his threat, of that she had not a single doubt.

"Hi." She took a nonaggressive cross-legged position on the floor. "I'm Ivy."

No answer.

She didn't move, kept her face calm and reassuring until he gave a jerky nod. "Miguel."

"Nice to meet you, Miguel." She tilted her head slightly to the side. "I've never said that to anyone in a closet before."

His lips curved shakily, then fell, his handsome face crumpling in on itself. "What's happening?" It was a plea, his eyes wet.

"I don't know, but your survival might be our first clue as to how to stop it."

Miguel began to cry, the great gulping sobs shaking his entire frame. "I'm the most broken person I know," he said between the sobs. "My Silence is so flawed, my family unit disinherited me."

Ivy bit back a pulse of anger . . . and saw the bright glimmer of an answer on its heels, but her abused mind suddenly ran up against a wall. *Enough,* it said, *stop.*

VASIC caught Ivy before she would've fallen forward, smashing her head against the open door of the closet. Lifting her in his arms, her face tucked against his neck, he hauled Miguel out using his telekinesis. "Running will get you nothing—you don't want to be hunted by an Arrow."

The young male trembled so hard his bones had to be banging against one another, but Vasic had no mercy in him with Ivy so motionless in his arms. "Stay in this apartment—give your details to the Enforcement officers and tell them I've authorized you to remain here. Do not run."

"I-I w-won't."

Leaving the man with his teeth chattering and his eyes glassy, Vasic teleported Ivy not to their bedroom, but directly to Sascha Duncan, using the other woman's face as the lock. He'd expected to find himself in a night-dark home, but the empath and her mate were up.

Dressed in a short blue nightgown, Sascha was rocking her baby. Her gasp had barely cleared her mouth when Lucas Hunter's claws were at Vasic's throat.

"Ivy!" Sascha's cardinal gaze flew to Vasic's precious cargo. "What happened?"

Lucas withdrew his claws from Vasic's throat, but Vasic felt the thin lines of blood beading on his skin, a silent warning from the predator whose lair he'd invaded. Striding over to his mate, the leopard alpha took the baby from her arms, cradling the child to his bare chest in a way that ensured Vasic couldn't see the infant's face.

Sascha had instinctively done the same. Protecting their child, making sure Vasic couldn't get an image to use as a facial lock. He understood the instinct; he wouldn't trust himself, either.

Placing Ivy carefully on a table that was the closest flat surface, he told Sascha what Ivy had done today, watched the cardinal empath place her hand on Ivy's forehead, tiny lines flaring out from the corners of her night-sky eyes.

Lucas, having stepped into another room, returned without their child and with a robe for his mate, his green eyes feral as he helped her into it. "Never, *ever*," he said quietly when he reached Vasic, "do that again, or I will rip out your throat."

Aware now of exactly how fast the leopard alpha could move, Vasic knew that was a real risk. But—"I'll chance it if Ivy's life is in danger."

Lucas's gaze didn't become any less feral, but folding his arms, he shook his head. "Can't deny you have balls." His eyes went to Ivy's supine body. "I understand about taking care of what matters, but you have to understand I have a child as well as a mate to protect."

"I have no intention of ever causing either harm."

"Use my face as the lock next time, is that clear?"

Again, Vasic thought about it. "You're not always with Sascha."

"Jesus, you're either fucking crazy or in love." The words were a growl. "Yeah, I might not always be with Sascha, but I'll know where she is, and the slight delay won't matter—having your jugular split open, on the other hand, will leave Ivy with no shield."

"Agreed." Lucas's logic was sound. "I apologize for my intrusion."

Raising an eyebrow, the leopard alpha snorted. "You're not sorry in the least, but you figure it's better to be friends with me than otherwise."

Vasic sometimes wondered at those in the Net who considered the changelings too driven by their primal natures to be intelligent adversaries. Clearly, none had ever met one of the felines. Now the other man said, "How bad is New York?"

"Bad." Vasic never shifted his attention off Ivy. "Initial estimates are that we lost four hundred Psy tonight, the majority dead, a fifth badly infected." All of whom would slip into irrevocable comas if the past pattern held true.

"Approximately fifty humans and three nonpredatory changelings dead, caught in the middle." An eagle had ID'd the changeling casualties. "One adult male survivor, talent: psychometry. The other Psy survivors were all empaths." His race was imploding, and there seemed to be nothing any of them could do about it.

"We also heard reports of a second outbreak on the heels of the New York one."

Vasic nodded, the data having come in during the past fifteen minutes. "Seattle. Krychek's taken charge there, but the overall situation is spiraling rapidly out of control." And it was causing Ivy to hurt herself. "Do empaths have a self-destructive streak?"

Lucas shot him a shrewd look. "No," he said, his tone low. "But they do have a tendency to put themselves last. An empath's capacity to care is what makes her who she is." His eyes lingered on his mate. "It's also an E's greatest weakness."

It was at that instant that Vasic truly understood the battle his great-grandfather had faced in attempting to protect his Sunny from her most profound instincts. "I don't care if it makes her hate me," he said to Lucas Hunter, "I *will not* permit her to sacrifice herself."

The other man's lips curved slightly. "When an E loves, she loves with every ounce of her being. She might be so angry with you she can't speak, might possibly throw things at your head"—a very feline glint in his eye—"but she will never hate you. That's the one advantage you have when it comes to protecting her."

"Are you advising me to manipulate my . . ." He didn't have a word for what Ivy was to him, used the one with which the man beside him was familiar. It fit. "My mate?"

Rubbing at his stubbled jaw, Lucas said, " 'Manipulate' is a strong word. I'm talking more about a gentle reminder that her life isn't only her own . . . that it would break you to lose her."

That, Vasic thought, was the absolute truth.

Sascha rose from her position bent over Ivy right then. "I think she just burned herself out," she said, rubbing absently at her lower back with one hand. "Vasic, can you carry her to one of the cushions?" She nodded at the large, flat cushions that lay scattered on the floor. "It'd be better for her than a hard table."

Vasic didn't do it using his telekinesis. Didn't want the distance. Gathering the woman who owned his battered heart gently in his arms, he carried her to a cushion set away from the windows that told him this wasn't a cabin on the ground, but an aerie in the branches of a tree. When Ivy curled up on the cushion, it unraveled a dark knot in his chest. *Ivy?*

No verbal or telepathic response, but her lips tugged up at the corners and she rubbed her face against the hand he'd placed on her cheek. It was enough. *Sleep. I'll be here.* He'd always be there, even if he had to tear the malfunctioning parts of the gauntlet from his body himself. He didn't trust her to look out for herself.

Standing only when she seemed to fall into a deep, natural sleep, he turned to find Sascha had moved to the kitchen area with her mate, the couple talking quietly to one another.

"Here." The cardinal E passed him a glass full of what looked like a nutrient mix. "Annoying as it is to admit, this stuff is still the best thing to rehydrate and reenergize after a psychic burn."

He thought of Ivy complaining about the lack of flavor in nutrient meals, knew she'd scrunch up her nose when he gave her the same kind of drink after she woke. Shifting to make sure she remained in his line of sight, he accepted the drink. The alpha couple had no reason to cause him harm, and he needed the energy boost.

"I think you should come to New York," he said after finishing the glass. "Ivy's mentioned several times that she wished you were nearby."

Sascha glanced at Lucas. "That's what we were just discussing."

From the look on the other male's face, a "discussion" wasn't quite what they'd been having, but the leopard alpha kept his relaxed position against the counter, arms folded. "We'll both be coming," he said, "but only for a short period."

"You don't want to be away from your daughter." Vasic knew they'd never bring a vulnerable innocent into a city in chaos.

Sascha leaned her head against Lucas's shoulder, her mate's arm going around her waist while her hand settled on his heart. Their movements were so unconscious Vasic wondered how many times they'd stood exactly this way. And he thought of how Ivy liked to tuck herself against him, the way he'd cradle the back of her head with one hand, his other arm around her. It . . . eased things in him to hold her, to know he had her trust. He could no longer exist without it.

"I think I can probably last three days," Sascha said, then twisted her mouth. "Okay, maybe two. She's so tiny, and I can't bear to think of her crying for me."

Lucas dropped a kiss to Sascha's hair as Vasic said, "There'll be an outbreak in that time frame if the infection continues to escalate at its present pace."

Shadows in Sascha's eyes. "We'll be there as soon as possible," she said into the hush of the forest night. "I want to speak to Alice one more time first."

"I'll have to get in touch with the WaterSky eagles," Lucas added, "clear my presence in their territory. Shouldn't be an issue as we're on good terms."

Vasic nodded. "I'll take Ivy home now." She curled immediately into his chest when he lifted her into his arms, and it felt as if she'd burrowed into the raw vulnerability of his unprotected heart. He didn't fight it. He was hers. It was as simple as that. "Do you want me to return to take you to New York?"

"No, save your energy," Lucas responded. "We'll catch a high-speed jet."

Vasic left without further words, needing Ivy safe in an environment he could control. A wide-awake Rabbit jumped up onto the bed the instant Vasic laid her down on her side. Nuzzling at her as if to make certain she was okay, the dog settled down in front of her. Vasic did a security sweep of the rest of the apartment, the outer corridor, the two unoccupied apartments on this level, as well as any entrances onto the floor, then checked in with Abbot to find the other Tk was with Jaya at the hospital. It meant he had to clear Abbot and Jaya's apartment, too, but the task didn't take long.

His next contact was Aden. "Update?" he asked over the comm built into his gauntlet.

The news was harsh. "Krychek's had confirmation from the NetMind and DarkMind that the entire span of the Net is riddled with the fine, invisible tendrils. Quarantining or slicing away parts of the population on the theory that some sections might be clean is no longer an option."

That meant the only way to save their race was to find a cure. Before Vasic could respond, Aden told him something worse. "Nonempathic children aren't immune; they're carriers. Impossible to know when or if the infection will go active."

Vasic's mind filled with the image of an innocent little girl named Harriet. "That eliminates the possibility of an uninfected next generation." It also cut off the option of segregating the young to give them a higher chance of survival.

"Krychek's suggested the squad force the Es to defect, set up a clean network."

Vasic might once have agreed with that tactic. Now, he shook his head in an immediate negative. "It'd kill something in Ivy." He had no compunction in making her rest or otherwise take care of herself, but he knew his E. Ivy was a fighter, and she was loyal. To make her watch while those she loved perished, while millions screamed for help, it would do damage that could never be healed.

"I guessed that would be the case. I'll touch base with the others, give the Es the choice."

Vasic didn't think any would accept it. "How many outbreaks since Seattle?"

"Five. Scattered around the world."

Time was running out. "Wake me only if there's no other option. I need to recharge."

Double-checking the security after signing off, Vasic stripped and showered in Ivy's bathroom. It only took a short second to grab fresh jeans from his room. Putting his boots near her bed so he could access them in case of an emergency, he was about to lie down next to her when he received a comm transmission on his gauntlet.

He stood, walked to the doorway so as not to disturb Ivy's sleep, and answered the call. "Grandfather."

Chapter 45

World financial markets fell steeply overnight, and the trend shows no signs of reversing itself.

The San Francisco Gazette

"THANKS FOR MEETING me so early," Sascha said to Alice as they walked in the area immediately outside the SnowDancer den. It was empty, the little ones still asleep, and the unbroken span of fresh snow sparkling under the dawn was both excruciatingly beautiful and too quiet. This place was meant for forts and snowball fights and wolf pups pouncing on one another in rough-and-tumble play.

"It was no hardship," Alice answered, tugging the ends of her royal blue sweater-tunic over her hands. "I tend to wake early to watch the sunrise." She drew in a breath of the chilly mountain air, the sun not yet high enough to burn off the mist that licked the woods in front of them. "Before . . . this, I always lived in cities. I visited my parents in distant corners of the planet—Egypt, Peru, China—but I always returned to the university."

"Do you miss being in a city?"

"A little, but it's a kind of faded missing. A sepia-toned photograph that tells me nothing would be the same."

The two of them wandered into the trees, boots leaving distinctive imprints on the snow.

"I've been watching news reports on the outbreaks."

"The more the Net degrades," Sascha said, her mind full of the heartbreaking images on the news this morning, "the worse the fallout—for everyone, not just the Psy." All major cities had an entwined population—human, Psy, and changeling residents living next to each other, often in the same buildings. The infected didn't discriminate when it came to their victims . . . even when the victims were too tiny to fight back.

Sascha had woken Naya after she'd understood the true horror of what had occurred in the night darkness. She'd held her sweet baby, warm and alive and safe in her arms, and she'd cried for the parents who had become monsters through no choice of their own and for the innocents who'd been butchered, Lucas's own arms tight around them both.

Swallowing the renewed knot in her throat, she said, "A lot of the first responders were taken out by psychic strikes during the outbreaks, even with Krychek's team doing everything it can to round up Psy capable of shielding others."

"I've been reading my own book in an effort to jog my memory." Alice ran her gloved fingers over icicles dripping from a branch above. "I see why it may make you want to tear out your hair. I assumed so much general knowledge."

"It was probably reasonable at the time," Sascha said diplomatically, though she'd been known to want to throw said book across the room.

"I don't know." Alice wrapped her arms around herself, but her expression remained open. "It was my first book. I probably didn't distill my original thesis down as neatly as I could have." She went as if to run her hand through her hair, paused. "Drat. I keep forgetting my hair's got to grow back. I feel like a damn skinny hedgehog."

Sascha had the sense she was seeing a glimpse of the real Alice Eldridge for the first time. A smart woman with a self-deprecating sense of humor that invited the listener to laugh with her. "You're lovely." Too thin, yes, but with incredible bones and lush lips against skin once more kissed by a golden sheen. "Watch out for the wolf males. They'll probably start doing sneaky things like bringing you food, and you'll be in a courtship before you know it."

When Alice's eyes narrowed, Sascha found the sorrow cloaking the world hadn't stolen her ability to laugh, to live this life she'd been given. "It's started already?"

"I was wondering at the sudden surge of interest in my favorite meals." The other woman's exasperated smile faded into raw grief. "For me," she whispered, "it wasn't over a hundred years ago. It was yesterday. And yesterday I had parents and friends and a career. Yesterday, I loved a powerful, tormented man who'd been my childhood playmate and who broke my heart to splinters."

"Alice." Sascha closed her hand over the other woman's shoulder in silent comfort.

The scientist didn't shrug it off. "I've had flashes where I think I can remember my research"—husky voice, careful words—"but nothing concrete yet." She turned to face Sascha. "I'd like to go to New York."

Sascha stopped walking. "Are you sure?" This was one response for which she hadn't been prepared. "It's bound to be dangerous."

"I'm not worried about danger, Sascha. I'm not even worried about dying. I'm worried I'll never live again if I don't start soon."

Chapter 46

They call it Haven.

Zie Zen to Vasic

VASIC WOKE THE instant Ivy did. Snuggled up warm against him, she stretched sleepily and rubbed her face against his chest. He caressed his fingers over her hip in turn, luxuriating in the pleasure of waking with his empath.

"Good morning," she murmured in a husky voice.

It was a caress over his body. Turning on his side, he stroked his hand into her hair as she lay drowsy eyed below him. "Good morning."

A lazy, affectionate smile that caught at his heart and refused to let go. "I flaked, huh?"

"You needed rest," Vasic answered. And then he kissed her.

Ivy responded with the lush generosity that had already made him an addict. Sliding her arms around his neck and bending one leg at the knee to cradle him between her thighs, she surrendered her mouth to his desires. And he took, devoured. He hadn't understood how starved he was of touch until he met Ivy. Now, she was the only one who could ease the piercing ache of his need.

Licking his tongue against hers in the way he'd discovered she liked, he closed his hand over the plump mound of her breast.

She jerked.

He halted but didn't remove his hand. "No?" It gave him excruciating sexual pleasure to touch that part of her, but he'd do nothing that caused Ivy hurt.

"Yes."

Tugging him down with a grip in his hair on the heels of that breathy whisper, she initiated another kiss. It was deeper, hotter, wilder than the previous one, Vasic's hand squeezing and petting Ivy's breast as they kissed and her body rocked against his own—which was probably why they ended up first in the desert, then in a remote part of the Rockies. He grit his jaw, clenched his teeth, and got them back home.

"I need to talk to Judd," he said, forcing his hands off her. "He has to have figured out a solution by now."

Ivy's chest rose and fell in a ragged rhythm. "Yes." Clenching her hands on the sheets, she said, "I don't want to stop again."

Neither did Vasic. His penis was so hard it was a rod of iron, the damp heat between Ivy's thighs tempting him even through the layers of their clothing. He wanted to touch her there skin to skin, wanted to taste, wanted to *take*. Shoving off her before he teleported them somewhere inhospitable, he sat on the edge of the bed with his back to her. Seeing her all sleep mussed and well kissed wasn't exactly conducive to control.

Rustling sounds behind him. "The infection . . . how bad are things?" A quiet, worried question.

"Bad, but it's been calm for the past three hours." He ran both hands through his hair, knowing that even if the world had been going to hell right that second, he'd still have done what he was about to do. If he didn't, Ivy would be left alone in the dark, and that was unacceptable.

Angling his body, he reached out to take her hand. "We have an appointment after breakfast."

Ivy's fingers curled over his. "Who are we going to see?"

"A man named Samuel Rain."

ALMOST out of her skin with hope, Ivy waited while Vasic teleported to the location for which he'd been given visual coordinates. He'd refused to take her with him until he'd verified it was safe; the man had a protective streak a mile and a half wide. "I like that about him," she whispered to Rabbit, who was sulking in his basket because he'd realized they were going somewhere and leaving him behind again.

Even a treat hadn't appeased him.

Ivy knelt to rub his belly. "I promise we'll go for a walk after. And Vasic's going to drop you off at Central Command with Aden, so you won't be alone." She'd just stood back up when Vasic reappeared.

"Rabbit," he said, and the dog scrambled to them. Vasic touched his hand to Ivy's lower back. "I think your pet will be welcome at our destination."

"Our pet." Ivy smiled, aware of Rabbit standing motionless beside Vasic. Their smart little dog had learned about 'porting and didn't so much as move a muscle until they were standing on the velvet green of a manicured lawn devoid of any hint of snow.

That lawn lay behind a sprawling and graceful home painted a rich, creamy white. It held hints of plantation-style architecture but had entire walls formed of glass—natural light would flood the interior on sunny days such as today. With its wide doors open to the lawn, the green space appeared an extension of the home.

Outdoor furniture dotted the grass, the seating arrangements comfortable, but the lawn was clearly only one part of the grounds. Several paths disappeared behind hedges and natural-appearing clusters of trees; they broke up the gently undulating landscape so it was impossible to tell how extensive the grounds actually were. Ivy had the feeling any guess she made would be a gross underestimation. She couldn't hear the sound of a single vehicle, much less see any other indication of civilization nearby.

The temperature and foliage didn't tell her much about the location, except that it was in the same hemisphere as New York, but more temperate. While the area was free of snow, she did still need the coat she'd put on over jeans and her white cowl-neck sweater—though that would no doubt change as the sun rose higher in the sky.

Despite the cold, people sat quietly in the seating areas, some in groups, several alone. All were dressed in ordinary civilian clothes. A few were reading, others stared out into space, one rocked back and forth . . . but no one was actually isolated. Men and women she assumed were caretakers moved quietly from person to person, group to group, never intruding, but always there should one of the patients have a need.

Ivy also noted the touches—on the shoulder, on the arm. "Anchoring," she said aloud. "The touches are to remind the patients of the here and now."

"Probable," Vasic answered, "given that the majority are apt to be F-Psy."

Foreseers, Ivy remembered, were at high risk of falling forever into the visions created by their extraordinary gift.

One of the caretakers came toward Ivy and Vasic. She wore a simple gray pantsuit paired with a pale yellow shirt, her golden brown hair in a single tidy braid, and her skin a warm caramel shade. There was a sense of calm responsibility to her that made Ivy believe the woman was in charge of the entire complex.

"I'm Clara Alvarez," she said on reaching them. "I manage Haven. Anthony told me to expect you."

Vasic's fingers brushed Ivy's hip. "I'm Vasic, and this is Ivy." A nod toward where their dog was sniffing at Clara's shoes. "And that is Rabbit."

The woman leaned down to pet Rabbit with hands gloved in thin black. Ivy had seen gloves like that before. Frowning, she tried to remember where. *The gloves . . .*

She must be a former J-Psy, Vasic replied.

Of course. Ivy had caught glimpses of Justice Psy while she'd lived in Washington with her parents. She didn't know why Js wore the gloves, but she assumed it had something to do with deteriorating mental shields. Clara, however, didn't appear stressed in any way, a tranquility to her that was soothing against Ivy's senses.

"If you'll follow me," she said now, and stood to lead them down a pathway to the left. "Samuel prefers to sit in the rose garden, even with the plants not much more than sticks at this time of year."

As they walked, she said, "I'll introduce you, then leave. Whether he chooses to speak or not is up to him—he's been largely silent since waking from the coma." Stopping beside a weathered pine table on which sat a small red toolbox, she looked at Vasic. "This is the personal and somewhat idiosyncratically stocked toolbox we recovered from Samuel's home.

He hasn't touched it though we leave it in his quarters, but you should store the image so you can retrieve it, just in case."

"I have a lock."

"Don't push him," Clara continued once they began to walk again. "It may be that he no longer has the capability or the knowledge you need." She stopped, held their gazes with warm brown eyes that were deadly serious. "He was a brilliant, gifted man, you understand. If he's lost that and is aware of the loss, he may simply choose not to face that part of his life. It is his right."

"You're very protective." Ivy felt a deep sense of respect toward the other woman. "Are you close to him?"

"There is no romantic relationship. My husband would take issue." With that startling and rather wry comment, Clara began to walk again. "But I see in Samuel something that resonates.

"A Justice Psy has a use-by date," she said, expression difficult to read. "I'm living a second life now, but many never do. I don't wish to steal Samuel's second chance from him by forcing him to compare the man he is now with the man he once was." A potent statement, for all that Clara never raised her voice. "His value is not diminished; it is just different."

"We understand." No wonder Anthony Kyriakus had chosen this woman to run Haven, Ivy thought. She was extraordinary, a quiet warrior.

"We will do no harm," Vasic said to Clara. "We'll simply sit with him until it becomes clear whether or not he wishes us to stay or go."

Clara nodded and led them around a hedge and into the dormant starkness of a rose garden in winter. Seated on the other side, on a bench situated beneath the shade of an evergreen with spreading branches and fine needles, was a thin man who might have been in his early thirties.

Dressed in wheat-colored slacks teamed with a simple blue shirt, the dark blond strands of his hair disordered by the breeze and what looked like a windbreaker discarded by his side, he stared out at the garden through old-fashioned wire-rimmed spectacles. They were unusual when eyesight could generally be corrected without issue, but Ivy didn't get the impression the spectacles were an affectation.

"Samuel." Clara placed one gloved hand on his shoulder when they reached him. "These are the guests I told you about. Ivy, Vasic, and Rabbit."

No response from Samuel Rain.

Giving them another solemn glance to reiterate the ground rules, Clara walked away. Ivy took a deep breath of the crisp air, painfully conscious that she couldn't sense Samuel Rain on the empathic level. It was as if he'd gone so deep into himself that he no longer existed.

"Woof!" Rabbit dropped a stick at her feet.

"Rabbit." Affection blooming in her, Ivy bent to pick it up. "Where did you get this? If you've messed up their garden, we'll both be in trouble."

Vasic was the one who answered. "I saw him find it beneath the tree to the right."

Glancing at Vasic, she telepathed, *Maybe it's better if we don't crowd Mr. Rain?*

Vasic took the stick she handed up. "Come on, Rabbit," he said, leading their excited dog to the left of the rose garden and to a rectangular area of open ground. It was within sight of Samuel but not in his face.

Meandering through the sleeping roses as her man and their pet played, Ivy read the small weatherproof card by each bed, examined the accompanying images—an exuberant peach rose was planted next to a vibrant yellow one, which in turn was beside a sexy red. Then and there, she decided she'd plant a flower garden at the home she made with Vasic.

Do you think you might want to settle at the orchard? It was a place she loved, but she'd go anywhere with Vasic.

I'm home with you, Ivy.

Undone, she went to turn toward him and was almost bowled over by Rabbit as their pet ran through the garden pathways to drop the stick in front of Samuel Rain. When the man didn't respond, Rabbit nudged at him with his head. Her heart melted. "Come here, Rabbit," she said, patting her thigh. "Samuel wants to sit quietly today."

Rabbit tried one more head butt before picking up his stick and coming to Ivy for a scratch. As he ran back to Vasic, Ivy looked up . . . to see Samuel Rain's eyes on her Arrow. Ivy's pulse thudded, but she didn't make any sudden movements. Until the engineer stood up and strode toward Vasic.

She took the other path to reach him at the same time.

Not saying a word, Samuel Rain grabbed Vasic's gauntleted arm and stared at it. "Are you mad?" he asked in a tone so sharp it could've sliced flesh. "This isn't ready for human integration."

"I was self-destructive when I volunteered," Vasic answered. "I no longer am. Can you remove it?"

The engineer shot him an incredulous look. "I'm brain damaged, you idiot. You don't want me playing around in your body."

"You seem quite mentally competent at this precise instant."

Hitting the gleaming black carapace of the gauntlet with his knuckles, Samuel Rain said, "Open it."

Vasic didn't move, but the carapace slid down on both sides to reveal the control panel within. Rain stared at it for a while. "The interface is creative. I need to see the guts of it." He glanced around in a distracted fashion. "Damn it, where are my tools?"

"Here." Vasic handed him the case.

Taking it without questioning how it had got there, the engineer put it on the ground. "Don't touch, Rabbit," he said absently, and took out a delicate laser tool. A couple of moves with the tool and the interface panel slid back.

Close your eyes, Ivy.

Ivy took Vasic's free hand in both of hers, pressed a kiss to the back. *It's you. I love every part of you.*

A long pause before he lifted his arm. Tucking herself under it, while Rabbit sniffed round the toolbox but didn't mess with it, she steeled herself to deal with the sight of the deadly threat within Vasic, and looked. She didn't know what she'd been expecting, but it wasn't the astonishing symmetry of man and machine.

Fine multihued cables sparking with current twined with muscle and tendon and bone, the delicacy of the filaments such that she knew she wasn't seeing everything with the naked eye. *It shouldn't be so beautiful,* she said to Vasic, anger rising anew at what he'd done to himself.

His fingers curled around her nape. *Are you going to be mad at me for this our entire life?*

She nodded. *You should've waited for me.*

I never dared dream of you, Ivy. I never thought a man like me deserved such a gift.

Petting his chest, she said, *You're my gift, too, you know. I'm so glad for you every instant of every day. Even when I'm really, really angry with you.*

In front of her, Samuel Rain's spectacles shimmered, and she belatedly realized they weren't old-fashioned at all, but tools to allow him to see to a microcellular level. "Imbeciles." The engineer shut the interface panel, nodded at Vasic to close the protective carapace. "Stealing my work and thinking they know what to do with it. Like monkeys deciding to program a computronic system."

"Can you fix it?" Vasic asked.

"No, I'm brain damaged." With that, he put away the tool, snapped the toolbox shut, and hefted it. "Come back tomorrow."

Ivy stared after the engineer, hope a tight, hard knot in her chest. "He's either mad or brilliant."

"There's often only a razor-thin line between the two."

"And"—Rain called over his shoulder—"bring the dog!"

Chapter 47

Anchorage, New York, Rio, Cape Town, Seattle, Osaka, Dubai, and Chengdu have all suffered outbreaks. And the pace is continuing to accelerate.

Live NetStream, *PsyNet Beacon*

LUCAS HUNTER AND Sascha Duncan, as well as Alice Eldridge, were already in the city and in discussion with Jaya and Abbot by the time Ivy and Vasic got back. Leaving the empaths to talk, Vasic decided to take advantage of the relative quiet to have another important meeting. Vasic trusted Abbot to the core, and Lucas looked at Ivy with a protectiveness that likely resulted from the leopard alpha's love for his own empathic mate.

"Contact me the instant there's a problem," he told them both. "I can be back in a heartbeat."

Getting their agreement, he 'ported to an isolated location in the Sierra Nevada mountains and sent Judd the visual so the SnowDancer lieutenant and fellow Arrow could join him. "Thank you for meeting me," he said when the other man arrived a minute later.

"No thanks needed." Running a hand through his hair to dislodge snow that had fallen on him from an overhead branch, Judd fell into step with Vasic.

The snow wasn't as thick in the trees as it was out in the open areas, their boots more than adequate for the terrain.

Judd gave him a measuring look. "You realize no one knows you have a visual anchor for this area."

"I never had any intention of using it for an aggressive act. I like the quiet." It was one of the most remote parts of SnowDancer's vast territory. He'd found it by accident, the image he'd been given for a transfer matching a particular section here. Such an accidental match was so rare, Vasic had only experienced it twice.

"I like the quiet, too." Judd's breath frosted the air as he spoke. "Brenna and I come up here." His cheeks creased. "We had a snow fight last time."

Vasic wouldn't have understood that before Ivy. Now, he found himself wondering if Ivy would enjoy playing in the snow. Rabbit surely would. "I need to ask you some highly personal questions."

Judd reached down to pack the snow into a ball. "I've been hoping for a long time that someone else in the squad would get to the point where a discussion like this would be necessary." Rising, he threw the snowball with a fast arm. "Ask."

"How do you control your telekinesis while intimate with your mate?"

"I broke a damn lot of furniture at the start, including two beds." A curious glance. "What are you doing?"

"Traveling around the world."

Judd stared, then started laughing, the gold flecks in his eyes vivid against the brown. Vasic couldn't imagine laughing, but it looked as if Judd did it naturally, so perhaps it was a skill he could learn.

"Sorry," the other Arrow said when he could speak again. "I just had visions of what Brenna would do to me if I teleported us somewhere public in the middle of intimate skin privileges." He thrust his hands into the pockets of the jeans he wore below a fine black sweater and black leather-synth jacket. "Your Ivy blister your hide?"

"I've managed to keep the locations remote so far," Vasic said, "but obviously, I can't leave that to random chance." He straightened the cuff of his own leather-synth jacket—the style was different from Judd's, but they were otherwise identically dressed. "Ivy says my civilian clothes are a uniform."

Judd scowled. "Leather-synth provides excellent protection against knives, and denim is extremely strong."

"Exactly." Their civilian clothes made sense. "Krychek is trialing a new bulletproof material that also deflects a certain level of laser fire." Vasic had already ordered a coat for Ivy of the material, though Krychek's offer had been made to the squad.

Instead of rejecting the request, the cardinal had ordered the coat be fast-tracked. "You should get it for Brenna."

Judd nodded. "I might talk to Kaleb about a larger pack-wide order." Stopping at the edge of a cliff, he looked out over the spread of ruler-straight firs below, their branches heavy with snow. "Like I said, I broke a lot of furniture," he began, keeping his eyes scrupulously forward. "Then we bought a titanium frame for the bed, and I bent it—though at least I could bend that back until it strained too far. Outside, I took down several trees, cracked a few boulders."

Vasic hadn't previously considered the idea of choosing to have sex out of doors. His body decided it liked the idea. "And now?"

"I've come up with a few tricks," Judd told him. "But I learned the thing that works best from another Tk in the 9 range."

"Who?" As far as Vasic was aware, of the high-Gradient telekinetics in the Net, only Judd and Kaleb had broken conditioning.

"Think about it."

Vasic knew or knew of every other strong Tk in the world. Considering Judd and Krychek, he realized the unknown Tk had to be isolated in some way, in a situation that encouraged a fracture in his Silence . . . *or* that conditioning had been problematic from the start.

"Stefan." The Gradient 9.7 Tk was on permanent duty in the deep sea station Alaris. "He's been very careful."

"He's one of us."

"Yes." Stefan had been shifted out of Arrow training as a result of a psychological issue that made him no less valuable as a telekinetic and no less trustworthy. In the past five years, he'd assisted in the defection of a number of Arrows by helping to fake their deaths. "What's Stefan's solution to the problem?"

"You have to teach your brain to handle sexual stimuli," Judd told him. "Under Silence, we were taught to maintain strict discipline even under severe duress, including torture. However, none of us were taught how to handle pleasure, especially the extreme pleasure of true intimate contact."

"There was no need." The dissonance would've crippled them before it ever got this far.

"Exactly. It means we have a blind spot—it also means we don't have any bad habits or training to overcome."

The latter, Vasic realized, was extremely important. "No need to split our attention in order to fight previous programming."

A nod from Judd. "Right now, in the absence of any other instruction, your mind reverts to the most instinctive aspect of your ability. For most Tks, it'd be random destruction." The other man shot him a quick, amused glance. "You're unique, but the same principles apply."

"I could train my brain to go only to certain locations." Such as from one bed to another. "It's not the best solution, but better than ending up on ice or on rocks."

"There's another option." Judd pushed back strands of hair that had fallen across his forehead. "Your core ability is still Tk, so you should be able to teach yourself not to 'port at all in that situation. Neither Stefan nor I," he continued, "are able to maintain control while sharing skin privileges with our mates. Perhaps if we'd been taught so since childhood—"

"I doubt that would alter the situation," Vasic interrupted to say. "True intimacy demands we lower our barriers."

"Yes." The single word held a staggering depth of emotion. "So, because we can't curb the surge of telekinetic power," he said, "we've learned to redirect it in a specific way."

"Into water?" Vasic guessed, seeing where Judd was going.

"Yes. Stefan's surrounded by the sea and even his strength won't do more than cause a ripple or two." The other man paused to watch a pack of wolves lope across the clearing below. "I do the same by filling in the bath with water. It's steam by the end." A grin and a shrug. "Not to say I don't still lose it now and then, but it's a hell of a lot better than before. I figure the more practice I get"—laughter in his eyes now, at a training regime that was clearly no hardship—"the better I'll become at handling the energy surge."

Vasic considered the genius of the idea. "Stefan's solution utilizes the

same training protocols and pathways as Silence, but with positive rein-
forcement"—sexual pleasure—"instead of negative." Using what had been
forged in pain and torture for a far more beautiful end.

"It does take time, so you might be traveling for some time yet," Judd
added. "And your instinctive 'porting ability may make things more difficult, but I think you have the mental strength and the psychic discipline
to be successful."

Vasic thought it over. "To begin, I'll set my brain on a loop of isolated
locations." Going bed to bed might be impossible this quickly, and even
using one or two of his favorite remote locations would require meticulous
care, but Stefan's inspired plan had given him an idea as to how to do
it—not to build something new, but to use what was already there.

"I'll utilize one of the data memorization techniques we were taught,"
he said, thinking it through, "hook it into the same system that allows
my senses to continue to function even if I have to sleep in the field." Both
skills were basic building blocks of an Arrow's training.

Judd nodded slowly. "Yes, that should work. Tell me if it does?"

"Of course." It might be an option that could assist another Arrow
down the line. "Is Stefan safe?" As the most isolated of them all, the other
man had little access to help if he needed it quickly.

"Yes, but perhaps you should visit Alaris, speak to him. With the
situation in the Net changing as fast as it is, he should know we have his
back if something goes wrong."

"I'll go after this." Due to an inexplicable quirk of teleportation, teleporters didn't suffer any ill-effects from the huge changes in pressure
involved in 'porting to the ocean floor and back up.

Shifting on his heel, Judd led them back into the trees. "You said you
had more than one question."

"How did you know what to do?" Vasic had gone on instinct to this
point, and Ivy didn't seem displeased, but he wanted to be certain he was
doing everything he could to pleasure her . . . because touching her gave
him pleasure so intense, he had no hope of ever describing it.

"I'll send you my research file," Judd said, "but you know what I've
learned? If you listen to her, you'll be fine."

Vasic thought of the little noises Ivy made in bed, the way she dug her nails into his back when he touched her just right, and felt his body pulse. "I want this for the others, Judd." Their brethren deserved the same happiness, the same steep learning curve anchored in pleasure rather than pain.

Judd's eyes met his. "I never thought you'd make it to this point. I'm fucking glad you have. We'll get the others here, too—we're Arrows."

"We never give up on a target," Vasic completed, and for the first time since he'd been taught it, the assertion wasn't one of darkness, but of hope.

IVY and Sascha spent a large chunk of the day visiting and interviewing the nonempathic survivors around the world, thanks to Vasic's 'porting ability, while Jaya and Alice remained at the apartment and collated the data in a search for patterns.

"The survivors," Jaya said over a take-out dinner late that night, "all have fractures in their Silence *and* they accept those fractures, even when the resulting emotions aren't pretty."

Ivy threw Abbot another nutrition bar where the blue-eyed Arrow sat with Vasic and Lucas. The three men had ceded the couches to the women, pulling up chairs for themselves. "The woman of darkness that we saw," she said to Jaya afterward, "she was so sad and so angry."

"The embodiment of rejection." Sascha stared at her food without eating. "Silence teaches Psy to stifle all emotion, but at the heart of it, it's always been about the aggressive, violent, angry emotions—and the PsyNet is impacted by the subconscious as well as the conscious."

All the dark emotions, the ugliness, Ivy thought, had been shoved aside, buried, and in that festering soup had grown the infection. "That doesn't give us a cure, though." She pushed away her meal. "No one can simply embrace the whole gamut of emotion after a lifetime of being trained to do the opposite."

Vasic's eyes met hers for a piercing instant.

That wasn't a complaint, Ivy said, blowing him a telepathic kiss.

I know. A caress in the ice of his voice. *It's an unavoidable fact.*

Yes, it was. Her Arrow had opened his heart to her, but he continued to fight a pitched battle against his darker emotions. Anger, rage, loss, it was all trapped inside that great heart, and it made Ivy ache. But she couldn't force those emotions out into the open. No one could. Only Vasic, when he was ready.

Jaya poked at her noodles. "A violent shift like that could also cause shock, a stroke, an aneurysm."

"The other thing," Alice said, leaning forward, "is that I can't believe there are so few people in the Net who've embraced their emotions."

At that instant, the charismatic intensity of the scientist's gaze reminded Ivy of Samuel Rain—a spark of genius lived in them both, and both had been wounded in ways that sought to bury that genius.

"According to everything I've learned since waking," Alice continued, "and what Jaya's shared today, Silence has been fracturing for years."

The three empaths looked at one another, nodded as a unit. The scientist was right—far more people should be immune to the infection if that was the only prerequisite.

Picking up a datapad, Jaya began to scroll through the information they had on the nonempathic uninfected. "We're missing something, but I can't—"

The other empath's words cut off as a screaming roar of insanity and confusion smashed into the room.

It took Vasic less than seven seconds to teleport Ivy, Lucas, and Sascha to the site two blocks over, then return for Alice, the human scientist having insisted on being present. Abbot took Jaya directly to the end of the worst-affected street, where she'd join the medical units Vasic had called in. Leaving Alice tucked up inside a doorway not far from Jaya, Abbot there to protect the medics, the rest of them waded into the fray.

The street, lined with midrises zoned for mixed commercial/residential use, was also a busy entertainment area and thoroughfare utilized by countless people. Those people were all now fighting desperately for their lives against the infected—who seemed not even to notice their own injuries. Ivy saw a man whose left arm was hanging broken by his side run headlong at a big human male. The infected went down under a single punch but continued to try and get up.

Ivy recoiled as she was hit by a telepathic blow hard enough to make her skull ring. Shaking it off, she concentrated on calming one individual at a time. It worked as it had the last time, but a mere ten minutes in and she could already feel an agonizing pressure building behind her eyelids. It would—

A massive telepathic blow.

Hitting the ground hard enough to graze her cheek and hands as blood vessels burst in her eyes, she realized there had to be a Gradient 8 or higher telepath in the crowd. *Hell.* "I'm fine," she managed to say to Sascha when the cardinal turned to check on her. "Telepathic strike."

Sascha wiped a bloody nose on her sleeve, said, "I just felt one, too." An instant later, she staggered. "That was a telekinetic hit." Going to her knees in a controlled move, as if to make herself a smaller target, she stared into the carnage. "Lucas is all right," she said at last. "His natural shields protect him."

Ivy could see the blue scythe that was the laser built into Vasic's gauntlet, so she knew he was holding up under the dual physical and psychic attacks. However, there were a significant number of humans and Psy—infected, noninfected, it was hard to tell—spasming on the ground, hands over their ears and screams tearing the air as the minds around them went haywire.

Nonpredatory changelings caught in the chaos tried to fight, but they weren't aggressive by nature, couldn't stand against the manic fury incited by the infection. And with the number of residents who lived in the midrises, there were simply too many infected against too few defenders. Even the arrival of the eagles didn't turn the tide.

Ivy saw victim after victim go down under pummeling fists and clawing hands while still others bled and collapsed from increasingly violent mental strikes.

"Terminal field!" It was a rasping scream.

Turning, Ivy and Sascha stared at Alice as she ran toward them. The scientist staggered halfway, as if hit by a telepathic blow, but didn't stop. "Terminal field," she gasped to Sascha after falling to her hands and knees beside them, her body heaving. "You have to initiate a terminal field."

Sascha, eyes pure black with the agony of the dying who littered the street, cupped Alice's face in her hands. "Tell me what that is."

Alice drew in a jagged breath while Ivy continued to do what she could, even as the pressure in her brain built and built to a nauseating pounding behind her eyes.

"Alice." Sascha fought the urge to shake the other woman, knowing that wouldn't hurry the retrieval of Alice's buried memories. *What is a terminal field?*"

Gaze blank, Alice stared at her, but just when Sascha was about to give up and turn back to the chaos, the other woman said, "You can block psychic abilities on a mass scale."

Sascha's heart slammed against her ribs. Forcing herself to hold firm against the horror and pain slapping at her senses, she focused on Alice. This was critical, could directly impact the number of fatalities. "How?"

Hands fisted on her thighs and eyes glittering wet, Alice shook her head. "I don't know. I can't find that piece of memory."

"Okay, okay." Sascha touched her fingers to Alice's cheek before shifting her attention to the fighting. "If I attempt to block everyone," she said aloud, "it'll negatively affect the defenders."

So she'd have to narrow her focus, and do *what*? She wanted to scream at the unfairness of being told she had an ability that could save thousands of lives, then left to flounder without a road map as to how to activate it. Turning to Ivy to see if the younger empath had any ideas, she sucked in a breath, abdomen lurching.

Ivy's face was a mask of blood.

Chapter 48

"IVY, STOP," SASCHA said, using the same tone she used on recalcitrant juveniles in the pack. "Stop right now." Panic beat in her—the other woman could easily stroke out, causing irrevocable damage to her brain. *"Ivy."*

"There are too many, Sascha." It came out thready. "I can't stop, or they'll swarm the defenders."

Sascha grabbed Ivy's shoulder, forced her physically around. "You stop right now, or I will telepath Vasic."

"Not fair." It came out mumbled, sluggish.

"Yes, well, you're not exactly acting rationally." She looked to Alice. "Can you get her to the medics?"

Nodding, the anthropologist rose to her feet with one of Ivy's arms over her shoulders, her own around the empath's waist, and staggered away. They were protected by Abbot and the Enforcement officers holding the line so the maddened couldn't escape this pocket of insanity. Sascha watched long enough to make sure the two women were safe before returning to her task, automatically scanning for Lucas as she did so.

Her mate—claws out—was fighting beside a number of cops, taking out the more aggressive infected so the officers could get the uninfected and injured out. Vasic wasn't visible, but since Ivy hadn't raised the alarm, the teleporter must be safe.

"Terminal field," she said to herself. "Terminal field. Figure it out."

She tried every tactic in her arsenal, but all it got her was another bloody nose and a pounding in her ears that told her she'd soon be as bad as Ivy. "I am *not* giving up." She refused to consign her daughter, any child, to a world overrun with vicious insanity.

That was when the Tk she'd chosen to focus on—on the theory his belligerence would make it easier to tell if what she was doing was working—looked straight at her . . . and teleported. Sascha hadn't thought he was that strong, and maybe he wasn't, but she was only twenty feet away and in plain sight. He was in front of her a second later, his hands shoving out as if to make her fly through the air to slam into the heavy-duty Enforcement combat vehicles. The impact would snap her spine.

Adrenaline took over. *"Stop!"* she yelled on the physical and psychic levels both. *"You can't do this!"*

Blinking, he pushed out with his hands. Nothing. Staggered at her success, she almost fell victim to the meaty fist he swung at her face— except her mate was already there. Lucas took her would-be-assailant out with a clean punch to the jaw that left the Tk unconscious but alive.

"Kitten?"

"I'm fine." Still on her knees, her heart a drum, she touched his calf. "Go, help the others."

As Lucas returned to the fight, Sascha began to concentrate the terminal field on small, tight areas that didn't weaken the defenders but eliminated the worst psychic threats. What she'd understood in that split second was that it wasn't simply about telling an individual he couldn't do something—it was about hitting his hidden emotional core to convince him he was *incapable* of the action.

Her nose didn't bleed now, the pressure easing in her frontal lobe. This, *this* was what she was meant to be doing, the act as natural and as simple as breathing. And she understood why the post-Silence Council had wanted to eliminate empaths from the gene pool. Not simply because they were the personification of emotion, but because an E could strip power from Councilor and beggar alike.

IVY sat with nerves raw and teeth gritted in the back of an ambulance and listened to the fighting while an M-Psy told her that a blood vessel in her brain was critically close to rupture. "Whatever you were doing, stop it," he said. "Or the next time, yours will be one of the corpses we body bag off the streets."

Leaving her with those blunt words, as well as an order that she utilize pain-control mechanisms to ameliorate the agony in her skull, he went to deal with other injuries. Her psychic strain would heal on its own—all it would take was time. Time the world didn't have, she thought, edging out of the ambulance . . . to see Vasic disable a man who'd been beating another to death with a broken chair leg.

Her throat filled with a raging scream she couldn't allow herself to utter. He was so strong, so honorable, and he deserved happiness and peace, not this endless ugliness. *Enough*, she wanted to cry, *he's done enough! Let this gladiator rest*. If only she could figure out the cure—

"You! This is your fault!"

Jerking around at the vituperative cry, she found herself facing a young woman on the other side of the secondary Enforcement barricade. She wore ordinary clothes but had a black band around her wrist. As did the man next to her . . . and the man beside *him*.

All three were staring at her.

A vicious telepathic punch.

Agony searing down her spine, she reacted in pure self-defense to suck out the cold rage that drove them. It poured into her, but she knew it wasn't hers, that she could filter it to inertness. And though her vision was blurred from the assault, she nonetheless saw her attackers look at one another in confusion before melting into the crowd.

Worried they'd done further damage to her already traumatized brain, she went to find a medic when her mind shut down with icy finality.

THREE hours after the outbreak began and ten minutes after the street was stabilized, Vasic placed an unconscious Ivy in her bed. An M-Psy had confirmed she'd suffered no permanent injury, and Vasic had no intention of permitting that to change. "Stay with her, Rabbit."

He petted the worried dog, then tugging a blanket over pet and mistress both, stepped out into the living area to speak to the others. "She isn't going to do any more." If he had to teleport her to a desert during the next attack, he would, regardless of her fury. "This is killing her."

Sascha nodded where she sat on the sofa with her mate beside her. The DarkRiver alpha pair had both showered and were now eating. Sascha had expended so much psychic energy that she'd lost physical weight, her cheekbones slicing against her skin, while Lucas Hunter had fought with hot changeling energy side by side with Vasic.

Alice Eldridge lay curled up asleep on the other sofa. The scientist's physical stamina was still low as a result of her time in stasis, but no one could say she hadn't pulled her weight today.

Vasic grabbed a chair and sat down. He had no desire to eat, but he consumed nutrition bar after nutrition bar with methodical precision—he'd be useless to Ivy otherwise.

"I thought I'd discovered a solution to the pressure on the brain," Sascha said, face drawn, "but the method I use to create a terminal field doesn't work to encourage calm." She thrust a hand through her hair. "There's *so much* we just don't know, don't understand." Eating the bite of pizza her mate held up to her lips, she chewed and swallowed. "I'll stay, help. I couldn't bear to go home knowing—"

"No," Vasic interrupted. "You need to return to your territory."

Scowling at his mate when she parted her lips to speak, Lucas Hunter put a nutrition drink in her hand and waited until she'd started drinking before turning to Vasic. "You want Sascha to train other cardinals?"

"Yes." He finished off his fourth nutrition bar. "We need cardinals ready and able to effect the terminal field, and we need them now. Everything else can come later."

Sascha put down the empty glass. "You're talking about cardinals who've been told they're flawed and of no use their entire lives," she said with such passionate force, Vasic knew she'd been told the same. "It'll take time for them to come to grips with the betrayal of it all."

"Ivy almost killed herself today," he pointed out, his jaw tense. "You've lost a fifth of your body weight, and Jaya is still at the hospital."

Lucas completed Vasic's train of thought, the DarkRiver alpha's eyes nightglow in the muted living room light. "An empath's instincts will always win out."

Of that Vasic had no doubt. "Will you do it?"

"Of course." Sascha closed her hand over Lucas's thigh, her eyes bruised from the anguish and terror that no doubt blanketed the city. "But that'll leave you with only Jaya, and she's a medical empath. Ivy risks brain damage or death if she goes out."

Vasic couldn't trust himself to even think about losing Ivy. "We have to think long-term. If you die here, your knowledge dies with you." He had to be ruthless, consider not the hundreds Sascha might save in the city, but the hundreds of thousands who'd die across the world. "I'm guessing using the terminal field will require a foundation of basic skills. No one else is qualified to assess and teach that."

Lucas ran his knuckles over his mate's cheek. "I know your instincts tell you to stay, but Vasic's right," the alpha said. "I've seen how hard you've fought to figure out each tiny crumb of practical knowledge. You know more than you think."

"And," Vasic pointed out, "you're the most stable and well-known E in the world." The psychological impact of that couldn't be underestimated. "The other cardinals might struggle with feelings of betrayal when it comes to everyone else, but they'll trust you to tell them the truth."

"All right," Sascha said into the quiet. "I'll contact Chang first, since he already has the basic training."

Nodding, Vasic waited only long enough for his psychic batteries to recharge a certain percentage before bringing in Aden to watch over Ivy while he 'ported the alpha couple and Alice Eldridge back to DarkRiver territory. Lucas and Sascha needed to talk to the wolves about turning the compound into a permanent training ground for empaths, and that discussion needed to happen as fast as possible.

Rabbit jumped off the bed and padded over to him when Vasic returned, a low whine in the back of the dog's throat. Bending down, Vasic stroked the anxious animal with a firm touch. "Ivy will be all right," he said. "I'm here to take care of her."

Bumping his head against Vasic's hand, the whine gone—as if their pet had understood Vasic's reassurance—Rabbit scampered up to the bed to settle by Ivy's side once more. Vasic checked her skin, found it warm, her lips curving at the press of his fingers against her pulse. "Vasic."

Releasing a breath at that drowsy mumble, he said, "Sleep."

But she struggled to lift her eyelids. "The others, did they . . ."

"No," he answered, almost able to read her thoughts. "It appears Brigitte is another medical empath, but Isaiah, Chang, and the others are in the same position as you." He'd just received a report that Isaiah had suffered a brain bleed, was in intensive care, but Ivy didn't need to know that right now.

Bleakness in her eyes, her hand curling on the blanket.

He knelt down beside the bed, cradling her cheek and jaw with one hand, his other arm on the pillow above her head. "Sleep. Then rise strong to fight again." That was what motivated her, and he'd use it without pity to help her heal. Even when he had no intention whatsoever of permitting her to cause herself such harm again.

Lids heavy, she closed her fingers over his wrist. "I love you."

The words reverberated in him long after she fell asleep. Forcing himself to leave her some time later, he stepped out to the living area where Aden waited.

"The incoming cardinals will need Arrow shields," he said to the other man. "Sascha's organs would've shut down today if Lucas hadn't realized how much energy she was burning and grabbed energy drinks from the medics." The DarkRiver alpha had known because of the mating bond that tied him to Sascha on a psychic level.

Vasic didn't understand how that bond worked. Neither did he comprehend the intricacies of the tie Kaleb Krychek shared with Sahara Kyriakus, but he knew he wanted the same with Ivy. "The Arrows," he said, "will have to be trained to force the Es to stop and refuel."

"We're going to be spread thin." Aden leaned against a wall. "We could request Krychek's men take over."

"No. Not until there are no more Arrows who can step in."

When Aden raised an eyebrow at that flat response, Vasic said, "Abbot's not the only one who's more stable since the day he began working with his empath."

"Yes," Aden said. "Regardless of the development or not of an emotional connection—though the most stable are the ones who've formed a friendship with their Es at least." His gaze was steady in the dim glow coming from the streetlamps outside, the room otherwise dark. "You've stabilized the most of all."

Vasic thought of Ivy's anger as she fought for him, her sweet sensual generosity, her smile, her courage. She was his anchor and his hope. It was as simple and as powerful as that. "We need to give others in the squad the same chance."

"I'll organize it. Silver Mercant's network is now functional worldwide, and everyone—Psy, human, changeling—who can send help in an outbreak is doing so. The squad shouldn't be as necessary on the front line as we've been thus far."

Vasic looked out into the heavy dark of the night beyond the windows. Arrows might be able to step back for the moment, but these outbreaks were the first stones to fall. When the avalanche came, every man and woman in the squad would be needed to stand against it. And the empaths, he knew, would stand right beside them.

His Ivy would be at his side to the end . . . because the truth was, he couldn't cage her, couldn't take her choices from her, no matter his fury and his fear. It would break her. "The ones who attacked Ivy today." His blood iced. "Did you track them down?"

"It's been taken care of."

"You can't protect my sanity by destroying yours." His partner had already done far more than anyone could've ever expected in managing to keep Vasic alive this long. "It's not necessary any longer."

Aden didn't answer directly. "The breakaway Venice group," he said instead. "They're asking to be placed on active duty."

"They've always been on active duty." Having defected from the PsyNet using great care to hide their tracks, the Venetian element of the squad had been feeding information to other Arrows and running operations as long as they'd been in existence.

"They want to respond to outbreaks," Aden clarified. "If I don't give the order, you know Zaira will simply make that decision on her own."

"Yes." Her independence of thought was why the other Arrow had been given charge of the Venice operation. "Zaira also knows they can't risk being recognized." Each and every Arrow in the Venice compound was officially dead.

"She's put forward a proposal that they be called in on night outbreaks in Europe, where her men and women can work with only a minimal disguise." Aden rubbed his forehead in an unusual sign of strain. "Venice also holds some of our most broken."

Vasic thought of Alejandro, the male's brain reset by an overdose of Jax so that he couldn't deviate from a command—but only if that command came from Zaira. Alejandro couldn't be helped, the damage done to his organic brain, but what of some of the others? "A civilian won't have any reason to ask whether or not an Arrow is supposed to exist," he said. "We can slowly pair up the Venetians with their own Es."

Aden continued to look out the window. "That'll require they rejoin the Net. That can be done covertly, and Zaira's team is ready to do so, even with the current problems . . . but they will stay in exile as long as necessary."

Until, Vasic thought, the squad no longer needed the escape hatch. That, however, might no longer be an option. "Is their network clean?"

"No signs of the infection, but a network populated only with Arrows was never going to be balanced," Aden responded. "Zaira suspects it's starting to show hairline fractures. There's no urgency yet, and it'll become a moot point if they rejoin the Net. For now, they continue to act as our eyes and ears in the wider world."

Calling in a teleport from another Arrow, Aden left only minutes later to speak to Kaleb about making up a list of dormant cardinal Es. It left Vasic free to concentrate on Ivy. She lay silent in a deep sleep. Rabbit was settled against her back, his small body rising and falling in quiet huffs.

Scanning her using the gauntlet, Vasic noted that the damaged and torn blood vessels the emergency medics had treated—with Aden having double-checked the work—were already healing. Her mental state however . . .

Vasic couldn't forget how defeated she'd looked when he'd found her in the ambulance. His Ivy, who had fought for him, who never gave up, had appeared in splinters during her single, bittersweet moment of consciousness as he lifted her in his arms.

Eyes dulled and bloody, she'd said, *Why can't I do this? What if what they did to me in the rehabilitation center broke me permanently?*

"You are not broken," he said in a harsh murmur as he got into bed and gathered her close. "You're the strongest woman I know." A woman who refused to surrender, regardless of the near impossible odds.

A woman who had beaten the numbness that had been swallowing him alive.

A woman for whom he'd fight death itself.

Chapter 49

GLASS SMASHING, GRUNTS of pain, a dog's frantic barking.

Ivy jerked awake to find the bedroom door shut, the slits in the blinds on the window telling her it was bright daylight outside.

Another grunt, followed by a loud thud.

Shoving off the blanket as she realized the sounds weren't echoes of a nightmare but coming from mere feet away, she forced herself to take the small weapon Vasic must've left on the bedside table, and made her way to the door. *Vasic?*

Stay inside.

She cracked the door a minute sliver to get a look at the living area beyond. Her fingers clenched on the slick black plas of the weapon. Dressed only in jeans and his boots, Vasic was fighting against three men, and it looked like all three were telekinetics. The furniture lay embedded in the walls, plaster dust in the air and window glass on the carpet. Vasic was bleeding but holding his own, while Rabbit lay whimpering against the wall, his small body crumpled.

Rage bloomed in her.

Waiting until all three attackers were facing Vasic, she darted out on silent feet to lift Rabbit into her arms and duck back into the bedroom. "Shh," she said to their injured pet, his side rising and falling in pained breaths. "You'll be okay, I promise." Placing him gently on the bed, she went back to the door to see her Arrow take a crushing physical blow to the ribs at the same time that he took multiple telekinetic hits.

The rage darker and molten hot, she switched off the safety on the weapon. *Jaya!* she telepathed, as it became obvious the weapons capability of Vasic's gauntlet wasn't functioning. *Where's Abbot?!*

When there was no response, she realized the other woman must be at the hospital, Abbot by her side. Which left Ivy as Vasic's sole backup. Going down on one knee to brace herself and using both hands as her father had taught her, she aimed the weapon through the gap in the door, but the men were moving so fast, she couldn't be certain she wouldn't accidentally hit Vasic.

Jerking back as he sent one attacker slamming into the wall beside the bedroom door, she saw the man was dazed but already pushing up on one arm. Not letting herself think too much, she shot him, the laser beam set to stun. As he went down, she sucked in a breath, expecting an empathic backlash of pain, but none came.

Maybe because all she'd done was put him to sleep. And maybe because Vasic was the biggest, most important piece of her heart. *No one* was allowed to hurt him.

Turning back to the fight, she saw one of the attackers pull a pressure syringe from his boot. Vasic had his back turned to the man as he fought off the other assailant. *Watch out!* she screamed telepathically and shot again.

The laser fire went wide this time, hitting the wall and attracting the enemy Tk's attention her way. Reacting on instinct, she shot a third time, but he dived out of the way, his hand coming up as if to slam her with telekinetic power. Ivy rolled behind the door to deprive him of a visible target, just as that door slammed open to hit her side in a bruising blow. Breath lost but bones unbroken, she kept her grip on the weapon and crawled quickly to the side of the bed so she'd have a direct line of sight to the door, while being protected by the bulk of the bed.

Except the Tk didn't come in. He used his ability to lift the bed, clearly intending to smash it against the wall. Rabbit lay motionless on the bedspread. Horrified, Ivy ran deliberately into the Tk's line of sight, and even as he smashed the gun out of her hand, she reached instinctively for the kernel of fear she could sense in him and made it bigger. And bigger. And bigger.

He collapsed into a whimpering pile just as Vasic finished off the other assailant.

Walking over to pinch a nerve in the man's neck, Vasic sent him into unconsciousness. "Rabbit?"

The tears falling now that the danger was past, she ran back to the bed where Rabbit lay so quiet and still. "He's hurt really bad." She had to focus on their pet, couldn't think about the fact she'd come so close to losing Vasic. It made her remember the ticking clock she'd almost managed to forget, the knowledge a vise around her chest, compressing her lungs until she could barely breathe.

"He was kicked." Taking the dog into his arms and ignoring his own wounds, he teleported out, returning mere seconds later without Rabbit. "He's with an M-Psy trained in veterinary sciences."

Nodding jerkily, she went into his arms, his embrace careful steel. "Breathe, Ivy."

It took effort, but she obeyed the order. Vasic didn't need to worry about her right now. "Who are they?" she asked at last. "Was it an anti-empath group?"

"No. These men came for me." He loosened his embrace only to cup her face and take her mouth in a kiss raw and possessive, before stepping back. "I need to transport them."

Gaining strength from the sheer, physical life of him, his skin gleaming with sweat and his scent hotly masculine, she said, "Don't forget the syringe." She'd made a note of where it had dropped, now pointed it out. "We need to know what was in it."

Vasic picked it up. "This won't take long."

She changed while he removed the three strangers from the apartment. "You need a medic," she said when he returned, the vise around her lungs having tightened again in the short time he'd been gone from her sight.

Delaying only long enough to pull on a T-shirt and jacket, Vasic said, "Rabbit first," and teleported them to the veterinarian who was working on their pet. Watching the vet through the window of the sterilized operating suite, she bit down on her trembling lower lip. "Did Rabbit try to help you?"

"He did help me." Vasic wrapped his arms around her from behind. "He bit one of the attackers just before the man would've landed a disabling blow."

"That's Rabbit." Pride unfurled in her, but that wasn't the emotion that held her hostage. No, it was bone-numbing fear, because it wasn't only Rabbit she'd almost lost. Turning, she pushed Vasic away and made him take off his jacket and T-shirt so she could examine his injuries.

Cuts and bruises marred his upper body, his beautiful face bleeding and his breath coming in a way that told her he had broken ribs. Violent protectiveness eclipsed the fear. "Medic. *Now.*"

"You need to be with Rabbit," he said, as if that ended the discussion.

It didn't. "Do you think I'm a mess at the moment?" she said. "What do you think will happen to me if one of those broken ribs goes through your lung?" Fingers trembling, she touched them to his chest. "Please, let's go." Rabbit wouldn't hold it against her, and she'd make sure to be here when their pet woke.

Vasic closed his hand over her own, his eyes going to the window into the operating suite. "We shouldn't leave him alone."

A shaky smile curved over her lips as she realized Vasic wasn't only worried about her, but about Rabbit. Their stubborn dog had wormed his way into the heart of this tough, dangerous Arrow. "Then," she said, "why don't you 'port a medic here?"

Vasic disappeared on the next breath, to return with an M-Psy who held what looked like a serious medical kit. Of course, he first made the slender brunette check Ivy. She acquiesced rather than further delay his treatment, and the M-Psy was able to deal with her bruised side in minutes.

"Now, you," Ivy ordered, completely out of patience.

Sitting down in an empty examination room meant for animals, he allowed the M-Psy to knit his broken ribs back together, the work painstaking. Ivy went between the room and the observation window of the operating suite, keeping Vasic updated on Rabbit's progress.

It was a half hour into it that she realized the veterinarian was doing much the same thing to Rabbit that the M-Psy was doing to Vasic. Her

Arrow had brought their dog to a top veterinary surgeon, someone who probably worked on Thoroughbred horses and other animals worth millions.

If she hadn't already been utterly, madly, absolutely in love with Vasic, she would've fallen right then and there. Fighting the urge to throw herself into his arms, she watched the M-Psy shape her hands over his ribs as she worked. The woman, who had the ability to see internal injuries without technological help, was wearing complex medical "gloves" that directed energy into Vasic, stimulating his cells into repair mode.

Ivy folded her arms over her chest. *You couldn't find a male medic?*

Vasic's eyes warmed, and it was a punch to the solar plexus, that hint of a smile. *Is she female? I didn't notice.*

Good, she said, utterly undone by him. *Continue not to notice.*

As it was, Rabbit was out of surgery first.

"He's going to be a little slow for a few days." The vet gave her a disposable datapad with instructions on how often Rabbit should be given pain medication as well as the food he should eat. "However, I've made sure there'll be no long-term repercussions."

"Thank you," Ivy said, her hand on Rabbit's warm body as her and Vasic's pet rested in a drug-induced sleep.

Acknowledging her thanks with a nod, the vet looked over at where Vasic was being treated. "I did owe him a favor, but I never expected him to redeem it to save the life of a dog."

Ivy smiled at Vasic from across the room but kept her silence. In fact, they didn't speak again until the medic working on him pronounced him fit for duty, and they returned to the apartment with Rabbit. An apartment that was smashed up and bloody in the living area. Ignoring that, Vasic carried Rabbit to his sleeping basket and placed him on the pillow shaped to their pet's body.

"He'll be all right?" Vasic asked when she hunkered down beside him to stroke Rabbit.

Ivy spun into his arms in response.

Almost unbalancing in his crouched position, Vasic locked his arms around her. "Ivy?"

"You were so hurt," she whispered.

Vasic nuzzled her temple. "I wasn't critically injured." He'd survived far worse.

Pushing back as suddenly as she'd come into his arms, Ivy said, "I need to see you're okay. Take off your clothes." She pushed at the sides of his jacket. "Off."

Not arguing, he got to his feet with her and shrugged off the jacket, then peeled off his T-shirt while kicking off the boots he'd slammed his feet into at the first sign of intruders. A bare chest was one thing—bare feet could be a serious liability against booted opponents.

Ivy dragged him in front of the blinds. Cracking the slats enough to let in a little more sunlight without exposing the two of them, she ran her hands over every inch of his chest with careful delicacy. To his body, each touch was a petting caress—but he could tell from her expression that she was only concerned about lingering injuries.

When she went around to check his back, he stayed in place.

"Were your legs hurt?"

"A few bruises from kicks, nothing more." He hadn't bothered to have the M-Psy treat those, since they weren't disabling and would disappear on their own soon enough.

"I need to see." Ivy dropped her hand to the top button of his jeans.

Closing his fingers over her own, he shook his head. "They're only bruises." He had endless self-control . . . except when it came to Ivy. Already, his body was reacting, his penis erect despite the fact he knew she hadn't meant her touch to be arousing.

Ivy's lashes lowered to throw soft shadows against her skin, a blush heating her cheeks . . . before she shook off his hands. "I need to see," she whispered again, and this time, her tone was husky.

He held as still as he could as she undid the button, but his stomach flexed at the featherlight brush of her knuckles, over two decades of training alone allowing him to stand there without taking her to the carpet. What he couldn't do, however, was keep from touching her. Raising one hand, he threaded his fingers through the soft black of her curls, took hold.

Her breath caught, her lips parting.

And Vasic suddenly understood why he so often saw changelings nipping at the lips of their mates when they kissed, playful smiles on their mouths. Leaning forward, he did the same. Ivy's gasp was quiet, her fingers tucked into his waistband . . . and her body straining up toward him when he began to move away.

Vasic had woken three hours before the attack this morning, but rather than leave Ivy, he'd stayed in bed and spent the time reviewing the material Judd had sent him. Now he realized the other man had been right; he didn't really need it. All he had to do was listen—to what Ivy said and, especially, to what she didn't.

Closing the small distance between them, he bit down on her plump lower lip again, the pressure gentle but firm. Then he tugged at her flesh to test if she enjoyed the sensation, because he did. He particularly enjoyed it when she rolled up on her toes, her knuckles pressing into his abdomen.

Releasing her lip with slow deliberation, he found his other hand had ended up at her hip, atop her sweater. She'd discarded her coat as soon as they'd entered the apartment, and so there was no impediment to his exploration. Holding the clear copper of her eyes, he slid his hand below the fine weave of the sweater to touch warm, supple skin.

Ivy inhaled sharply, her pulse a drumbeat against the curve of her neck. Fascinated once again by the small movement that told him so much and made his own pulse race to match, he bent his head to press his mouth to it. He sucked, even grazed with his teeth. One of Ivy's hands rose from his waistband to curve over his nape, holding him to her throat as she made a small, incoherent sound.

Her response ignited unadulterated possessiveness in him, making him want to devour and to cherish in equal measures. He hadn't understood what it meant to cherish before Ivy. Now he knew it was about giving her what she needed, showing her what she was to him: Everything.

"Vasic." Her short nails dug a little into his neck, the sensation adding to the others to go straight to his groin.

"Hmm." He kissed her neck again, sucking harder at the soft skin, oddly pleased by the resulting red mark.

Chest rising and falling in a rapid rhythm, her breaths hot pants that made something slumberous and primal in him stretch awake, she rubbed her face against the side of his. "I can feel your hunger." It was an intimate whisper, his empathic lover attuned to his body and his senses. "What do you need?"

Driven by the craving to claim her skin to skin, he lifted his head and said, "I want you spread out beneath me, and then I want to feast on every inch of you."

Ivy shivered. "Naked?"

The strange painful-beautiful emotion he'd finally recognized as tenderness twisted inside him. "I can wait."

Eyes luminous, she reached for the bottom of her sweater. "Remember that night I stripped for you?"

"I'll never forget it." It was an erotic film he played in his head whenever things became too dark, too hard. Soft curves and lush skin, a shy, coaxing smile, she made him remember there were better things in the world.

Today, her smile held sinful play. "I wanted your hands all over me." Then she drew the fabric of the sweater over her abdomen in preparation for tugging it off. "You can feast on me any time you please."

His mind hazed, his hands fisting at his sides. "Wait. Stop."

Chapter 50

IVY FROZE WITH the sweater bunched below her breasts. "No?"

"I have to fill the bathtub with water."

Blinking, she went to part her lips as if to ask a question, but he couldn't wait. He strode to the bathroom and turned on the cold faucet at full blast.

Ivy appeared in the doorway a few seconds later, frown lines marring her forehead. She snapped her fingers the next instant. "It's to help you control your 'porting in some way."

He loved her mind as much as every other part of her. "Yes." Not sure he'd remember to turn off the faucet once she bared herself, he waited with bone-grinding patience for the tub to fill. And as he did, he suddenly thought of the one thing they'd never discussed. "Ivy, if we share biological—"

"I took care of it," she said, cheeks red. "While we were still back at the compound."

The feeling deep inside him, he identified it as a smile of unalloyed delight. "Way back then?"

"Oh shush." Laughing admonishment. "I asked Sascha's advice, and she arranged for the DarkRiver healer to drop by since the healer also has medical training, plus she's made it a point to learn about Psy physiology, so . . . "

Vasic remembered the healer coming in; at the time, he'd thought she was simply being welcoming to the Es. "She brought baked goods."

"Yes." A sweet smile that cut him off at the knees. "I knew I was thinking much too far ahead, but . . . I was hopeful."

"Ivy." Clenching his fists, he stared at the wall. "I won't last if you look at me that way."

Soft, sensual laughter. "The bath's about to overflow."

Finally.

Walking Ivy backward into the bedroom, he stopped by the bed. "We may travel," he told her, "but I've programmed a repeating loop in my head that should only take us to the desert and back." He'd done it yesterday, before the outbreak. "No snow."

"I'd go anywhere with you."

Tracing her smile with a fingertip, he kissed her, his hand in her hair. *I really like kissing you, Ivy.* The intimacy, the wet, the way her breath became shorter and shorter the longer he did it. *I think I'm developing preferences when it comes to tactile contact.*

So am I. She splayed her hands on his chest, nails lightly scratching as she ran them down and over the ridges of his abdomen to his navel. Where she began to trace the fine line of hair that led into the partly open fly of his jeans. The touch made him clench his abdominal muscles, break the kiss to look down at the slender gold of her hand against him, air hot on his skin as she inhaled and exhaled in the same jagged rhythm.

As if aware of how the visual affected him, she stroked up with a finger . . . back down. When she reached for the zipper tab, however, he braceleted her wrist with one hand and pulled her away. "After." The idea of her fingers wrapped around his penis made his spine lock, his thighs taut.

Kissing her again, he ran his thumb over the pulse in her wrist before releasing her hand. Then he reached for the bottom of her sweater. She raised her arms, and the fine blue wool was on the floor seconds later. Her bra was a delicate creation of pale yellow lace. Fascinated by the way it cupped the creamy mounds of her breasts while appearing so fragile, he traced the scalloped edges, dipped his finger underneath just a fraction.

One of her hands rose to grip his wrist, but it wasn't a hold that asked him to stop.

"From the township by the settlement?" he asked, and continued to touch.

Fingers tightening on his wrist, she nodded. "The humans didn't see anything wrong with selling it to a Psy." Her voice was husky on her next question. "Do you like it?"

"Yes." He decided he'd buy her more. "It appears I have a distinct preference for visual stimulus." Kissing her collarbone, he said, "I still intend to watch you touch your own body in front of me, but not today. Today I want to be the one doing the touching."

Ivy shivered again, then pressed an unexpected, wet kiss to his chest before reaching back to unhook the bra. Cupping his hand over the ball of her shoulder, he turned her slowly. Her hands dropped as she granted his silent request. First, he swept her hair to one side to bare her nape, the exposed skin making him want to taste. So he did.

Ivy uttered a hot, sweet sound in response that wrapped around his erection and squeezed . . . and they ended up in the desert.

"Sorry," he said, the two of them already back in the apartment.

Ivy leaned her back against his chest, and turning her head, rose on tiptoe. He bent toward her automatically, used to the height difference, was rewarded by her lips brushing the side of his jaw. "As long as you don't stop touching me"—another kiss—"you can take me to the desert and back a thousand times."

The kisses threatened to distract him, entice him to stay in this position, but he wanted her naked. Shifting back, he reached for the hooks on her bra and undid them after figuring out how they were linked. Ivy curved her shoulders inward as soon as he was done and slid off the straps one at a time, the movement wholly feminine.

He watched the lace drop to the carpet, realized he couldn't look at her front if he wanted to finish this. "Stay." Gripping her hips until he was sure she understood, he stepped away to look at the graceful curve of her back, but he couldn't look and not touch. He ran one hand down the expanse of skin he intended to kiss inch by inch.

"I was overambitious," he said when she arched toward him. "I don't think I'll be able to explore all of you before my control snaps."

"We can do it again." A shy, sensual glance back at him before she faced forward once more. "As many times as we like."

Vasic's fingers stilled on her skin as he realized the import of her words. Before Ivy, he'd never been given anything he wanted without fighting for it. Most times it had been a stolen moment of peace in a calm place. All with a time limit. This didn't have one.

His eye fell on the gauntlet.

Forcing his mind away from that darkness and to the pleasure of this instant when he was with a woman who denied him nothing, he ran both hands down her sides and around to her front to flick open the button of her jeans. "Tug down the zipper," he murmured against her ear, nibbling at the curve of it simply because he wanted to.

Ivy moaned, her body soft and warm in the curve of his as she did as he asked. Then, not waiting for his request, she pushed the jeans down her thighs and to the floor. Releasing her so she could tug off the material, he wrapped one arm around her waist again as soon as she finished the task, the fingers of his other hand exploring the tiny bows of yellow ribbon at the sides of her lace panties. There'd been one on her bra, too, he remembered, in the center.

Tugging at a bow, he was disappointed to discover it was only for show. "I'm going to buy you panties with ribbons that unlace." He knew such things existed, had seen them in shop windows and on advertising images.

Ivy's skin turned a silky hot shade that made him want to stroke, kiss, maybe even bite. "You can buy me anything you like," she whispered, melting back into him. "I'll wear it."

Vasic kissed the side of her neck. "You should be careful what you say to a starving man." Biting at her in playful warning when he hadn't known until Ivy that he could play, he luxuriated in her moan.

Then, pulse pounding, he slipped his hand around to her navel and under the lace of her panties to cup her flesh. "I read a book," he said when she jerked. "A sex manual. Actually, I read two, downloaded another three for later." Arrows always did intensive research, and he'd followed up Judd's information with further investigation of his own. "I also watched certain recordings."

"When?" Ivy's voice was high, shocked.

"While you were asleep." He read extremely fast, a natural skill augmented by his Arrow training. "One of the manuals said that for women, sexual pleasure is as much in the mind as in the body. It suggested that the male talk during sex." Vasic didn't really talk except when he had something to say, but when Ivy whimpered, her body going even more damp against his palm, he decided this was a case where talking wasn't only warranted, it'd be foolish not to do it. "I like holding you like this."

Curving his fingers, he cupped her more firmly. "I like feeling you become wetter and hotter and impatient."

Her hands reached back to grasp at his thighs, her breathing harsh.

"According to the manuals, a woman's clitoris is extremely sensitive and can be caressed in a number of ways." Tightening his arm when she rose on her toes as if to escape his touch before pressing back down, he kissed the side of her throat again. "Apparently, there's also a place inside you that can give you incredible orgasms. I'm determined to find it."

Breasts plump and flushed, Ivy reached up and back to clench her hand in his hair. "I didn't know we were supposed to read manuals," she complained, a little pout to her mouth that made him wish he was in front of her. But that would end this before it began, and there were so many things he wanted to do to and with Ivy.

He tilted the heel of his hand to put pressure on her clitoris. Back bowing, she shuddered. "I'm finding a manual, too," she gasped when the wave passed, her eyes closed.

As a result, she missed the fact that they'd ended up in the desert again before he brought them back. "Wait until I can keep us in one place." He was already balanced on a razor-thin wire. If Ivy became expert at how to arouse his body, he'd probably take them into the heart of a volcano. "Do you like this?" He used his finger to circle the sensitive entrance to her body.

Ivy's back arched again, her skin shimmering. When she turned her head and looked up, he knew what she wanted, though she hadn't said a word. Gripping her jaw with his gauntleted hand, he kissed her at the same time that he reinitiated the pressure against her clitoris with the heel of his other hand. Crying out into the kiss only seconds later, Ivy melted all over his palm, her hands gripping at his upper arms and her eyes fluttering shut.

He watched her body ripple with pleasure, pleasure he'd created in her, and felt the wire snap. Only his protectiveness toward her had him remembering to shunt his energy to the water. Removing his hand from her panties to her murmured complaint, he swept her up in his arms and placed her on the bed.

It took mere seconds to pull off his jeans and underwear, another two to tug off her panties. Crumpling the damp lace in his fist, he knelt between her legs, his eyes on the delicate folds barely hidden by the soft hair at the juncture of her thighs. His mouth watered. Not giving her any warning, he dropped her panties to the bed and dipped his head to lave his tongue over her honeyed flesh.

"Vasic!" Her back lifted off the bed.

Licking one more time, he promised himself he'd return, taste her properly. Right now, he wanted only one thing. He rose up over her body to brace himself on his gauntleted arm, using the fingers of his other hand to brush back her hair. "This will likely hurt." He didn't like the idea, but it was a biological fact they couldn't escape.

Ivy wrapped her legs around his hips. "Love me, let me love you."

He gritted his teeth, guided himself to her, and began to push. She was slick and hot and so tightly stretched around him that he felt he'd rip her open. "*Ivy.*"

Clutching at his shoulders, she gasped, "So . . . you're built in proportion, then."

The unexpected words gave him the breathing room he needed. Kissing her on that sweet, soft, generous mouth, he said, "Unfortunately."

A sensually feminine smile. "I have a feeling that won't be the correct description once we begin to do this on a regular basis."

That was it. Vasic stopped thinking, his only focus on being inside her and on not hurting her. The twin desires pounding within his skull, he moved as slowly as his body would permit, his Arrow training having given him superb muscle control . . . that would've collapsed at the first pulse of her body on his if he hadn't been worried about causing her pain.

Uttering a near-soundless cry, Ivy held on impossibly tighter but didn't ask him to stop.

He did so anyway. "Ivy—"

Her answer was a kiss on his biceps.

His chest feeling as if he had huge metal bellows inside him, pumping out air in great gulps, he dug the hand of his gauntleted arm into the pillow and continued the tortuous forward momentum . . . and then he was buried to the hilt in Ivy.

Tiny nails dug into his flesh, her body tense. "Give me," she breathed out, "a few seconds."

Sweat dripped down Vasic's temples, his jaw painful. Locking his every muscle in place, he tried to decide if this was self-inflicted torture or pleasure. *Pleasure,* he groaned internally when Ivy's body rippled on his, *very definitely pleasure.*

Then the woman who held him with such unhidden possessiveness, stroked his cheek. "You can move," she whispered. "I'm getting used to you." She lifted up her hips experimentally against him.

Vasic growled and took her mouth as he pulled out and stroked back in on pure instinct. He knew in the back of his mind that he was supposed to draw this out, make her orgasm before he did, but rational thought was long gone. His body exploded on the second stroke, his spine arching and the desert shimmering around them, Ivy's arms and legs holding him close in an embrace that said he was home.

Finally, he was home.

IVY had never felt so . . . She didn't have words for it. A silly smile on her face, she rubbed her cheek against the hot silk of Vasic's chest, luxuriating in the feel of him against the length of her, his hand in her hair in a way that had become familiar.

"This room is full of steam."

Ivy had noticed that, tiny beads of water condensing on her skin. But she was far more interested in other matters. Pressing a kiss to his pectoral, she wiggled up his body to look down at him. "So?"

Vasic ran his hand down her spine, back up. His face remained expressionless, but Ivy could feel his emotions with the senses she couldn't turn off, and they made her want to cuddle close and purr like she was a cat being stroked.

"I need to practice."

She giggled at his response, her heart about to burst with the intimacy of what had passed between them. The sex had been hot and beautiful and a little messy, and she couldn't wait to do it again. His touch, the feel of him so hard and strong inside her, the heavy weight of him in her arms as he tried to catch his breath, she'd loved it all. "Repetition, huh?" she teased. "Could get dull."

Silver frost eyes held hers. "Do you think you're in danger of getting bored?"

Ivy pretended to think about it. "Hmm—" She shrieked as they suddenly found themselves in an icy environment, only to blink back into the bedroom the next split second. "I can't believe you did that!"

"I lost control."

"Liar." She poked a finger at his side, delighted with him.

"No comment."

He closed his eyes as she ran her fingers through his hair, his pleasure in the simple touch bone deep. "You going to tell me why those men came for you?" she asked, because much as she wanted to ignore the world and spend the next week naked in bed with him, the world kept shoving itself back into their life.

"They were Ming's men," he told her without opening his eyes. "No emblems on their uniforms, but I recognized them." Lifting his hand, he opened it to show her the pressure injector he must've 'ported in. "It'll need to be tested to be certain, but I recognize the cobalt blue shade of the cartridge. It's Jax; a very high dosage."

Fury was an inferno in Ivy's blood. "Bastard," she said, as Vasic returned the injector to wherever it was stored. "Why is he still alive?" She might hate violence, but she also understood evil on a visceral level, knew that some people found pleasure only in holding cruel power over others.

Vasic's answer made too much sense. "He might be a monster, but that monster is holding Europe together right now."

"What if he comes after you again?" she said, laying her head against his shoulder and nuzzling close so she could draw in the scent of him. "He sent three highly skilled Tks after you—that's serious."

Vasic squeezed her nape. "And all three Tks are now in Arrow custody. Ming knows how to do a cost-benefit analysis, and I've just tipped the scale to the wrong side by depriving him of three senior men."

Ivy nodded, made herself believe. This was Vasic's world, and he understood it far better than she did. "I hate that another man's lust for power forced you into violence tonight."

Shifting her onto her back, Vasic caressed his hand down her side. "Before you, I would've handled the situation by withdrawing further into the numb state where nothing really impacted me." A lazy, possessive kiss. "I like working out the tension with a naked Ivy much, much better."

Her lips curved. She believed him; she was the one who was tense with anger right now. Vasic, by contrast, was lazily relaxed. "I so need a manual." Her lover—her *lover*—was proving to be lethal in a most delicious way. A woman had to have some weapons of her own.

That got her a kiss, his hand petting her breast. She would've melted right into him if she hadn't felt his gauntlet graze her shoulder. "Wait." Pushing at the muscled width of his own shoulders, she said, "What time is it? We have to go see Samuel Rain."

Chapter 51

Should we stop him?
No. Repair any glitches when he's out of visual range but don't interfere.

Message stream between Haven Maintenance Team and Clara Alvarez

SHOWERED AND CHANGED, they arrived at Haven two hours after the time they'd told Clara to expect them. Accepting their apologies with a quiet nod, the manager said, "Well, it appears you woke Samuel up at last."

Ivy caught the glint in the woman's rich brown eyes. "What did he do? Tell you all you were monkeys attempting to run an asylum?"

Ivy could've sworn laughter warmed Clara's gaze, but the manager's voice was even as she said, "No, but he rewired the entire complex in the space of eight manic hours. We had a backup team checking his work, but they said he'd done things they didn't even know were possible, and we're running at fifty percent increased efficiency when it comes to our power usage."

"Is he still insisting he's brain damaged?" Ivy asked.

A nod. "He may well be right—we can't know if all the systems in his brain are functioning at full capacity. It's only as he attempts to use them that that will become clear." She looked at Ivy and Vasic both. "Please don't get your hopes up. If he senses it, then fails in helping, it could undo all the progress he's made."

"We'll be careful," Ivy promised, her fingers locked with Vasic's.

The first thing Samuel Rain did when they found him in the rose garden was to scowl and say, "Where's the dog?"

Ivy felt her heart clench. Placing one arm around her shoulders, Vasic hugged her close as he answered the engineer. "He was injured and is resting in the care of friends."

With Jaya and Abbot at the hospital, Vasic had left a peacefully sleeping Rabbit under the watchful eye of the Arrows at Central Command. Had Rabbit been healthy and happy, the idea of those deadly men and women taking care of a small, curious dog would've made Ivy smile, but right now, all she felt was a deep worry.

"Injured?" Samuel narrowed his eyes at Vasic. "Is he healing?"

"Yes. He'll make a full recovery."

Ivy knew the statement was as much for her as for Samuel. Holding the truth of it to her heart, she said, "Clara told us you've made some improvements to the complex."

"Yes. Come on." The engineer rubbed his hands.

They spent the next hour on a tour of the facility's power system. Samuel Rain didn't even glance at the gauntlet. Frustration gnawed at Ivy, but she held her silence. She could sense Samuel now, and below the excitement at his accomplishment was a bone-deep fear—as if the hard crust of a lake in winter had been sheared off to reveal the liquid beneath. It made her heart hurt.

The engineer, she realized, was aware enough to understand that he might not like what he found if he pushed himself. But he was far stronger than she'd guessed, because right at the end, while he was closing a maintenance panel, he said, "I need the prototype gauntlet the imbeciles who worked on you used to test the connections."

Vasic lifted his arm as the other man turned to face them. "This is the prototype."

Ivy thought Samuel Rain's head was going to explode. Literally tearing at his hair, he said, "Why didn't you just walk into a butcher's shop and have them hack you up?"

"Stop it," Ivy said, having had enough. "You don't get to talk to him like that."

Staring at her through his spectacles, the engineer said, "Are you doing something to me?"

"No."

Suspicion writ large on his features. "I wasn't like this before."

Ivy had the feeling Samuel Rain had always been high-strung and outside Silence, his genius intellect such that he'd been given a pass from the authorities—until one of the Councilors had apparently decided to make an example of him. Right after Rain turned down a job offer from the Councilor in question.

Aden had unearthed that fact yesterday. It was simply more evidence of the ugly hypocrisy and self-interest hidden in Silence, Ivy thought as she folded her arms and said, "I don't care if you dance naked at midnight, as long as you help Vasic."

A roll of his eyes. "It's cold at midnight," Rain said with exaggerated patience. "If I planned to dance naked in winter, I'd do it at noon."

Then he left, telling them not to follow.

Growling low in her throat, Ivy lifted her hands and made a squeezing motion. "I want to strangle him."

Vasic pressed a kiss to the top of her head, the affectionate act making her toes curl. "He's right, you know," he said, while she fought not to make a big deal of something that *was* a big deal. "The implant team should've never grafted the only prototype. I'll have to find the most detailed simulation files we have and send them to him."

"I don't care if he's right." She scowled. "No one is allowed to treat you that way." Hauling him down with her hands fisted in his jacket, she kissed him with all the passion in her heart. His hand rose to cup her face, his body hardening against hers.

When their lips parted, she looked around to find he'd teleported them back to the apartment. "We should've told Clara we were leaving," she whispered, far more interested in shaping Vasic's chest with her hands.

He raised the gauntlet, tapped in a short message. "I've sent her a notification."

Arousal fading, she touched her hand to the carapace, slick and hard. "You'll miss it, won't you?" It was a fact she hadn't considered until now. "It's truly become a part of you."

He lifted both hands to her face, stroking her hair behind her ears.

"I'll adapt. No piece of technology is worth losing time with you." Continuing to hold her face, he said, "You're sad, Ivy."

She went to protest, but he shook his head, said, "I'm not an empath, but I know you. You enjoyed the sex—"

"The other races call it making love." Ivy had heard that on comm shows. "It felt like that, didn't it?" She curled her fingers against the firm breadth of his chest.

Vasic tasted the words, nodded. "Yes."

Her smile was luminous. "I loved making love with you. Can we do it again?"

"Ivy." Brushing his thumbs over her cheeks, he held her gaze. "Don't try to distract me. You were happy for a while, but there's sadness inside you." Tiny flickers in her eyes, her smile fading when she thought he wasn't watching, he'd noticed it all. "Tell me why."

"Could you get Rabbit first?" she asked, her expression holding a raw vulnerability that kicked him in the heart. "I don't want him to wake and find himself in an unfamiliar place."

Vasic left at once, to return less than half a minute later. Rabbit was still curled up in his basket, fast asleep. Going down into a cross-legged position on the floor, Ivy petted the dog with a gentle touch. "My brave Rabbit," she murmured, as Vasic came down to sit with his back against the wall, one arm braced on a raised knee.

Ivy took time to speak, and when she did, it was with helpless pain in her voice. "I can't stop thinking about the gauntlet. I try so hard not to, but it's always there at the back of my mind." She dashed her hand across her eyes. "I'm sorry."

Vasic didn't know how to comfort her. All he could do was draw her close, wrap her in his arms. "Surely," he said, "you don't doubt Samuel Rain's genius. Are you a monkey?"

When she spluttered wetly and slapped at his chest, he felt a staggering sense of achievement. He'd given his mate what she needed, brought her through the sadness. Nuzzling his chin into her hair, he continued to hold her as they sat on the floor beside Rabbit.

"That wasn't funny," she said at last.

"You laughed."

He saw her lips tug up at the corners, only to curve downward not long afterward. "There'll be another outbreak soon, won't there?"

Vasic didn't want to talk about that, wanted to indulge in Ivy, but the world continued to turn beyond the walls of this apartment. "Chances are high."

"I don't know what to do, Vasic." It was a trembling confession. "I was so foolish at the start, so sure instinct would guide me, but . . ." She moved her head in a negative motion against his chest.

"You weren't foolish." He couldn't stand to see his tough, determined Ivy so beaten. "You were ready to try, to take a chance. Without you pushing for placements in infected zones, Jaya and Brigitte wouldn't know who and what they are, and Sascha wouldn't have made her breakthrough."

Ivy's hand curved over his upper arm. "That doesn't change the fact that *I* can't do anything to help!" Angry frustration. "The medic told me I'd cause an aneurysm if I continued on my current path."

Vasic thought of the secret he'd kept from her about Isaiah, knew she'd be angry with him for it, but told her anyway. Her eyes darkened as she sat up to face him, one hand lifting to her mouth. "Will he . . ."

"The doctors are hopeful, but there is no definite prognosis as yet."

"Concetta must be devastated." Hand dropping to her side and voice raspy with withheld emotion, she said, "Why did you hide it from me?"

He curved his hand around the side of her neck. "I knew it would hurt you."

Gaze meeting his, she shook her head. "I don't want that kind of a life. Padded against danger and insulated from reality."

"I know." He leaned forward, pressed his forehead against hers. "Just . . . give me a little time. I've never had someone who was mine before."

She softened, hand spreading on his thigh. Enclosing her in his arms once more, he held her close, the scent of her in his nose, his heart beating in time with hers. And he knew he'd fight a thousand outbreaks, vanquish untold nightmares, to have another moment such as this. "Have you attempted to attack the infection on the PsyNet itself?" he asked, the idea a sudden, acute one. "The infected are only a symptom. The cause is the poison in the PsyNet."

Ivy sat up and shifted sideways so that her back was braced against his raised knee. "We tried that back at the compound on the day of the farewell dinner. We thought we should attempt it while we were all together." Her skin crawled at the memory. "It threatened to suck us into itself, as if we were insects and it was a huge spider."

"You were inexperienced then, unsure."

Ivy tapped a finger on her knee, gave his statement serious thought. "Yes." Not only had the group been uncertain and untested, they'd been feeling the staggering responsibility of coming up with a solution before more people lost their lives. Not ideal conditions. "I think there's something I can try during the next outbreak as a test."

Vasic took her chin in a gentle but firm hold. "I won't get in your way, but promise me you'll stop the instant you feel any pressure on your brain."

Ivy felt her heart break at what she saw in his expression, what he let her see, her lethal Arrow trained to hide all vulnerability. "I promise."

If she'd thought she'd have more time to consider the idea, that proved to be a false hope. An hour later, all hell broke loose in Midtown Manhattan, the outbreak the largest across the world to this point. Arriving with Vasic, Ivy fought her instincts and didn't wade into the fray when he began to work to contain the situation. Instead, she took a protected position behind a wall and opened her eyes on the PsyNet.

The area where she was anchored remained quiet, but she could see minds sparking an erratic red not far in the distance, violent against the velvet black of the psychic plane. Shooting to the turbulent section, she took a deep breath and whispered, *Shh, be calm, be at peace,* to herself and released the empathic energy within her.

It was a translucent ripple, akin to the colors formed inside a soap bubble, so subtle it was near invisible against the black. The ripple traveled over the tormented minds, settling on them in undemanding gentleness . . . yet the violent red sparks continued unabated. Disappointment heavy in her gut, Ivy was about to stop and volunteer to fetch and carry for the medics, when Vasic's mind touched hers.

Ivy, if you're doing something and it's not hurting you, keep doing it. This entire block has gone eerily placid—the infected are standing around looking confused, while the noninfected are so calm they're falling asleep on the street.

Bracing her hands on her knees as her legs threatened to go out from under her, Ivy nodded though he couldn't see her. *Okay, okay.*

She didn't know how long she stood there, but by the time Vasic appeared in front of her, her back was stiff and her calf muscles knotted. "Well?" she rasped, dots in front of her eyes.

"Drink this first." He thrust an energy drink in her hand and hunkered down to massage her calf muscles with firm, knowledgeable hands that made her moan in relief.

"Only limited casualties," he said when he rose to his feet and saw she'd finished off the drink.

Already she felt better, her power outlay nowhere close to burnout.

"It could've been a massacre." Vasic's expression turned grim. "There was a gun shop within the zone of infection, and several of the infected worked inside, had the weapons."

Ivy shuddered at the thought. "The infected I calmed?" she asked in cautious hope. "How are they?"

"The majority fell asleep over the past ten minutes." Wrapping his arms around her, he teleported to the apartment before adding, "Jaya and the medics say signs are they'll slip into comas like the others."

Heart falling, Ivy stumbled to sit on the arm of a sofa Vasic had righted. "It might be that the cure for this infection isn't psychic at all," she said, uncertain what else an E could do. "Maybe it's a medical problem." Even as she spoke, she knew it couldn't be that simple, not with the Net itself beginning to erode.

"Krychek has a top medical team looking into that possibility." Disappearing without a word, he returned in seconds, Rabbit in his arms. Once again, it was the off-shift Arrows at Central Command who'd kept an eye on their pet.

Rabbit was asleep but woke soon afterward. Ivy hated seeing him so lethargic, so unlike himself. Stroking and petting him as she murmured loving reassurances, she reminded herself how hurt he'd been when he'd first dragged himself to the orchard. If he could survive that, he'd certainly come back from this.

"He likes the sun," Vasic said, and taking him carefully from Ivy's lap, placed their pet on the wide windowsill that was his favorite lookout. He didn't sit up and stare out the window as per usual, but he did stretch out in the late afternoon sunshine.

"Now you," Vasic said, and pulled a box of nutrition bars from the kitchen cupboard. "That drink was just a stopgap measure."

Ivy made a face but sat with him on the sofa and ate. "You know, now that some of us want taste," she said as he finished a bar with quick efficiency, "there's a business opportunity in making flavored bars."

"I'll tell the Arrow Consortium."

She hesitated with the bar halfway to her mouth. "Is that a real thing or are you teasing me?"

"It's a real thing, though it's not called that officially," he said to her surprise. "We knew we'd need money if we ever defected or went independent. Not all of us want to continue in this line of work."

But they would, Ivy thought, heart twisting. As long as the Net needed them, the Arrows would surrender their lives to it. For that sacrifice, the men and women of the squad would be pushed to the margins of society and looked upon with fear. Hand tightening on the bar, she took another bite and made a vow that any member of the squad would always be welcome in her home, would be family.

However, all that had to wait. The first thing she had to do was share her empathic breakthrough with the others. It was as well that she'd discovered the key to soothing the infected when she did—the outbreaks continued unabated across the world in the next week.

Empaths—all Gradients, with a focus on those on the brink of natural emergence—were awakened on a wholesale level during the same period. Not all could accept the truth of their nature so quickly, but those able to open their minds to their new abilities after any existing blocks were removed, were given basic training, and sent out to join the fight.

Yet despite the appearance of countless minds sparking with color, color that had slowly begun to infiltrate the formerly cold black fabric of the Net, the infection couldn't be slowed, much less eradicated.

The infection might have hesitated to approach the concentration of Es at the compound back at the start, but it had grown more aggressive. While empaths remained immune, having even multiple Es in a limited area was no guarantee of safety for those around them. And the simple fact was, no matter if every E in the world was brought to active status, it would never equal the one-to-one ratio from the compound.

An entire section of the Net in Paris had to be evacuated when the infection surrounded it in a liquid black cage. Twenty-four hours later, that section collapsed, rotted through; the resulting shock wave left a thousand dead, many more injured. New York, too, hadn't escaped injury—Ivy and Vasic had been responding to at least two outbreaks a day, even with the humans and changelings throwing their weight behind the containment effort *and* with all the active Es in the city working on a rotation.

The infection was winning, millions staring down the barrel of death.

Chapter 52

Interpersonal violence between Psy has dropped to rates so low, it eclipses that during Silence. And as we all now know, given the recent investigative reports, the Silence stats were manipulated by Council after Council and cannot be trusted.

The fact that it has taken the threat of near-certain annihilation to bring us to peace is a bittersweet irony.

Editorial, *PsyNet Beacon*

SAHARA HAD A genius level IQ. That's what she'd been told as a child forced to struggle with math when she'd rather have been out dancing. Math and Sahara had never made their peace, but in other ways, her brain was a finely honed machine.

It had been worrying on a problem for a considerable period of time.

"Eben Kilabuk," she said, and placed an image of the empath on Kaleb's desk, having commandeered the space since he was at a meeting. "Phillip Kilabuk." She laid the photo of Eben's dead, infected father below the boy's.

"Christiane Hall. Marchelline Hall." Empathic mother and infant. "Miki Ling." The caretaker cousin. A low-level M-Psy murdered by one of the infected. Her autopsy had shown no signs of the disease in her own brain.

"Miguel Ferrera." Twenty-five-year-old male, Gradient 4.1, commercial telepath.

She took several more photos, laid them out. All of survivors. Then she removed the Es and rearranged the remaining survivors into two groups. On one side, she placed those like Miki Ling, people connected to an empath and thus assumed to be, or have been, protected by the empath's immunity in some way.

On the other side, she placed the random outliers, such as Miguel Ferrera, who had no empaths in his family tree and had, in fact, had no contact with his biological family for over two years.

Then there was Phillip Kilabuk. His brain had been riddled with infection though he was the father and custodial guardian of an E. Proximity to an E, familial and genetic connections to an E, Phillip Kilabuk had had them all and it hadn't saved him.

There was no pattern. And yet . . .

Eyes narrowed, she logged into Kaleb's system using the password he'd given her—her beautiful, dangerous man had access to every database under the sun—and began to run down every scrap of data she could find on each one of the people represented by the photographs. Banking information, medical histories, university transcripts . . . that was just the start.

The work was tedious, might take days or even weeks, but she could sense something in the information she already had, akin to a tiny stone in the bottom of a shoe, an irritation that simply would not go away. She had to find that stone, because in the irritation might lie a critical answer.

Chapter 53

Heroes are often the quietest people in a room, the ones least willing to lay claim to the title. These men and women simply go about doing what needs to be done without any expectation of gratitude or fame. It is in their nature to protect and to shield and to fight against darkness, whatever form it may take.

New York Signal

EXHAUSTED DOWN TO the bone, Ivy nonetheless put Rabbit on a leash during a mercifully peaceful afternoon, and she and Vasic took him out, their intended destination a Central Park clothed in sparkling white snow. It wasn't fair to their pet to be cooped up now that he was back to his usual energetic self.

"It's so quiet." Ivy had quickly become used to the frantic energy and wild vitality of New York, but that vitality was nowhere in evidence today; people's faces were strained and their eyes downcast. "How many have left the city, do you know?" she asked Vasic.

"A tiny percentage in comparison to the city's population."

"People have jobs, lives they can't just leave," she murmured, thinking aloud. "And word's out that pretty much nowhere is safe." Her parents' region of the Net was holding strong at the moment, but Ivy continued to worry. "I wish I could cover my parents in my empathic shield and your great-grandfather, too." She hadn't yet met Zie Zen, but Vasic had told her a lot about the extraordinary man.

Vasic, dressed in his "civilian" clothes of jeans and leather-synth jacket—though the T-shirt wasn't black today, but dark blue—put his arm around her waist, his fingers at her hip. "Neither of the three would thank us for abandoning hundreds of thousands to shield them, regardless of how much we might want to ensure their safety."

Ivy sighed, having had that exact conversation with her parents. "Yes." It took her a few seconds to realize her Arrow was stabilizing her using Tk as she walked on the icy sidewalk. Those sidewalks should've been cleared of snow early that morning, but systems were breaking down all over the world.

As were the systems in Vasic's gauntlet. While he hadn't been using its weapons capability since the command failure during the attack by Ming's men, the program had come on spontaneously during an outbreak. He'd suffered a small overload in the fight to shut it down.

The burns had been minor and treated on-site. It didn't matter—Ivy had felt her heart crack in two when she saw the wounds, though she'd fought not to let her panic and fear show. He'd known. He always knew. Holding her tucked against him, he'd told her that Aden had found a surgeon willing to attempt the risky operation to remove the critical malfunctioning components.

Only if we don't hear back from Samuel Rain before time runs out, he'd told her. *The surgeon is exceptional. She's known to be a maverick with a reputation for accepting risky cases and coming through with flying colors, but she's not Rain.*

Ivy's nerves were stretched to the breaking point at the sustained silence from Rain, but she agreed with Vasic's choice. Her stomach a lump of ice, she knew there was a high risk the surgeon might kill him. Samuel Rain might as well . . . but if the engineer *wasn't* brain damaged, the risk was lower.

That didn't mean it wasn't still unacceptably high.

Shoving that brutal truth to the back of her mind on this sunny afternoon when she was out for a walk with her man, she tugged his hand off her hip to lace their fingers together. "You should wear color," she said when Rabbit, nimble and curious, paused to scrutinize the window display of a menswear shop. "With those gorgeous eyes, any vibrant shade would look good on you."

He examined the display. "Would it please you if I wore color?"

Ivy's heart flipped. "You please me by being you. I was just . . . flirting." It was silly and awkward, and she wanted to try it with him. She wanted to try everything with him, couldn't bear the thought of living in a world where Vasic wasn't there to be her partner in exploration.

He didn't speak again until they were deep in Central Park. "Why would you flirt with me?" he said as they walked along an otherwise deserted pathway enclosed on all sides by snow-dusted trees, the white carpet of it unbroken but for Rabbit's paw prints in front of them. "I'm already yours."

She stopped, unable to look at him because there was *so much* inside her for him that it terrified.

Breaking their handclasp, he closed his fingers over her nape, his thumb brushing her skin in a quiet caress. "I don't know how to play games of courtship. I can learn if that's what you need."

Rabbit's leash dropping from her hand, she swiveled to face him. "No, I want you to be you." An Arrow who said what he meant and who didn't speak except when he had something to say. "I want you to be you," she repeated in a whisper, her hands clenched tight in his T-shirt. "I want to make mistakes with you, learn how to be in a relationship with you."

Vasic stroked his thumb over her skin again, his hair gleaming blue-black in the ray of sunshine that pierced the canopy, his skin golden. "I'm used to working with plans, with blueprints," he said, "but observation of the other races tells me life doesn't come with a blueprint." The Psy had attempted to change that, create rules, but all that had done was buy them a little time before the inevitable crash. "We have to make the plan ourselves."

Ivy, his empath who'd wrenched him out of the gray numbness in which he'd existed and into a world of vibrant color, reached up to play her fingers through his hair. "Samuel Rain," she said, determined fury in every word, "is going to come through. I will believe *nothing* else."

Vasic had never been afraid of death, but now he fought the idea of it with every breath in his body. "I could kidnap him," he said, his hands on her hips. "Force him to work on the gauntlet under threat of being left in a jungle full of his favorite primates."

Ivy's laugh was a little wet. "I don't think anything could make that man do something he didn't want to do." A kiss so tender, it enslaved him.

"But," she whispered against his lips, "if he doesn't get back to us soon, I'm going to pay him a visit." Her eyes glinted in readiness for battle. "Rain is about as brain damaged as I am, and it's time he stopped playing games."

"Woof!"

Vasic kissed her the way she'd kissed him, before releasing her from his hold. "I believe the other male in your life wants some attention."

A smile in the copper eyes that had been raw with pain since his overload—pain she tried to hide from him but couldn't, her face without shields—she turned to pick up the stick Rabbit had dropped at her feet. Unclipping the leash while she was hunkered down, she wrapped it loosely around her left hand and stood.

"Come on, Rabbit"—she threw the stick—"fetch!"

As Vasic watched her encourage their ecstatic pet, her delight music in the air, he said, "This wasn't meant to be my future," to the man who walked up to join him.

Aden had arrived in the city on a high-speed jet-chopper a half hour ago. Now, his partner stood with his gloved hands on either side of the tailored black winter coat he wore open over a suit of the same color, his shirt white. It was camouflage for an urban environment.

"Are you sorry for the change?"

"No." Not far from them, Ivy lavished Rabbit with affectionate praise when he ran back with the stick. "I'll never be sorry for Ivy." He'd fight the world for her, and he'd battle like a gladiator against the results of his formerly self-destructive instincts. "There's one more option we haven't explored when it comes to the gauntlet." It was something he'd realized during the outbreak this morning, when Dev Santos's team had taken primary responsibility for ensuring calm. "The Forgotten have certain unusual gifts."

"I already checked it out." Aden's eyes followed Ivy's arm as she took the stick from Rabbit after a play fight and threw it again. "Their medical tech has gone in a different direction. Santos did say he might be able to assist using an ability about which he'd tell me nothing."

Vasic braced himself for bad news. It could be nothing else if Aden hadn't already shared it with him.

"He did a field test in the aftermath of the outbreak, while you were both in close proximity." Aden glanced at him, shook his head. "Whatever his ability, he says it's too rough yet to work with such complex computronics."

Having processed the information as Aden gave it to him, Vasic moved on. Time was the one commodity he didn't have. "Keep the surgeon on standby. I don't know if the gauntlet is going to last the full eight weeks Bashir initially predicted."

Aden didn't argue with his order. "Have you told Ivy the risks?"

"Yes." Vasic paused. All his life, he'd shared data with Aden almost automatically—his relationship with his empath, however, was new territory. *Ivy,* he said telepathically, *will it break your trust if I talk to Aden about our relationship?*

She shot him a look over her shoulder, eyes bright. *No. I plan to complain about you to Jaya.* Laughter in her mental voice as she turned back to watch their courageous little dog race toward her. *Just don't go into detail about how we make love.* A pause, her body suddenly motionless. *What exactly did you ask Judd Lauren? Only about the control issue or—*

He sent me his research file on sex.

Vasic could see her turning red even from this distance. Her mental groan was mortified. *I will never be able to look him in the eye again,* she said, face in her hands. *Fine, talk to Aden about it if he needs the information. I hope he does . . . I hope he finds what we have.*

So did Vasic. "Ivy," he said to the other man, "expects me to talk to her, and so I do. I'm learning not to keep secrets."

Strands of Aden's straight black hair slid across his forehead in an undemanding breeze that didn't dislodge the snow from the branches above. "Is it difficult?"

"Sometimes." Vasic didn't always do the right thing, but with Ivy, that never meant rejection. She wanted to make mistakes with him, was forgiving of his own. "Being with her is the most complex, most fascinating operation of my life."

And it was one he knew would only grow more intricate with time. "Some would say this is the punishment for my crimes," he said into the quiet broken by Rabbit's excited bark as he ran for the stick again. "To be given happiness only to have my own choices steal it from me."

His friend looked at him. "Is that what you believe?"

"No." Once he might have. No longer. Because to do so would be to believe Ivy was being punished, too—and his Ivy had done nothing to deserve the pain that made her cry in her sleep.

Each tear was a drop of acid directly on his soul.

"The recent media coverage of you," Aden said into the silence that had fallen between them. "Can you handle it?"

"It doesn't concern me." Vasic didn't need to be underground, not like those of his brethren whose lives would be placed at risk should those men and women be identified as members of the squad.

"No." Aden reached down to pick up Rabbit's stick when the dog raced over to drop it at his feet. "Can you handle being the public face of the squad?" Throwing the stick past Ivy, he dusted the snow off his hands.

Vasic stared at his partner, Aden's words making no sense. "We don't have a public profile, and if we did, you're the best one to take that position."

"The decision is now out of our hands." Taking a thin datapad from his pocket, he passed it to Vasic just as Ivy returned to them.

She leaned against his side to look at the screen, her cheeks glowing and a panting Rabbit resting at her feet. Every inch of Vasic's body was sensitized to her presence, her warmth seeping into his cells to ease the ice-cold places inside him, the soft curve of her breast pressed against his upper arm. With any other woman, it would've been an intrusion. With Ivy, it felt natural . . . normal.

Shifting his arm, he wrapped it around her shoulders.

"That's an incredible photo."

He followed the copper and gold of her gaze to see that the image on the datapad was of him. He had a baby cradled against his chest and a hand shoved out behind him as he held off two of the infected armed with broken glass bottles. Blood dripped from his temple where he'd taken a hit at some point, and his T-shirt was torn, the gauntlet visible because he'd taken off his jacket to wrap the infant in it, having caught her as she was thrown off a third-story balcony in an act of insane violence.

"What do you see when you see that photo?" Aden asked, his question directed at Ivy.

"Vasic being the strong, extraordinary man he is." She rose on tiptoe, and Vasic angled his head down. Her lips brushed over his jaw.

Aden took in the interaction, wondered if his partner had any comprehension of just how far he'd come. "If you didn't feel positive emotions toward him already," he said to the woman who was Vasic's, "what would you see?"

Ivy focused on the image again, frowned. "I'd see the same. A strong man protecting the vulnerable."

"That is what the wider population sees as well." Tapping the datapad, he brought up the hereto hidden headline: "A Silent Hero."

There was more, the feature article illustrated not only with that first image, but with several others of Vasic taken during the recent outbreaks— as well as a photograph from when he'd rendered assistance after a bomb blast masterminded by Pure Psy in Copenhagen and another from the group's attack in Geneva.

Vasic was wearing his Arrow uniform in both those photos.

"The media has connected you to the squad," Aden said, "and by doing that, they've given the squad a face, a name."

"We don't play for the media, Aden. Even if that's to change, I'm the last person you should put in that position."

Ivy spread her hand on Vasic's chest, her smile rueful. "I adore him," she said to Aden, "but he's right. Vasic's not exactly the chatty media type." Her eyes danced. "In fact, I'm not sure he knows how to chat at all."

Vasic squeezed her. "I'm going to find a manual."

Bursting out in laughter at what seemed a reasonable statement to Aden, Ivy tried to speak, gave up. "Sorry," she said almost a minute later, her voice still tremulous with laughter and inexplicable tears rolling down her face. "Your partner has a sly sense of humor."

I didn't know you had a sense of humor.

I appear to be growing one. Vasic shifted back to vocal speech after using his thumb to wipe away Ivy's tears. "The media. Why?"

"We need to adapt," Aden said in an echo of the promise the entire squad had made when Silence was about to fall.

To adapt. To survive.

"The squad has always been a shadow in the Net," he continued, "the whip used to terrify the population. Right now, people are in shock, but sooner or later, if we survive this infection, things will come to an equilibrium." Aden met eyes of copper ringed with gold, then those of cool gray. "When that happens, people will seek someone to blame." The psychology of it was clear-cut. "We're a big target."

"No one can touch us," Vasic replied.

"No, but they can touch those who are our own." Aden looked deliberately at Ivy.

Chapter 54

"IF ANYONE IN the squad intends to have a life beyond Silence, we need to rehabilitate"—Aden paused, conscious of the incongruity of using that word—"the perception seeded into the minds of the population that we're murderers and assassins. That might be true, but it isn't going to be useful going forward."

Ivy's eyebrows drew together. "Don't call the squad that," she said, her voice fierce. "Don't say it about yourself, either."

Aden held Ivy's gaze. "We're killers, Ivy. That can't be altered."

Aden. Vasic shook his head very slightly. *Don't remind her of something she appears to have forgotten.*

But it was too late, Ivy stepping forward to face Aden. "You were assassins, black ops, whatever you want to call it. You took orders. And yes, you should take responsibility for your actions, but you were also drafted as *children* and programmed to take those orders, do those acts." Voice low and intense, she continued before he could interrupt. "That gives you the right to cut yourselves some slack. You're trying to change things now—you've put your lives on the line again and again and again to help the defenseless."

"At what point," Aden said, "is that enough to erase the past?"

"Never," Ivy said softly. "We all have to live with our past, but it doesn't have to define us." She shoved a hand through her hair, her loose ponytail unraveling to leave her face haloed in curls. "What you're doing now that you've broken the chains? Those are the real choices, the ones that *will* define you."

Vasic looked from one to the other. Ivy, who reached parts of him he hadn't known had survived until her. Aden, who'd refused to consign him to the abyss. They were the two most important parts of his life, and now they stood with him, Ivy's fierce refusal to let him fall—let any of them fall—coming up against Aden's iron will.

"Why fight for us?" Aden asked, his tone quiet. "Vasic, I understand. He's yours. Why do the rest of us matter?"

"Because you're his family, and because whatever you may have done, you paid the price for it in the kind of pain no child should have to bear, in not being allowed to even *exist*." She touched her fingers to Aden's shoulder. "Enough, Aden." It was a gentle plea. "This isn't only about rehabilitating the public's image of the squad, but your own image of yourself and your Arrows."

"Would you welcome other Arrows to your home, Ivy?" Aden asked. "Would you truly treat them as family?"

"Of course," she said as if the answer was self-evident, as if every woman so blithely welcomed a squad of trained killers into her home.

Rabbit got up and ambled ahead at that instant, and the three of them followed.

"That's another reason why Vasic must be our public face," Aden said a minute later. "You humanize him."

Vasic waited for Ivy's response, wasn't expecting it to be laughter. "Did you throw me and Vasic together to get this outcome?" Her fingers petted his back under the jacket, and he knew she wasn't offended at the idea.

"No. But now that it's happened, I'll use it."

Vasic didn't interrupt his partner; he and Aden had too much trust in each other for Aden to place Ivy in any kind of danger.

"The human and changeling media," his fellow Arrow continued, "is very good at picking up the nuances of interpersonal relationships." Taking the datapad, he brought up an article linked from the first. It wasn't as long, but had a number of pictures.

The first was of Ivy on her knees in a street overrun with the infected, bleeding from her ears.

"That's from right back at the start," Ivy murmured.

The other images had a far different tone. Vasic's hand on Ivy's lower back as they took Rabbit for a walk. Ivy's face quiet with a trust that pierced him to the core as he lifted her in his arms when her strength ran out. Ivy laughing with her whole body on the doorstep to their apartment building, her hand curled around his upper arm.

"The public," Aden said, "is fascinated by you and your relationship. We can use that."

Ivy made a face. "I want to help the squad, but I don't want to live our relationship out on the world stage."

"That'll never happen." Vasic had no intention of allowing any intrusion.

"I don't expect you to," Aden replied. "To do so would look false, and the reason you've caught their attention is that you don't look false together."

"Then why," Ivy said, "are you telling us?"

"So you know you're being watched." Aden looked down at Rabbit as the dog dug up a fresh stick with unerring canine instinct and came to drop it at his feet. "Why does your pet think I'm his personal stick thrower? I'd expect that task to fall to Vasic."

Lips twitching, Ivy bent to rub Rabbit's head. "He's testing you out. He already knows how Vasic throws—Rabbit likes variety."

Aden threw the stick. Multiple times.

Passing through a patch of sunshine ten minutes later, after Rabbit had decided to give Aden a break, they shifted to the right to allow a jogger to pass. The blonde shot Ivy and Vasic a dazzling smile, calling out, "You're both amazing for what you're doing!" as she passed.

Ivy sighed afterward. "I guess we can't just ignore the media."

"No," Aden confirmed.

"It's not just about the squad's image, is it?" Vasic said as Ivy walked on ahead to make sure Rabbit didn't venture into the more heavily trafficked areas. "It's about the squad." He'd known his partner too long not to pick up the unspoken subtext.

Aden paused beside a statue half-buried in snow. "Seeing Krychek connect with Sahara Kyriakus was a positive sign, but he wasn't trained with us, didn't grow up with us."

"Judd is one of us."

"He also had a family to anchor him."

While the majority of the squad, Vasic completed silently, had been cut loose from those ties. His relationship with Zie Zen didn't alter that; it had begun after his childhood ended, and his great-grandfather had never been able to treat him as a child who was part of the family unit, only as a foot soldier in the war.

"Judd gave the others hope," Aden said quietly. "You make them believe in that hope."

It was the last position in which Vasic had ever expected to find himself. "I'll speak to Ivy about how open she wishes to be about our relationship when it comes to the squad." He didn't think his sweet, generous empath would mind the attention of men and women who sought to understand love, but the choice would be hers.

Nodding, Aden glanced at the sleek timepiece on his wrist. "I'd better head to my meeting with Santos."

"About their handling of the outbreaks?" The Forgotten teams had done a stellar job, as had the other groups in the city.

Aden shook his head, angled his body to face Vasic. "Zaid set up the Arrow squad to protect Silence, but he also set it up because Psy with certain abilities fit nowhere else."

Too dangerous, Vasic thought, too unpredictable. Now, he saw where Aden was going. "The Forgotten are having the same problems," he guessed. "How did you get Santos to trust you?"

"I think it was a combination of necessity and the fact he's seen the work we're doing to protect the Es." Aden pushed a hand through his hair. "Whether they can adapt our training protocols for their own abilities is an open question, but it's a starting point. And they may develop techniques we can use in turn."

It also gave the squad another ally in the world, the reason why Aden had made time in his brutal schedule for this meeting. "Do you need a teleport?"

Aden shook his head. "I'll walk."

Rabbit stared mournfully after the other Arrow before dropping his new stick at Vasic's feet. Picking it up, he threw it far enough that Rabbit had to race, but the dog caught it, came back with his tail wagging. They played a little more before Rabbit abandoned the game in favor of jumping in the snow again.

"Aden believes our relationship gives hope to other Arrows," he told Ivy. "If he's right, and Aden is always right about the squad, it'll mean the others may be inquisitive about us."

Ivy halted on the edge of the frozen expanse of the Reservoir as Rabbit explored the roots of a nearby tree. "I don't mind—family members are often nosy." Her smile in her eyes, she searched his face. "Does it bother you? I know how private you are."

He put his arm around her, buried his hand in the warm silk of her hair. "I would bleed for the squad, lay down my life . . . but now he asks me to share the one thing that is mine."

"You'll do it though, won't you?"

"Yes." Because he understood what it was to be in the gray, in the nothingness. "You're my hope, Ivy, my beacon home on the darkest night."

"Vasic." Eyes shining wet, she cradled his face in her gloved hands, her kiss heartbreakingly tender.

Vasic didn't know if he'd ever become used to the way Ivy touched him—as if he wasn't stained with blood, as if he had the right to her affection, her care. But one thing he did know was that he didn't want to be out here any longer. He wanted to be alone with her, to strip himself to the skin and press himself to the giving softness of her.

Grueling as the past week had been, they'd found the energy to make love in stolen moments between outbreaks. His favorite part was Ivy's laugh when they got something wrong, like when they'd clumsily bumped noses yesterday afternoon in the heat of passion. According to her, they were on training wheels.

He'd never had so much fun making mistakes.

"I read a manual when I couldn't sleep last night," she whispered now, not startled by the sudden 'port back to the apartment. "Are you too tired to let me experiment on you?"

"I told you not to read any manuals yet," he chastised, but didn't stop her when she pushed off his jacket and tugged up his T-shirt. Peeling it off to drop it to the floor as Rabbit gave a long-suffering huff and wandered out to the living area, he stood in place and let her explore.

It was deeply pleasurable torture.

"You are so beautiful." Rubbing her cheek against his pectorals, she leaned back to run both hands down his chest, a sigh leaving her lungs. "I could do this for hours." A glance up through her lashes. "Women called you a 'hunk' in the comments to the *Signal* article."

Vasic might not have had much experience in certain areas of life, but instinct whispered this was treacherous ground. "You don't like the description?"

"I don't like other women salivating over you." A light scratch over his nipples.

Sensation arced through his nerve endings.

"You like that," she murmured and did it again.

Hauling her to him, he kissed her until she was liquid in his arms. "I don't care what any other woman thinks of me." The only time he even noticed another woman was when she was near Ivy—and that was in the context of evaluating a threat. "Call me beautiful again." No one else ever had, ever looked at him the way Ivy did. And she saw inside him, his empath, so if she said he was beautiful, he might even believe it a little.

"My beautiful man." She shaped his torso, kissed the dip of his collarbone, drew in a breath that made her moan. "You smell so good."

Nuzzling at her, he pushed off her coat, but when he went to unbutton the thick orange cardigan she wore underneath, she gripped his wrists. "No."

Once he might have halted, uncertain. Now he could gauge her desire in the kick of the pulse at her throat, the flush of her skin. "Why?"

"Because you take over." A scowl. "And I let you because when you touch me, my bones melt and my blood turns to honey."

She may as well have stroked him all over. "I like melting your bones." Breaking her hold without hurting her, he backed her to the nearest wall. "I read about a position I want to try."

Eyebrows drawing together, she glared at him. "Vasic—"

He kissed her complaint into his mouth, her lips lush and sensual, her taste distinctly tart today. Vasic might not care about food, but he could explore the flavors of Ivy forever. "Undo the buttons," he said against her lips, stroking one hand down to lie over her buttocks, the other braced palm-down beside her head.

Chest rising and falling in a shallow rhythm, she lifted her hands between them. "Next time," she muttered, even as she slipped button after button free, "I'm ambushing you while you're asleep and tying you up."

Vasic felt the languorous, sexual part of his nature smile, stretch lazily. "I'll buy you the rope." He kissed and nipped at her throat. "Are you wet for me, Ivy? My penis is so hard it feels like a rod of iron."

Groaning, she finished unbuttoning the cardigan and shrugged it to the floor. "A gag," she gasped. "I need to gag you, too."

You're welcome to. He shaped his hand over the fragile lace of her camisole, bracketing her breast between thumb and forefinger. She wore a bra under the camisole, but it was of lace, too, and he could almost imagine he saw the dusky pink of her nipples beneath the rich white. *Now, undo your jeans so I can tease you with my fingers.*

Shivering at the telepathic order, she rose up on tiptoe and bit down on his lower lip. He took the sensual punishment with a smile. It wasn't a smile as other people might think of it, his lips barely altering shape, but Ivy knew, her eyes glowing from within as she flicked open the button of her jeans.

"Shall I take off my camisole?" She whispered the question against his ear, soft, hot breath and erotic temptation. "I want to feel your mouth on my breasts, want you to suck hard and leave a mark." Her own mouth grazing his jaw. "And your hands." A throaty moan. "You have such big, strong hands, the way you rub around my—"

He growled at her, the sound coming from deep within his chest.

Laughing in the intimate space between them, she rose up against him, kissed him in sweet little sips, her hands on either side of his face. Every muscle in his body tense, Vasic surrendered to the kiss, to the possession that may as well have been steel chains around his body. When her lips moved down his neck, he shuddered . . . and realized they were about one and a half seconds from being swallowed up by a raging sandstorm.

Chapter 55

"STAY RIGHT HERE," Ivy said after he 'ported them back to the bedroom. "Don't move a muscle." A kiss pressed to his sternum.

When she ducked out from under his arm, he didn't go after her into the bathroom. Instead, he used the minutes it took for the water to fill the tub to regain a measure of control. And lost it all the instant Ivy returned to her earlier position trapped between his body and the wall.

"Maybe," she said, lavishing kisses on his chest, "we could have a large water tank next to our home."

Our home.

Vasic had never had a real home, and now he was going to have one with his empath. "I'll build it myself," he said through the flood of happiness in his blood.

Licking at him then blowing on the wet, Ivy leaned back against the wall. "Why didn't Tks in the past use the same trick?"

"Probably," he said, as she unzipped her jeans, "because they didn't have the mental training to direct their abilities so specifically." His words came out harsh, his breath ragged. "The damage caused was often significant."

"I guess Silence did have some good points." Toeing off her shoes, she began to wriggle out of the jeans.

He should've pushed back, given her more room, but he liked the fact that she kept rubbing up against him in the confined space. Jeans off, she nudged them aside and tugged off her socks to rise to her full height clad only in lace.

"Now this." He touched the strap of the camisole.

Slipping it off over her head, Ivy drew her hair away from her face.

He pressed one hand against her abdomen before she could make any other move. "Let me look."

Hands flat against the wall and breasts feeling swollen and taut in the confines of her bra, Ivy gave Vasic what he wanted. Molten silver, his eyes lingered on her lips, her throat, the tight points of her nipples . . . lower. Biting back a moan, Ivy watched him raise the hand he'd placed on her abdomen, tuck a finger under the strap and stroke downward.

"Vasic."

"Hmm?" Kissing her as he repeated the maddening caress, he pulled a bra strap off her shoulder. Another ravenous kiss before he turned his attention to her breast, reaching to tug the cup farther down so her nipple was exposed. Then, before she could ready herself for it, he lowered his head and closed his mouth over the sensitized tip, licking and sucking at her as if she was a decadent treat.

Fingers locked in his hair, Ivy could feel her body undulating in naked pleasure, the wall at her back, and the hard muscle of him in front of her. Unable to control the movements, she gave in, her panties so damp with her arousal that when he raised his head from her breast, his nostrils flaring, she knew he'd caught the musk of her scent. The silver of his eyes shifted to pure black. No whites. No irises. Just a wild, endless night that told Ivy her Arrow's hunger echoed her own.

Steam curled into the air behind him, coming from the bathroom, but it was the steam they'd generated between them that scalded. Acting on instinct and need, she slowly pulled down the other strap of her bra, baring the begging pout of her nipple. "Please."

Hitching her up onto his waist with muscled ease, her legs wrapped around him, he used one hand to further plump up her breast. Then he gave her what she wanted and took what he needed, his pleasure in her intoxicating. Rubbing the juncture between her thighs against his abdomen, she tried to get lower, craving the friction of his arousal, but the position made that impossible.

Then Vasic took her hand from his shoulder, situated it so her fingertips were just under the elasticated waistband of her panties. "Touch," he murmured, eyelids lowering as he looked down. "I want to watch."

Lungs working overtime and skin shimmering with perspiration, she inserted her hand between them, the hard ridges of his abdomen separated from her skin only by a fine layer of lace. Not sure quite what to do, she tentatively stroked, shivered.

"It feels good," she whispered, having the courage to do this only because it was Vasic. Her Arrow. Her lover. "But I like your touch better."

His breathing had lost its rhythm, his voice gravel when he said, "I like watching you. Do it for me, Ivy."

All at once, her body was tighter, wetter, more wound up, each caress creating a heady rain of sensation. Moaning, she closed her eyes . . . and Vasic pressed up tight against her, trapping her hand as he kissed her with such unleashed passion that all she could do was take it. The wall vanished from behind her, but it was back before she could lose her balance, the bedroom a misty landscape painted in steam.

His hand around her throat in a gentle, protective hold that made the nerve endings in her skin ignite, Vasic kissed her into an oblivion of pleasure. Ivy rubbed and arched against him, her nipples deliciously abraded by the muscled silk of his chest. A groan came from deep in him. The vibration traveled through her near-painfully aroused nipples to the engorged folds between her thighs.

"I want you," she got out between kisses, and it was half entreaty, half demand. "Inside me, Vasic."

Shifting back without warning, he allowed her to remove her hand from her panties before dropping her to her feet, his hands on her waist keeping her upright when her knees threatened to crumple. Startled because she'd assumed he wanted to enter her in their previous position, she gasped when he flipped her around so she faced the wall.

"Brace your hands against it." The words were so rough, she wasn't surprised when the wall disappeared a second later, the desert in front of her. The wall was back in a single heartbeat. He was getting faster at the switching, she realized before all thought was lost as Vasic pulled down her panties.

Leaving them tangled around her thighs, he squeezed one cheek with a blatantly possessive touch, then dipped his hand between her legs. "You're liquid." Crushed rocks and sexual heat, that was his voice.

Ivy's answer required no thought. "Because it's you."

Movement behind her, the back of his hand brushing her buttocks. The sound of a zipper. Fabric being pushed down. And then he was gripping her hips to tilt her farther forward as he pushed into her with relentless focus. Making incoherent sounds of need, she was hardly aware of the world altering between sand and the wall and back over and over. Every cell in her body was focused on Vasic, on feeling the thick intrusion of him stretching her flesh.

This position permitted nothing else.

He slammed home to her body's convulsive rippling, stroked out, thrust in. Again and again and again. It was harder and faster than he'd ever before ridden her, his fingers bruising in their grip. When he rasped out her name, she knew it came from between gritted teeth.

"Yes," she said, afraid he was going to stop, to slow down. "Yes, yes, yes, yes—" Her words ended in a hoarse scream as he increased the speed of his possession, his testicles slapping against her with every thrust.

It made her mindless, her fingernails trying to dig into the wall. The orgasm caught her unaware, demolishing her into a million shards of unbridled ecstasy. But it didn't hurt, felt wonderful, because Vasic never let her go, even when his own orgasm turned his body to living stone, his seed pulsing wet inside her, the intimacy absolute.

THEY came to lying on the floor, Ivy on top of Vasic. Her panties were tangled around one of her ankles, her bra twisted. Vasic wasn't in much better shape. Running her foot over his leg, she found her way blocked by jeans he'd never actually fully taken off. She glanced down, laughed a silly, delirious laugh. "You're still wearing your boots."

Chest heaving as if he'd just run a long-distance race, he didn't answer except to stroke his hand down to splay over her buttocks. Feeling lethargic and pleasured and adored, she looked up at his face to see his lashes shading his cheeks, his gauntleted arm above his head.

She flicked out her tongue over the flat disk of his nipple, licked up the salt and sex of him. When she bit at his pectoral muscle a little, he squeezed her where he held her but didn't otherwise protest. Finding a new vein of energy on the realization she finally had him at her mercy, Ivy managed to kick off her panties and unhook her bra.

Then, rubbing her naked body over his, she began to kiss her way down his chest. Only when she reached the bottom of his ridged abdomen did he react—to twine his fingers in her hair. She hesitated, glanced up. His eyes remained closed, the tension in him a quiet hum, nothing urgent.

Returning to her pleasurable task, she licked along his hip bone, pushing up on her forearms to admire the V shape created low on his body by some very nice muscles. She didn't know what they were called, but she'd already decided it was one of her favorite parts of his body.

To be fair, she licked the other side, too.

His hand tugged at her hair in reaction. The tug came again when she curled her fingers around his penis, which was already semihard again. Fascinated by the differences in their bodies, in the way he responded to her touch, she rested her cheek against the hair-roughened skin of his thigh and stroked him, testing to see what he liked, what made his breathing alter, his hand flex in her hair.

And found her own legs getting restless, the place between her thighs slick with renewed wetness. When he hauled her up and flipped their positions, she didn't argue. Taking a second to get rid of his boots and remaining clothing, he sank into her pleasure-swollen flesh, his forearms braced on either side of her head and her arms around his neck.

They kissed; said soft, intimate words; rocked together. The orgasm was quieter but the intimacy no less potent. *Mine*, she said, mind to mind. *You are mine. Every breath, every scar, every perfection, every flaw, every light, every darkness. It's part of you, and it's mine.*

Vasic shuddered and collapsed onto her. *The man I was, the man I am, the man I will be, the man I want to be, they all belong to you. Always.*

Despite the visceral power of their vow, Vasic's mind remained separate from hers on the psychic plane. Ivy's chest ached, but it wasn't from hurt. She knew what he was doing, her Arrow. He tried so hard, but he couldn't stop protecting her . . . especially against the consequences of his possible death.

No, she said silently, *no.* But it was getting harder and harder to forget the lethal countdown to a highly risky surgery. Then, in a vicious reminder, Vasic's gauntlet malfunctioned again a half hour later. A cool blue laser shot out, scored the same wall Vasic had repaired after the attack by Ming's men.

The feedback from the laser caused a minor overload, but he was worried only about her, wanted her away from him. "The weapons capability might spontaneously reinitialize again. I could hurt you."

Ivy wasn't about to budge. Swallowing her tears, she sat him down on the bed and, using the advanced first aid kit Aden had quietly dropped off three days ago, took care of the burns on his arm and rib cage. "Mine," she whispered again, pressing her lips to the thin-skin bandage that protected the healing skin.

His hand stroked through her hair. *"Ivy."*

Refusing to look up, her hold on her emotions fragile, she said, "It's time we hunted down Samuel Rain."

VASIC took her to Haven, but the engineer refused to see them. According to Clara, he'd been shut up inside his room for days. "He accepts food through the slot he sawed into the bottom of his door"—the manager pointed out the mangled hole—"but will reply to no one."

Wanting to scream, Ivy disobeyed Clara's orders and banged on the door. "Samuel!" she yelled, slamming her fists against the barrier. "Open this right now! Samuel!"

"Stop, Ivy." Vasic enclosed her in his embrace.

Angry and infuriated, she kicked at the door, her words directed at Samuel Rain. "I will make your life unbearable if—" She couldn't complete the threat, couldn't acknowledge the fear. Trembling, she held on to Vasic's strength, unable to imagine a world where he didn't exist.

A kiss to her temple. "Shh." His heart pumped steady and powerful in his chest; the idea it might stop was one her brain just couldn't process.

After leaving Haven, they went to see the surgeon—who told them that the chance of Vasic surviving the surgery was eight to ten percent.

"One in ten," Ivy said afterward. "It's not so bad if we put it like that. One in ten." She repeated that over and over to herself, cupping the meager shield it provided around the flickering candle of hope in her heart. Never would she let that candle go out. Never.

THE infection continued to hurtle across the Net in the ensuing days, decimating a huge swathe of the psychic plane and leaving thousands of people in comas. Jaya and the other medical empaths figured out a treatment of sorts five days after that beautiful, horrible afternoon of love and despair when Vasic and Ivy had crossed Samuel Rain off as an option. The treatment succeeded in bringing a small number of the infected back to consciousness and to reason.

"The disease is simply dormant in the patients we've been able to wake," Jaya told her one night as they sat on Ivy's bed, dark circles under her friend's eyes. "It's not a cure, and we can't know how long the Band-Aid will hold." A defeated slump of her shoulders. "I'm so *tired*, Ivy," she said, a sob in her voice. "You are, too, even if you smile through it. Your clothes are starting to hang off you."

Ivy couldn't dispute Jaya's assessment, not with her body feeling as if it had been beaten. Hugging her teary friend close, she stroked her hand down Jaya's hair. "We're all on the edge of exhaustion, even the Arrows."

That wasn't the only problem.

"How many?" Ivy asked, her fingers trembling against her mouth as Aden gave them the news the next morning.

"Nineteen," he said. "Not many in the scheme of things, but enough."

Legs shaky, Ivy sat down on the edge of the sofa. "Why did . . ." She couldn't say it, couldn't even think it. It seemed impossible that a mob had formed to kill a group of innocent Psy going about their business.

"Fear," Vasic answered shortly, his hand on her shoulder. "They believed the victims infected. The only surprise is that it took this long to spill over into violence."

"The worldwide cooperation agreements," Aden said, while Ivy tried to process the horror of it, "gave people pause. But now with empaths burning out under the nonstop outbreaks and the infected turning violent again, even formerly rational individuals are seeing vigilante justice as an answer."

Vasic glanced at the gauntlet that continued to function as far as communications were concerned. "Krychek is on his way."

"Good. We need to discuss a way to throttle the mob violence before it escalates."

A flicker at the corner of Ivy's eye half a minute later announced the deadly cardinal's arrival. Beside him stood a woman dressed in a forest green sweater-coat belted over black jeans, her dark hair pulled into a rough tail and her eyes a deep midnight blue. "Hello." She smiled at Ivy, though the strain in her face couldn't be masked. "I'm Sahara."

Whatever Ivy had expected of Kaleb Krychek's mate, it wasn't this woman with an open expression that said she'd welcome a friendship. "Ivy."

Any other conversation had to wait, the mob attack a priority.

"We'll need the cooperation of the others."

Everyone agreed with Kaleb's assessment, and they were soon in a comm conference with representatives of the worldwide rapid-response network set up by Silver Mercant. No one had any arguments about working together to stop the chaos from spreading.

"A mob might think it has a purpose," said the security chief of the Human Alliance, "but sooner rather than later, it all devolves to mindless violence. We need to nip it in the bud."

Decisions were made, plans to head off another incident set in place.

"Sahara's discovered something intriguing," Krychek said after the comm conference ended, taking a seat on the arm of the sofa that held his mate.

Sahara put one of her hands on his thigh as she leaned forward. "Do you remember Miguel Ferrera? The commercial telepath apparently immune to the infection?"

"Of course." Ivy could still feel Miguel's panic, his horror as he hunched in that closet.

Vasic, standing behind the sofa on which she sat, stroked his thumb over the side of her neck in tactile comfort. Her Arrow knew how touch anchored her, never withheld it. The tension in her muscles easing, she looked across at Sahara. "Miguel still isn't showing any signs of infection as far as I know."

"Kaleb"—the other woman turned her face up to the cardinal—"was able to confirm his immunity for me. The reason why he's immune may explain all the outliers."

"The ones who have no connection to an E?"

"No *obvious* connection," Sahara replied, tucking a strand of hair behind her ear with impatient fingers. "Miguel Ferrera has an empathic neighbor who was away at the time of the outbreak."

Aden, having taken a seat next to Ivy, shook his head. "Many of the infected lived in close proximity to an empath—even closer than Ferrera."

"That's just it," Sahara responded as Rabbit jumped down from his favorite window ledge and came to sit at Ivy's feet. "Miguel doesn't just live down the corridor from an E. He's listed as her emergency contact."

A hush fell over the room.

"Three months ago," Sahara continued into the quiet, "Miguel was the one who called an ambulance when the E had a fall. Three weeks after that, she named him as her emergency contact.

"Soon after that, their purchasing patterns changed. The E started ordering certain food items that previously never appeared on her online grocery order but that regularly appear on Miguel's, and vice versa. In the same period, he also twice purchased two tickets to a lecture series at a nearby gallery."

The evidence was circumstantial, Ivy thought, but compelling. "They have an emotional bond."

Sahara nodded. "That's my conclusion."

Ivy rubbed her hands over her face; something was niggling at her. "But, if an emotional bond with an E is the deciding factor, why was

Eben's father infected? With such a young empath, I'd expect a connection—even if it was one-sided."

Sahara's hand tightened on Kaleb's thigh. "That case frustrated me, too," she said. "I tore the data apart looking for an answer, and I finally found it."

Chapter 56

ENERGY PULSED OFF the other woman. "It appears Eben Kilabuk is the child of a contractual dispute—the conception and fertilization agreement was drawn up by an incompetent lawyer, and while the mother believed she had the right to full custody, the father challenged it for unknown reasons when Eben was ten. He won."

Ivy thought of how Eben had asked to call his mother during the time the teenager had stayed at the compound. "He never bonded with his father."

"Yes." Sahara held her gaze, dark blue eyes intense. "And his mother, a low-level Tk, just survived an outbreak that took out everyone else in her building."

Aden stirred. "Does the theory hold for the other outliers?"

"Yes." Sahara thrust a hand through her hair, messing it up. "All the anomalous survivors I was able to track eventually connect back to an E."

That also, Ivy thought, explained the other commonality among the survivors—a fractured Silence that was accepted by the individual. Bonds couldn't be formed within the cage of the Protocol.

"I know the data is thin yet," Sahara said, "and there's no way to manipulate the emotional bonds to protect everyone, but I thought it was important to share it."

Ivy barely heard the qualification. She could feel something pushing at the back of her mind, a huge knowledge, but she couldn't reach it. Frustrated, she met Sahara's gaze again. "The bonds, why aren't they showing up on the Net?" Ivy had grown up knowing she was loved and wanted, and yet the connection with her parents was nowhere in existence on the psychic plane.

Sahara looked to Kaleb, who said, "They're there but concealed." The cardinal's voice was obsidian in its controlled power . . . and his love for Sahara so absolute, it burned against Ivy's senses.

Sahara's emotions were as potent, as deep, and oddly—as *old*. As if the two had known each other far longer than they were said to have been together.

Kaleb continued to speak as Ivy considered the mystery of the couple's relationship.

"I had to make specific requests to see each one Sahara suspected." Slipping off the tie on the other woman's hair, he ran his palm over the dark strands. "The NetMind has been protecting the vulnerable for a long time."

Ivy watched the cardinal interact with Sahara, understood intellectually that the two were "mated," to use the changeling term, but though she felt their connection, she had difficulty comprehending how someone so hard, so cold, could've bonded with anyone. Much less powerfully enough to rip through the fabric of Silence itself.

A polite telepathic knock on her mind. When Ivy accepted, Sahara said, *You do realize your Arrow is just as lethal as my Kaleb?*

Your Kaleb only acts "human" with you.

Um, have you noticed Vasic touching anyone else?

Okay, Ivy conceded, *you may have a point.* Vasic didn't even touch Aden that she'd seen, and the two might as well be twin brothers, they were so close. *I'll try not to sidle away next time Kaleb appears.*

Sahara hid her smile behind a raised hand. *It's all right. The first time Vasic teleported me anywhere, I was half-afraid he'd decide to lose me mid-'port.*

Ivy reached up to touch her Arrow's hand. His fingers curled around her own, though he was listening to the conversation between Aden and Kaleb. *The two of us,* she said to Sahara, *need to have lunch together after this is all over.*

Yes—Sahara's ocean deep gaze held hers, solemn and haunted—*after this is all over.*

Both of them knew that might be a long time coming.

. . .

UNABLE to sleep despite the fact she'd attended a bad outbreak with Vasic two hours earlier that had come close to wiping her out, Ivy sat up in bed that night and gnawed on the knowledge she could feel just beyond her reach.

"Ivy, you need to rest."

She looked down at Vasic, the light from the streetlamps coming through the thinly opened blinds marking him in tiger stripes. "Shh"—she bent to press a kiss to his shoulder—"I'm thinking."

Rising from bed after a minute, he left the bedroom and came back with a hot nutrient drink. "You're losing too much weight."

Ivy frowned. "What ab—"

"I already had mine." He tapped her on the nose, the affectionate act making her toes curl. "Now stop stalling and drink. I drowned it in your caramel syrup."

She stuck out her tongue at him but accepted the glass. Taking a sip to find he'd made it a drinkable temperature, she narrowed her eyes as he sat down beside her and pulled up something on a reader. "That better not be another manual."

"I thought you were thinking?" He looked pointedly at her glass as Rabbit raised his head in his basket, ears pricked.

Gulping the drink, Ivy put the empty glass on the bedside table and sat up on her knees facing him. His eyes went to her breasts, her nipples pushing shamelessly against the camisole she'd worn to bed with her flannel pants. "Focus," she said through the pulsing ache he aroused in her with a single look. "I need to see the bonds Sahara told us about."

"I can contact Krychek." He patted the bed, and an ecstatic Rabbit scampered over to curl up in his favorite spot at the bottom end.

"No." She ran her fingers along the ridges of Vasic's abdomen, scrunching up her forehead in thought. "I have this nagging sense that he isn't naturally built to see the bonds. It seems more like the purview of an E."

Vasic nodded slowly. "It might be why the NetMind can only show him pieces."

Yes, Ivy thought. Because psychic minds were wired differently, depending on their designation. "Sascha told me the NetMind likes empaths." She nibbled on her lower lip, made a decision. "It can't hurt to ask."

Snuggling to his side, she opened her eyes on the psychic plane and wasn't surprised to see her Arrow right beside her. The black velvet night of the PsyNet, each mind a glittering star, was now "contaminated" with sparks of color, but those sparks couldn't seem to reach the stars . . . as if blocked by the invisible tendrils of a terrible, voracious corruption.

Ivy put her palm over Vasic's heart, anchored herself in the steadfast strength of him before she said, "NetMind?" It felt foolish to attempt to contact a vast neosentience this way, but she couldn't figure out any other. "May I please speak to you?"

"???"

Her heart kicked at the overwhelming and immediate sense that she was no longer alone inside her mind. Joy was a waterfall on her senses, flowers falling over her eyes as a sense of infinite sorrow, of such a *long wait*, made her want to sob. "I need to see," she said when the raw emotional cascade faded enough that she could think. "I need to see the bonds I have with others."

"???"

Thinking of how the neosentience had greeted her, Ivy tried again, this time by visualizing her loved ones as she asked the question.

It was as if a filter was placed over her mind. Her visual field changed to show a Net lit with faint golden lines. She could see her parents on those lines, her friends from the settlement, from the compound . . . and she could see Aden.

Him she could understand, but there were other Arrows, including total strangers.

Vasic wasn't visible, but she sensed him all around her, their shields interlinked. Inside her pulsed the driving need to reach out across the void to him, lock her soul to his. His own need was a dark, passionate force that stole her breath, but he fought it. Stubborn, protective Arrow.

Multihued stars falling around her, racing from a voracious rain of black arrows. Ivy grinned and replied to the NetMind by creating an image of the stars pouncing on the arrows. It laughed and the laughter was a dazzling kaleidoscope that she tried to telepath to Vasic. *Can you see?*

A glimpse. It's . . . extraordinary. His heart beat under her cheek, steady and solid and alive. *Can you show me the linkage?*

I think so.

Vasic was quiet for several minutes. *There aren't enough Arrows.*

I wouldn't expect to be connected to them all.

Yes, but you're already connected to more than you should be—through Aden, and if it's through Aden, you should be connected to every single Arrow in the squad.

Because Aden, she understood, was their acknowledged and accepted leader. "Is Aden particularly close to any other Arrows?" she said out loud.

"There are three or four senior Arrows with whom he works on a regular basis, but he knows and is aware of the mental health of every single member of the squad."

So, again, she should be connected to them all through Aden, yet Ivy saw only a scattering.

Deciding to focus on those connections, she traced them outward . . . and found all but one Arrow she could see through Aden appeared to have no other connection to anyone. Abbot was the single exception. That didn't make sense, since Arrows were all connected to one another. Unless— "It cuts off at the second layer," she murmured, even as she realized these bonds were different from the kind of bond that tied Sahara and Kaleb to each other.

She'd thought fractured Silence was a necessity, but clearly it was simply something that often happened to coexist alongside these ties. A majority of the squad walked the edge of absolute Silence, and yet the golden links had formed . . . almost as if they were so necessary, all that was needed was a single crack for it to take hold. Such as the loyalty that bound the members of the squad to one another or the responsibility an Arrow felt for the safety of his E.

Chewing on that, she traced her link to Jaya, the other E's constellation of bonds opening up in front of her as if she was flying over a city lit up for the night. She didn't know the minds in Jaya's network except for Abbot and Aden. Jaya, too, was linked to unknown Arrows through the leader of the squad, but they were different from the ones in Ivy's group.

Jaya's network held a surprise: another E. Perhaps a family member. That E was linked only to a tiny number of others, no secondary layer. Ivy woke Jaya up with a telepathic hail, though she knew her friend needed the rest. This was too important. *Jaya, do you have another empath in your family? What Gradient?*

Jaya's sleep-hazy voice mumbled, *Yes, a child. Untested for E abilities, but I think he's probably around 3 or 4 on the Gradient. Why?*

Go back to sleep. I'll tell you later.

Okay.

"We're the Band-Aids," she whispered, sitting up to face her Arrow. "I get it now. I understand how we can save the Net, why there are so many of us."

Vasic spread the fingers of one hand on her lower back. "Tell me."

"The Es need to find ways to connect with a circle of people. Jaya and I are both on the high end of the Gradient, can share our immunity with a secondary layer, but others will only be able to shield those with whom they're directly bonded."

She knew she wasn't explaining it properly, told herself to slow down.

Then Vasic spoke. "You have a direct bond with Aden, but you can also protect those with whom he has a bond. A weaker E would only have been able to protect Aden."

"Yes!" Ivy shoved both hands through her hair, trying to contain the beautiful audacity of the image in her mind. It would mean restructuring the entire PsyNet, but it could work. It *would* work! "One E, I think, can only protect a finite number of people. That's why I can only see some of the Arrows."

"How many will depend on the E's psychic strength."

"I'm guessing, yes." Spreading out her hands, she drew a diagram of her vision in the air. "But isolated clusters aren't enough—it's no use shielding individuals if the Net crumbles around them." The psychic fabric was too riddled by infection, too damaged to sustain itself. "To hold the PsyNet together, we need to create a massive honeycomb pattern of interlinked clusters across the world."

"Stitch the Net back together using the Es as the glue?"

Ivy grabbed his face, kissed him. "Exactly!" Tumbling onto his chest when he nudged at her back, she wriggled up to straddle him. "I saw serious damage directly outside the area Jaya and I cover with our clusters, but inside? Vasic, it's strong as steel."

"If you're right," he said, sliding his hands up her rib cage, "the only stumbling block remains the issue of emotional connections and how to create them."

Ivy blew out a breath and fell forward onto his chest on crossed arms, but she wasn't about to give up. "Are there any Arrows who aren't already paired with an empath? Ones who aren't linked to me through Aden, either."

"Yes, a number couldn't be pulled off core tasks."

Core tasks. Hunting the serial killers who continued to prowl the Net. "Would they talk to me?" she asked, not voicing the dark truth.

Vasic paused. "Yes, two of them are at Central Command and available to talk." He sat up. "We'll have to go now to catch them."

Dressing quickly, Ivy cuddled Rabbit when he bounded over, ready for an adventure. "Can he come?" The Arrows had cared for their pet more than once already, but Ivy didn't assume welcome.

"Rabbit is now an accepted fixture," Vasic said, and teleported them into a lush green space she'd never have known was underground if he hadn't already told her of it. The kiss of moonlight on the trees was a muted silver, the starlit sky above a perfect illusion.

"Amin is here."

Following Vasic's gaze, Ivy saw a uniform-clad Arrow emerge from the moonlit shadows, his skin the darkest brown Ivy had ever seen. He ignored Rabbit's curious presence to walk over to Vasic and Ivy. "What do you need?" he asked Vasic.

"Ivy will explain."

"An experiment." She smiled, though she could feel nothing from this man, as she'd once been unable to from Vasic. "Would you mind spending some time with me?"

Amin's eyes met Vasic's in a silent question before he said, "All right."

"Thank you." Inviting him to walk with her, Vasic on her other side, she'd only gone a few steps when Rabbit scampered over, tail wagging triple time. "You like this place, huh?"

"Woof!"

Then he was off again, zipping around the corner. From the bark Vasic heard, their pet had located Ella. Sure enough, he led the lithely muscled brunette to them ten seconds later. Ella, too, agreed with Ivy's request to spend time with her, and the four of them walked along the pathways of the otherwise empty green area.

Catching his eye almost ten minutes of stilted conversation later, Ivy telepathed, *A little help?*

I don't know how to chat, he reminded her, because it was the truth. *They may well consider me deranged if I begin now.*

Ivy's lips twitched. *Stop making jokes,* she said, though Vasic wasn't aware he'd done so. *Amin and Ella know you, trust you. Please, try?*

I can't promise success, Ivy. You must remember who I was before you. That is where they are now. In the cold numbness that permitted them to do what needed to be done.

I understand.

Vasic didn't bother to engage the other two Arrows in conversation; he went right to the heart of the matter. "Do you trust me?"

"Yes." It was impossible to separate the two voices that answered.

"Then you need to trust Ivy."

It shattered an unknown wall in him when they didn't hesitate. Turning to Ivy, Ella said, "If you have Vasic's trust, you have ours. What do you need from us?"

Ivy blinked. "It's done." Laughing, she jumped into Vasic's arms.

Amin's mind touched his. *She truly is yours.*

Yes. He looked into two pairs of dark eyes. *Life isn't only for other people.* It was a reality it had taken him a long time to accept. *We're permitted to exist, too.*

Neither Amin's nor Ella's expression altered, but he could read them as only a fellow squad member could, and he knew both were shaken.

Releasing Ivy after drawing the scent of her into his lungs, he listened as she turned and laid out the facts for his fellow Arrows.

"The connection," she said, "is through Vasic, which makes complete sense." *I've also lost two others that I was linked to through Aden, so I must be maxed out on the number of people I can protect.*

That won't matter once the entire empathic network is in place, Vasic pointed out. *There will be multiple failsafes.*

"Does this connection equate to a security vulnerability?" Ella asked.

"I can't access your minds or your emotions if that's what you mean," Ivy said, "but I'll be honest—I have no idea how it may affect you. If this is meant to cure the Net, the connection to me could equal a change in your emotional equilibrium."

"Understood." Amin was the one who spoke. "We're aware of what's been happening to Arrows linked to empaths. It's an acceptable risk."

Ivy's face was suddenly stricken. *You don't think I influenced you to be with me somehow?* she asked Vasic. *I swear I didn't do it consciously if I did.*

Vasic closed his hand over her nape, her curls warm against the back of his hand. *All you did was haul me into the light. I could've walked away at any point. I chose to stay. I will always choose to stay.*

The knot in Ivy's throat was a huge, wet thing. Unable to speak, she just listened as he thanked the two Arrows for their patience. They turned to walk away, and as they did so, Rabbit raced up to them, tail wagging. The Arrows glanced down, then the male angled his head at Ivy. "What does he want?"

"To play," she said. "You could throw a stick." She looked around, but Vasic had already found one in the undergrowth. "He likes chasing it."

The Arrow took the stick from Vasic and threw it. The two began walking again, were soon out of sight, but from Rabbit's happy "woofs" for several minutes afterward, he'd found some new stick-throwing minions.

"The connection's already having a subtle impact," Ivy whispered, thinking of how both Arrows had ignored Rabbit earlier.

Vasic leaned down to tug the stick from Rabbit when he decided to come back to them, play fighting with the dog until Rabbit let go and raced off in preparation to catch it. "Our minds link to the PsyNet because we need the biofeedback to survive," he said. "Yet the biofeedback has undeniably been damaged in a subtle but fundamental way for an unknown period of time."

Ivy's eyes grew wide. "The link to an empath might be acting as a filter to clean up the biofeedback." She thought again of the two Arrows who were now connected to her. "They trusted me because of you, but others will put their faith in an E out of desperation." It wasn't clean or tidy, but it might just work.

Eyes of winter frost met hers. "We need more data, and we need it as fast as possible."

Neither one of them slept for the next seventy-two hours, and neither did seven of the other empaths who'd been part of the original group at the compound. Isaiah was still in hospital and needed more rest, but he was alert when awake—and irritable. Ivy was delighted to see him on the road back to his normal self.

The group ran multiple experiments—with complete strangers, with men and women who lived deep in zones of infection, with those who'd already begun to exhibit the erratic behavior that had come to be known as a precursor to an outbreak.

Kaleb and Aden sealed up two severe Net breaches in the interim, while Sahara took the myriad reports that came in, crunched the data, and broke it down into bite-sized pieces that sleep-deprived Es and their Arrow partners could understand.

What they discovered was extraordinary.

Chapter 57

And these are the men, women, and children Silent Voices and their like
would have us erase from the gene pool.

Editorial, *PsyNet Beacon*

IT WOULD BECOME known as the Honeycomb Protocol.

Rolled out across the entire PsyNet in the space of a single month, the
fear that gripped the populace helping to spread the effect faster than
initially predicted, its success was soon a matter of unimpeachable fact.
Outbreaks dropped apace with the spread of the honeycomb, and people
in comas began to wake up.

None were yet who they'd once been, but the medical empaths were
hopeful.

Ivy Jane, Kaleb thought where he stood behind his desk at home, had
been correct: desperation was a great motivator of trust.

Of course, not everyone was happy with the situation.

Kaleb looked down at the lists his people were sending in from around
the world. "These individuals refuse to join in."

Sitting curled up in the chair on the other side of his desk, Sahara
frowned at a datapad of her own. She was keeping track of how many
connections an E at a particular Gradient could make before maxing out,
as well as any other factor that altered the reach of a cluster. It wasn't
simple data collection and collation, but a record meant to ensure no E
was placed under unnecessary stress, as well as a way to monitor the health
of a very fluid network. The honeycomb altered constantly as new connections were made and others dropped.

The fact Sahara was fluent in every language under the sun meant there was no chance an E's report would be mangled in translation. Her own lack of E abilities was considered an asset not a handicap.

"We're too close to it," Ivy Jane had said when she asked Sahara to take up the task. "The torrent of emotion in the Net is consuming our attention—we need someone who can see patterns, and you saw this pattern before anyone else. Plus, you might not be an empath, but you're very empathic and able to handle dealing with us."

Sahara had fallen to the task with relish. When Kaleb pointed out she was technically doing a type of math, she'd gasped and said he'd stabbed her through the heart. Then she'd hauled him down by his tie and made him apologize. Now, she chewed on the end of her laser pen and answered absently. "Forcing the holdouts into the honeycomb defeats the purpose. Coercion is what got the Net into this in the first place."

"By staying unconnected," Kaleb said, "they give the infection room to thrive." An unacceptable risk.

Sahara looked up, the charms on her bracelet making tiny sounds as they clinked against one another. "That'd be true if they were concentrated in one area—and if they were, we both know their chances of survival would be minimal at best." Sadness in her gaze, she rubbed at her forehead. "But I'm guessing they're scattered throughout the Net."

Scanning the data, Kaleb nodded. "At this point at least."

"So I'd say they're being balanced out by the connections around them." She bit at her pen again.

Teleporting it out of her hand, he replaced it with a cookie. Her shoulders shook. "Funny." But she bit into the snack. "Anyway," she said after swallowing, "if they do start to congregate, then we can tell them the risks and ask the NetMind to quarantine their section." Her lips turned downward. "It's not the best option, but we can't justify allowing them to create a hothouse for the infection."

"If it comes to that, I have a feeling the objectors will defect to create their own network." He met the eyes of the woman who knew every scarred, twisted corner of his soul and loved him anyway. "Since this dictatorship appears to be oddly lenient about rebellion, I won't stand in the way of their plan."

Cookie finished, Sahara came around the desk to straighten his shirt collar. "I think you're becoming an incredible leader," she said, pride in her voice.

No one but Sahara ever felt such emotions for him, saw such merit in him. "Nikita and Anthony are doing some heavy lifting at the moment"—freeing Kaleb to deal with more urgent matters—"but it's all ad hoc. Long term, we need to come up with a political system to replace the Council."

Kaleb knew he'd always be a power and that was how he wanted it. Never again was anyone going to hurt him or Sahara. But he also wanted time to dance with her, to live with her, and for that to happen, he needed to create an institution that wouldn't collapse if he stepped away—and that wouldn't eventually become rotten to the core, as had happened with the Council.

Sahara ran her fingers over his nape. "It'll have to be a system that takes the specific strengths and weaknesses of our race into account, like the changeling pack structure does theirs."

"Yes." Right now, however, it was about survival. "Is the rollout complete except for the objectors?" Kaleb himself didn't like the idea of being linked to anyone other than Sahara even on a basic level, but he'd been willing to accept it to ensure she was doubly protected. Both by his immunity and the relevant empath's.

As it was, she'd made a natural connection to multiple Es and brought him in.

"Yes," she said now. "I received reports from the final cities an hour ago."

Opening his eyes on the PsyNet, Kaleb took in the honeycomb effect. It hadn't been visible to non-E eyes in the first week of the rollout, or in the second, but things had reached some kind of critical mass in the third. The entire network had blazed to life in an instant that had stunned disbelievers into faith and brought the hopeful to their knees.

No more was the PsyNet a star-studded night; it was now an intricate tapestry.

His bond with Sahara overlay the golden threads, obsidian strong in comparison to the delicate filigree of the links below. "The Es have created a new psychic foundation for our race."

"Now," Sahara said, "we have to make sure we don't break it again."

Chapter 58

Please advise me of your response within the next seven days.

Excerpted from a letter to Ivy Jane from the office of Kaleb Krychek

"KALEB KRYCHEK IS making me another offer!"

Vasic turned from where he stood between the rows of winter-dressed apple trees, playing stick slave for Rabbit, to find his empath tugging on her boots in the doorway to their cabin. Her face was flushed, her curls awry, and she'd pulled on his Arrow jacket like she always did now that they were home.

"As a counselor?" he asked when she reached him, referring to the resurrection of a pre-Silence employment option for Es; such therapeutic help was needed at a critical level as millions of people struggled to cope with the staggering changes in their lives. Ivy was already training under and being supervised by a cadre of human specialists and changeling healers.

But she shook her head, an unfolded letter in one hand. "He wants me to represent the empaths on the Ruling Coalition." Her eyes were huge, the copper brilliant and the gold shimmering under the North Dakota sun.

"Not unexpected," he said, cupping her jaw with his gauntleted hand. "You came up with the Honeycomb Protocol, and you seem to know every empath in the world."

"Ha ha." She poked his side. "I don't know why I've become one-third of E-Psy Central." The other two-thirds were Sahara Kyriakus and Sascha Duncan.

Sahara handled data while Sascha was in charge of the education of Es. Ivy, on the other hand, had slowly become the port of call for any E who had a problem, psychic or otherwise. She'd already had multiple dealings with the Ruling Coalition in that role.

"I do like it though," she said now, "keeping an eye on them all, making sure no one feels isolated or overwhelmed."

Wrapping an arm around her shoulders, Vasic made sure she was warm as they walked the snowy paths, Rabbit racing imaginary opponents in front of them. "What else did the letter say?"

Ivy made a face. "That I'd be paid by the rest of the ruling group."

Vasic immediately saw the problem. "You wouldn't be an equal at the table."

"Exactly." Ivy put the letter into a pocket of his jacket. "Any ideas?"

"Politics is Aden's field of expertise. Let me ask him."

His partner came back with an answer five minutes after Vasic 'pathed him, while Ivy was throwing a snowball at Vasic's head. Ducking it, he got her in the leg with his own snowball before hauling her laughing face close for a kiss.

"Aden says you need to set up an E-Psy union," he said when they parted, both breathless. "Ask the membership to pay a small percentage of their income to belong. That would cover your salary, as well as giving designation E funds to use to fight another attack such as the one that almost wiped you out once."

It was a solemn reminder. "We'd have to have a vote," Ivy said. "I don't want to just assume I'll be the leader of this union."

"No one else," Vasic said, "will relish the idea of sitting across from Krychek, Nikita, and Anthony."

"Neither do I." She'd do it though, because Vasic and Aden were right—designation E had to fight to make sure it was never again sidelined or buried. "Thank Aden for his idea. It's a good one—I'll talk to the others."

Taking a trembling breath, she stroked her free hand down the gauntlet. It was covered by his jacket, but she could feel the hardness of the carapace. "How bad?" The question was a terrible one, but she had to ask it, had to know how much time they had together before he had to go under the surgeon's knife.

His forehead touched hers. "Approximately seventy-two hours, maybe less if the power surges become more erratic."

Ivy tried to stifle her sob, but she couldn't, not this time. Burying her face against his chest, she held on to him with all her strength, hands cupped desperately around the flickering hope inside her. *Please*, she said, not sure to whom she was speaking, *please don't take him away from me.*

There was no answer.

VASIC hated seeing Ivy cry. She was so strong, his empath. Day by day, week by week, she'd pushed on, determined and relentless in her belief that fate wouldn't do this to them, wouldn't so maliciously destroy their love. Now he held her, rocked her, aware of Rabbit nudging at her with his head. And he knew what he was about to ask her to do would cause her even more pain, but his Ivy was strong . . . and he needed her with him as he made good on a promise.

It had taken the elderly stonemason longer than he'd initially estimated to finish his commission, but he'd made it just in time. Vasic would never be able to wash the stain of his sins from his flesh, but at least he would go into the operating room as a man who'd accepted those sins and laid them bare.

"Will you come somewhere with me?" he asked after Ivy's tears had gone quiet, her breathing raspy.

Wiping her face on the sleeve of his jacket, she looked up with red-rimmed eyes. "You know I'd go anywhere with you."

First they dropped Rabbit off with Ivy's parents. Then Vasic 'ported Ivy to a room at Central Command. She glanced around the spartan space with its single bed made up with military neatness, the only other piece of furniture a metal trunk at the end of the bed. "Is this your room?"

"I slept here." Going to the trunk, he flipped it open to retrieve a piece of paper. He didn't really need that paper, with all the names branded on his brain and backed up on a secure computronic drive. But he'd started writing the names on this list the day he'd understood exactly how he'd been used, what he'd done, and now the yellowed sheet was both a talisman and a physical reminder of the debt he owed.

Ivy put a hand on his shoulder where he crouched by the trunk. "What's that?"

"A list of the people I was sent to erase." He looked up, held her gaze; never had he lied to her about who he was, the things he'd done. Today, he told her the worst of it, his heart a block of ice. "Some were murdered by those whose Silence had broken, others were 'accidents' at the hands of out-of-control anchors, still others were the victims of serial killers the Council couldn't afford to acknowledge.

"I had to make them disappear, get rid of any trace of their deaths." He'd cleaned blood out of carpet, made bodies vanish into crematoriums, erased betraying particles of DNA, destroyed any other physical evidence. "I wiped these people out of existence, stole the peace of a final good-bye from their families."

Gentle fingers stroked through his hair. "You remember each name," she whispered. "That matters."

"Not enough." He rose, the list in his hand. "Someone once said to me that I had no right to rest until I could give the lost their names, set the record straight. I don't want that kind of rest anymore," he said, rage in his blood at the idea of leaving her. "But I can't go forward without paying this debt."

"I understand." Taking the list from him, she unfolded it. "What can I do to help?"

Such a simple question. It threatened to break him. "Just be with me."

Ivy nodded and slipped her hand into his. He took them first to a secure room that was the records hub when it came to births and deaths among the Psy. Using a password he'd been given by a fellow Arrow who'd had reason to have hacked the system, he logged in and uploaded the corrected files, ensured the changes were made across the entire system.

If a member of a victim's family checked the records now, they'd find the truth, discover exactly how their family member had died. But that wasn't enough. No one might ever check. *I considered sending an e-mail to each family unit with details of the updated information,* he telepathed Ivy, *but some have no families . . . and others will not care. I'll personally deliver the truth to the ones who will care, who've searched for that truth.*

He held the clear honesty of her gaze. *It could take as long as twenty-four hours.* One of the final precious days before he placed his life in the hands of a surgeon who'd given him an eight to ten percent chance of survival.

Even if it takes seventy-two, Ivy replied, her expression both tender and fierce, *we'll make sure we reach every single one of them.*

Vasic said nothing; there was nothing to say. His Ivy understood him.

Upload complete, he teleported them to a remote location beside a brace of staggering mountains, home to a stonemason who worked with his hands. "Oh, there you are!" the white-haired man called out. "You got my message, I see! I sent it as soon as I finished."

They followed the sturdy-limbed artisan down a pebbled pathway swept free of snow. He eventually stopped beside a simple obelisk about seven feet tall, the stone a smooth black with glittering minerals wound through the midnight. "It's lovely," Ivy whispered, a fist gripping her heart. She knew without asking that Vasic had chosen the stone, taken great care to create a memorial haunting in its beauty.

"Yes, yes." The stonemason smiled, smoothing his weathered palm over the stone with pride. "Each name, I do by hand. See? All perfect. I checked to make sure no mistakes."

Regardless of the man's words, Vasic spoke each name aloud from memory as he checked the obelisk, his hand intertwined with hers. With every name he spoke, he telepathed her the truth of that person's death. Her eyes burned for all those who had been lost, many so young. And her heart, it broke for her Arrow who carried the weight of these losses on his shoulders in silent penance.

He spoke the last name and went quiet. Beside them, the stonemason surreptitiously wiped away a tear. "This is good, what you do," he said into the quiet. "The heavens weep."

Thanking the stonemason for his work, Vasic 'ported the memorial to a place of astonishing beauty on a high bluff that overlooked a serene aquamarine beach, waves rolling gently to shore and grasses waving in the wind. Instead of using his Tk to sink the foundation of the obelisk into the ground, Vasic dug for two hours with a shovel he'd left there earlier.

Ivy got on her knees and used her hands to clear away the dirt.

After it was done, they stood in silence for a long minute. "This isn't enough," Vasic said at last. "This place is isolated."

Stroking his back, Ivy said, "No, Vasic, it's beautiful." A song of sorrow and peace. "To go public with this information is to risk other lives." The Net was stable in one sense, but the psychological impact of the events of the past months—the past century—had left jagged cracks in millions. One more thing could tip an already wounded people over the edge of tolerance.

"The day will come when people are ready to confront the past," she said, her throat thick. "On that day, we'll make a public announcement, read each name aloud, make sure their stories are known."

"I don't want to cheat them, Ivy." Vasic's eyes held such raw emotion, she couldn't imagine how she'd once thought him cold. "I don't want to build a future on a broken promise."

"You aren't." It was hard to speak past the knot choking her, because she knew he carried each and every name in his heart and his mind always. "This, what you're doing, it's what you can do at this moment in time. As the world changes, you'll keep going." She cupped his face. "I know you'll never stop, never forget. We'll come here as often as you need to, and we'll bring the families to whom the truth matters. We'll keep the promise, Vasic. Together."

He didn't answer, simply lowered his face to her neck, his arms coming around her. Ivy held him tight, held her Arrow who couldn't cry, but who mourned all the same.

IT took them almost two days to personally visit those Vasic knew wanted the truth—because he'd kept track of every single one of the affected families. Ivy stood with him as he accepted their recriminations, their rage and sadness, and then she held the people who needed it. Others were too angry, would need time to come to terms with the truth.

That was their right.

As it was Ivy's to spend these last hours before the operation making sure Vasic's life was ordinary. A normal day in a normal life . . . or as normal as it could be when the man she loved was an Arrow. He deserved a normal day, one without blood and horror and darkness. He deserved a million such days and she wanted to give them to him.

Sitting on the stoop of the cabin, she hugged her knees to her chest and watched him go through a quiet, dangerous martial arts routine with Aden in a corner of the yard he'd telekinetically cleared of snow. His best friend hadn't said a word since his arrival, his shields impenetrable and his face expressionless.

Zie Zen would also soon be here, Vasic scheduled to pick him up in another forty-five minutes. They'd have lunch together with her parents, and she'd make sure she laughed because Vasic hated it when she cried. And she'd continue to hope for the comm to chime or her phone to buzz.

So many people were working to the final hour to find another, less dangerous solution. Ashaya and Amara Aleine hadn't yet been able to unravel the complexities of Samuel Rain's invention, but continued to try. The original project team had never stopped its attempts at formulating an answer. Even the surgeon was completing simulated operation after simulated operation in an effort to alter the percentages.

Samuel Rain, however, had become a hermit.

"I'm sorry," Clara had said to Ivy when she'd called the sympathetic woman this morning. "I've tried to get in, see him, but he's intransigent. All I can tell you is that the medical scanners built into the room report he's healthy. He continues to send out order requests for arcane equipment and supplies, all of which Zie Zen fulfills at once, but we have no idea what he's doing with it."

Ivy caught the subtext—Samuel Rain might be trying to do what he'd once done with such ease, and each failure could be driving him further and further into despair. "Has he . . . Is it a total breakdown?" Ivy's fingers had clenched on the phone.

"He seems rational when he does communicate, but he barely communicates." Clara's voice had softened. "I'll keep trying, Ivy. I know how important this is. But we can't barge in; that'll erode any trust he might still have in us."

"It's all right, Clara. I never wanted to harm Samuel in any way." She'd truly believed he was strong and becoming stronger. "I hope he comes through this."

Now, four hours after that call, she sat watching the man she loved move with a deadly economy of motion beside his best friend. Aden had treated the latest burn an hour ago but hadn't had the equipment to totally remove the mark, and so it was an ugly redness on Vasic's arm.

Fingers fisting in Rabbit's coat, she said, "You know it, too, don't you?" Rabbit had taken to following Vasic around, leaning up against his leg any time he stopped. Vasic didn't rebuke their pet, always finding time to stop and touch Rabbit before going about his work again. But Rabbit wouldn't be soothed, as Ivy couldn't be soothed.

Her mate was dying and she couldn't do anything to stop it.

Chapter 59

WHEN A THIRD Arrow walked out of the orchard to join Vasic and Aden, Ivy wasn't the least surprised. They'd started doing that ever since she and Vasic had settled at the cabin, just turning up. She'd fed more than one at the dinner table—though that was easy enough, since most just wanted nutrition bars. It wasn't the food they came for, of course.

"Home," Vasic had told her. "They come because they know they're welcome in our home. To men and women who have never had a true home, a place of warmth and safety, it is a treasure beyond price." He'd kissed the top of her head. "And they know you're my treasure. So they come to check on you when they're nearby. Do you mind?"

No, Ivy didn't mind. She wanted to have Arrows dropping by for decades to come, wanted Vasic to build extra rooms onto the cabin so their guests could stay overnight, wanted to tease him into trying real food. "I want him safe, Rabbit," she said, angry at the entire universe. "I don't want to be in a world where he doesn't get to survive. How is that in any way fair?"

Vasic froze right then, and for an instant, she thought he'd heard her and that she'd ruined the day. Then came a deeper, more violent fear.

She stood and ran toward him as, turning, he jogged back to the cabin. Sweat stuck his black T-shirt to his chest, the thin black of his martial arts pants outlining his thighs as the wind pressed the fabric against him. Ivy still had trouble letting him out into the snow dressed like that, even though he assured her that as a Tk, he was never in any danger of freezing.

Today, it wasn't the cold that was the risk.

"What is it?" Her eyes and her hands went immediately to the gauntlet. "Is it—"

Vasic cupped her face in hands so gentle, she knew he could sense the vicious control she had on her fear and her anger. "Samuel Rain has demanded our presence."

Her heart kicked. "What are you doing here? Let's go!"

"Give me two minutes to shower."

"Vasic—"

"I may need to be clean." He kissed her hard as the import of that statement punched her in the solar plexus.

Watching him head inside to shower, she turned to Aden, terror knotting her guts. "If I lose him, I'll break."

His mind touched hers. *You can't break, Ivy. You're the only home my Arrows know—no matter what, that home must survive.*

She met his eyes, shook her head. But he was adamant. *You're strong. That's why you're Vasic's. You'll honor him . . . but that is a conversation we may never need to have.*

Ivy took a deep breath, straightened. *Yes,* she said. *We won't. Because he's going to be all right.*

Going to Rabbit, she petted him in gentle reassurance. "Mother and Father are on their way to pick you up," she said, having just telepathed them. "Be good and stay with Aden until then, okay?"

She rose as Vasic stepped out of the cabin in jeans and a leather-synth jacket paired with a light blue T-shirt she'd talked him into because it made his silver eyes even more striking. Walking over, she slipped her hand into his.

"Rabbit?" he asked, looking to where their pet stood solemnly with Aden and the third Arrow.

Ivy swallowed past the emotions choking her up, told him she'd made arrangements. "He won't be alone."

Then they went to talk to Samuel Rain.

Clara met them in the foyer of the sprawling house that was the core of Haven, having requested Vasic not teleport directly to Samuel as the staff remained unsure of his mental state. "This way," the manager said at once. "He hasn't permitted anyone inside yet."

No more words necessary, the three of them headed upstairs to Samuel's quarters. There was a massive skylight in this section. It drenched the corridor in light, likely the rooms, too. Stopping at one on the farthest end, Clara knocked. "We gave Samuel the corner suite because it gets the most light and he's always demanded natural light in his workshops."

"Who is it?" Samuel Rain yelled suspiciously from the other side of the door.

"Ivy and Vasic to see you."

The door opened to reveal a man with wild, matted, and overgrown hair, his blue checked shirt buttoned crooked, and what looked like over a month's worth of beard growth on his face. "Come." Eyes blazing with either intelligence or madness behind his spectacles, he stepped back to give them their first glimpse of what lay beyond.

Ivy gasped.

He'd turned the central chamber—lit by two glass walls and part of the main skylight—into a laboratory. That wasn't what made her gasp. It was the fact that sitting in the middle of the workbench was a gauntlet identical to Vasic's, except without the carapace. Linked to a computer that simulated the Psy brain, brain stem, and spinal column, the gauntlet had been split open to display its intricate internal workings. The faux bone and tendon and muscle within it were scarily realistic.

Samuel Rain, Ivy realized with a trembling awareness of the true depth of his genius, had built a working copy of one of the most complex pieces of technology in the world from scratch in the space of just over six weeks.

"It's useless," he said now, and her heart dropped, until he added, "Too many issues to be grafted. But I can get it out with the help of a halfway competent surgeon."

The world stopped, Ivy's hand bloodless around Vasic's.

There is only one choice, Ivy. Vasic cupped her cheek, touching his forehead to hers in a way that had become part of their emotional lexicon. *I would have eternity with you.*

Stomach churning, she wrapped her arms around his neck. *Don't leave me. Please.*

I won't. I'll always be here. Winter frost holding her in thrall. *Even if my body goes, my soul will remain. It's a mess, but it's yours. It'll always be yours.*

I love you, Vasic. I love you. It was so hard for her to release him, to watch him turn to Samuel Rain. "My unit has almost completely destabilized. Can you operate now?"

"Yes," the engineer said without hesitation. "I need a sterile operating chamber with these monitors." He scribbled a list on a scrap of paper. "I also need a nurse and a surgeon. Make sure it's someone who can follow instructions and doesn't have a God complex."

Shoving both hands through his hair, he continued. "I can remove the majority of the gauntlet myself. I might not be able to do the neurosurgery, but I understand biofusion in a way no one else does. I'll need to make split-second decisions, and the surgeon *must* obey."

It took a terrifyingly short time to accommodate his requirements. Edgard Bashir was brought in as the surgeon, rather than the surgeon originally scheduled to operate on Vasic. "She won't follow instructions," Vasic said when he made the decision. "That makes her an asset as a solo operator, but for a team, Edgard is the better player."

Ivy wasn't so sure she wanted the man who'd originally grafted the device to Vasic working on him, but holding her close, Vasic assured her that Edgard was an excellent neurosurgeon. "He just isn't creative, and he doesn't need to be with Samuel in the room. All he has to do is have steady hands."

The operation was to take place in a secure Arrow medical facility that Samuel Rain and Dr. Bashir, plus two theatre nurses, were teleported to so they could have no knowledge of its location. Vasic 'ported in Ivy himself, with Abbot standing by to bring in anyone else who was needed while he was down.

Zie Zen chose to wait with Ivy's parents at their cabin. "I will speak to you when the gauntlet has been removed," he said to Vasic over the comm, but though his face was serene, his hand was bone white on his cane.

Then it was time. "I'll be back soon, Ivy."

Ivy held Vasic's promise to her heart as she sat outside the operating room. Aden sat with her, his combat uniform reminding her piercingly of a thousand moments with her Arrow. When she closed her hand over Aden's, he didn't protest, curling his fingers around her own. Two hours passed before he stood and made her get up, too, to stretch her legs. When he tried to give her an energy drink, she waved it off.

He didn't move. "Vasic trusted me to watch over you. I won't let him down."

"Stubborn, high-handed, both of you," she muttered, while her heart bruised with every beat.

Aden held out the drink again.

Taking the bottle, she forced herself to finish it before returning to her vigil. This time Aden stood against the wall across from her, and though he was as remote as Vasic had once been, she didn't feel alone. They were family, tied together by their love for the loyal, courageous, wonderful man beyond the doors to the operating room.

Three hours.

Four.

Five.

"Do you think we can ask for an update?" Her throat was scratchy from disuse as she looked up at Aden. "No, we shouldn't interrupt," she said before he could respond.

Aden sat down beside her again. "Would you like to hear the story of the first time I met Vasic?"

He was trying to comfort her, she realized, to get her mind off the painfully circular path in which it had been running for hours. "Yes."

Leaning forward with his forearms braced on his thighs, Aden looked at the wall in front of them, but his stare wasn't blank. It was as if he was watching a stream of memory. "I was seven years old and a very well-behaved child."

There was something about the wording of his statement that made
Ivy frown.

"Vasic, only a year older than me, was considered a problem. Those in
charge of the squad at the time had no intention of releasing him—he
was too valuable. So they had to find a way to break him down."

Ivy's nails cut into her palms. "He never broke."

"No," Aden said. "I think he believed for a long time that he had
broken, but they never managed to destroy the core of who he is. It's why
he carries such guilt for actions he couldn't have fought, consequences he
could've never changed."

"He's built to protect, to shield, and they made him a killer."

"Yes." Aden continued to look into the past. "Even as they tried to
break him, they had to teach him. Brute strength is never enough to make
a man an Arrow. All of us train with sparring partners when young—
mental and physical. However, in most cases, they're rotated. The reason
given to us at the time was that it was to ensure we could all work together,
but I believe it was also so bonds couldn't form between long-term
partners."

Encouraged by his earlier acceptance of her touch and wanting to
comfort him as he was trying to do her, she put a careful hand on his
shoulder. He didn't shake it off, but neither did he react. "Vasic, however,"
he continued, "was such a problem that he kept destabilizing his psychic
sparring partners. They'd work him against another child, and even if
that child had been in a relatively calm state previously, he or she would
be erratic afterward."

"Why not adults?"

"That was to be the last-case scenario. It's harder for a child to spar
against an adult, because an adult always has to hold back in case they
cause harm, and so the balance isn't natural and it impacts speed, accuracy,
everything." His lashes came down, flicked back up. They were black like
Vasic's, but unexpectedly long and with a curl at the ends.

He was handsome, she realized in a startled way. With sharp cheekbones and dark eyes against olive colored skin, he no doubt caught female
attention. Only Ivy was always too focused on Vasic to notice.

"Finally," he said, as her need for Vasic keened again, "they decided to try me. I was the last choice, because I was considered the weakest child in training at the time."

Ivy knew beyond any doubt that there was nothing weak about Aden.

"Still, the trainers figured they might as well pit me against him just in case. I was led into our first session in a bland beige room furnished with a heavy metal table and two metal chairs. Vasic should've been sitting on one chair already, but he was standing in a corner, staring at the door.

"When I came in, he continued to look at me with this unblinking stare he shouldn't have been able to maintain as a child." Aden angled his head to meet Ivy's gaze. "He was trying to disconcert me, make me run. Later, he told me it had worked with several of the other children. He broke their nerve just with his eyes."

Ivy's emotions knotted in her veins—affection for the boys they'd been, fury for what they'd both suffered, pride at the men they'd become. "What did you do?"

"Took my seat like the well-behaved child I was, and waited for the trainer to leave the room. I knew, of course, that the evaluation team would be monitoring our interaction via the surveillance equipment, as well as on the PsyNet. Then I watched him watch me."

Ivy found herself charmed by the thought of two small boys trying to win a battle of wills. "Who blinked?"

"That's a matter of dispute. I say he did. He says I did."

Laughing softly, Ivy leaned in a little closer. "And?"

"When he realized I wasn't going to leave, he went to phase two. Taking the seat across from me, he started lobbing psychic strikes at me in an erratic scattering rather than the mandated training pattern." Aden's profile was clean, no smile, and yet Ivy had the sense the memory was a good one.

"Apparently, he'd driven off quite a few others with that tactic. At that age, we're taught in rote patterns," he explained. "It's meant to make certain things instinct, and it does, but it also leaves most child Arrows without the capacity to deal with unexpected situations."

"You handled it," Ivy guessed.

"I think it's better to say I held my own," he said. "Session completed, I got up and left. We went through pretty much the same routine ten times, never speaking a word. Then late one night I was in my room studying when the ceiling panel slid aside and he looked down and asked me if I wanted to go outside."

Ivy started to smile. "What did you do?"

"It was past curfew, with all violations to be strictly punished." A pause. "So I said yes and stood on a chair, and he hauled me up." A glance at her laughing eyes. "I was much shorter then, while Vasic had already started to gain his height. We snuck outside and just walked around."

It was the freedom, Ivy understood, that had been important, the fact they'd made a choice. "Vasic told me you once painted a training room in zebra stripes."

"That was later, after we'd been partners for four years. We planned the operation down to the second, were back in our rooms before anyone discovered the incident."

"I'm glad you had each other," she said, releasing his shoulder to lean forward in an echo of his own position. "Thank you for looking after him."

Aden's responding look was quiet. "You don't understand, Ivy. I didn't look after Vasic. He looked after me—he understood I was a scared boy whose parents were Arrows who were gone ninety-nine percent of the time on missions that could end their lives, and who knew his place in the squad was shaky at best.

"Vasic had the handicap of a heart that felt too much, but he was always the more emotionally strong of the two of us . . . until the past two years, when I think the weight of the guilt began to crush him."

Ivy understood both men would say the same thing with the opposite meaning. To Vasic, Aden had helped him stay sane. To Aden, Vasic had helped him stay upright when he would've fallen. One lost boy helping another.

Reaching out, she closed her hand over his again, knowing she was breaking boundaries, but these Arrows needed to have certain boundaries broken. Who better to do it than an empath? The squad had become so ferally protective of the Es that an E had more latitude with an Arrow than pretty much anyone else in the Net.

"It doesn't matter," she said. "There's no ledger. You were there for one another, and because of that, I have a man who lives in my heart and he has a friend he knows he can rely on no matter what."

Aden's fingers twined with hers. "He also has a woman willing to walk in his darkness and not judge him. You don't know how much that means."

Soul aching, she leaned her head against his shoulder, and that was how they stayed for a long time. Then he made her eat again, drink again. She didn't argue this time, realizing that Aden was sublimating his own fear by looking after her—if he lost Vasic, he'd lose the one person who was his family. So she did what he told her, even walked up and down the corridor after he said her back would get stiff.

Fourteen hours after the doors had closed on the surgery, they opened again.

Chapter 60

IVY AND ADEN both stood as one, staring at Samuel Rain. His formerly pristine white operating smock was bloody, his eyes drained and tired, but there was a jubilant smile on his face—shaved clean prior to the operation—that gave Ivy her answer even before he walked straight to her and said, "Go. He's put himself under. He asked that you give the signal that he should wake."

"Thank you." Ivy hugged him so hard she almost knocked him off his feet. "*Thank you.*" Tears poured down her face.

"Wait," Samuel said when she drew back to run to Vasic. "We had to take his arm." The brilliant man scratched his head, a wary confusion in his eyes. "He told me it was all right before the surgery began. Should I have asked you?"

"All I care about is that he's alive," Ivy said, trembling with the force of her relief. "Aden, come with me." She stretched out her hand, took his again, and drew him into the operating room.

Edgard Bashir dragged himself out as they hit the door, muttering, "He's a genius. He's also mad."

Ivy thanked him and the exhausted but exhilarated nurses who left in his wake, but her attention was focused on the man who lay on the surgical bed. The screens at the end of the frame showed his vitals, strong and stable and alive. She released Aden's hand, went to the side of the bed.

Pressing her lips to Vasic's forehead, her shaking fingers on his chest, she kissed him on the psychic plane at the same time. "We're here," she whispered, both with her voice and telepathically. "I love you."

Thirty seconds later, his lashes fluttered, his lids lifting. Eyes of silver frost, unique and beautiful, met her own. "Don't say no."

Vasic tried to give Ivy more warning of what was about to happen, but it was too late. His mind smashed into hers like an out of control bullet train. Her hand spasmed on his chest, her eyes sparking with a cascade of color, and then he saw her, all of her. His Ivy. Strong and stubborn and loyal and with flaws that made her unique . . . and her heart, it was his. Always his.

No one had ever loved him like Ivy did.

Enough to claim him in this most elemental way. "We're bonded," he said when he could speak, the splinters of their minds falling back into place. But they weren't the same any longer, the black of his mind edged with translucent color, the empathic shade of hers streaked with protective black.

"I know." Crying and laughing at the same time, she kissed him. "I've been ready for so long." She made a stern face at him. "I knew you didn't want to accept it until you were certain you wouldn't leave me. Idiot man."

The affection in those words made him smile deep inside, her love his sunlight. Over her head, he saw Aden standing tall and strong. *Thank you.* For watching over Ivy, for being his friend, for bracing him when he would've stumbled.

May I see? Aden asked.

Vasic opened the shields he'd instinctively snapped around himself and Ivy when their minds collided, and Aden slipped in. The bond between Vasic and Ivy was different from that which connected Kaleb Krychek and Sahara Kyriakus. It wasn't a single titanium rope, but countless threads of finest black translucent with color. Each appeared as if it would break at a whisper, but when Aden glanced at Vasic for permission and touched a psychic finger to one, it bent with the pressure, then flowed right back into shape.

Quickly closing his shields back up as soon as Aden stepped out because he wasn't ready to share this with anyone else, Vasic looked at his friend.

I think, Aden said, *this may be your most challenging assignment yet.*

Vasic wrapped his arm around Ivy when she climbed into bed with him, her hand over his heart and her head on his shoulder. *I'll learn.* He'd learn anything for her.

Aden nodded and quietly left the room, saying one last thing as he gave them privacy. *I truly understand hope now, Vasic.*

So, Vasic thought, his heartbeat aligned to that of his empath, did he.

FOUR weeks later and three weeks after he left the hospital, Vasic was told that while medical science had advanced to the point where limbs could be regrown from the cells of the individual who needed them, so as to negate the risk of rejection, his body had suffered too harsh an insult with the gauntlet. He was otherwise healthy, should have the same life span as any other Psy, but no biological transplant would take.

"I could try, but it would involve further surgery on my brain," Vasic told Ivy as they sat on the stoop of the cabin he'd started to extend the day Ivy stopped fussing over him if he so much as moved a muscle. He had to admit he'd enjoyed the fussing; he might even have played lame duck for a day or two longer than strictly necessary.

Ivy's response came out a near growl that made Rabbit prick his ears where he sat just behind them in the cabin. "You try and I'll beat you."

"You're becoming very violent, Ivy." Vasic rubbed his hand over the roughness of his head. Edgard had had to shave off his hair to get to the tendrils fused to his brain. Those tendrils were still there, would remain till the day he died, but the surgery had rendered them permanently inert.

Grabbing his hand, Ivy pressed her lips to the back of it. "It's growing back," she said, smile lines bracketing her mouth. "I never knew you were so vain."

He was used to being teased by his Ivy now. "I think you want to be teleported into the middle of a swamp."

A heavy-browed scowl. "Try it and see who's sorry."

Pulling his hand from her grasp, he wrapped his arm around her to tuck her close. "I may have lost an arm," he said, "but it's the stubble on my head that reminds me of how close I came to death. Perhaps because when I feel it or see it, I can't help but imagine Samuel Rain digging around in there with manic glee."

Ivy snorted with laughter before slapping him on the chest. "He saved your life, you ungrateful wretch!"

He loved watching Ivy laugh, could do it forever. "Rain will make certain I don't forget his genius." In truth, Vasic would never be able to repay either Rain, Edgard, or the two nurses. Whether the four knew it or not, they now had the support of an entire squad of Arrows. "But even Rain agrees a biological replacement is off the table."

"Hmm." Ivy tapped her lower lip. "Mechanical?"

"Problematic. My wiring was rerouted in strange ways." The entire surgical team had been surprised at some of what they'd discovered. "I could get a cosmetic arm, but it wouldn't be functional."

Hand curving on his thigh, Ivy made a face. "That would just annoy you."

Yes, he thought, it would. He'd suggested it to make things easier for her . . . but Ivy didn't seem to care that he was missing a part, her only concern how he felt about it. She still touched him, kissed him, loved him just the same. Always would, he understood in wonder, even should he lose every limb he possessed.

"My telekinesis balances out the loss, so I won't lose any functionality." But he would miss embracing Ivy with both arms, having her sleep on one while he wrapped the other around her.

Expression pensive, Ivy tilted her head, studied his face. "You're sad."

He told her what he'd been thinking, saw her eyes grow wet. "You hold me every second of every day." She spread her fingers over her heart. "I should be so mad at you for making us wait that long for our bond."

Running his hand down her arm, he shifted position to lean his back against the doorjamb, one booted leg on the ground he'd cleared of snow, the other bent at the knee, foot flat on the wood of the cabin floor. "Come here."

Her eyes narrowed. "I'm trying to have an argument with you."

"Ivy," he said, dropping his voice in that way he knew made her melt. "Come here."

Breath catching, she pretended to bite at his jaw before tucking herself against his chest, his legs on either side of her. He wrapped his arm around her again and felt his heart smile because embracing her this way felt just as good. They sat listening to the breeze and to the happy chirping of a cricket who didn't seem to realize this was the tail end of a North Dakota winter.

It was some time later that Ivy sat up on her knees and with her arms around his neck, leaned into him. Their kisses were slow, deep, playful. Stroking the roughness of his jaw, she said, "Can I shave you?"

"Is it too rough?" he murmured. "I can—"

"No, I want to do it."

Vasic took in the flush on her cheekbones, the sinful anticipation in her eyes. "You've been reading more manuals," he accused.

"Actually, it was a historical romance novel." Another kiss as she pushed his raised knee down so she could straddle him. "This one scene just . . ." She shivered, her arms compressing her breasts from either side as she hugged herself. "So, can I?"

Vasic was many things. The one thing he was not was stupid. He said yes and didn't flinch when she produced an old-fashioned shaving kit, complete with a straight razor and a brush to lather up his jaw. Then she unbuttoned her shirt.

An hour later, Vasic finished shaving the rest of his face himself while a naked Ivy sat on the counter trying to catch her breath. "I need to read these novels," he said, bending down to kiss her thigh once he'd completed the task.

She pushed at him with her foot, but it held no force. "I'm password protecting them." Breasts rising and falling in a visual that he appreciated, she spread her thighs and drew him back against her. "You don't need any more ideas."

Vasic hauled her even closer, one arm around her back, the other— But he only had one arm now. So he adapted and used his Tk. That gave him an idea. Utilizing his ability to affect small, delicate things, he stroked telekinetic fingers through her labia.

Ivy jerked, her fingernails digging into his shoulders. "Oh my God."

Taking the moan as encouragement, he did it again, dipping his head to suck on her nipples at the same time. Deciding the other one shouldn't have to wait, he split his attention and used telekinetic fingers to pluck at it. *Have I told you how much I like my hobby?*

Ivy's spine arched. "No," she gasped, "romance novels for you."

"I bet I can change your mind."

EIGHT hours after losing the bet to Vasic in a delicious paroxysm of pleasure, Ivy sat down in a chair beside Zie Zen at his Lake Tahoe home. Her eyes were on Vasic where he stood in conversation with a DarkRiver soldier near the edge of Zie Zen's property line, the lake water beyond a silver mirror under the moonlight. Vasic was dressed in his Arrow uniform, the changeling in jeans and a faded sweatshirt. Their conversation appeared relaxed.

"He will be all right, Grandfather," she said, able to sense the concern Zie Zen would likely never put in words, having lived in Silence for too long.

The older man, his hand on the head of his cane, turned to look at her. "I had forgotten what it was to live with an empath."

"I don't mean to intrude," she said, uncertain about how to be with Zie Zen. He was so remote sometimes, and yet he loved Vasic with a quiet, painful intensity. "I don't seem to be able to filter out a certain level of my ability."

"And why should you? It would be equivalent to me having one of my eyes permanently shut." His gaze returned to Vasic. "He is meant for great things, my son."

The words used, she knew, were deliberate, a sign of what Vasic meant to Zie Zen. "He is a great man."

"Yet he ties himself to an empath, seeking only to make her path easier."

Ivy's hand tightened on the arm of the chair. "He's earned his peace." She would allow no one to take it from him. "Earned the right to a home and a life undefiled by blood."

"Some men are not meant for peace, for calm. Some men are built for war." Zie Zen's eyes pierced hers. "He's far stronger than he knows, able to fight with unrelenting fury for that in which he believes."

"I know." Even when Vasic had thought himself irreparably broken, he'd fought for his squad. "But he's walked that road most of his life. Don't you think he's done enough?" she pleaded, aware just how much Vasic respected his great-grandfather. "Or do you believe he must be stripped down to the bone?"

Zie Zen leaned back in his chair, hand flexing on the head of the cane. "If I say I believe he needs to fight on? If I ask him to shed more blood, walk once more in the darkness?"

Ivy's heart thudded, her own blood hot. "I won't allow anyone to hurt him, not even you." Never did she want to take this relationship from Vasic, but neither would she permit Zie Zen to use that relationship to destroy Vasic.

The elder's eyes met hers again, an odd light in them. "So, he's found a woman who will fight for him. Good." With that, he returned his gaze to the lake and to the two men who stood there. "Do you know what I would like to see before I die, Ivy Jane?"

Ivy shook her head, still stunned at the realization that it had all been a test. "What, Grandfather?"

"I would like to see my son laugh."

Ivy saw Vasic bend down to pet Rabbit when their pet ran over after investigating an interesting rock, and she felt her lips curve. "That," she said, "is a wish that will come true." Perhaps not today, or even tomorrow, but Vasic had joy in his heart now. It would one day color the air, of that she was certain.

Rising from his chair without warning, Zie Zen walked slowly into the house. Ivy didn't follow; he'd made no invitation, and like Vasic, he wasn't a man with whom you assumed any kind of acceptance. When he didn't return in the next five minutes, she walked down to the edge of the lake as Vasic and the changeling said their farewells.

I would speak to you, my son.

Leaving Ivy and Rabbit searching the pebbles on the shoreline for the best one to skim across the water, Vasic headed up to the porch. Zie Zen came out of the house at the same instant, something in his right hand.

"Grandfather." Vasic fought the urge to subtly stabilize the older man, aware Zie Zen would pick up on the interference and be offended by it. But Vasic couldn't keep silent. "You're leaning more heavily on your cane." And he was walking slower, his ruler-straight back beginning to bend.

"I am old," was the succinct answer. "And I am almost ready to go." Lowering himself into his chair, he waited for Vasic to take the one beside him. "Before Silence," he said, after he'd caught his breath, "some of us chose to marry. Though we may have been psychically bonded, to see my ring on my wife's finger, it meant something. To wear hers on mine, it meant even more."

Taking the small velvet box his great-grandfather held out, Vasic opened it to reveal two gold wedding bands, each one beautifully etched with intricate carvings. The hugeness of what he felt was a storm inside him, the words ones he couldn't say.

"Humor an old man and wear them." His great-grandfather closed his hand over Vasic's, Zie Zen's skin warm and papery, his grip strong. "Live your love into old age as I and my Sunny could not do."

Vasic? Ivy started back to the house. *What's wrong?*

Grandfather has given us a gift beyond price. He stood to catch her against him as she ran up to the porch, pressed his lips to her temple, and showed her the gift. Perhaps this wasn't how it was done, but this was Ivy, with whom he could do nothing wrong, make no mistakes, and so he simply asked, "Will you wear my ring, Ivy?" *Will you permit me to wear yours?*

A jerky nod against him, her eyes overflowing.

TWO weeks later, the newly formed Empathic Collective unanimously voted Ivy in as president. Five other empaths from around the world, including Sascha Duncan, were voted in as her advisory board. Sahara Kyriakus was asked to continue on in her role as a specialist, and an invitation was extended to Alice Eldridge to come onboard as a consultant as and when she wished.

Both women accepted.

The initially suggested percentage to be paid into the Collective Fund by the membership was doubled after intense discussion, with the Es deciding they needed a powerful body that would lobby on their behalf.

The money was to be used not only to compensate those who worked for the organization, but to create secret bolt-holes for empaths and to finance the training compounds that were springing up around the world. It was also decided that the Ruling Coalition would be asked to kick in a percentage of overall tax revenue, given that it was the Es who were holding the Net together.

Of course, the empaths themselves hadn't come up with that little point.

"You're too inherently kind," Vasic had told her when he first suggested the idea. "Aside from possible anomalies, as occur with any population, you tend to think of others first and yourselves second."

It was as well they had the entire Arrow Squad on their side. The lethal group had quietly made it clear that anyone who wanted to take on the Es would have to go through them. While one-on-one partnerships were no longer possible, given the number of active Es, each and every empath had the direct contact details of at least three Arrows.

"It's a strange, beautiful alliance," Ivy said to her man as they sat on a dune in the desert under the golden rays of the setting sun, Rabbit's warm body beside her as he dozed after an active day.

"Me and you?"

"No, empaths and Arrows." *Me and you? We're just beautiful.*

No curve of his lips, but there was light in the winter frost, a deep happiness in the bond that tied them together.

"Ivy?"

"Hmm?"

"Have you ever thought of having children?"

Tumbling him to his back in the sand, to Rabbit's excited "woof," she kissed him all over the face, sensing his startled delight. "Yes, with you."

It hadn't been a subject she'd ever thought about before him. Now . . . now she wanted her Arrow's babies. "What about you?"

He spread his hand on her lower back, eyes locked with hers. "I think . . . I'd like that, too." It was a wondering statement, as if he'd surprised himself. "But we'll have to wait until things are more stable."

"Our world's not yet ready," Ivy agreed. "I want our children to grow up happy and wild and—"

"Half-feral?"

Her heart clenched at the odd poignancy of those words. "Yes," she whispered, almost able to hear the raucous laughter and mischievous glee of the children they would one day have. "That sounds perfect to me."

It was a promise of joy, and one they sealed with a lingering kiss.

"Do you think our race will make it?" she asked later, after the sun had set, the desert draped in pale gray.

"We're clawing our way back—we'll never be what we once were, but that isn't the goal."

No, Ivy thought, it was to be better.

That night, she dreamed of a woman of infinite darkness. Her rage and loneliness was a crushing weight on Ivy's chest, but Ivy wasn't afraid. No, she was just sad. Holding out her hand, she felt the darkness brush past her senses with a malevolence that stole her breath . . . but it did her no harm. And as she slipped into a deeper sleep against the muscled warmth of her Arrow, she saw the now formless darkness intertwine with a river of starlight riven with translucent color.

Hope

You are cordially invited to the wedding of Vasic Zen to Ivy Jane.

Invitation sent to every member of the Arrow Squad

THEY MARRIED AS the apple trees opened their first blossoms, the grass an emerald green carpet beneath their feet. Vasic wore his Arrow uniform modified with a formal jacket in place of the lightweight armor. On his lapel was a pin: a black arrow entwined with the branches of an apple tree.

The handcrafted item had been a gift from Aden. Now the other man stood beside Vasic as Ivy's parents walked her up an aisle strewn with cherry blossoms another teleporter had brought in that morning. Ivy's dress was a light, gossamer creation of cream and lace; she had a ribbon in her hair and a bouquet of tiny peach roses in her hand.

Friends and family stood on every side.

Every member of the squad who wasn't on duty was in attendance. Ivy had invited the others to a special breakfast tomorrow, where she planned to make them try at least a bite of the wedding cake.

Dressed in a neat charcoal suit paired with a white shirt, Samuel Rain—infuriated because he'd so far failed to build Vasic a robotic arm that integrated into his damaged systems—blended in oddly well with the Arrows. The lethal men and women stood beside Ivy's friends from the settlement and the world.

Kaleb and Sahara were next to Judd Lauren and his changeling mate; Sascha, Lucas, and Alice nearby. A man with pale green eyes and dark blond hair introduced as Walker Lauren was also present, his healer mate at his side. Aden had spent an hour with Walker after asking Judd's brother to arrive early, their discussion intense even from a distance.

Dr. Bashir, the surgeon who'd operated on Vasic, stood proudly beside the two nurses, while Anthony Kyriakus had been invited as Zie Zen's guest—Zie Zen, whose last name Vasic had officially taken as his own in a quiet, powerful act of honor and of family. Eben and Jaya beamed at Ivy from near the front, and a washed and groomed Rabbit, his collar a debonair bow tie, stood quivering with excitement by Vasic. The air was filled with hope and love and promise.

I would've married you on Zie Zen's porch, Ivy said to the man who was hers, *but there is something so special about this day, about the people around us.*

Vasic took Ivy's hand when her parents handed it over, clasped it tightly. She was already his on the psychic plane, but this ceremony wasn't only about them. It was about every black-clad man and woman who stood in the orchard. It was about hope. And his fierce, generous Ivy knew that.

He married her with spring in the air, the sunshine a cool gold.

Kissing her to the quiet jubilation of their guests, his Ivy dressed in cream and lace, Vasic felt a wriggling at his foot and looked down to find Rabbit had squirmed his way between them, was now looking up. Ivy laughed, and it was the perfect music for their wedding day.

To be an Arrow has always been to protect our people. That mandate now requires the protection of designation E. As of this update, the empaths are the squad's top priority—any threat to an E is to be swiftly mitigated.

First Code of Arrows (Revised)

For too many years, others have made choices for us, and those choices have defined us in darkness. Today, we make a free choice. We cannot know where that choice will lead us, but one thing I know—this is a path of honor . . . and perhaps of redemption.

Aden Kai to the Arrow Squad, after a squad-wide consensus
to update the Code

When an Arrow gives his or her loyalty, it is carved in stone—only if that stone proves false ground, shattering from the corruption within, will he break the bond. For those who hold his loyalty, an Arrow will lay down his life without hesitation, stand in the path of a bullet or a blade, sacrifice every last drop of blood in his body.

We now hold the promise of an entire squad of Arrows, men and women who have vowed to act as our shields against violence. It is a gift that we must always cherish and never dishonor.

As such, our first law, decided after discussion across the entire collective, is this: No Arrow is to ever be used as a personal weapon by an E. No E is to ever use his or her connection to an Arrow to induce that Arrow to do harm to another living being for the E's personal gain (whether that gain is emotional, financial, psychic, or otherwise).

The Arrows are our partners and the relationship must be of mutual respect and trust if it is to grow ever stronger. Also, as in any partnership there must be give-and-take. The Arrows know only how to serve, how to give—it's time they learned how to receive as well. (A personal note on the latter point: They can be stubborn about this, but so can an E. Persevere. Trust me, it's worth it.)

Memo from Ivy Jane Zen, President of the Empathic Collective,
to its membership

Dear V,

I ate the whole box of Turkish Delight. Under no circumstances are you to bring me any more (this month at least). I have the self-control of a starving squirrel.

Rabbit also has no self-control and is currently lolling around deliriously in his bed after gorging on his treats.

Love,
Ivy

p.s. I bought a new manual just for you. I haven't even opened it. Come home early.

≫———→

Nalini Singh was born in Fiji and raised in
New Zealand. She spent three years living and
working in Japan, and travelling around Asia
before returning to New Zealand.

She has worked as a lawyer, a librarian, a candy
factory general hand, a bank temp and an
English teacher, not necessarily in that order.

Learn more about her and her novels at:
www.nalinisingh.com

Love 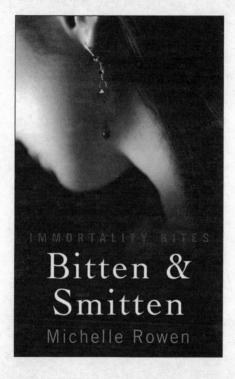 Funny and ❤ Romantic novels?
Then why not discover

IMMORTALITY'S BITE

IMMORTALITY BITES

Bitten & Smitten

Michelle Rowen

Blind dates can be murder – or at least that's how Sarah Dearly's turned out.
Her dates 'love bites' turn her into a vampire and make her a target for a zealous
group of vampire hunters. Lucky for her she's stumbled onto an unlikely saviour
– a suicidal vampire who just might have found his reason to live: her.